THE GRIMSAH Forest

K.L. Beckman

The
Next
Chapter
Publishing

The Next Chapter Publishing P.O. Box 765252 Dallas, TX 75376 Print ISBN – 978-1-941398-05-0 Ebook ISBN - 978-1-941398-06-7

Cover Design and Interior format by The Killion Group
http://thekilliongroupinc.com

Please send your thoughts to
thenextchapterpublishing@gmail.com

Find us on Facebook at:
https://www.facebook.com/TheNextChapterPublishing
Find us online at: www.thenextchapterpublishing.com

DEDICATION

To my husband—Thank you for your support and for believing in me. To my family—Thank you for your support and your love.

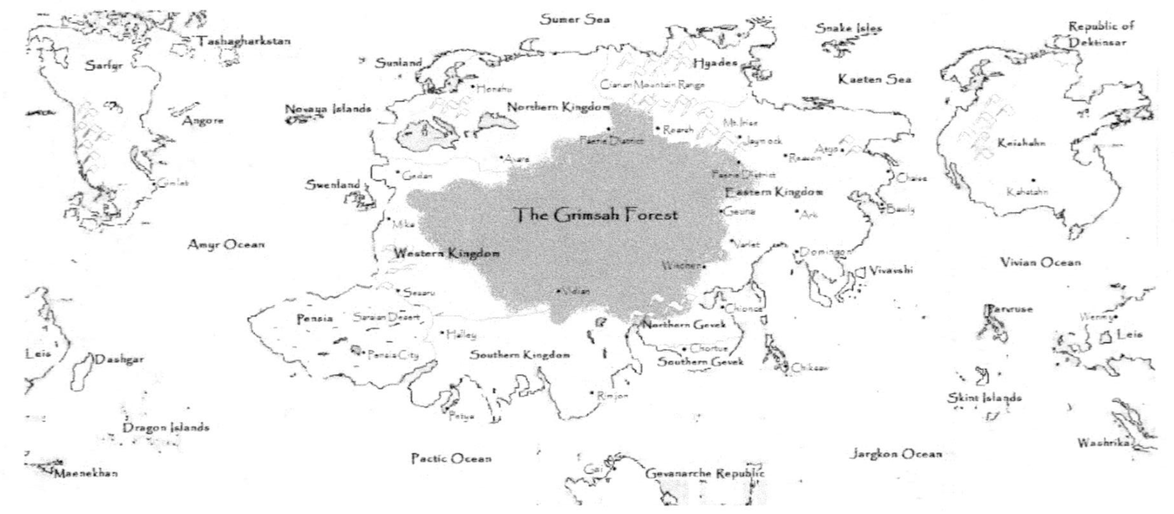

Sumer Sea
Snake Isles
Republic of Dektinsar
Tashagharkstan
Sarfgr
Sunland
Hyades
Kaeten Sea
Angore
Novaya Islands
Cianan Mountain Range
Honshu
Northern Kingdom
Keishahn
Mt. Irian
Reach
Jaynock
Atga
Faerie District
Kahstahn
Rexson
Avra
Chave
Gedan
Faerie District
Swenland
Eastern Kingdom
Basily
The Grimsah Forest
Geuna
Ark
Amyr Ocean
Mike
Vivasshi
Western Kingdom
Varlet
Vivian Ocean
Domingan
Sesaru
Vidian
Wiecher
Chionoe
Parvruse
Pensia
Saraan Desert
Northern Gevek
Wenny
Leia
Dashgar
Halley
Chortue
Leia
Pensia City
Southern Kingdom
Southern Gevek
Chikeau
Skint Islands
Rimjon
Dragon Islands
Patya
Washrika
Pactic Ocean
Jargkon Ocean
Maenekhan
Gai
Gevanarche Republic

PROLOGUE

Becoming Eve

I can feel the pain beginning to creep on me. It starts from within, from deep within my soul. I had never noticed the pain that had persistently dwelled within until now.

It had been lying in wait, hoping to be awakened. It could only be awakened and set free by me. I had to do it willingly and I did. I did because I didn't understand that what I was doing is wrong.

I didn't care. I didn't care about anything. Apathy devoured me and spit out a coward. I stopped caring and, when I stopped caring, I stopped growing in my soul. When I stopped growing in my soul, I began to fall backwards.

Who would be there to catch me but the Darkeness?

The Darkeness catches anyone who falls, but it pulls on people like me. How sad that I've realized this only now.

As I lie here in the snow, dying, only now do I realize everything I am is a curse. It is a deserved curse, of course. I brought this upon myself with earthly wants, apathy, and my damn sense of self-preservation.

Everything seems to be moving in slow motion now. Everything is beginning to blend together like a painting. Figures above me fade into each other. Colors erupt and blend together into a murky grey. I can see the edge of the

Forest reaching out to me. Another figure stands over me, yelling, screaming, and begging me to respond.

I scream out in pain as my soul begins to tear. I had never been aware of my soul or felt it within me. It was just one of those things I accepted that I had. I accepted that people had souls and then I didn't think anything else about it. I didn't care.

I do not care.

My soul splits itself and I scream. Lights seem to jab into my eyes and I writhe in pain. My soul jerks violently within me and I scream again. My scream breaks and doesn't make a sound. My throat is ripping. I clutch the ground, wanting the pain to end. I can feel a sense of want within myself. My soul could stay in one piece. The split half of the soul wavers for a moment.

I scream again when an outside force touches me. A hand, I think. I push my soul out. If it leaves, the pain will stop.

The soul leaves me and I arch my back. My mouth is wide open but no sound is there. Silence covers me like a blanket. It's deafening. It makes me look in at myself, but I'm stuck. I can't move.

A new me, a new being takes control, and I step out of the way to watch.

I do not care.

CHAPTER ONE

Mary

I dangle my feet off the cliff. The cliff edge is soft unlike its jagged base, but it won't move for another thousand years. The wind is blowing steadily and softly although it is beginning to pick up. The salty waters below beat relentlessly against the sharp edges of the cliff. I squint into the horizon. The ocean just seems to disappear. It almost seems rounded, like it just curves off and you see no more of it. I watch the edge of the ocean. Could I sail right off?

The skies in the far distance are dark. A storm is coming. I always leave a flower propped up between blades of grass, standing in my path out to the cliff edge. When it falls, I know a storm is coming. It has fallen. Not that that little sign is necessary. The heavy winds always come before the storm, warning us.

I inhale deeply. The salty air tastes like home, as it should. I lean forward, propping my elbows on my knees, watching the waters rise and fall in their rhythmic sloshing. No matter how many times I sit out here and sketch the waters in my sketch pad, I can never seem to capture the light dancing on the surface of the waves as they bob.

The ocean is mysterious and dark. It deserves respect. I admire the waters. No matter how hard they beat the cliff, the cliff does not bend to the ocean's will. Yet, the waters, after thousands of years, continue to thrash against the cliff. I feel as though this has significant meaning. Too many people nowadays give up. The ocean is the true icon of determination and work.

Though there is not much hope to fight for. Giving up is so much easier than caring and fighting a losing battle. Even the Gods seem to have abandoned us. I know the thought itself is blasphemy. How can I think such thoughts? Yet trying not to think the thoughts only seems to bring the thoughts on stronger.

The Grimsah Forest, the forbidden forest of all lands, seems to be growing in power and the Unspeakables are becoming more and more. Their population is growing far too quickly and the Gods do not seem to notice or care.

I twist around and look at the dark, gnarled Forest beyond my village. The Forest has been pushing closer and closer to Mika. The Forest itself is an evil being, intent on destroying everything created by the Gods. Just where did it come from? I don't remember the Forest in my childhood, but I'm sure I had happier things to focus on.

I have to wonder how the Gods can let this Forest destroy us all.

I stand up and pick up my satchel with my sketch book and pencils. The sun will be setting soon and I need to be inside Mika's walls before dark. The Unspeakables have been bold lately and many lives have been taken just minutes after dark.

Papa says it's only a matter of time before they start attacking in the daylight. As it is, no one leaves their homes after dark because Unspeakables have been known to come over the walls after a target under the cover of night's darkness.

I run back to Mika down my worn path in the grass. I hold up my skirt and grip my satchel as I run. I can't be tripping.

I make it inside the walls minutes before sundown. The gate-guards, Mick and Huling, raise their eyebrows.

"Just in time, Miss Mary," Huling chuckles. "You're cuttin' it closer n' closer e'ry time."

I smile and straighten my tunic and smooth my skirt. I pull my satchel over my shoulder and look around. People are beginning to pack up their shops and head home. The baker is putting out stale bread for the poorer families. I see Huling's son, Granger, ask for some bread. The baker, Mr. Kohnen, hands him two loaves of stiff bread. Granger thanks him repeatedly before racing off. Mr. Kohnen nods at me and I smile back.

I make my way through the plaza, avoiding the small children playing Grinma. They have the bright red Grinma balls. There are boys sitting on the ground, already hit. There are boys leaping over them with their balls. Two little boys strike each other at the same time. They quickly charge each other. One overpowers the other, winning. He gets to stay on his feet. The other boy sits down, looking irritated because he's out now. I walk through the middle and the boys halt their throwing, waiting for me to pass. As soon as I'm out of the playing space, I hear squealing and giggling once more.

I walk past a gaggle of girls. I can almost feel their hate radiating off of them. I'm not popular among people my age. Riley Johnston, the son of the richest man in Mika, has made it clear that I should be disliked. I don't understand why Riley has chosen me to hate. I remember he used to hate a girl named Briny, but she was killed by an Unspeakable and I became the replacement. Kaleb and my brothers, thankfully, still like me.

The girls stop talking and watch me walk by. Do you have to be so obvious? I sigh and quicken my pace. Once I'm past them, I run all the way home. I yank the door open with a mighty pull, since it sticks badly, and step inside. I blink quickly; my vision is purple from being outside all day. The house is dark and quiet.

I blink around the small house. The kitchen with its pale yellow walls is tiny. A little black stove sits in a corner beside large shelves on which foodstuffs sit. The kitchen has a narrow doorway by the door I have just come through and another doorway leading to the back bedrooms. There is a large window, glass-less of course, that looks into the living room.

The living room has a table in the corner, against the wall of the back door. A large couch, brown with patches of fabric, sits against the opposite wall. Opposite the couch are two small chairs with a small, short table between them. There are several game boxes stacked on top of the table, put there by Connor months ago. The games still sit there with dust collecting on them.

I creep through the small kitchen past the living room and to the back bedrooms. Papa isn't home yet, but my brothers should be. I open the door slightly to peer into Mason's and Connor's room. Their bedroom is small and cramped with two beds pressed against opposite walls. The room is dark, especially with no window. I can see shoes and books strewn about the floor. My eyes find Connor sprawled out on the bed, his face pressed between the wall and his pillow. He's fully dressed. Is he not feeling well?

Connor makes a small noise, nestling his head further. From my vantage point, I can see his upper lip sticking up and out, revealing his teeth and an unsteady dripping of drool. I cover my mouth, trying not to laugh. Mason is going to hear about this later! Connor adjusts himself again, pushing his face deeper into the crevice between the bed and the wall.

Connor looks exactly like Mother did. He is lucky to have curly dark hair that seems to jut out wildly from his head. He has mossy green eyes and dimples when he smiles. He's got Mother's straight nose and high cheekbones. Sometimes I think Connor's looks make Papa sad, make him miss Mother. Sometimes they make me wish she were still here.

Suddenly someone grabs my waist and lifts me off my feet. My body reacts outside my brain, and I struggle and scream. Connor bolts up, smacking his head into the wall. The wall gives a solid noise and Connor looks stunned for a moment. He bounces back onto the bed and falls off. He manages to get to his feet and starts toward me.

"It's me! It's me!" Mason yells and sets me down. He starts to laugh at Connor's manner of waking up.

"Mason!" Connor pushes me into the doorframe indignantly and tackles Mason.

Mason has been gone for a week. He went to Gedan, capitol of our lands, the Western Kingdom, to barter and trade for supplies with others. Mason is still laughing.

"Wake up call!" Mason manages to say with a muffled voice as Connor climbs on top of him.

"Quick, Mary!" Connor's knees are pinning Mason's arms down. "Hold his head down!"

I run over and hold Mason's head against the floor with all my might. I can feel him struggling beneath my hands. He howls for me to let him up. He knows what's about to happen.

Connor sits on his legs and punches his stomach. Mason's long arms reach for Connor at first and then his arms wrap around my neck. I scream again, laughing.

Connor punches harder and I can hear the blows. Mason pulls me over and I get a sharp hit from Connor in the hip.

"Ouch!" I cry, trying to wiggle out of Mason's steel grip. "Stop! Stop! Stop!"

"You deserve it, too!" Connor roars and tries to grab my legs to pin me down. He gets a handful of skirts. "Too many damn skirts! I know you're wearing pants under them. Help me, Mason!"

"No!" I squeal and thrash against them. "I'm not wearing pants!"

"Yes, you are! You liar! You always wear pants under your skirts!"

They know me too well.

Despite Connor being the youngest, he is stronger than both of us. Still, Mason manages to wiggle out from beneath me and he grabs Connor, pulling him into a headlock.

Since Mother's death, we've become even closer. Nastia Loke once commented that it was 'weird' that we were all so close. I, of course, said nothing back. Nastia's family hasn't lost a family member. They are very lucky.

"Mason!" Papa's booming voice makes my brothers pause.

"Pap!" Mason breaks free of Connor's grasp and runs to hug Papa.

"My boy," Papa rubs Mason's head. Mason is identical to Papa in every way. He has dark straight hair and dark brown eyes with the same Old World Irish nose, as he calls it, and the same handful of freckles splashed across his nose.

I have Mother's green eyes and her body and Papa's nose and freckles. But I have red hair, like my Uncle Seth and no one else. So I guess if Connor looks exactly like Mother and Mason looks like Papa, I am sort of a blend.

"How was the trip? Tell me about it," Papa motions to the worn couch in the living room.

"I'll toast some bread," I say quietly.

"Thanks, dear," Papa says as he and Mason flop themselves down on the couch. Connor lies on the floor on his belly.

Papa has been all over the Western, Southern, and Eastern Kingdoms, Hyades, and even Vivashi! Papa is the greatest doctor in all the Western Kingdom! He goes all over the world and learns about all different practices of medicine. He's truly a genius.

I put the bread onto a tray and into the oven; then I strike a small flame and light the gas to warm the oven.

"It went really well." Mason's voice sounds like he's stretching. "We traded the medicine for weapons like Mayor Sixsmith asked us to. . ."

"How was Gedan, though?" Connor interrupts.

"Big," Mason chuckles. "It was really big. There were people everywhere! Oh, Mary, you would have loved it. There were even people sitting on corners painting people for money! You could paint people's portraits for money! There weren't any cars or anything like what the Eastern Kingdom has, but there were people with bicycles!"

"Real bicycles?" I pull the bread out. "Real bicycles?"

Mason nods, wide-eyed. "Real bicycles."

"I saw a picture of one once," I say quietly. "They are very odd looking, no?"

Mason nods, his eyes searching the wall for an image. "They did look strange now that I think about it. I guess I was so surprised that I didn't really look at them hard."

Papa laughs. "Mary, we ought to take you to Gedan."

"Eh," Mason doesn't like the idea already. "Ron got pick-pocketed. He got his wallet stolen right out of his pocket."

Papa shakes his head as I walk in with the tray of bread. "That's one of the bad things about living in the big city."

Mason's lips press together. "I guess so. But poor Ron always seems to get the short end of the stick."

The next morning Connor leaves early for work and Mason sleeps in. Papa is also gone at work when I awake. I make some eggs and eat quickly. Mason can fend for himself. I imagine he'll sleep all day since they traveled all night.

I straighten myself in front of a mirror. My skirt comes to the middle of my shins. I pull on a white tunic and tie a belt around my waist to hold my skirt up. I pull on boots and look at myself. My figure looks odd in this skirt. I feel awkward. But that is nothing new so I grab my satchel and run out of the room.

I push against the crotchety back door with all my might and fly through it, landing in the back alley. I turn and shut the door as hard as I can. It's impossible to shut this door quietly, so I slam it and trot down the alley.

Riley Johnston is suddenly in my face. I back into the brick of the house behind me. He leans heavily against his hand on the wall. His face is close to mine. His handsome face seems so horribly grotesque when twisted into the grin he wears.

I try to jerk away from him.

"No words for me today?" he asks, his blue eyes searching my face menacingly.

I have never spoken outside my house in the village. Only Papa, Mason, Connor, and sometimes Kaleb hear me speak. Mother used to sing and teach singing lessons in the village and surrounding villages. I was her student and she used to say I'd teach, too. After she passed, I just can't bear to hear singing or sing. I can't even speak. I can't hear my own voice. I just can't let go, I suppose. Papa says it's normal and that I'll slowly work through whatever it is…

No, Riley, I will never have words for you. Not now, not ever.

Riley stares at me. I look away. He makes me feel so uncomfortable.

"No words?" Riley seems irritated. "So what are you up to today, you little freak?"

My jaw clenches. He pokes at my satchel and sees my pencils and sketchpad.

"Out to the cliff edge again?" Riley leans in closer and I look into his face. "Why don't you throw yourself off this time, Mary Stoneburner? It'll save your family from feeding yet another mouth. After your mother's and your death, they'll be living like kings!" Why? I want to ask him, why do you hate me so much? His words sting me and I feel a churning in my stomach. I feel that same empty sadness bubbling up.

"I think that's enough," a voice suddenly says. I know exactly who it is.

Riley pushes off the wall and turns to face Kaleb. Kaleb steps forward and takes my hand.

"We're leaving," Kaleb says and then looks down at me. "You don't need to listen to this stupid jeck. He doesn't even know where he is."

Riley starts to step forward, bowing up.

Kaleb laughs. "Please, Riley."

Riley, unsure of what to do, storms off. Kaleb is the only one who can treat Riley like he deserves. Riley knows Kaleb is stronger.

I smile at Kaleb. "Thanks."

Kaleb lets go of my hand and we walk through the village towards the west gate to head to the cliff edge. I look at Kaleb. I can imagine Nastia and the other girls fuming to see him walking beside me. They hate me and adore Kaleb. Who wouldn't? He's strong, handsome, kind, funny, and just perfect.

He has blonde hair, blue eyes, freckles, dimples, and strong arms. He is a prince charming all in himself.

I wait until we leave the village to speak.

"Are you not working today?" I ask him.

He shakes his head. "Not today. I asked for a day off to see you. I feel like I haven't seen you in eons!"

Kaleb is a Runner. He patrols the Forest edges and runs back to the village to report anything unusual. The Runners are the most respected in Mika. Kaleb is the youngest and the apple of every girl's eye. But Kaleb, it seems, doesn't think about girls. His mind is always on fighting the war on the Forest and the Unspeakables. Kaleb has never been the same since he lost his parents. He doesn't talk about his family, about his parents or his sister. He's no longer carefree or easygoing, although he seems happy enough when he's around my family. He is focused on the war and only ever thinks about defenses and Unspeakable numbers and population sizes.

Connor says Kaleb's parents were killed by Unspeakables back before Mika had walls. We were only able to bury Kaleb's father. His sister's and mother's bodies disappeared. Kaleb has never told this to me himself. It's never really come up. I haven't had the desire to ask either. The Runners, at least, take care of him well. His home, food, and income are all with the Runners. He doesn't need to worry about those.

"Ah!" I throw my arms out and let the strong salty wind push against me. "The ocean is so beautiful!"

Kaleb laughs. "Only you!"

I turn back and grin at him. "Admit it; it's pretty grand, isn't it?"

Kaleb smiles crookedly. "It is. It's pretty big."

He changes his persona suddenly. He bows and extends a hand. "Dance with me?"

"Why," I press a hand daintily against my chest, "if you insist, good sir!"

I take his hand and he spins me toward himself. He spins me around and leads me in little circles. I laugh as he twirls me again. He dips me backwards and brings me back up. I look into his eyes. Gods, this man is perfect. My eyes detect motion behind him. They stray past his beautiful face. I scan the Forest edge.

Suddenly I see a familiar limping figure. My hand shoots out and smacks Kaleb chest hard.

"Mary, what th-" Kaleb turns around. "Mary, don't move."

"What do we do?" I whisper. Terror has me in its grip. I am unable to move. My heart is increasing and my hands begin to sweat.

"We'll see if it has seen us and…"

"And?"

The Unspeakable stops and lifts its head to the sky. Our scent. We are upwind from it.

"Run," Kaleb says in a low voice.

"What about you?" I whisper to him, frozen in fear.

"I'm right behind you," Kaleb pushes me in the direction of the village. We are far enough away from the village to be afraid. The Unspeakable can easily catch us.

I take off running toward the village and I can hear Kaleb behind me. I hear his breath catch. I look over my shoulder to see the Unspeakable tearing after us.

"Unspeakable!" Kaleb screams. "Help!"

Kaleb doesn't have his weapons on him and is defenseless. And neither of us is going to give up our secret like this, though I have a feeling that Kaleb will if needed.

A bell rings from the top of the gate. Kaleb's hand is on my back.

"Don't look back!" Kaleb yells.

I can't run any faster. My skirts are tangling in my legs. Oh Gods! I'm going to fall! Oh Gods! Oh Gods! I see men running out of the gates with spears. Oh thank the Gods!

I hear Kaleb shout as the grass rushes up to meet me. I slide forward in the grass – still 20 yards outside of the gates! Kaleb stops abruptly and stares at me in horror. Time seems frozen as our eyes lock. He's contemplating giving up

 K. L. BECKMAN

our secret. No, we cannot. It seems as though everything is in slow motion. His eyes slide up to the advancing Unspeakable.

I turn over. The Unspeakable, a whole seven feet of fury, is tearing after us. Its white eyes have locked on me. Its skin is a dusty grey and its limbs are long and gangly. I know the Unspeakable's strength is its secret. It doesn't look strong, but it is stronger than five men put together.

But its stupidity is its weakness. Kaleb says they are learning to be smart though, so it's only a matter of time.

Oh Gods, Kaleb has probably run for the walls. Where are those men? The Unspeakable is flying through the air. He's pouncing on his kill. Oh Gods! My secret can save me, but is it worth the repercussions?

My fear can't hold it back. I can feel the heat bubbling up in my veins. Faster than humanly possible, I twist sideways seconds before the Unspeakable's nails dig into the ground. The demon creature makes an awful sound, confused.

The white iris-less eyes find me and make eye contact. The Unspeakable suddenly grabs me. Its skin is too hot, burning mine. Its nails dig into me. I scream and try to wiggle away. I can see its muscles are about to contract to yank me in and devour me. Oh Gods! Oh Gods!

A spear flies lightning-quick over its arm. The thrower missed, but the Unspeakable is distracted. I scream again and try to wrench my arm away from the creature. Kaleb is suddenly there with a small dagger. He grips the knife hard and stabs the forearm of the Unspeakable. The Unspeakable lets go of me instantly and swings at Kaleb. I stumble backward as Kaleb is knocked off his feet.

Spears sail through the air. Kaleb scrambles to his feet and sprints toward me. He jerks me to my feet and pushes me toward the walls. My arm complains to me from being yanked so hard.

"Run!" He yells, leaving no room for argument, as if I would.

I run like I'm told, never looking back and never slowing down until I'm behind the walls. I run through the village all the way to my house. I run past people, their faces just a blur, and can hear the Unspeakable screaming. I sprint down the alley between the Blacksmith and the torn-down schoolhouse all the way to my back door. I wrench it open with inhuman strength, nearly tearing it off its hinges. I slam the door and collapse on the floor.

Fear does the impossible to people. I clutch my forearm in wild terror. That really just happened. Oh Gods! Oh Gods! Is Kaleb okay? Oh Gods, I can't leave. What if the Unspeakable bested all of them and is ripping through the village looking for me?

When an Unspeakable sets itself on a target, it will not rest until the victim is an Unspeakable or its meal. The Unspeakable will die trying to hunt down the target, and I made eye contact with it. Oh Gods. Oh Gods.

My skin is red, angry with blisters. I gasp in pain and stagger into the kitchen. I mash the pump repeatedly, praying for water to come up. Oh Gods. Oh Gods.

"Mary?" Mason appears in the doorway and takes me in. "Oh Gods! What happened?"

Had I been muttering out loud?

I open my mouth to say something but the cold water rushes out of the pipe, stinging my arm. I gasp loudly and grip the countertop. Mason moves closer and looks at my arm.

"Mary! What happened? What is that?" Mason turns my arm over to see the clear marks the Unspeakable left. "Is that from an Unspeakable's hand? Are you okay?"

I nod weakly, suddenly feeling the adrenaline of fear leaving me. The pain of the burn is beginning to make me dizzy.

"An Unspeakable attacked Kaleb and me," I manage to say. "I don't know where Kaleb is. He t-told me to run and I did. All the way. Here."

"Are you okay? Can I leave you to find Papa?" Mason hops around, ripping his socks off. I hear the double meaning in his question. He knows fear can bring our hard fought secret to the surface. He stands barefoot in front of me, waiting for a response. He is going to run barefoot through the village.

I nod. I'm in control now.

He tears out the backdoor, slamming it shut. The house shakes and I'm left mashing down the pump for more water. The burnt skin hurts more when the water isn't running over it. I become aware of my own breathing in my ears.

Oh Gods. I ran like a coward. I don't even know if Kaleb is alright.

I have to go see if he's okay. But what if the Unspeakable is in the village? No, there's no way that Unspeakable can make it past everyone. I need to see if Kaleb's okay.

The water stops right as I run out of the kitchen. I wrench the backdoor open. Down the alley, I can see Papa and Mason sprinting for me.

"Mary!" Papa yells. His voice is strained with worry.

"I'm okay!" I yell back.

Papa runs up the steps and pushes me into the house.

"Does anyone else know about this?" Papa turns on Mason, who is shutting the door with his shoulder.

"No," Mason shakes his head. "That's why I got you immediately."

"We can't let this get out," Papa is rummaging through all the drawers. "The people will believe you're Marked."

"But that's hogwash!" I hold my arm tightly. "An Unspeakable can't Mark you!"

"Everyone believes it," Mason says gently, guiding me into the kitchen.

"Only Darke Angels can Mark you," I frown. "And they haven't been seen since… well, since the Old World. That was nearly a century ago!"

"Unspeakables are Darke beings, Mary." Mason pats the counter top. "People think they can Mark you, too."

I hop onto the counter. "I've always wanted to know for what. Marking for what?"

"What?" Mason stops what he's doing and leans against the counter. His attention is undivided now.

"So you're Marked." I extend my arm to look at it. The skin is red and covered in blisters. It looks nasty. "What do you do when you're Marked? What does it mean?"

Mason shrugs. "I guess it means you're Corrupted."

Corruption, the turning of the soul. The Forest claims you as its own and your soul is lost. You become a demonic creature of the Grimsah.

"Just from the touch of an Unspeakable?" I ask skeptically. "That's ridiculous."

"Yes." Papa pulls out a roll of moleskin and white medical tape. "But the people believe it and they'll kick you out of the village. This is serious, Mary."

"What should I say when people ask what I've done to myself?" I extend my arm again to him. "Not that many will ask…"

"Just say you burned yourself cooking," Mason suggests. "You were reaching into the stove and weren't watching where you were reaching. It looks like a regular burn."

Papa nods. "That'll do. Say that."

Papa wraps the moleskin around the burn, cutting the necessary holes into it, and then wraps the white tape around it to hold the moleskin onto my skin. I flip my arm, looking at the tape job.

"Perhaps wear long sleeves?" Papa says, frowning.

I nod. "Okay."

The door opens and Connor bursts in, looking wild. "Papa!"

The three of us look at him.

"There was an Unspeakable! In the day!" Connor slams the door shut. "Can you believe it? Whoa, what's wrong? Why are you all looking at me like that?"

"Mary was attacked by it," Mason blurts out before any of us can say anything.

"What?" Connor's voice is like a whip. "Kaleb didn't say that!"

"Smart boy," Papa murmurs.

"We don't want people knowing that the Unspeakable touched her," Mason says. "If anyone asks, she burned herself."

"Oh," Connor realizes what they are saying. "Mary burned herself cooking. Got it. Such a clumsy girl, she is."

I look up into Papa's eyes. He smiles at me, but I can sense fear in him. Something is bothering him.

CHAPTER TWO

Mary

"Cutting it close again, Miss Mary," Mick laughs at me.

I salute him and he laughs. Mick understands my silence. He told me as much back when the wound was fresh. Since then he has always been my friend.

Mick shuts the gate and lights the fire. The fire whisks around all the walls, creating a fiery wall on top of the brick walls. He climbs down from his post and claps me on the shoulder.

"Better run on home, missy," he smiles and heads home.

Vasily, the night guard replacing Mick, nods at me as he climbs up to his post just behind the fire. He's hidden and can see as far as the fire's lights allow him.

Darkness is falling quickly and I walk toward home. The pencils in my satchel tap lightly against the sketchpad cover as I walk. I can hear loud laughing. It sounds like Riley and his gang are getting drunk off his father's stash of alcohol again. I know it should not bother me, but it does. Alcohol isn't allowed in Mika, but no one blinks an eye when Riley is drunk.

I quicken my pace. Riley thinks even less than he usually does when he's drunk. He has a strange 'thing' with me, as Connor calls it.

A mouse scampers across my path, causing me to gasp loudly. The mouse scuttles off, heading in the opposite direction. I swallow. The boys sound like they are near my house. There doesn't seem to be any way to sneak by them.

I lick my lips and walk as quietly as possible. I roll from my heels to my toes, minimizing any noise my feet can possibly make. I can hear my breath in my ears. Connor has warned me about being around Riley when he is drunk. Riley tends to get drunk before the sun is down. I don't understand why. Of all the books I've ever read, people would always get drunk at night. The books are all from the Old World, so I know they reflect what life really was like. But why would you get drunk during a time when darkness has fallen?

My pencils are tapping against the sketchpad. It's like gunshots in the darkness. My hand mashes the pencils against the pad, trying to stop the tapping. The bag sticks to the bandages on my arm for a moment.

I press myself against a house. The boys are nearby. I can hear them and they're close. I inhale a deep breath before dashing across the small path.

"Hey!" One of them spots me.

I curse under my breath and sprint toward the alley that leads to my house.

"Hey!" the voice is closer. "Hey! Wait! Mary, is that you?"

I can hear their footsteps thundering behind me. I can't tell if it's just one person or two.

"Hey!" one of them spots me.

I curse under my breath and sprint toward the alley that leads to my house.

"Hey!" the voice is closer. "Hey! Wait! Mary, is that you?"

I can hear their footsteps thundering behind me. I can't tell if it's just one person or two. I sprint around a corner. My back door is in sight. I'm running too fast. Oh Gods, this is not the time to fall down. I keep running. I can hear them catching up to me. I am fast but they're a little faster.

I open my mouth to yell for help but I can't. My voice won't cooperate with me.

I see the backdoor is lit by a torch on the wall. They're home and should be able to hear me.

Papa, please hear Riley's voice and understand what is happening!

The back door opens. I'm not close enough to the door, and Riley is gaining on me. Oh Gods, don't let him catch me!

Please, Papa! Connor! Mason! Help me, please!

Connor appears in the doorway and realizes what's happening. He throws it open and runs to me. Mason's head pokes out and then he's running down the steps. Everything is too dark and my breath is too loud.

Papa stands in the doorway, watching us. I can see someone else is behind him.

I run to Connor. He grabs my arm, the burnt one, and swings me behind him. Mason runs to Connor's side.

Riley's feet are loud as he skids to a stop in front of my brothers. Connor steps forward, shielding me further.

"Connor," Riley's voice is clearly drunk. "Mason. How're you?"

"Riley," Mason says sternly," you're drunk. Go home."

"I just wanted to see," Riley hiccups, "if Mary would say anything for me. I heard she used t' sing."

"She can't talk, Riley," Connor says menacingly. He can sound terrifying when he wants to. He steps forward. "Go home."

I peek around Connor. Riley is swaying slightly. He catches my eye.

"She doesn't talk?" Riley takes a step forward. "I coulda sworn I heard her talk to Connor once."

Connor takes a step forward, closer to Riley. "She doesn't talk."

Riley, drunk as hell, bows up to Mason. "Get outta my face, Stoneburner."

Mason shoves him backward. "Go home. You're drunk."

Riley backs away, knowing that he can't win against both my brothers. He points at me. "I'm gonna get you to talk, girl."

Connor shoves him hard, sending him staggering back. "She doesn't talk!"

Riley steals one last glance at me before disappearing into the dark alley. The light from our house is flickering, dying.

Mason turns around. "Are you okay?"

"What are you doing out so late?" Connor twists around to see me.

"The gates shut like five minutes ago," someone behind Papa says.

"C'mon." Connor's hand is on my back. "Let's go inside."

They follow me inside. Kaleb steps out from behind Papa.

"Kaleb!" I cry, hugging him. "I haven't seen you since…"

I trail off as Connor shuts the door. He squints through the little peep hole.

"Uh, oh. I think Riley heard you say that," he says, then turns. "Has he been giving you trouble again?"

All four men look down at me. Gulp.

"No," I say, fearing their reactions if I tell the truth. The last thing I want is more attention and for them to challenge the son of the richest man in these lands. "No, he's just been heckling me like he does every other girl."

Connor grunts, satisfied with my answer, and flops on the couch in the living room. Kaleb takes my arm and looks at it.

"Does it feel better?" he asks me as Papa pats my hair.

"It did until Connor grabbed it," I say loudly.

"What?" Connor isn't paying attention.

"They've got a game of chess in the other room," Papa says, smiling. "Are you okay, darling?"

I nod. "He just scared me is all."

He rubs my cheek and smiles. "Let me check your arm."

"I'll go take the bandage off in the bathroom," I say, backing away into the bathroom beside the kitchen. "I've got to go anyway."

I shut the door to the bathroom. I peel the bandage off. The wound has been feeling horribly scratchy earlier. I fling the bandage into the small trashcan by the toilet and look down at my arm. My hand shoots up to cover my mouth.

There is black dust all over the burn. Is this a Mark? Am I Corrupted? What is this?

I stick my hand under the faucet while I pump water. The water rushes out and hits my skin. The dust slides off of my skin. My skin is clear and without a blemish. I turn my wrist over. What the hell is the black dust?

I look at myself in the mirror. I clearly look panicked. I smooth my hair, which looks like fire on my head. The red curls are unwilling to be flattened. I sigh and step out of the bathroom.

"Papa," I stick out my arm. "Look!"

I certainly am not going to tell them about the black dust. For one thing, it could be dirt from the cliff edge. I don't need to worry them about dirt that got in my bandages. It's fine. It's absolutely fine.

"Remarkable," Papa touches my arm gently. "I'd say you've certainly got your mother's gift."

"Kaleb knows, Papa," I say flatly.

Papa smiles. "Of course."

I make eye contact with Kaleb who grins like a fool.

"I suppose there isn't anything to look at." Papa kisses my forehead. "Are you tired?"

"Yeah." A yawn nearly interrupts me. "I think so."

"It's not even late," Connor pipes up from the other room.

"Yeah, well," I search for an appropriate comeback, "you didn't draw all day. That requires a lot of brain power."

"No," I hear Connor say as he moves a piece. I hear the tap of the piece on the board. "But I hauled supplies all day."

"Boo hoo," I say. Papa meanders into the kitchen looking exhausted. "You pushed some boxes around? Oh, you must be so tough."

Mason snorts.

"Goodnight all!" I say before Connor can think of a retort.

I crack my door and slip out of my clothing. I pull on a white nightgown and twirl a couple times before climbing into bed. I pull the old blanket over myself and curl into a ball. I sigh happily, listening to the boys bantering in the living room.

Yet, there are a number of things that don't seem to want to settle in my mind. Riley, the Unspeakables, and Kaleb are spinning in my head. Since the attack, a mere two days ago, four Unspeakables have been seen during the day. We've killed three of them. The fourth one outran our Runners to the Forest. I say we as if I had any hand in it. I stood behind the walls watching with all the other women.

I have a sick feeling that Riley isn't going to stop harassing me. It's a nauseating feeling; it rolls over me in waves. He is going to do something drastic. I need to get inside before dark from now on. Nothing good happens after the gates close. Nothing good ever happens after dark.

Kaleb has been doing more and more runs in the Forest lately. They've been sending him farther and farther in. It just makes me sick when he's even a minute late to see me. I'm constantly worrying. Something tells me that I like him more than I care to admit.

The next morning I wake with a start. When did I fall asleep? I sit up and look around. I distinctly remember having an odd dream. I was lying in my bed when I heard a blood curdling scream outside my window. Connor and Mason were in my room but the screaming wasn't me. An Unspeakable had attacked someone outside my window.

Our house sits close to the northeast corner of walls. It isn't too unreasonable that an Unspeakable could have crawled over the wall. The thought is terrifying.

I will myself out of bed. My room is colder than usual. Perhaps a cold wind has swept in. Winter is supposed to be coming any day now. Perhaps I can debut my new pants. I sewed myself new clothes just last month, but it is all winter wear. I do love pants, but women in Mika tend not to wear them. I don't understand why.

My nightgown is sticking to me as I dig through the trunk at the foot of my bed. Mother's clothing is stashed at the bottom. I rarely wear her things. My new clothing sits in a corner on top of her old dresses.

I push the door shut and pull off my nightgown. I pull on the pants and tuck them into my boots. The boots belonged to Mother. Our feet are the same size. The leather is soft and worn, perfect for running, hiking, and climbing.

I pull on a long-sleeved tunic and pull my hair back into a loose ponytail. I'm just all different today. Usually I leave my hair down. Kaleb says my hair reminds him of a house of fire. The red ringlets seem to just be everywhere.

I step out into the hallway and nearly run into Connor.

"Oh." He is ringing his hands. He only does that when he's upset. I frown. "I was coming to check on you."

"What?" I frown at him, not moving. "What has happened?"

"Do you remember anything from last night?" He looks at me closely.

"No." I turn my head, looking over his shoulder. Mason is standing behind him. "What happened?"

Connor turns and looks at Mason.

"There was an attack last night," Mason says. He doesn't move from where he's standing. They're hiding something. I just know it. "Right outside your window."

"That wasn't a dream?" I say quietly, mostly to myself.

"No," Connor lowers his head, trying to look me in the eyes. "Do you remember anything else?"

"No." I make eye contact with Mason and then Connor. "Should I? Everything's hazy. It was a dream."

"There was a lot of screaming," Mason shudders.

When there is a scream in the middle of the night, we all know what it means. We all know that an Unspeakable has come into the village and attacked someone who wasn't in their house. No one leaves their house after dark and we usually come back to find a body, blood, remains, or nothing but evidence of a turning. But Unspeakables don't usually turn people into Unspeakables. They usually eat them.

"Was there a body?" I'm almost afraid to ask.

Connor presses his lips together.

"It was Andrew," Mason says. "One of Riley's buddies. We don't know why he was so far over here on this side of the village."

Did Riley send him to spy on me?

"Is there a lot of blood?"

"There was," Connor says. He doesn't like blood and probably didn't help cleaning it up. "Papa, Mr. Greene, and Mr. Kirkland cleaned it up."

"And the Unspeakable?" I look between them.

"Nowhere to be seen," Mason says. "And there's something else, Mary. You can't leave the village walls anymore. Papa says it's dangerous now. The Unspeakables are acting strangely and coming out the day. He thinks something is about to happen. You can't leave by yourself to go to the cliff edge."

"Am I to bring someone with me or stay inside the walls?" I hope Kaleb can come with me.

"I don't think you should stretch Mika's men," Mason says, looking away. He knows how hard that's going to be for me.

"Oh," I say, crestfallen.

I don't belong in this village. I don't talk to anyone. It's small enough that I can't escape from people. Kaleb is working today. What am I to do? What am *I* going to do? What about *me*?

"I'm sorry, Mary." Mason turns to leave. "I'll be working with Mr. Boes. Get me if you need anything."

"I'm going to head back to work, too," Connor backs away from me. "I'll be with Mrs. Merrimay."

The door shuts as my brothers leave. Well, what am I to do today? I suppose I can walk to the walls and help Mick look for any holes or weaknesses. Mick used to get his son, Barry, to do that before he was killed. Barry was our best Runner, but a group of Unspeakables bested him. It was awful. The blood was everywhere. Mick still can't talk about it. Who would be able to?

I leave the house, shutting the door with all my might, and walk toward the east gate where Mick sits with Huling. For once I don't have my satchel on me. I feel naked and my hands have nothing to hold onto.

I take the back alleys between houses to the gate. I don't want to see anyone today. Mick is the only other person, besides my family and Kaleb, who understands me. Every once in a while I say a couple words to him but, other than that, he's content to let me sign to him. He and a handful of others know sign language. There used to be a deaf boy named Aaron, but he died of sickness. It was an unexplainable sickness. Papa could do nothing for him and Aaron slowly died from the inside out.

"Miss Mary! Where's your bag?" Huling calls as I near them, coming out from behind the Greene's house.

"Hulin'." Mick elbows him. "No one's allowed out of the gates 'cept for the Runners."

I stare at the two of them. Huling seems nice enough, but I just don't feel comfortable talking in front of him. Silly, I know.

"What can I do for you, Miss Mary?" Mick smiles at me.

I look at the wall. Usually he's pretty adept at understanding what I want.

I mouth silently, "Can I walk the walls?"

Mick read my lips. "Of course! Looking for weakening?"

I nod.

"Hop on up, then!" Mick extends a hand.

I place a foot on a brick that sticks out slightly from the wall and he hoists me up on top of the wall. The wall has a narrow path on top of it that goes all around the village. If there is a weakening in the wall, the path will tell usually.

"Come back if you find anything," Mick says as I head toward the north wall.

I nod and continue to walk, my eyes on the path. My eyes stray off and I stop. Could it be? I'm on the north wall, and usually the only thing between the backs of houses and the wall is trash. I look carefully. That doesn't look like trash. That looks like a body.

I run as fast as I can on the narrow path, turning the corner almost too quickly, and running all the way to Mick and Huling. Mick stands up quickly when he sees me coming.

"What is it?" He starts after me and I turn again, running back from where I had come.

Mick is by no means young, but he's spry and strong. Huling stays at the gate, looking anxiously after us.

I point to the body.

"Oh Gods," Mick says, out of breath. "Oh Gods, I think that's Mayor Sixsmith.

"Mary," Mick puts both hands on my shoulders and makes me face him. "Mary, you need to run to Mr. Taylor. Got it? I'm going to go get your Papa. Run! Here, I'll help you down."

Mick holds my wrists tight and bends over, letting me find footing on the wall. I plop onto the ground beside the body. It doesn't smell yet.

I sprint between the houses and to the main plaza where all the shops are. Mr. Taylor is the bricklayer and sort of an unofficial officer. He's also the judge of all wrongdoings. Mr. Taylor is good friends with Papa.

I see Mr. Taylor working in his shop. No one is in front of the shop, but I can see people looking at me. I must look crazed. I run straight to Mr. Taylor and gesture frantically for him to follow me. Now people know something's wrong.

Mr. Taylor is a large man with a thick mustache under his nose. He has on a black apron covered in dust. He doesn't hesitate and drops his tools.

"What is it?" he asks me.

I run out of the shop, turning to be sure he is following me.

Mr. Taylor, the large man he is, can't keep up with me. I slow to a jog and he hustles after me. We squeeze between the houses. Papa and Mick are already there. Papa has two fingers on Mayor Sixsmith's throat.

"Oh Gods," Mr. Taylor stops in his tracks.

I turn and look at him. I can see others have followed us to see what has happened. They stand on their toes trying to see past Mr. Taylor.

"Mary," Mr. Taylor looks at me, changes his mind, and looks at Mick. "Mick, will you send these people home? I'll tell them everything they need to know when I know what has happened."

Mick nods, looking pale in the face, and shimmies past Mr. Taylor. He waves his arms.

"Go on home now," he yells. "Mr. Taylor will tell you what you need to know soon enough. Go on home!"

Mr. Johnston, I can see, isn't budging. I recognize him easily. He looks just like Riley. Curly blonde hair, blue eyes, and very tall. Riley and Mr. Johnston tower over most men in Mika. Mr. Johnston pushes past Mick. Mick lets him and continues herding people out of the alley.

"What has happened?" Mr. Johnston brushes past me.

Papa makes eye contact with Mr. Taylor before answering. I'm not sure if Mr. Johnston caught that. Papa is going to lie.

"It looks like an Unspeakable attack," Papa says gravely. "It seems the Unspeakable got more than one person last night. I'm surprised that I didn't hear Mayor Sixsmith yell out. People would have come for him."

Mr. Johnston says nothing for a moment. Then he says smoothly, "We need a new mayor before anything."

What a jeckin' parasite.

Papa's face is a mask. I can't read it. "We'll need an election but that seems a little hasty. The man just died."

Mr. Johnston's jaw clenches but he says nothing.

"That sounds about right," Mr. Taylor says. "We need to bury Marcus first. James, what should we tell the people?"

Papa hesitates and shrugs. "The truth: an Unspeakable attack."

Mr. Taylor nods and disappears down the alley. Papa looks at me. Why would he lie to Mr. Johnston? Mr. Taylor seemed to know why and didn't question it. Something else is going on. Papa was right. There is something coming.

We bury Mayor Sixsmith facing north in the Mika cemetery just hours after finding his body. If you don't bury a body quickly, its soul is trapped in this plane of existence; it is trapped by Darkeness. Luckily, he didn't have much family to account for in Mika, so arranging the burial was pretty simple. Most of his family lives in Sesaru and is only extended family.

Mr. Johnston begins pushing for the election as soon as Mayor Sixsmith is in the ground. In fact, he wants the election to be tomorrow. Most people are just too shocked to really care about how Mr. Johnston is "grieving" for the loss of our beloved Mayor.

So Mr. Taylor and Mr. O'Brien, who is a lawyer, come back to our house after the funeral to discuss the election. Papa shuts the door behind them. Connor and Mason go into the living room to clear off the couch and chairs. I take out a loaf of bread to toast for the men. Then door opens and all turn to see Kaleb walk in.

"Can you believe that jackass?" Kaleb says.

"That wasn't an Unspeakable," Mr. Taylor suddenly says. "Why did you say it was?"

"Mr. Johnston is a dangerous man," Papa says back, his eyes cutting toward Connor and me. Papa *did* lie to Mr. Johnston.

"You should have said what it really was," Mr. O'Brien sits down on a stool. "The people need to know what this man really is."

"A devil," Mr. Taylor finished.

"But-"

"Mr. Johnston is a dangerous man. I repeat, a dangerous man!" Papa interrupts Mr. O'Brien. "If I had said that, I would have been next. Mr. Johnston has very powerful allies that just so happen to be Mika's enemies."

"But-"

Mr. Taylor suddenly interrupts Mr. O'Brien again. "He's just like his son. He's charming and knows how to work the people over. He's going to be elected. We need to accuse him before it's too late."

"But-"

"I am not going to risk our lives to try and convince the people!" Papa says, nearly yelling. "He's fooling them! They don't see that he's not grieving! The man's a phenomenal liar!"

"But-"

"Out with it, man!" Mr. Taylor roars at Mr. O'Brien.

"But what if James ran for mayor!" Mr. O'Brien bursts out in frustration. "You are more liked than Johnston," he says to Papa.

"I'm Mika's doctor. I cannot be both." Papa's voice is quiet again.

Kaleb moves to stand next to me, listening to the conversation. I bend to take the bread out of the oven. Kaleb swats my hands away and takes the bread out himself.

"You don't need to do everything," he whispers.

"James, he's got a point," Mr. Taylor says. "You're the only person that stands a chance against Johnston."

"At what cost?" Papa folds his arms.

Kaleb cuts the bread into slices and sets the tray on the table beside the men. He picks two pieces up. Connor grabs several pieces and hands one to Mason, watching Papa. Mason chews his bread slowly.

"What do you mean?"

"At what cost!" Papa is shaking his head. He's set against running. "If I win, who's to say I won't end up like Marcus? Stabbed repeatedly and so damn bloody that it looks like an Unspeakable mauled me? If I lose, who's to say he won't kill me anyway to shut me up. He'll figure out that I saw through it. Whether he killed Marcus himself or had someone else do it, Johnston is responsible for the murder of our mayor."

Mr. O'Brien and Mr. Taylor are silent for a moment.

"What if he wins?" Mason asks quietly. "What then?"

Mr. Taylor shakes his head. "I'm sorry, fellas, but I would leave if I were you. If he becomes mayor, I will move to Sesaru. They have an actual police force there."

Mr. O'Brien nods. "Me, too. I'll get my family out before his first day as mayor."

Papa hesitates. He can't leave Mika. We can't leave. Everything is here and Papa is the doctor. He cannot leave people to suffer, and he knows it.

Mr. Taylor shakes his head. "Well, that's it, then. I'm going to start packing tonight. I'll be out as soon as dawn breaks. I need to make it to Sesaru before nightfall."

Mr. O'Brien claps Mr. Taylor's shoulder. "You won't be alone. My family and I will be with you."

"You can't make it to Sesaru before nightfall," Papa says, looking between the two.

"We know," Mr. O'Brien sighs. "We'll stick close to the coastlines."

"Are you going to go through the mountains?"

"No choice but to go around," Mr. Taylor sighs. "There's no way Daria can make it through the mountains."

Daria, Mr. O'Brien's pregnant wife, is due any day. It is too risky for them to go, I think.

"I'll be praying for yours and Daria's, especially, safety," Papa presses his lips together.

Kaleb squeezes my hand. Things are about to get dark.

CHAPTER THREE

Mary

One year and a season later. Winter.

Mayor Johnston is as bad as Papa said he would be. We have heard from Mr. Taylor and Mr. O'Brien. Daria gave birth to a stillborn boy, but they are safe and settled in Sesaru.

Johnston has the Runners patrolling the walls. Only the Runners are allowed out. I haven't seen the ocean in months. Riley has been unbearable. I can't escape outside the walls, so I've been reduced to sitting in my room and reading.

I set my book down and stare at the wall. I have to get out of this house. I look at the clock. It is a little late to be wandering about. I bite my lip. Surely Riley won't be out. It's so cold outside. Sure, he's been unbearable but that's only during the day, during the warmest part of the day, when I'm out and about.

I pull on a coat and slip into high-kneed boots. I lace them up tightly, securing them against the wet snow. I button my coat all the way up and wiggle a hat onto my head.

I step out of my room as Connor is coming to his room. He raises an eyebrow.

"Where are *you* going?" He folds his arms and stands in my way.

"I'm going crazy in that room," I sigh dramatically.

"What about your books?" Connor leans against the wall.

"I've read them all," I say flatly.

"You've read them all?" He's skeptical.

"Try me." I raise an eyebrow now.

"Ugh." Connor goes into his bedroom. "That's too much effort."

I laugh at him and make my way out to the living room. Mason is lounging on a chair, sprawled out sideways. He looks up from his book.

"Where are you going?" Mason frowns at me.

"Just to wander," I shrug, trying to be nonchalant about it. "I'm going insane in my room."

"What about your books?" he asks me.

I glare at him. "I've read them already."

"All of them?"

"Well, I haven't gotten any new ones lately."

"Be safe." Mason is still frowning. "Papa is not going to be happy."

"Where is he?"

"He's over at the Sullivan's." He runs a hand through his hair as he stretches. "They just had a baby not too long ago."

"Oh okay," I say, stifling a yawn. "I'll be back before long."

"See that you do," Mason says, cutting me a glance.

I stick my tongue out at him and slip out the door. I bounce down the stiff wooden steps and sink my feet into the snowy ground. I bury my hands into my pockets. The cold air burns my cheeks pleasurably. A cold night always makes me feel alive.

Despite my pleasant overall feeling, I still am on high alert. Just because it is cold outside does not mean that'll keep Riley indoors. The man is crazy, and crazy is unpredictable.

As I round a corner, someone grabs me and slams me hard against the wall. I gasp and fear seizes me. The aggressor pulls down the scarf around his mouth. Riley smiles at me.

"I knew you'd come out of there eventually." Riley fingers the buttons on my coat as his eyes slowly work their way up to mine. "You're mine now."

My mind goes completely blank. I know I should do something. Instead, I stand there and stare at him blankly.

"Did you think you could stay there for the rest of your life?" Riley raises his hand to my neck. His fingertips tickle my neck. "I knew you had to come out. I put people on watch to see when you would come out. And tonight I just so happened to be on watch."

Why? I want to ask. Instead, I stare at him blankly.

He jerks me closer to himself.

"Because you're mine." Riley smiles wickedly.

That isn't the reason. It can't be. Yet, craziness isn't based in logic so who knows what the reason could be. Gods, I need to do something! Connor and Mason spent a whole day with me teaching me self-defense for a time like this. Oh, what were the moves?

I suddenly step forward and simultaneously send a hard palm-strike to the base of his jaw. He steps backward, off balance, and I fit an ungainly kick to his stomach in. He reels backward and lands on his rear. I tear off in the opposite direction. I'll reroute back to the house. I cut through several alleys between houses. I can hear Riley behind me. He's much faster and larger than I am. I cut suddenly to the left and clamber over a woodpile. I find myself back on the main street. I sprint toward the small road that leads to my house. I turn onto the road, slipping and sliding as I go.

I can hear Riley close behind me. Suddenly, he tackles me from behind. I hit the ground hard and immediately roll over. A silent scream fills my throat.

"No one is going to come. No one is going to come out." Riley has a hand around me throat. I couldn't scream even if I could bring myself to speak in front of Riley.

I kick with both feet, pushing him backward, but I can't push his weight off of me. Riley slaps me hard across the face.

We didn't practice this! I gasp again.

I fight against his weight and his strength. Riley laughs at me. He lets himself fall on top of me. I grunt beneath his weight. Then my stomach flips as he begins to undo my pants. I buck and flail wildly, screaming in my head for Papa or Connor or Mason to sense my panic.

Someone has to come out! Someone has to come out! Gods, I'm going to be raped right here and no one will help.

I claw his face with my nails and buck up. I jerk my arms down, trying to give myself some form of momentum. Riley stays on top of me and slaps my face again.

"Stay still!"

Like hell! I buck and kick wildly. He gives me a sharp punch. I cover my face, still screaming. The punches fall harder and faster now.

"Hey!" someone else yells.

"Get that jeckin' bastard off of her!"

Riley's body is lifted off of me suddenly. I sit up, dazed from the blows. Someone lifts me from beneath my armpits and picks me up.

"Are you okay?" Papa turns me around and scans my face.

Mason and Connor leap on top of Riley and begin to beat him. The sounds of the blows are loud and solid. Riley begins to scream. Connor knocks him out with a sharp blow to the face. Riley's body goes limp and they stand up, giving him a couple more kicks for good measure. Mason storms over to me with Connor in tow. They stand in front of me looking angry.

Papa pulls me gently back to the house. I look over my shoulder at Riley's body.

"He can freeze to death for all I care," Connor announces as we climb up the steps. Mason shoulders the door open and lets us in.

"Mary," Mason turns and starts to say something.

"I don't want to talk about it," I say, putting a hand up. "Let's just pretend this never happened, please."

My brothers nod reluctantly. "Of course."

Papa frowns. "I'm here when you want to talk about it."

This is one of the many times I wish Mother was still alive. There are some things you just don't want to talk about with males. How humiliating. How horrible. This is the worst day of my life.

I wake up with a start, remembering Riley's actions last night. I fold my arms across my chest and wander out to the living room. Papa and Mason are sitting at the table eating soup for breakfast. Connor sits down between them and smiles at me.

"Morning, Mary," he says a little too brightly.

They are trying to act normal, to pretend like nothing happened.

"G'morning," I mumble sleepily.

I curl up on the couch and watch them eat. I don't really want to eat or talk or do anything.

"I'm joining the Runners," Connor announces.

Papa's head snaps up from his soup. "Excuse me?"

"I'm old enough." Connor twirls his spoon. "I want to be a Runner."

"When do you go?" I ask, knowing he has already sent word to Kaleb.

"Next week," Connor says quietly.

Papa shakes his head. "I wish you had told me sooner."

"Are you okay with this?" Connor asks. Mason's head turns between the two of them.

Papa hesitates before nodding slowly. "Only if you promise not to do anything stupid."

Connor smiles, his smile as wide as the ocean. "I promise not to be stupid!"

Papa laughs. "Okay, I'll clear up. Oh, and Mary? I ordered some more pencils from Mr. Sharp. They are there now if you want to run and get them. I think he said he put them in his letterbox."

"Right now?" I twist in my seat to look out the window. The sky is dark with heavy clouds. Darkness has fallen and a storm is coming.

"No," Papa thinks better of it. "You should probably go in the morning."

"We haven't seen Unspeakables in forever, Pap," Mason says. "Let her get them. I'll go with her. I want to stop by Penny's anyway."

Connor dramatically starts gagging, clutching his throat, and finally collapses on the table with his tongue sticking out. He has been particularly childish lately.

Mason snorts. "Just wait until you've got a girl of your own."

Connor gags again and falls out of his chair. He twitches on the ground. Papa chuckles and I laugh. He is *so* dramatic!

"Go on, go on," Papa shoos us, "before Connor has a seizure."

Connor twitches again.

Mason grabs his coat and mine, throwing mine to me, and we leave. Mason shuts the door with a hard shove.

"One of these days," Mason shakes his fist at me. "Connor will be nothing but a puddle of drama."

I laugh. "He's getting more dramatic."

"Maybe the Runners will knock some sense into him." Mason bumps me. "Man, I haven't seen Penny in so long."

Penny is Mason's girlfriend. She is one of the kindest people I know. But it has been a while since I last saw her. Penny only moved to Mika half a year ago from Gedan, and she and Mason have already been dating a couple of months. She teaches the younger kids in school. Mason always checks on her because she lived alone in Marcus Sixsmith's old house.

We stop in the middle of the plaza by the center tree Mika has kept alive all these years.

"I'll run by Penny's. I'll meet you back here in fifteen? Or if I'm not here, head to Penny's." Mason smacks my arm. "Sound good?"

"Sounds good!" I shove my hands deep in my coat pockets.

I walk toward Mr. Sharp's General Store. The shops all look the same: thatch roofs, clay walls, and little wooden doors. I peer in his drop box. I can see someone else is picking some butter up. I grab my pencils and leave the tube of butter in the box.

I walk back to the center of the plaza by the large tree and lean against it. People are hustling through the plaza trying to get to their homes as quickly as possible. We haven't seen Unspeakables in several months, but everyone is still wary after the double killings of Andrew and Mayor Sixsmith a year ago.

I walk toward Penny's house. I shove the pencils in my pocket and squint in the dim lighting. There is a torch always lit in the plaza to provide a little extra light, but the torch is flickering and not providing nearly enough to see anything clearly.

Someone bumps right into me. I'm pushed backward.

"Mary." Riley is standing over me, breathing hard. "Did you see anything?"

I shake my head. What is he talking about? I swallow. I'm too close to him and too alone. His breath doesn't stink of alcohol. He's sober and very aware of our situation.

"Good." He reaches out and pulls a strand of my hair. He stares at it and then looks at me. "I don't have time to deal with you now, but I will later."

Riley disappears before a thought can come to my head. I stand there for a moment. Did he just threaten me? I look towards Penny's house. The lights are on inside.

I dash toward her house and burst in without even knocking.

Mason leaps to his feet when I burst into the living room. Penny is sitting on the couch looking embarrassed. I ignore them both.

"Riley," I say through ragged breathing. "Riley just threatened me."

"What?" Penny sits up. Her honey-colored hair is a mess.

"What did he say?"

"He-he said that he didn't have time to deal with me but he would later," I look between them both. "What does that mean?"

Mason frowns. "Let's go home. Penny, will you be safe?"

Penny smiles. "I'll be okay."

Penny, too, carries the secret we all carry. But she wasn't able to keep her secret. Her past came with her and many people know what she is. We can still choose to keep our identities a secret, especially with Papa being the doctor.

Mason grabs my arm and we leave Penny hugging herself in her kitchen. She smiles at me as Mason shuts the door. We walk briskly all the way home. Mason pushes me in the house rather roughly and slams the door behind him.

Papa looks up pleasantly. He has been reading.

"Riley's threatened Mary," Mason says, clearly agitated. Why is he so upset? It wasn't much of a threat. I must be missing something…

Papa's book lowers slightly. "Excuse me?"

Mason nods. "He said he didn't have time to deal with her but he would later."

"Where did you see him?" Papa looks at me. I'm definitely missing something here.

"He bumped into me as I was walking to Penny's," I look back and forth between them. They're not telling me something. "He touched my hair."

Connor walks into the room, mouth full of bagel. "What?"

Papa and Mason ignore him.

"Connor," Papa turns in his chair to look at him. "Is Kaleb staying with us tonight?"

"He should be. It's Ashes Week," Connor says. "He'll be with us for two weeks."

Papa nods, thinking to himself.

"Mary," Mason says as he runs his fingers through his hair. "Why don't you go on to bed? Tomorrow is prepping day for Ashes Week."

Ashes Week, my favorite time of the year. Everyone worships the Gods in their very own way, putting aside work for a whole week to devote all time to the Gods. Not everyone worships the same Gods so many pick and choose who to worship that year.

Papa smiles at me. The smile doesn't reach his eyes. "Goodnight, darling."

I nod, sensing a conversation not to be heard by my ears. I'll read in my room until they think I'm asleep. I kick off my shoes by the door and pad back to my room. I shut the door and turn to face my room. I pull my nightgown off of the bed and strip off my clothes. I pull the soft gown over myself while thinking about what to read. I look around my room.

I have more books than my bookshelf can hold, so I have stacks of books in front of it as well. I pick up a historical fiction novel on the Ravage that I haven't yet read. It's one of the few New World novels that has been published.

I flip through the pages, looking at the pictures. The first half of the book is composed of pictures from the Old World, black and white photos showing wars. I prefer learning about the wars in the Old World. You can learn much from the wars and what they were based on. My favorite Old World war is World War Two, followed closely by World War Four. The pictures are vastly different. The World War Two pictures are black and white shots of men suffering in laughable armor. The pictures' backgrounds are usually of trenches or burned lands. The World War Four pictures are clear color shots depicting horror. The soldiers have on alien-like armor and in the background is orange-brown dust that seems to cover everything. Their armor is tan colored in an attempt to blend in. After World War Four came the Ravage. The pictures from the Ravage are shown with a warning. Viewer discretion is advised. The images are bloody, violent, and uncensored.

After World War Four, the first true biological war, the effects of the poisons were starting to take their toll. I look at the pictures, ignoring all the text in between. The pictures show men turning Gods into Unspeakables. Most of the pictures are bloody with an infected man hunched over a single body or many bodies. Blood drips from his mouth and stains his torn clothing. His skin is a strange blotchy combination between grey and pale flesh. I flip through the pictures. The pictures show more and more Unspeakables and fewer and fewer humans.

The next picture is of the interfering. A photographer has captured a man parting earth. The man has golden hair and stands with his arms wide open. The earth before him is cracking and people are running everywhere. The Unspeakables are on the other side of the parted earth.

The pictures after that are of people burning the earth, trying to burn the Unspeakables. High fires rage over three figures in one picture. A smaller picture in the corner of the page shows an Unspeakable on fire.

I turn the page. A photographer, probably human, has captured a fight between a large werewolf and an Unspeakable. The werewolf has the Unspeakable's throat in its jaws. This was when the Gods sent all the creatures: Werewolves, Elves, Fairies, Keepers, Lightnings… everything. The Gods had kept so many things from the Old World, and now we can't imagine life without these creatures.

The next picture has clearly been taken from the back of a dragon. The photographer is high in the air and has captured a picture of a huge forest burning. This is the first known attempt to burn the Grimsah Forest. I know this Forest, and this is the Forest in the beginning.

I really ought to read this book or ask Kaleb about the full history of the Ravage. Kaleb has read this book cover to cover several times and owns many other history books. He should teach at the Western Kingdom University in Gedan instead of being a Runner, but he loves being a Runner. I know he loves history more but he won't listen.

I shut the book and listen to the conversation in the kitchen. I had been tuning it out. Now I strain my ears trying to listen, but I can't hear them. They're whispering. I sigh. I might as well go to sleep.

I close my eyes and flop backward onto my pillow. I sigh heavily. I can't get comfortable. I slide out of bed and stand up. I twirl several times before climbing back in. It's an odd little bedtime ritual, but it seems to work most of the time. I pull the covers over myself and bury my face into a second pillow. The pillow had belonged to Mother but has long since lost her scent. It is just nice to have.

I slowly become aware of a low growling noise. Or is it a moan? I sit up quickly, eyes wide open, listening. It is outside my window! I slowly slide out of bed, trying my best not to let the bed creak. I creep softly toward the windows, walking on the sides of my feet to be quiet.

I duck under the window and crawl to the other side. I stand up slowly and smoothly, pressing myself against the wall. I peer down, looking for the source. At first, I see nothing. I can see the dirt, but it's not its usual brown. It's a dark color or wet. It looks wet. Is it blood? My mind jumps to terrible conclusions immediately. Have the Unspeakables learned to control their noises? Unspeakables always have the impulse to scream when they've made a kill or been injured. In fact, Unspeakables scream at just about everything.

I take a deep breath and dare to step in front of the window to look around. A human body lies under my window! How many people are going to die under my window!

A foreign feeling seizes me just then. An overpowering impulse to run outside and investigate comes over me and I can't resist. I bolt from my room, still in my nightgown and barefooted, through the kitchen and out the back door. I hear Papa and the boys cry out after me.

I run around the side of the house, and the danger of being outside alone, even for a couple minutes, suddenly hits me. I falter momentarily in my investigation, pausing before approaching the softly moaning person. It is a woman. The smell of blood is strong. The metallic smell is distinct.

She moans again. Someone suddenly grabs me and I nearly scream.

"What are you doing?" Papa snaps. He sounds angry.

"She needs help." I pull away from his grip. I'm confident now. Papa is here with me and nothing can happen.

I approach the woman. She's barely conscious, lying on her back. I squat beside her and wave a hand over her eyes.

"Oh Gods!" Papa gasps, seeing the woman for the first time. "Stay with her! I'll be right back!"

Stay with her? Alone? She smells like blood! Can't the Unspeakables smell her? I swallow loudly and look down at the woman.

Connor appears from the side of the house. He rushes to my side and takes the woman's hand.

"She's still alive," Connor murmurs. He looks up at me. "Do you see any bite marks? We need to kill her now if she's infected."

I'm surprised at such a cutthroat attitude from Connor. He usually is inclined to stick it out to the end. For him, death has never been the immediate answer. I would expect that from Mason.

"W-what?" I stumble over my words. "N-no. She's fine. I... I don't see anything."

"That's not going to cut it," Connor says rather gruffly. He pulls the woman up, supporting her head with one hand and pulling her up by her arm, being careful not to touch her blood. If she is infected, her blood can infect us.

"We need a light. I don't see anything," I say, looking at her back. Her back is covered in blood. It's hard to say what happened to her. "There's blood everywhere."

Papa and Mason suddenly run around the corner of the house with a sheet.

"We need to get her inside now," Papa says quietly. Why is he being so quiet?

"Here," Connor says quietly. He seems to know why. "Put the blanket beside her and we'll lift her onto it."

Are Unspeakables near?

Almost like an answer to my question, I hear a high sickening scream not too far off. That scream is much too close for my liking!

Papa, Mason, and Connor gently lift her onto the blanket.

"Mary," Papa says, picking up an end of the blanket. "Hold that end!"

The four of us pick up corners of the blanket and rush her inside. The woman gives a pitiful moan as we jostle through the back door.

"Here." Papa starts to lower his corner. "Let's put her here."

We set her down in the middle of the living room.

"Mason, get my bag."

Mason runs from the room back to Papa's bedroom for his medicine bag.

"Where is the blood coming from?" Papa mutters to himself, as he pulls on rubber gloves.

"Her back," I say quietly.

She moans again.

"Shh." Papa pets her hair. "It'll be alright. Just a moment."

"We can't let Johnston know about her yet," Mason suddenly says.

Connor and I look at Papa. Johnston doesn't like foreigners, especially ones that show up in the middle of the night terribly wounded. He'd ask her so many questions. He may even kill her. He killed an old werewolf passing through just a couple months ago. He claimed that the old man had attacked him. We know better. Johnston was threatened by a being more powerful than he.

"We'll heal her here and go from there," Papa murmurs. He gently rolls her onto her stomach.

"Get me a pillow," Papa says to Connor. "A small one."

Connor grabs one off the couch. It is our only decoration in the entire house. Papa puts it under her head and turns her head to the side. She groans in pain.

She is wearing a formless, grey dress and no shoes, which suggests to me that she is either poor or an escaped slave. I glance at her feet. But her feet don't look as though she's been walking barefoot. They aren't cut, crusted, dry, or calloused. Her feet are clean, aside from the dirt. Her back is covered in blood. The blood is matted against her skin and the dress. The blood is also in her hair.

Her hair is a true golden blonde color but matted against her back in clumps of blood. It almost looks as though she's been burned.

Papa begins cutting the dress off of her. She moans a little louder. She is conscious.

"Don't worry," Papa murmurs. "We're going to make you better."

I crawl to her side and take her hand. It just feels like the right thing to do. I give her hand a little squeeze. Her eyes are still shut, but I know she appreciates the touch.

Papa stares at her back. The dress and blood are sticking to her skin.

He looks up at me.

"This may hurt a little," he says to her. "Squeeze Mary's hand, ok?"

She doesn't give a response, but Papa prepares to pull the fabric away from her skin. He begins to cut off as much as he can. He slides his knife between her skin and the dress. Very carefully, he cuts it off of her. I hear the sticking sound give a release as he pulls the fabric off of her skin. She squeezes my hand with more strength than I thought she had. She doesn't moan.

Finally, Papa has cut the back of her dress off. He leaves her sleeves and stops just at the top of her buttocks. Blood is still everywhere and it's not clear to me, at least, where the source of it is. Mason brings Papa a bowl of water, as though he knows what Papa is about to do.

Papa dips a soft square of fabric from his medicine bag into the glass. He gently begins wiping the blood off of her. Her grip loosens slightly but her grip on my hand is still tight.

Blood trickles off of her and stains the sheet beneath. The smell of the blood is strong in the room. I look up at Papa. The smell is too strong.

"The smell, Papa," I say, worried. What if the Unspeakables go into a frenzy or something?

"Connor," Papa looks up at him. "Make some bread."

Connor dashes into the kitchen and begins banging around. I can hear him rushing to get the bread going.

"Do anything you can to make this smell go away!" Papa calls.

Papa wipes across her shoulder blades, and she cries out loudly. Papa pauses and looks closely. He puts the rag in the cup and examines her shoulder blades.

She's whimpering now. I squeeze her hand.

"It looks like," Papa frowns, "like her skin has been torn off here, but that doesn't explain this much blood. There must-"

He stops talking suddenly and rummages through his bag. The woman relaxes considerably. Her grip on my hand loosens to a point where it is me holding onto her.

"Papa?" I watch him carefully. "What is it?"

He doesn't answer me as he pulls out a small glass bottle filled with white cream. The cream looks strange. It almost seems to sparkle. I've never seen him use this cream before.

"What is that?" I ask him. The cream almost looks translucent.

He dips two fingers into the cream and carefully spreads it over one of her shoulder blades. He seems to know where the blood is coming from now. He spreads the cream over a large cut on her shoulder blade evenly. It is a long and narrow gash going from the top of her shoulder blade to the middle of her ribs. Papa dips his fingers in the cream again and does the same to her opposite shoulder. The woman sighs.

Papa wipes his forehead, seeming relieved. "Okay, go on to bed now," he says to us.

"What?" Mason, who has been sitting in a chair behind Papa, leans even further toward him. "That's it?"

Papa nods. "Connor, I'll take care of that bread. You three go and try to get some sleep!"

"What?" Connor yells from the kitchen. He leans out, looking at us.

"Go on to bed," Papa repeats himself. "I'll take care of all that."

I stand up reluctantly, my hand sliding out of hers. The boys walk back to bed, exhausted. I hear both doors shut. I look down at the woman. Papa glances up at me.

"Go on to bed, Mary," he says gently. "It'll be okay."

I hesitate and he raises his eyebrows.

"Go on," he smiles, "She'll be okay."

I kiss his cheek and look at the woman one last time before retiring to my bedroom.

CHAPTER FOUR

Mary

Hope, as we have come to know her, healed rapidly over the next several weeks. I suspect her rapid recovery is due to that strange cream Papa applies to her wounds. I also suspect Hope is not a human.

Hope has taken to following me around. Since I can't go out to the cliff edge, I haven't minded her company. In fact, she's kind of won us all over. I wouldn't be surprised if she and Connor hit it off before long. Hope is so kind and sweet, she could win anyone over. The other girls don't shoot me dirty looks as often because she's with me. Mika is a pretty good sized community and Hope already knows everyone by name. She's only been walking about for a couple weeks now, yet she knows every single person.

Mayor Johnston almost seems charmed by her. He doesn't mind her staying with us. Papa and Mason concocted a story for Hope. She didn't want to lie but, when she realized the dangers behind telling the truth, she happily obliged. Everyone knows her as our cousin from Gedan and she plays the part well. Johnston doesn't suspect a thing.

Hope almost seems unearthly. Her skin is white as snow and nearly glows in perfection. The girl is perfect, I swear. She has thick golden hair that seems to spiral down her back.

To match her angelic form, she has bright blue eyes with long dark blonde lashes. Hope is the exact image of what I imagine an angel would look like. Her voice is sweet, and I've never heard her say anything derogatory toward anyone.

She is perfect.

I was worried about her perfection at first, thinking everyone would notice, but they all just seem to think she's sweet. No one questions her humanity. I haven't voiced my wonderings, but I really think she's not human.

"Mary," Hope interrupts my thoughts again.

This time I look up. "Oh, sorry. What?"

"It's your turn," Hope smiles brilliantly, flashing her white teeth. "Were you daydreaming again?"

The wind blows her hair and she tucks it behind an ear. It is so bright outside. The sun is reflecting off of her hair. Is it possible to go blind looking at the reflection of the sun off of someone's hair?

I smile back and move my pawn. "Yeah, sorry. I just get so caught up. I think I tune everything else out."

I hunch over the little wooden board between us, my fingers still on the pawn. People pass us, peering at our game. We are sitting outside the bakery, my back against the wall and hers against a barrel of wheat. It's not hard to miss us what with her golden sun-hair and my red hair.

I lift my fingertips off of the pawn. The pawn has moved into dangerous territory.

She watches my move carefully. Her eyes flicker around the board, looking for weaknesses.

"Yes, I know what you mean. Sometimes I think so hard I become deaf!"

I nod. "So what do we want to do after this game?"

Hope moves her bishop forward, bumping my pawn out of the way. She holds her fingers on the piece, looking around the board one last time. Then she lifts her fingers off and makes eye contact with me, waiting for me to take her bishop. But I see no offensive moves for myself.

"Well," she looks back down at the board again, "we walked the wall yesterday and drew the day before…"

She wants me to decide.

"We could do both?" I move my rook backward into its original spot.

Hope watches the board and says nothing, thinking.

I sigh heavily and she looks up. "What are we going to do?"

She doesn't respond and waits for me to continue.

"I mean," I lean back against the stone wall. "I'm too old for school and you are, too. We can't be Runners-"

"Why not?" she asks. She likes Kaleb and the Runners. She likes to listen to him talk about his job. I do, too. It is always fascinating. Sometimes, he even tells us plans of other Runner Bands from neighboring villages.

"Well," I frown, "we're girls and we're not fast enough."

"You don't know how fast I am." Hope folds her arms and smirks. "Besides, you're very fast when you're not wearing skirts… at least, according to Kaleb."

I laugh at that. Kaleb likes to say I become ten times clumsier and slower in skirts and dresses. I'd say it's true!

I shrug. "I guess you could be a Runner if you wanted. There used to be a couple girl Runners, but they're mothers now. It's just not an interest of mine."

Hope sticks out her lower lip in thought. "I suppose, though I don't think I'd want to do it either."

"Yeah," I look back down at the board. "But what are we going to do? Where is life going for us? Are we just going to play games and draw every day?"

"Sometimes we walk the wall." Hope moves her own rook forward three spaces.

"Yeah," I immediately move my endangered pawn forward one. "But you know what I mean."

Hope props an elbow on her knee and puts her cheek in her hand. She picks up her queen but sits up, looking at me.

"So what will we do?" She throws her arms out. "Are we going to let life pass us by like this?"

"We can't very well leave Mika's walls without Papa's permission." I sit back on my hands.

Hope stands up. "C'mon, let's go ask him. There hasn't been an Unspeakable attack since I've gotten here. Surely he'll let us go out to the cliff edge you always talk about! I've never been outside these walls."

Hope never speaks about her life previous to the night we found her. We have never asked her and she has never said anything. She has let on that she has never seen the world. Mason suspects she was a slave. Connor thinks she was a royal and is now exiled. I think she's not human and somehow was injured and can't remember her life.

I stand up. The chess board always stays here for others to play. The baker takes it in during the night and brings it out in the mornings.

Hope grabs my hand and begins pulling me through the square.

"Do you even know where he is?" I ask, not resisting her.

"Of course." Hope doesn't look back. "He's with the Greens!"

She pulls me up the stairs to the Green's little cottage. Mr. Green is suffering from that strange disease. We don't see it much here in Mika but sometimes people die. The disease usually strikes when they're either very old or very young, and it just takes over them from the inside out. Nothing Papa does can heal them.

Papa opens the door right as Hope reaches for it. He jumps visibly.

"Papa!" I say, surprised. I've never seen Papa jump like that.

"Hello," Hope says in a singsong voice. "I was wondering if Mary and I could go out to the cliff edge."

Before Papa can answer her, she throws her hands up.

"Okay," she waves her palms at him. "I know what you're thinking, but there have been zero Unspeakable sightings! The Runners haven't seen them, and I've never been outside these walls!"

Papa frowns, shutting the door behind him, and looks past us. He thinks for a moment and opens his mouth.

Hope clasps her hands together. "Please?"

Papa's face softens into a smile. "Only if you can take one of the boys with you."

Hope pumps the air with her fist. "Yes! Let's go get Kaleb!"

"Thanks, Papa!" I manage to say before Hope pulls me back down the stairs.

He laughs and waves as we disappear around a corner to find Kaleb. We'll find him in the Runner's huts on the very southeastern side of Mika. Hope lets go of my hand and we run through the village. It's nice not having to fuss with skirts as I run.

Lately, I haven't been wearing skirts as much. Hope and I both prefer to wear trousers. She rolls hers up to her knees, folding them carefully as she goes. I haven't tried that yet, but it looks comfortable.

"What's today?" I ask her. Would Kaleb even be available today?

"He's off today," she answers, knowing my thoughts too well.

"Kaleb?" Hope begins to call loudly.

Too loud. Too loud.

Other Runners poke their heads out of their individual little huts.

"Kaleb?" Hope moves through the huts, still calling. The huts are probably five feet tall and wide enough to fit a bed and a little dresser for clothes and hooks to hang weapons. I've only seen inside once. Hope pauses and calls for him again. There is no way he can't hear her! They can probably hear her all the way in the Eastern Kingdom!

"What! What! What!" Kaleb emerges from his hut, waving his hands for her to be quiet.

"Let's go to the cliff edge!" Hope is practically bouncing.

"What?" Kaleb frowns. "I thought Mr. Stoneburner said not to-"

"Nope!" Hope beams. "He said we could go if you came with us!"

Kaleb looks at me and I feel my heart skip a beat. Why does he make me feel this way?

"Have you got your sketch pad and pencils?"

I nod and pat my satchel. I always have them with me.

"Alright then." Hope claps her hands together. "Let's go! Oh, this is so exciting! This is more exciting than pigs in a pen!"

Kaleb and I exchange a look. Half the things she says make absolutely no sense to anyone but her. She is practically trembling with excitement.

"Hold on." Kaleb ducks back into his hut and comes out with a bow and arrow in hand. "Just to be safe."

I have not been allowed to leave Mika's walls in over a year. Johnston has allowed people to leave recently, but Papa hasn't let me. What I don't understand is that Hope could leave if she wanted, but she never left me despite many invitations for her to join others to pick flowers or something or other.

As soon as we step out of Mika's walls, Hope glances at me. She gives me a calculating look. I've never seen her look at me like that. She usually just looks thoughtful.

"I'll race you there!" She looks ready to run. "Is it straight ahead?"

"Yeah," I say as she takes off. I call after her. "But watch out! It'll sneak up on you!"

I take off running after her and Kaleb runs between us, not wanting to leave either of us completely alone.

I watch his form. He's a fast runner with strong legs and powerful arms. I've seen him without his shirt a couple times and his body is toned and tan. And I completely understand why all the girls drool over him.

Hope stops abruptly at the edge and flings her arms out in a moment of pure excitement. She is a small figure against the mass blueness of the ocean. Hope's hair blows behind her with the sea wind. She breaths in the air visibly, her small form expanding with the incoming oxygen. Like me, she takes pleasure in such simple things. Kaleb and I look out at the ocean beside her. She sighs happily.

"Have you ever seen anything more beautiful?"

I smile, remembering how I used to stare at the ocean for hours. The waves bob up and down endlessly. Hope sighs and sits down, watching it. Kaleb sits down, facing away from the ocean and watching the Forest.

I sit down and take out my sketch pad and pencils. The ocean's salty wind blows the grass, tickling my shins.

"Hope," Kaleb says suddenly, not looking away from the Forest.

She doesn't glance at him. "Yes?"

"Where did you come from?"

In my peripheral, I see her back stiffen slightly.

"I'm going to be blunt," Kaleb says in a low voice. He sounds tense. "Are you a slave? An exiled royal? Or are you even human? Personally, I think you're not human, but I can't figure out what you are. I've narrowed it down to only a couple species."

Hope doesn't say anything.

Kaleb is on my side! He thinks just like I do!

"You're not demonic," Kaleb continues, "but you're not Godly. You don't seem to possess any visible powers, so you're not a Lightning or a Rider. You don't have strange skin so you're not a faerie, a Thunder, or a Keeper. I know you're not a werewolf."

I look up at him. What is he getting at? I stare at Hope.

Lightnings are beings with glowing skin that possess all powers and abilities of lightning. They're very powerful. Riders have dragons, and Hope doesn't seem to have a dragon anywhere that we can see. It'd be pretty hard to hide a dragon. Faeries are nearly seven to eight feet tall with blue skin, so Kaleb is right to cross that off the list. Thunders have scaly skin because they're part dragon, part human. Keeper are spirit-beings, and we would be able to sense her if she were a wolf.

"You're not an elf because you don't have the facial features. You're not a fairy because you're normal sized. You aren't a God or a demigod. Who are you protecting?" He turns around and looks at her.

Hope looks up at him.

"I'm human, and let's leave it at that," she says forcefully. "Angels don't bleed."

An Angel! Of course! That would be the only logical explanation for her! Kaleb blinks. Did he know if Angels bled or not? I didn't. Angels are the Gods' workforce. They guard Marked beings, preventing them from becoming corrupted. Their presence alone, over an extended period of time, can turn the being back to goodness. If she is an Angel, who is she guarding and why did she bleed?

She can't be guarding me. I'm not Marked. Would a Mark wash off? Of course not. I'm not Marked. Someone else in Mika is Marked and could be corrupted. Should she be near them or is her general presence in Mika enough? Maybe it's Mayor Johnston! That would make sense! He has been kinder lately and Riley has given me no trouble since Hope arrived.

The silence between Hope and Kaleb is awkward. I feel a need to say something, but I can't think of anything to say. I start to draw Hope. She props her arms on her knees and watches the ocean. The wind blows her hair, tossing it in waves of gold. Intensity is hard on her face as she watches the ocean. Her jaw is set and her eyebrows are drawn down. Her entire body seems tensed.

"I just think it's interesting that we haven't had any trouble since you've arrived," Kaleb says finally, breaking the silence.

"Coincidence," Hope says. Her voice falls flat. She's hiding something. What if she is an Angel? It would make sense.

"Kaleb," I say, thinking back to my conversation with Hope. "Are you going to be a Runner the rest of your life?"

Kaleb turns, looking away from the forest. He looks at me with a strange expression.

"Why do you ask?"

"Well," I raise my eyebrows, "are you?"

"No," Kaleb's eyes flicker toward the ocean and then to Hope. "No, I guess not. Why?"

"I was just wondering." I bend over my sketch pad. "I mean, this can't be the rest of my life. Something has to happen. What are you going to do?"

"Kaleb," Hope suddenly says in a hushed tone. "Look behind you!"

Kaleb whirls around and I look up. Three Unspeakables are just outside the tree line of the Forest. They've caught our scent.

"What do we do," I whisper fearfully, looking at Kaleb. We're too far away from Mika to make a run for it.

"When's the last time someone has left the walls?" Hope suddenly asks.

"What?" I snap at her. Is this really the time? We need to get out of here.

"I don't know," Kaleb stands up slowly. "A couple weeks? They may be hungry."

"This can't be," Hope murmurs to herself. "I don't understand."

She looks at me suddenly.

"What?" I snap again.

"What do we do?"

"Run," Kaleb says. "We have to run. No stopping. Now!"

I bolt as soon as the word leaves his mouth. Hope is behind me and Kaleb behind her. I look sideways to the Unspeakables. They've spotted us, and they're heading straight for us! There is no way we can outrun them!

Pure adrenaline pushes us now. We can't stumble or trip now. The Unspeakables are tearing after us. Two are running on two feet and the third on is running on all fours. The third one is much faster and will definitely get to us.

"Kaleb!" I scream.

"Keep running!" He screams back. His voice breaks.

Hope is right behind me, breathing hard. I look to the walls. No one has seen us.

"Help! Help!" I scream. "Someone help!"

"Help!" Hope screams. Her voice is much louder than mine. I just can't get the volume others can.

"Someone please help!" Hope screams at the top of her lungs.

I see two heads poke up over the wall. I recognize the red hair of Huling. Huling grabs the bell that hangs over the south gate and rings it hard.

"Run!" Huling screams. His voice carries over the grasses.

I look back. Kaleb is much slower than Hope and me because he's shooting arrows at the Unspeakables while running. Kaleb is much better with a sword, I think. He shoots clumsily.

The Unspeakables are too close now. Mika minutemen are running out toward us, ready to fight. They rush past me as I sprint to the gates. I look back but find that Hope isn't with me. She's stayed behind with Kaleb, just standing beside him. She's yelling something to him.

I keep running. Suddenly there are gunshots inside Mika. I slow in my running, unsure of what to do. There aren't any guns in Mika. Guns haven't been used since the Old World. People just collect them now.

"Mary!" Huling screams at me. "Get in!"

I run inside without thinking. I can see part of the plaza from where I am. I can see smoke. More gunshots are fired and people are screaming. There is screaming from inside Mika and from outside the walls.

What's happening? I whirl, turning to look up at Huling.

He opens his mouth to say something, but he stops and grabs his chest. A deep maroon color slowly spreads across his white tunic. His face seems to go suddenly blank, but his eyes find mine.

"Huling!" I scream, horrified. My mouth is wide open. I cover my mouth with my hands.

He falls off of his post and lands at my feet with a heavy thud. I drop to the ground and grab at his tunic. I shake him, not believing he's dead. People can't die that fast! He's not dead! But his body is limp.

"Huling!" I scream. "No! Huling! Come back! No!"

I shake him. He can't die! I press on his chest, trying to keep the blood from spilling. The blood seeps through his shirt and between my fingers. A man has just died before my eyes! I scoot backward from him on my rear, horrified. What is happening! Huling's eyes are wide open and staring beyond me now. The yellow dirt sticks to the blood on my hands.

Where is Mick? I stand up and look around. Oh Gods, don't let him be hurt! The gunshots are almost indistinguishable from each other. The shooting isn't stopping.

I run toward the plaza, ducking behind houses and peering out. A fire has been set to a house. A man thrashes on the ground, burning and screaming. Oh Gods! Where are you? Please! This can't be happening! Someone has a gun and is shooting everyone else. Spears are being thrown. Everything is moving too fast. People are falling left and right. People are screaming. I can hear Unspeakable screams outside the walls. Screaming is everywhere. A girl, Charlotte is her name, runs past me. I press myself against the house. Suddenly, her back arches forward, pushing her onto her toes and she falls to the ground. She's been shot! I dart forward and grab her. I drag her behind the house; she is so heavy! I put two fingers beneath her jaw. She's dead. Blood is coming through her hair from the back of her head. Her dark hair seems to turn into blood in my hands. Oh Gods. She's dead! Dead! Gone! There is so much blood. There's blood on me! I turn around and run back to the wall. I'll get shot if I go toward the plaza.

I run along the wall toward the east gate. The huts and houses should prevent stray gunfire from hitting me, I think. I don't really know a lot about guns. I know they can kill a man in an instant, but what can the bullets go through? The shots aren't stopping. They aren't pausing or hesitating. Screaming is everywhere. What is happening?

Dust swirls high into the air from the panicked feet of the villagers. People and Unspeakables are still screaming, and the shots are still ringing. My ears feel strange, as though I'm in a tunnel. Everything seems too surreal. Everything seems to be moving too slowly and too quickly simultaneously.

Mick isn't at his post. Where are Connor, Mason, and Papa? Then the panic hits me. Where are they? I don't know where they are. I know Kaleb and Hope are outside the walls, but that certainly doesn't mean they're okay. They could be dead right now and I'd have no idea!

"Mason!" I scream, my voice straining to be heard. "Connor! Papa! Papa!"

I run to the house, going the long way and sticking to the wall. I burst into the house.

"Papa!" I scream. He has to be in here.

No one answers me. The house is eerily quiet.

"Papa!" I scream again. I run through the house, cutting through the kitchen, and back to the bedrooms. "Connor! Mason!"

"I knew you could talk," a familiar high voice comes from the kitchen.

"P-Papa?" I ask, disbelieving. I walk toward the kitchen slowly.

My stomach flips and I feel my palms grow clammy. Riley emerges from the kitchen and advances toward me. I run around the countertops toward the backdoor. I look behind me, but he's just calmly walking after me. I turn to grab the back door to flee. Riley's presence stunts my secret. I can't use it on him. I can feel my fear trying to rustle it up from its sleeping state, but Riley seems to stop it.

He grabs my wrist. "You're not going anywhere."

I pull back. "I have to find them."

Riley shakes his head. "You'll see them eventually. I've figured out what you are, Mary."

His blue eyes penetrate me and I know he's not bluffing. He's figured me out. I don't know how but he's got me. He knows what I am.

I struggle against him to wrestle it from its dormant state. Riley smirks at me. I wonder if he's aware of his own ability.

"They could be dead!" I plead, trying in vain to twist my arm away from his.

"They are," Riley says unflinchingly. "Father killed them himself. Half-breeds will always be rooted out."

"No!" I pull hard, trying to reach the door. "You're wrong!"

Riley yanks me close and grabs my hair with his other hand. He pulls my face close to his own. I can't scream. I can't escape his eyes or his stunting presence.

"I watched them die," he spat. "Father shot them with a *silver* bullet."

Riley shoves me away from the door and stands in front of it. "Father doesn't like freaks living among us."

I can feel my insides churning uncomfortably. It has to be him. It has to be his presence. Something about him is preventing me from changing. He can't be human. Humans don't have this effect on me.

"Oh, are you supposed to be human?" I manage to say. My voice cracks, but I am determined to look unafraid. I ball my fists and stand my ground.

Riley's nostrils flare. "How could you possibly know anything?"

"You're not human!" I scream.

Riley lunges at me and yanks me off my feet again. His light hair hangs in his eyes, making him all the more threatening. He looks insane with anger.

"You're a jeckin' wolf," Riley says. He pulls a knife from his pocket. The silver-colored blade gleams in the pale light from the kitchen window. I swallow. I don't feel so strong anymore.

"Werewolves," Riley holds me against the wall, "are the most unnatural beings on earth."

Unnatural? We've been here since the Ravage! What's he supposed to be? He's the unnatural one here, whatever he is. But it's definitely not human!

"Then what are you supposed to be?" I spit out before I realize what I'm saying. "Some sort of *mutt*? What are you? You're definitely not full human!"

He presses the blade against my cheek and I cry out. The silver blade burns my skin. I squirm, trying to escape him. He lifts the blade from my cheek. That mutt comment certainly didn't win me any favors with him.

"I'm not going to kill you," Riley says in a sickening tone. "But you will remember me."

He presses himself against me, and I feel a scream rip up my throat. The back door bursts open, but Riley doesn't move. It's probably one of his buddies. Oh Gods, this is getting worse by the second. I squirm against him. His body is hard against mine. I dig my fingernails into his flesh, willing my secret to take hold of me. It won't come up. It just won't listen to me.

Riley's face suddenly is away from mine and his body is off of mine. His body hits the back of a chair and flips over. Mason grabs my wrist and yanks me toward him with more force than necessary. His anger is controlling him now. He swings open the door and pushes me out.

I turn after stumbling down the steps and look at him. He barrels out the door, smacking into the doorframe with an audible thud. He looks angry, but there is something else in his face, in his eyes. Mason looks angry that I'm still there.

"Go!" He doesn't even go back for Riley. Something's wrong.

Mason leads me out the eastern gate, running straight to the Forest.

"Where are we going?" I stop. "I'm not going in there!"

"It's not safe in Mika anymore! We have to go!" Mason comes back and pulls me. "The rest are waiting! Come *on*!"

This is happening too fast. I don't understand what's happening. Gunshots are still firing in Mika. Smoke is everywhere. Did someone start a fire? My senses can't grasp anything. I run blindly behind Mason, watching his back closely. I feel numb. My feet feel like giant hunks of wood. They don't feel like my own.

We run to the Forest. What about Unspeakables? We get inside the Forest, just beyond the tree line and out of Mika's gaze. The gunshots are more distant now.

"I knew she was alive!" Hope suddenly is hugging me.

"What's happening?!" I scream, pushing her away from me. "Where's Papa?"

Hope stumbles backward from me and into another person. She stares at me, hurt. Mason whirls on me, looking wild again.

"Move! We have to move!" Mason yells, taking off running.

I look back at Mika. People are running out of Mika toward us. I can't tell if they are running to us or after us. Gunshots are still firing and the smoke is getting thicker. On instinct, my feet pull me into action and I lurch forward into an ungainly run. There is a pain in my leg. Cramp? I don't have time to deal with this.

I look at the people running in front of me. Mason, Penny, Kaleb, and Hope are running ahead of me. Connor's friend Ardon, a Runner, and Sarah, the baker's daughter, are running beside me.

"What's happening?" I yell, desperately wanting anyone to answer me.

"Be quiet!" Ardon snaps. "We don't want to be heard!"

I feel my stomach turning over rapidly. Why are we leaving? Why aren't Connor and Papa with us? A flip of my stomach gives me a terrible feeling. Something is very, very wrong.

CHAPTER FIVE

Mary

It is close to nightfall now. Mason has made us stop and build a quick lean-to out of broken branches and sticks. I quietly walk to him. Penny makes eye contact with him and quickly leaves to gather wood with the rest. It is hardly stealthy.

I wait until she is out of hearing range before looking at Mason.

"Mason," my voice is shaking, "I'm scared. Where are Papa and Connor? Please tell me they're ok."

Mason's jaw muscles clench and unclench. He looks down at me wordlessly.

"Mason, please."

"I can't tell you that."

His voice breaks on the last word. I grab him and he hugs me hard.

"Johnston shot Papa," Mason says, his bravery finally giving. "Connor was shot, too. I watched them both die before my eyes, Mary. Johnston specifically shot them. Then there was just… everyone just went crazy. Johnston started shooting everyone. Someone set a fire. Riley pushed Mick in the fire and then he went after you. It was just all-"

"They're dead?" That part rings in my head slowly. I can't believe it. They can't be dead. I didn't even say goodbye.

Can they be gone just like this? No goodbyes or a final farewell? I didn't even see them. What was Connor wearing? Did he feel the pain? Did Papa know what was happening? This can't be right. They're dead and there is nothing I can do.

Mason doesn't say anything and hugs me tightly. No, they can't be dead. People can't just die so fast. I saw Connor this morning. I hugged him. I made him breakfast. I saw Papa this morning. He kissed my forehead like he does every morning. He had a strong cup of coffee. The smell had filled the house. They can't just be gone. I'll never see them again. That just can't be.

I'm not aware I'm crying until Mason strokes my hair. I sob into his shirt. I feel numb. What has happened? My world has been overturned in a matter of minutes. The tears subside quickly as I realize I'll never see, touch, hear, or smell them again. A different emotion is starting to take over. I can't tell what it is.

"Did Riley hurt you?" Mason pulls me away and presses two fingers against my face. "Did he burn you?"

My hand slides underneath his fingertips to feel my face. The burn is hot and sensitive.

"He had a silver knife." I pull away from him. "He almost… he almost hurt me."

Mason understands what I mean. He almost raped me. In the midst of everything that was happening, he was going to do that to me. The insanity of it just doesn't make sense even now.

Mason steps toward me and hugs me again. "I'm never letting you out of my sight."

"Mary," Penny is suddenly hugging me. "I'm so sorry."

I don't say anything. What can I say? It's okay? No, it's not okay, and it will never be okay!

"Let's all go to sleep for the night," Mason murmurs, breaking away from us. "Kaleb and I will stay up the first part of the night."

"Will Unspeakables bother us?" I ask timidly. Do I really want to know the answer?

Penny smiles, but it doesn't reach her eyes. "We'll be okay. Hope is an Angel. Her presence protects us."

Penny has such warm brown eyes. I can't help but believe her. How could anything worse happen to us?

"I knew it," I mutter to myself. She doesn't hear me.

The lean-to is pathetic, but it makes me feel better than sleeping out in the open. I'm about to crawl in when a large wolf appears at my side. The wolf has brown eyes that almost blend into his chocolate-brown fur. Mason licks my hand. He and Kaleb are going to keep guard outside in their wolf form, which is probably safest. Our senses are most amplified in that state.

I look around for Kaleb. I've never seen him in his wolf form. I imagine he'll be white. He seems like he'd be snow white or black as night. He seems like he would be some extreme. Or perhaps it's just my imagination wanting him to be an extreme.

I crawl in to the lean-to. There is just enough room for everyone to lie side by side. Penny has saved me a spot between her and Ardon. Hope lies between Ardon and Sarah, who both seem to be asleep already.

I lie down beside Penny. Penny turns toward me and wraps her arms around me. I've never been close to Penny before, but this gesture almost makes me start crying again. Kindness in this dark time seems almost out of place. How can humanity exist in this dark Forest?

Penny falls asleep quickly. Somehow it's comforting to have her arms around me and her hair all over me. It's like a cave. I listen to the breathing of the others and to the creaking of the trees. I'm inside the Grimsah Forest, my family is all dead but one, and an Angel is protecting us. How has this all happened? Just this morning I was playing chess outside the bakery!

Sarah's father must be dead. She doesn't seem torn up about it. Perhaps she's internalizing it. I wouldn't want to cry here. I wouldn't want to cry in front of people. I don't and I won't. My pain won't get the best of me again, remembering my crying with Mason. Mason is strong and is our leader now. I have to be strong too, for his sake.

Where are we going? My mind can't seem to grasp how this has all happened and so fast. We were talking and then the Unspeakables chased us. There were so many gunshots and people dying. Riley attacked me and Mason stopped him. Now we're lying in the Forest, and Papa and Connor are dead. This has all been one day.

This is the worst day of my life.

I didn't realize I had fallen asleep until I wake up. Penny is still lying beside me, breathing deeply. I sit up. This isn't a nightmare. This is real.

Kaleb and Mason are asleep by the lean-to's opening. I crawl over them and outside. Ardon and Hope are sitting outside.

"Morning," Ardon says quietly.

"What are we going to do?" is my first question.

Ardon is quiet for a moment. "Mason wants to get to Gedan. We'll be safe there."

"We?" What will we be safe from?

Ardon looks at me. "Gedan is more tolerant of nonhumans."

"Is this what this is all about?" I ask him. "What started all of this?"

Hope leans forward to hear him.

"Johnston discovered what your family is," Ardon says, looking at the ground. "He shot your brother and your father. Everyone reacted, and he just started shooting people. Some people were looking for you and Mason."

Ardon doesn't look at me. He runs his fingers through his strawberry blonde hair nervously. Hope doesn't say anything. I look down, gritting my teeth and willing my eyes not to let any tears escape. I'm sure Johnston would want me to cry. Papa and Connor definitely wouldn't want me to cry. They would want me to rejoice. They are reunited with Mother at last.

"Can you never go back?" I ask him, looking up. He's human. They won't kill him.

Ardon shakes his head. "I'm a full werewolf. I'm not human, but no one knew except for Connor and Kaleb, and I know they would never tell. How did they find out about me?"

"How did they find out about me?" I echo quietly.

"Are you full werewolf?" Ardon looks at me this time.

"No," I look into his dark eyes. "I'm half. Papa was human and Mother was full werewolf."

"Can you change?" He looks at me closely. He notices the burn on my face.

"Yeah," I touch my face self-consciously. "I can change and silver hurts pretty badly. Mason can change but silver doesn't hurt him. Silver hurt Connor, but he could never change."

My voice breaks on Connor's name and I stop talking abruptly. Ardon picks up on it and doesn't say anything else to me.

"So Hope," Ardon starts a new subject, "Mason tells me you're an Angel?"

Hope sighs heavily. "Yeah, I'm fallen."

Ardon leans forward. "Are you Fallen or fallen?" The emphasis on the words are slight, but we know the meaning.

Fallen is Darke and fallen is not.

"I was shot down." Hope looks at the two of us. "I suspect some Darke being shot me down. Luckily, I landed outside your window, Mary."

"So are you guarding someone?" Ardon asks, forcing the conversation. "Kaleb says Angels usually come to earth to save a Marked soul."

Hope dances around the question. "Usually they do. But that doesn't really matter in my case."

Doesn't matter? She doesn't want to tell us.

One of us is corrupted. I glance at Ardon. His blue eyes suddenly seem a little colder. Perhaps Ardon is the corrupted one. Is that why she doesn't want to say?

Ardon doesn't press her. "Do you suppose we should wake Mason? I don't want to stay another night in this Forest."

"I'll wake him," I say, backing into the lean-to again. I suddenly feel uneasy around Ardon. What if he is the corrupted one? Oh Gods, I hope Hope can redeem his soul and purify it! What if he is going to be a powerful Darke being! He could turn at any moment.

I turn around and step over Sarah and Kaleb. Kaleb looks so calm in his sleep. Lately, he's been looking so anxious. His face is so beautiful.

I tear myself away from his face and lean over Mason.

"Mason," I whisper, pushing his shoulder gently. "Mason, we should go."

Mason sits up and smiles at me. He almost seems to have forgotten yesterday and why we're here. His face is still looking sleepy, but I watch as the memories of yesterday sink back into his brain. His face darkens immediately.

"Okay." He stretches and looks over at Penny as a reflex. "Will you wake everyone?"

"Yeah," I say as he climbs over Sarah and Kaleb. He stumbles outside and I hear a surprised yelp from Hope.

"Penny," I shake her arm. "Penny, it's time to get up."

She sits up, looking exhausted. She looks like she hasn't slept a wink. She doesn't say anything but simply nods. I pat Kaleb's arm.

"Kaleb," I say, looking at him. He looks so sweet. "Kaleb, it's time to wake up."

His blue eyes blink a couple times before focusing on my face.

"Mmkay," he murmurs. He starts to get up but is interrupted by an intense stretch. The stretch paralyzes him and he remains locked with his arms above his head and his toes stretched out. He groans loudly.

"Sarah," I say, reaching across to touch her. "Sarah, it's time to wake up."

Sarah sits up and I can tell she cried most of the night. Her nose is red and her eyes are red around the edges. She avoids my gaze. She pulls a curtain of dark hair between us, pretending to fix her hair.

Penny crawls out of the lean-to first, followed by Sarah. I hear her greet the others.

Kaleb is attacked by another need to stretch. He groans and yawns.

"Did you sleep well?" he asks me.

"I've slept better," I say, my voice falling flat.

Kaleb nods, remembering the events of the previous day. "Are you okay?"

I look up at him. "I don't know."

Kaleb pulls me into his arms and just holds me. I fight the urge to cry again. I can't cry. I have to cry in private and away from the eyes and ears of others. I stifle my tears and swallow down my sadness. I close my eyes. We sit like that for a moment.

"We should probably go," I say quietly and he lets me go.

Kaleb watches me carefully, looking worried. "I'm here if you need me."

I nod, blinking back tears. "I know."

Kaleb crawls out and I follow him out.

"We're heading out now. We should get halfway to Gedan in a couple days," Mason is saying. "We'll be in the Forest a little longer. Mika is still too close, and we don't know the extent of Johnston's insanity."

"Who changes?" Kaleb says, folding his arms.

"You, Mary, and Penny," Mason says without hesitating. "I'll stay human, but I'll hear you three."

Mason has the ability to be able to understand us in wolf form despite him being in human form. Kaleb and Penny look at me. No one knew I could change. I have refused to change since Mother died. Mason raises his eyebrows. Oh, he means right now.

"Sarah," Mason says, catching her attention. "Will you put their clothes in Mary's bag and carry it?"

Sarah nods but doesn't say anything. I think she's feeling exactly what I am. She probably feels just as numb as I do. I don't even know what I'm feeling. Fear? Grief? Mourning? Anger? I don't know one emotion from the other. I feel numb and empty. Blank, really.

I glance over at Penny and Kaleb. We all look away from each other. I haven't changed in so long. I step behind the lean-to and strip down and fold my clothes neatly at my feet. I clench my fists. This may hurt.

My senses explode from me, and I squeeze my eyes shut. No pain.

I shake my back and stretch. It's been so long since I've been a wolf. The air is full of smells and everything is so clear. The leaves' textures are precise and nothing hides from my eyes.

I turn and pick up my clothes. I trot over to Sarah. She takes the clothes from my mouth timidly. I'm not a particularly large wolf, but I come up to her chest. Perhaps that's large for her. I look around for Kaleb.

Penny is silver colored. She blinks at me and picks up her clothing. Penny gives her clothing to Sarah, who takes it with a little more confidence. Kaleb is a white wolf with blue eyes like I had expected. I don't think he's ever seen me in wolf form.

The white wolf comes over to me and looks me over. We are complete opposites. He is a pristine white with glittering blue eyes, and I am a pitch black with green eyes. Connor used to say I could look terrifying if I snarled at someone.

Kaleb licks my ear and picks his clothing up. Sarah stuffs the clothing into the bag and slings it over her shoulder.

Mason appears suddenly and scratches behind my ear. I jump a little and he laughs.

"You'll be walking up front with me," he says quietly. "Penny, walk beside Hope. Kaleb, you walk in the back with Ardon. Ardon, you should change too. The more wolves the better."

Ardon hesitates. "The Unspeakables can smell us more than they can smell humans, though."

Mason smiles. "Exactly. Unspeakables won't mess with more than a couple wolves at a time. We're pack animals. Unspeakables are smart enough to know that a pack would come to our rescue."

"But we don't have a pack," Ardon takes his shirt off.

"Unspeakables aren't smart enough to realize that," Mason takes his shirt from him and hands it to Sarah.

Ardon steps behind the lean-to and then I hear a groan as he shakes out his fur. I wonder when the last time it's been since he was in form. He's a full wolf, but I still have to wonder.

"Ardon, walk the other side," Mason says. "Humans are on the inside. Everybody up for a fast walk?"

"Do you know where we're going?" Hope asks as we start walking.

I shake my head at her words. Mason always knows where he's going. He has assumed control and already has a plan for us. I always knew he was a leader, but I never imagined a crisis would have to bring it out of him.

Mason answers her and assures her that he knows where we're going.

This just seems so surreal. My brother and father are dead. I'm walking through the Grimsah Forest in my forbidden form. Mika is no longer my home and will never be again. How has this all happened so quickly? I feel as though there should have been a sign somewhere. Was Mayor Sixsmith's death the sign? Should I have been looking for signs?

Or is Riley the sign himself? Should I have realized he would have looked into my heritage? How could I? Who would imagine he would have looked into my life? No one cared about me in Mika enough to investigate my life. Why did Riley have to find out? How did they find out about Ardon?

Perhaps Riley's father did the investigating. Johnston seems to be terrified of other species. He has never liked anything that isn't human. I don't blame him when it comes to Darke beings, but the Light beings are fascinating. How can he not like them? And he doesn't just dislike them; he fears them.

I wonder if Riley is the same way.

But it doesn't make sense. I know Riley and his father aren't human. Every time I was around them, I felt as though my own abilities were stunted. I need to ask Kaleb about that and see if he felt it, too.

I step over a fallen branch. Mason and I walk in silence, both in deep thought. The silence between us is thick, but it's not uncomfortable.

What about Ardon? Is he corrupted? I glance over at him. Even as a wolf, he just seems colder and more menacing. He looks over at me and makes eye contact. His icy blue eyes already seem soulless, but it could be my imagination. They flicker black. Did that just happen? Is this my imagination running wild?

There's a sudden snap of a twig to the right. I stop instantly and peer into the darkness of the Forest. The Forest is lighter on the outskirts, but the dense canopy prevents almost all light from hitting the floor. The Forest floor is always dark.

My eyes scan the dead bushes, thorns, and fallen trees that seem to be everywhere. I spy a small ghoul hiding in one of the dead bushes. I lunge forward at him, licking my teeth and snarling. It's probably best to spread the word around the Forest that our group is not to be messed with. I know ghouls scout out and look for new victims. I don't quite understand their ranking in the Forest, but I know they're little devils.

The ghoul gives a high-pitched scream and scuttles off. I chase it for a few feet and stop, growling and snarling after it.

"Damn," Mason murmurs. "Connor was right. You are scary."

I return to his side and he pats my head. Oh, Connor. Mason chuckles quietly in spite of everything. I want to laugh, but it just won't come. The moment is awkward, empty, and wrong.

I feel a remote sense of sadness, yet it doesn't really affect me. Is something wrong with me? I feel like the true sadness is just… over there. It's away from me and not truly within me. I know I felt true sadness last night. Was that it? Is my grieving over? What is wrong with me? "So much has happened," Mason murmurs only to me, seeming to have read my mind. "So much. I think we haven't had time to really let it hit us… that they're gone. I don't feel different. I just feel numb. Should we feel different?"

His voice breaks on the last question. I press my head against his hand. I feel the same way. I think Mason can sense my feelings. I sigh and then growl to myself, trying to shake these feelings away. My growl startles Sarah behind me.

Ardon bumps into her to reassure her, but I think it just startles her again. She is probably a little jumpy because of his corrupted aura or because of the Forest. One can never be too careful in the Grimsah.

CHAPTER SIX

Mary

We're a little over halfway to Gedan now, according to Mason, when we spot a small village about a mile away from the tree line.

"Thank the Gods!" Sarah bursts out. She's been silent the entire trip and makes everyone jump with her sudden exclamation.

"We could get food," Mason says quietly.

I know what he's thinking. A couple days ago we realized an Unspeakable troop is following us. It's a little unnerving for Sarah and Hope, seeing as they cannot change their weak forms. Mason and we wolves have been on high alert.

We can't change into our human selves to approach the village. The Unspeakables will attack while we're weak before we can get to the village. But the village also has a high chance of being intolerant of other species. The smaller the village, the more conservative they tend to be about foreign species.

It's a chance we'll have to take.

Mason leads Sarah and Hope out of the trees first. We follow carefully, listening for the Unspeakables. Not one of us can break or they'll see that as a weakening in our force and attack. I'm sure we could hold them off but not without injuries. And we have to get to Gedan in one piece. Mason says Uncle Seth will take care of us. Mason sent a dove telling him about all that has happened, so he should already know we're coming.

Mason, Sarah, and Hope begin to run for the village upon hearing an Unspeakable grunt at us. Ardon and Kaleb run beside the three of them while Penny and I slowly back out of the forest, watching carefully for any movement. It's probably best that Ardon stay as close as he can to Hope. I'm sure he has to be the corrupted one. He has to be. His eyes seem to flash black and his presence makes me feel sick when I imagine the evil inside him. His smiles seem knowing and sinister now.

Something moves in the bushes in front of us.

We snarl and lick our teeth, flashing our canines and showing how dangerous we are. Penny barks aggressively and I snarl when an Unspeakable tentatively steps out. Penny lunges forward at the disgusting thing and it steps back.

I can feel Penny wanting to run with the others. If too much distance separates us, we'll become weaker in the Unspeakables' eyes. We'll become the prey.

Penny steps backward, about to take off running. I catch the signal and we turn tail together. We sprint for Mason and the others as fast as we can. They are already halfway to the village. They are screaming and yelling. The villagers know we are coming. They have their gates open and men on top of the walls with bows armed.

I turn my head. Four Unspeakables are running after us. There is no way in hell I'm turning around to fight them. I can feel Penny wanting to protect the others. I bark to alert Kaleb. This is probably Ardon's fault. He probably somehow warned them.

Ardon and Kaleb immediately turn around without stopping to join Penny. I charge forward, feeling the need to stay with the runners. They have to be protected, too. Kaleb, Ardon, and Penny engage the Unspeakables.

Mason, Sarah, and Hope are slower on just two legs. Mason slows, hesitating. He's debating on changing. The other two hesitate with him. I bark at him to keep running as I run toward them. Mason turns and pushes the other two onward. They sprint toward the village walls. I stop and let them keep running ahead of me. I can catch them easily. I stand between them and the fight. If any Unspeakables get past Kaleb, Ardon, and Penny, I'll be the last guard.

I really hope I'm not the last guard.

We wolves can't sprint for the gates until the runners are in. They're much slower. I watch the runners, waiting for them to be safe so that the wolves can run. I look back and forth quickly between the two groups.

Kaleb tears at an arm of an Unspeakable. Ardon is swiped into the air by an Unspeakable's long, powerful arm. Why would they attack one of their own? Perhaps they're smart enough to keep up the disguise? But Unspeakables aren't that smart. Perhaps he isn't fully corrupted yet? He bounces away and an Unspeakable looks up and past me. The runners are an easier dinner. I can see on his face what the Unspeakable is thinking.

I whip my head around to see how close the runners are. They're close enough. I howl, telling the other wolves to beat it back to the gate.

Ardon gets to his feet and runs as fast as he can toward me. I can see a little blood on his grey fur. Penny turns with Kaleb and both begin running to the gate. The Unspeakables are hot on their heels. I turn and sprint to the gate. I'm much faster than the others normally and with a head start I get to the gate much faster. I pass the runners at the entrance but they run in seconds after me.

A villager screams and pulls her child away from me. Mason looks back but then looks up at the men on the wall.

"They're with us!" Mason yells to the villagers. "Help them! Let them in!"

The men on the walls don't look happy to be using their arrows but they send arrows over, striking the Unspeakables.

"Shut the gate!" a villager howls as the wolves get closer. They plan on timing it just so, I hope.

The gate starts to draw down. This village has an Old World castle gate which means it will be slower.

Kaleb skids into the village first followed by Penny and then Ardon. The gate shuts seconds after Ardon rolls in. The Unspeakables scream outside, wailing and beating themselves against the walls. The villagers look wary of the large wolves in their walls, but Mason walks over to one of the villagers and speaks in a low voice.

Kaleb, Penny, and Ardon walk over to where I am standing. Ardon sits beside me and I sit, too. I can't very well get up and move away. That'll be too obvious. I can't let him know that I'm on to him. We watch the villagers backing away from us. One woman stands in front of her child, looking as though we may attack the child. Werewolves are hated in some villages, and I suppose this is one of them.

The Unspeakables are screaming outside, but their screams are growing softer and softer. Retreat.

The man Mason is speaking to points across the semicircle the villagers have made around us. Another much older man steps into the center of the semicircle and casts a disgusted look our way.

Mason meets him halfway and extends a hand. The man reluctantly shakes Mason's hand. Mason is speaking quietly to the man, trying to reason with him. I can see Mason's fingers on his left hand are tapping together. His fingers tap when he is agitated.

The man folds his arms, and I glance at Penny. She gives me a sad look. Some people cannot look beyond appearances. This village doesn't want us here, but hopefully Mason can get them to let us stay for at least a night. The Unspeakables will be watching for at least another hour or so before they give completely up.

Sarah and Hope come over to stand beside us. Sarah shifts her weight to one hip and folds her arms watching the idiots talking.

I sigh and lie down suddenly, startling several of the villagers. I want to scream. They should understand that we may look like wolves, but inside we are still human! I look at each face watching us. Each villager hates us. I can see it clearly on all of their faces. We don't belong here. They think we are abominations and forever damned.

Who has the right to condemn another human being because they are not exactly like everyone else? Who has the right to say werewolves, because they live different life styles and aren't cookie-cutter humans, are damned? I think only our Gods can make that final judgment. And how can being kind and understanding damn us? It isn't like we chose to be werewolves; that life was chosen for us.

The villagers suddenly are leaving the semicircle. Most glance back at us as if checking to make sure we're not stalking after them to eat them. I am really getting tired of the looks. Maybe I should eat one of them…

Mason comes back over to all of us shaking his head.

"They're only letting us stay for one night." Mason looks over his shoulder. "Disgusting. You'd think *we* were the Unspeakables!"

"It looked like you really had to convince them," Sarah says bitterly. "I don't even want to stay here. These people…ugh."

Mason frowns, nodding. "When people don't quite understand something, they automatically think it is wrong and against the Gods. One day people will all understand that this isn't a choice."

"Some people think that they chose this lifestyle?" Hope gestures to the four of us wolves. "People really think that? How? That doesn't even make sense. Why would anyone choose a lifestyle that would subject them to hatred and violence?"

"You would think most intelligent people would understand that," Sarah mutters.

Mason just shakes his head and says nothing. I feel Sarah's presence behind me.

"Are we camping right here for the night?" Sarah asks, sitting down beside me.

Mason nods. "Right in this very spot. You four can change into your human selves, if you like. Sarah, would you mind going with them to give them their clothes?"

Sarah nods. "Not at all. Where do they change?"

"Just find somewhere where they won't be seen." Mason turns and looks around for a place for us to change. "I doubt anyone will let them in a building or a house."

"Ok," Sarah says and starts to walk out. We follow her, looking around for a corner or anything.

Just ahead of us is a corner between the gate and a small house. I don't know if anyone lives there, but we can definitely change between the two walls. I nudge Sarah with my nose and jerk my head toward the spot. Sarah nods but doesn't say anything. She leads us over here and touches my back. She wants me to change first.

"I'll stand in front of you to make sure no one sees you," Sarah says but thinks better of it, "Actually, let me go get Hope. She can help me block you."

Sarah runs back out into the open sunshine and in front of the gate. "Hope! Will you come stand in front of Mary and Penny when they change?"

I hear Hope oblige and both girls come walking back. Hope stands on one side of me and Sarah stands beside her. I have four walls around me. Hopefully no one can see me. The other three wolves sit down facing the other way.

It always takes me several tries to collapse my senses and regain my human skin. I close my eyes and brace myself. My senses suddenly collapse in on me, ramming into me. I stand up on two legs and nearly fall into Hope.

"Sorry," I mutter as I pick up my clothes.

I pull on my clothing in jerking motions. My human form always feels so strange after being a wolf. I feel so weak, cold, and ungainly. I step out from behind Hope and smile at her. She smiles back and starts to say something but is interrupted by Mason.

"Mary!" he calls me over to him.

Just as I near him, he points toward the cluster of shops around a well in the center of a plaza. "Will you go see what food you can buy?"

He drops some money in my hand and sends me on my way. I watch my feet as I walk. They seem so unstable after being in my wolf form. I can't recall the last time I was in my wolf body.

I go to the butcher's place first. We can dry the meat and keep it longer. I step into the shop and the butcher looks up. He is a skinny man with a severe face and intense blue eyes that seem to glow.

"We're closed," he says, putting down his cleaning rag.

I glance around the shop. Three other customers are there and there are two people in line waiting.

"Excuse me," my voice is timid and soft, "but it doesn't look like you're closed. I don't mean to trouble you, but we just need so-"

The butcher comes around the counter at me. "Excuse me, but we're closed. We don't serve half-breeds here."

If Connor were here he would have had something to say about this whole situation. I nod and bow out of the shop, apologizing as I go. How did he know I'm one of the wolves? He probably didn't recognize me and figured I am.

I sigh and look around the small plaza. On the other side of the well, there is a small bakery. The baker is setting stale and burned bread out on a shelf. I cross the plaza and approach the baker.

"Excuse me," I use my most polite and respectful voice, "Do you have any fresh bread I could possibly buy?"

The baker smiles at me and nods. "Of course, Miss. Come inside."

Relief fills me and I follow him in. He is a large man, much larger than Papa. I feel a knot rise in my throat. He looks like Papa but larger. I swallow hard.

Emotions in this body are so strong. I had forgotten that the wolf body doesn't have such strong emotions. I condemned myself to suffering when mother died. I purposefully decided never to use my wolf form again so I would suffer emotionally as she did physically. It was my fault, so I deserve a portion of that pain.

"Miss?" the baker is looking at me.

I blink. Oh dear, I've been wallowing while he was talking to me! "Oh, I'm sorry. What?"

"What kind would you like?" He smiles.

"The cheapest there is, please," I say pleasantly as an older woman walks in.

"Eugene!" she cries, making the baker and me both jump. "No animals in the shop!"

"What?" The baker looks around the shop. "I don-"

"It," the older woman points at me. "That thing came into town earlier. Get out!"

I take a step back, unsure of what to do.

"Get out! Get out, you filthy little half-breed!"

The baker stares at me in shock as I take another step back.

"I just need bread for our group," I plead.

"Out!" The woman is coming at me, faster than the other man had. I take another step back.

"Please," I say just before she raises her hand to hit me.

I flinch and wait for the blow, but it doesn't come. I open my eyes and look up. The baker has grabbed her hand, stopping her from hitting me.

"Enough of that," the baker's voice is cold now, unlike when he first spoke to me.

I stumble backwards and out of the shop. There is a sign on the stale bread that says "Free." I glance into the shop and the couple is arguing. Still watching, I snatch several loaves of bread, both burned and stale, and run from the plaza. Clearly, no one is going to serve me here.

Mason stands up when he sees me come around a corner. I know I haven't been gone long.

"Bread?" he says as I get closer. I can't tell if he's disappointed or not.

"It was free because it's stale or burnt." I give him back his money. "No one will serve me."

Mason's nostrils flare. "That's fine. I wouldn't want to give them my money anyway. We cannot get to Gedan fast enough."

"Is there anything to eat?" Hope suddenly asks, appearing at Mason's side. Her eyes are on the bread.

"It's a little stale," I say with a shrug.

"Hey," Hope takes a loaf and smiles. "Food is food."

She turns and calls to Sarah. She splits the loaf and gives half to Sarah. The two sit down cross-legged, talking in hushed voices, and sharing secrets probably. Mason takes a loaf from my arms.

"Thank you," he says, smiling at me.

CHAPTER SEVEN

Becoming Adam

I wake up suddenly in the middle of the night. I can see Mary's and Hope's sleeping bodies in the pale moonlight. They are huddled together beneath a blanket generously given to us by a sympathetic villager.

I look at the others as they sleep peacefully. How easy it would be to jerk their heads and break their necks. It would be so easy to slide a knife across their necks.

I gasp. What is this? What is this feeling?

I struggle to collect my own thoughts for a moment. The intrusive thoughts take hold of me again. They aren't my own but they sound so natural to me.

Easily make them suffer. Cut them, bruise them, beat them, burn them. Make them dance until their legs are nothing but little nubs. Dance until they die. Dance until they die.

I grab my head. No! No! No, no, no! These are my friends! What is happening to me! Oh Gods, am I corrupted? No, no that can't be! I can't be corrupted!

But corruption can be good, can't it? Yes, it can. No responsibilities to your worthless Gods. Leibus – no, Lucifer – is a gracious and understanding God. He will grant you everlasting life and will make me powerful!

I rub my hands together. I can become one of the most powerful beings on the planet.

No! That… that isn't what I want. No, I love my Gods and I love my friends. No, this isn't happening.

I feel the corruption churning inside me.

I stand up, out of my own will. Kill the Angel first.

No!

Kill the Angel!

No!

I struggle to say something to Hope as I stand over her. No! My voice comes out as a quiet, strangled 'no'!

Hope suddenly sits up and touches me. Her purity shoots up my leg and flows through my body. I collapse.

Who am I? What have I become?

"You'll forget everything," she whispers. "Don't worry. You'll be okay. I'm here."

I drift off into the darkness of sleep as the corruption becomes dormant again.

CHAPTER EIGHT

Kaleb

There is a grief that cannot be spoken. I watch Mary carefully as she stands beside Mason. Mason is talking, but I'm not really listening. Both of them look as though they have nothing left. Their grief has taken the form of numbness. I remember the feeling well when my own family was murdered.

I see the Unspeakable through the crack of my door. It walks through the living room silently. I catch my breath and its head turns sharply at the noise.

I swallow and push the memory away roughly.

Mary stares at the ground fixedly. Her green eyes have dark circles beneath them and her face is paler than usual. Her eyes suddenly flicker up to me. I stare unabashedly back. She holds my gaze for a moment with her intense green eyes. Even in her misery, she is still beautiful.

Her eyes drop back to the ground and she twirls a strand of her red hair nervously. She has never liked to be stared at.

Who am I kidding? She would never have me. I need to give up on this girl. I've been in love with her for so long, but I need to move on. She'll never love me. She looks up again at me nervously. My heart flutters again.

Mary looks so broken. Her grief has remained behind her eyes, but it is still plainly seen.

Mason is trying to cover his sadness with his leadership. I have to wonder what will happen when we get to Gedan and there is nothing more for him to do. He seems as broken as Mary. I make eye contact with him for a moment. His sadness is as clear in his eyes as it is in Mary's. He's talking about the trip.

I glance over at Sarah. She is hugging herself and listening attentively to Mason. I know her father is dead. He was killed in the shooting. Sarah saw him fall in front of her. He had stepped in front of her to protect her. She would have died if Ardon had not pulled her out of Johnston's sight.

"Ready?" Mason says.

"We're all in wolf form, right?" I ask. I have not listened one bit.

Mary nods without saying anything. She turns and walks over to the corner where we all changed earlier. She must be changing first. She disappears behind the wooden walls. I hear her sigh and she comes back in her silky black form. Her clothing is in her mouth. She drops it at Sarah's feet as Ardon disappears behind the corner.

Her green eyes find me. They don't look quite as pained, but I know it's only the influence of the wolf form.

Ardon trots from around the corner. I wonder what happened to his family. I don't even know if he had family in Mika. I run a hand over Ardon as I walk toward the corner. I pull off my tunic and pants as soon as I'm around the corner. I fall into my natural form easily, like a shrug.

I pick up my clothes in my mouth and trot toward the group. Mary is lying down and Ardon sits beside her. Penny's long, lean human form walks past me toward the corner. She brushes her fingertips against my head. When she comes back around the corner, she gives her clothing to Sarah. Sarah stuffs our clothing into the bag she slings over her back. Mason gives a halfhearted wave to the few villagers who have gathered to see us off.

We step out of the gate with hesitation. No Unspeakables. They're dumb enough to give a call before attacking. No sounds.

Mason waves Hope and Sarah forward. We surround the humans and begin our way to Gedan. Hopefully, we won't run into any more Unspeakables. Yesterday was a little too close for my comfort.

I also could not help but notice that Mary was the first inside the gates. Although she is my best friend, she is a coward. Always was and always will be.

Everyone has their flaws.

Mama used to say cowardice and arrogance are tragic flaws. When I asked her what that meant, she said they are flaws that will lead to someone's downfall.

I have to hope that won't be the case for Mary.

I glance over at her, but she's staring at the ground as she walks. Though I can't tell what she's thinking, I know she's feeling sadness and despair, even in her wolf form. It radiates off of her.

Hope suddenly coughs and I jump, my hair standing on end. Gods, I hadn't realized we were walking in silence until she coughed. My heart slows down again.

Is she getting sick? Can Angels get sick? Well, they're not supposed to bleed. She said that was from being shot down, but I have to wonder how she was shot down.

Who or what shoots down an Angel? That has to be taboo even among the most wicked.

"Hope," Mason says suddenly. I can feel his mind reach into my own. "What do you think shot you down?"

Wolves can't read each other's thoughts, but Mason has a rare ability. He can see what we're feeling and guess at what we're thinking about and put it into words. The only other person I have known who could do that was Mrs. Stoneburner, his mother.

I look up at Hope. She purses her lips before answering.

"I suspect some sort of two-legged being," Hope says quietly. "Perhaps a Blood Elf or something. Someone knew I was coming. Someone knows something."

"What do you mean?" Mason asks. "Do you mean Lucifer himself?"

"Don't call him that," Hope says sternly. "That's a name he gave himself. His name is Leibus."

"Okay," Mason asks again, "Do you mean Leibus himself?"

Hope nods. "Something is happening. Something is definitely coming."

Why so cryptic? It's just us.

"Hope," Mason almost laughs… or cries. I'm not sure. "What is coming? Let's stop playing games now."

He stops and the group stops. Penny looks startled. We have all been listening quietly, but now this has come to something else entirely. Hope is talking of Godly things.

Hope frowns for the first time. She folds her arms across her chest and her jaw seems to tense.

"There is a war brewing, Mason," Hope finally says.

"So why are you down here if there is a war up there?"

Hope sighs and looks away. "I'm here for… collateral damage control."

"Hope," Mason folds his arms. "We have a right to know if it's one of us."

"The danger has passed," Hope says unconvincingly.

"Hope, who is it?"

"Kaleb," Hope says.

What? Wait, what? What just happened? Did…? Am I the one she's guarding? Am I corrupted?

"W-what?" Mason didn't expect that answer.

Hope's usually glowing skin seems a little paler. She looks down at me. "He was corrupted. I cannot tell if he is anymore. Getting to Gedan is our best bet right now, so let's get a move on."

Was? She's not sure if I am still? How was I corrupted? I know that Unspeakable touched me in my human form so long ago. I washed off the Darke dust. I purified it with holy water from the temple! How am I corrupted? There has to be some sort of mistake. I don't feel corrupted. Can you feel corrupted?

"Wait," Mason unfolds his arms and puts his palms toward her. "Kaleb is corrupted? How is getting to Gedan going to help?"

Hope sighs impatiently. I have never seen her so irritable before.

"In Gedan," Hope looks down at me, "there are people that can help him – *if* he is still corrupted. There is only one way to know if he is corrupted and only one way to cure him, both of which can be done by the… people in Gedan."

Why did she hesitate to say people? Are they real people? What if they're not people? I can feel my stomach twisting in nervous knots.

"But you need not panic," Hope lays a hand on me. "With me around, nothing will happen to you. You won't turn. I can't tell if you're corrupted because my presence prevents it."

Mason swallows audibly. "Why is he so important that you, in the middle of an oncoming war, have to come down?"

"Do you know what Darke Angels are?" Hope asks carefully.

I feel sick. I feel absolutely sick. Darke Angels are beings of Leibus' own direct creation. He takes corrupted souls and makes them into Darke Angels. I don't know much else about them, but I know that two Darke Angels named Adam and Eve have the capability to destroy the world.

Then again, I only heard that from a few Runners.

"He is supposed to become one if he becomes fully corrupted."

Fully corrupted? What the hell does that mean?

"What does that mean?" Mason asks.

Mary sits down across me, looking genuinely concerned.

"Being corrupted is a process," Hope says, beginning to get frustrated again, "You don't just become corrupted. You are exposed to something Darke, and then it starts to eat away at your soul."

WHAT? My soul is being devoured?

Mason, sensing my panic, asks, "Eating away?"

"That's the only way I know to put it," Hope says, then continues. "The Darkeness will take the soul and almost kill it. Almost. Sometimes the soul can be salvaged and saved by Psyche. Sometimes the soul is taken by Leibus and it just disappears from Psyche's 'view'."

"Psyche?"

Hope rubs her temples. "This is so complicated. Psyche is the Goddess of the soul. She controls everything. She is one of the most powerful Lesser Gods up on high. Personally, I think she will be a Greater God soon."

"Then how come we don't know her?" Sarah asks, piping in for the first time.

"Because humans have lost that spiritual connection," Hope says rather sadly. "Humans are only focused with material items. They're obsessed with earthly items. Humans want things to be done as quickly as possible so they like things like war, destruction, and famine. It gets rid of things quickly. Things like the soul, something you can't see or hear, are of no concern to people anymore."

No one says anything. What are we supposed to say to that? I couldn't say anything to that even if I had words. My main concern at the moment is how rapidly my soul is being eaten.

Okay, not literally being eaten but, hell, I don't know what's happening! I don't even understand what a soul is!

"Anyway," Hope says, "Once the soul is destroyed, the being becomes Darke and is automatically drawn to Leibus and his Forest. Leibus will then decide the fate of the being. He only chooses certain beings to become Darke Angels. Because of Psyche, we know which beings will become Darke. Sometimes we even know if the being will become one of Leibus' disciples. Those are his select Darke Angels."

Like Adam or Eve? I wonder.

"Like Adam or Eve?" Mason blurts out my thoughts.

Hope nods slowly. "He, Kaleb, is supposed to be Adam."

Mason looks at me slowly. "He is supposed to be Adam?"

"Don't be alarmed," Hope puts a hand on my head. "As long as I am here, he is safe."

"What will Adam do?" Sarah looks at me. She almost looks repulsed. "What will happen to Kaleb?"

Why does she look repulsed? I can't help it! Can I? Was I predestined to be this? Oh Gods. This is too much. I paw at the ground in frustration. A small whimper escapes my chest.

Hope digs her nails into my fur. Somehow I feel comforted.

"If he were to become fully corrupted, Kaleb," Hope rubs my ear, "wouldn't be Kaleb anymore. He would sort of look like Kaleb, and he'd have Kaleb's memories, but he'd be just… a very wicked Kaleb. The real Kaleb would either be with Psyche up above or trapped somewhere with Leibus. But this is not going to happen. I will not allow Kaleb to turn. Please, don't be concerned or disgusted with him. It is nothing he can help. It is something chosen for him by the Fates."

Hope rubs my ear and looks down. She watches the grasses move near my paws.

Mason doesn't say anything. No one says anything.

The silence is deafening. I've never heard silence quite this loud.

"Let's just get to Gedan," Mason says, casting a glance my way.

He comes toward me and scratches my head. Again, the touch somehow feels comforting. I feel something rub against me. Mary rubs against me, lending me some reassurance.

"Everything will be okay," Hope says quietly but everyone hears her.

CHAPTER NINE

Mary

The city gates of Gedan probably aren't as beautiful as we think they are. However, as soon as they come into sight, they are the most beautiful thing we have ever seen. Everyone begins yelling and laughing. It has been such a long and trying journey from Mika.

Kaleb hasn't spoken since that day outside that conservative village. But now he is laughing and talking excitedly. I can only imagine his happiness. Within the city walls are the very people who can cure him. I don't know what I would do if I was corrupted. I thought Ardon had been corrupted and I felt as though I were being suffocated when I was around him. I feel like I owe him some sort of apology, but I can't very well apologize to him and then explain to him why I'm apologizing. Probably best to keep it to myself. The power of imagination at its best. It turns out it was Kaleb this whole time. Kaleb is so much braver than any of us. He didn't say anything else about it and none of us did either. Hope remained by his side the entire time. She never left him after that day. She is the only person who talked to him. She even slept next to him. It probably made him feel better to always have his protector touching him. She probably has some sort of calming effect on him. He also seems different. He seems almost colder to me but not in a cruel or mean sort of way. He just seems less tuned into me. It almost seems as though he has turned from me to Hope. He engages with her and looks at her in such an endearing way.

Hope is smiling and laughing. She is shining brightly again. When she laughs, her skin glows brighter. It's slight, but we all notice.

Mason lets us change into our human forms so we can talk with one another and the gate officials if needed. It feels nice to be on two legs again.

The city gates are white and sparkling with a new coat of paint. I can see the painters working down to the dirty bottoms of the gates. The white gates stand in marvelous contrast to the dark skies holding rain and thunder. Gedan is marvelous. It has tall buildings and wide streets and cars driving around. The cars are amazing. They are so sleek and so unnatural.

Most of them are a shining silver. Their beauty takes my breath away. I wouldn't be surprised if they were somehow inspired by the Gods.

The gate officials let us in when they realize Hope is an Angel. They recognize on sight that she is an Angel. Amazing. I can only imagine the other creatures and beings that must live here.

We stop just inside the gates to look at the glamor of Gedan. No one even gives us a passing glance. So many people are walking along the sidewalks. I have never seen so many people. It is almost overwhelming.

"Uncle Seth lives on Sixth Street," Mason says, blinking hard. "East Sixth Street."

"I have some great aunts that live here," Sarah says quietly. "Would you mind if I…?"

Considering her father's death, she's held up quite nicely but at this request her eyes start to water.

"Of course," Mason goes toward her and hugs her with affection.

The tender gesture breaks her resolve, and Sarah starts to cry right then and there. She completely breaks down. Her crying is quiet, but her shoulders are shaking.

She steps away from Mason, wiping her eyes. "I'm okay. I'm okay."

"It's been a… hard trip," Mason says. His eyes water, and I look away.

Penny smiles and hugs Sarah. "There you go." She wipes Sarah's face with her thumb, sweeping away the tears. "You look normal now."

"I hope I see you guys again," she smiles and steps backwards.

Mason waves. "Bye, Sarah!"

She disappears into a crowd of people and we lose track of her.

"Shall we go?" Mason puts an arm over my shoulder.

"Let's." I smile but it feels fake on my face.

Uncle Seth's house is squished between two other houses. Penny says it's called a townhouse. I have never seen one like this before. It has a strange roof. It's not made of thatch or woven grasses. It has strange little squares and rectangles on top.

We pause before walking up the steps to the olive green door. Mason walks ahead of us and knocks gently on the door. As though he had been expecting us, Uncle Seth opens the door almost immediately. He has insane red hair that seems to stick out in every direction in wispy little strands. He has huge glasses which amplify his eyes. Connor used to say he was an evil bug genius.

Uncle Seth gives a strange laugh and pulls Mason into a strong hug. Mason hugs him hard and steps backward. He puts an arm out to introduce Hope, Penny, Ardon, and Kaleb.

"This is my girlfriend, Penny," Mason says. I notice his eyes are watering a bit. "This is Kaleb, a family friend, and Hope. Hope is an Angel. Ardon here is a Runner from Mika and Connor's best friend."

I step forward to hug Uncle Seth. He takes me in his arms and gives me a long hug. He has always smelled like Mother. He releases me and hugs Hope, Penny, Ardon, and Kaleb each in turn.

"Come in," he smiles, opening the door widely, "Come in!"

We pile into the house quickly as fat raindrops suddenly begin to fall.

"Erm," Hope begins to say, "Mr. Seth-"

"Call me Uncle Seth, dear," he says, sitting down heavily in a fluffy chair.

"Do you know where the Thunder reside?"

"Yes," he looks at her strangely. "Now why do you need to know that?"

"Don't be concerned," Hope says brightly. "Kaleb and I need to pay them a visit. Angel stuff, Uncle Seth."

Uncle Seth presses his lips together and glances at me. I keep a straight face and stare blankly back at him. He looks away, and I have the opportunity to look around.

The walls in the living room are a smooth, light, creamy brown color. The furniture is much darker than the room giving it a cozy look. There is a couch and two chairs with looming bookshelves against the walls. A coffee table sits in the middle of the furniture with several books piled on top of it.

I can see into the dining room, which is decorated in a light blue theme. The table has delicate white lace on it and the china cabinet appears untouched. After Aunt Margaret died, it seems that Uncle Seth hasn't touched that room. In the house's entryway, there is a spiral staircase that twists up into the ceiling, up to a second floor. That must be where all the bedrooms are. I feel a sense of excitement. I've never been in a house with more than one floor!

"Go all the way down Second Street to the far outskirts of the city," he tells Hope, as he links his fingers together and leans back in the chair, relaxing. I look at him for a moment.

The paintings on the walls look like they were done by Aunt Margaret. Most of them are pictures of potted plants or flowers. There is a grand painting of the sea in the dining room. It almost looks like the sea by Mika.

"Thank you," Hope's voice makes me turn back. She takes his hand and squeezes it. "We'll be back!"

Hope grabs Kaleb's hand and they leave quietly, shutting the olive green door with a small click. My heart feels pained. I couldn't help but notice when she grabbed his hand, his fingers curled around her small hand.

I've suspected there is something going on between them. I shouldn't be too hurt. It's not like Kaleb was ever mine. We have always been just friends. Best friends. But still friends…

Then why does it hurt so much that there is a possibility those two are a couple? Why should it hurt? I have been through so much and lost so much these past several days… Why should this hurt as much – or more? – than the rest of all that? It doesn't make sense that Kaleb liking Hope in that way should hurt me. My brother has died and my father has died. My village could be ashes right now for all I know.

Uncle Seth sets a cup down in front of me. It smells like hot tea. I take the cup gingerly between my hands. My hands feel cold so suddenly. Perhaps it is the sudden onset of rain. I glance out the window. I can hear Mason telling Uncle Seth everything that has happened. Uncle Seth received Mason's dove, so he already knows about Papa and

Connor's deaths. They discuss what to do next. They talk about going to Aunt Imry's in Reason, Eastern Kingdom.

I stare out the window. Do we have to talk about this immediately? They're talking about an honor funeral for Papa and Connor. How can they talk about it already?

Connor always loved the rain. I watch it steadily rain harder and harder. The rain is pouring straight down. The grey rain pouring down reminds me of a picture from the book back in Mika. The book is probably a pile of pathetic ashes by now. I really should have read the book.

"Uncle Seth," I say suddenly, startling him and everyone else sitting in the room.

Mason and Penny are sitting on the couch together and Ardon is sitting on the floor leaning against the corner of my chair. They are all staring at me now.

Uncle Seth looks at me patiently. He has always understood my silence, but now I think he is genuinely interested in what I have to ask. I rarely spoke around him after Mother died. I think he was okay with that, too. He and Mother were very close.

"What caused the Ravage?" I look into his bright green eyes.

Uncle Seth is an anthropologist and a historian. He knows all there is to know about late Old World wars and the Ravage. He pushes his lower lip out and pushes his fingertips together like a steeple in front of him. He thinks for a moment.

"Should we start with World War Three?" he asks me and I nod.

Mason leans forward and Penny begins to scratch his back as we prepare for Uncle Seth's stories. He knows everything.

"World War Three was in the late Old World period," he nods to himself as he speaks. "During this time there was a constant conflict somewhere on the earth. There had not been complete peace on the earth since before World War I. Our information before that time is extremely weak and variable. But there was a constant conflict between major world religions. Religions, and lack of religion, were constantly fighting. Keep in mind that all of the major religions only believed in one God. They did not know our Gods. The only civilization that knew most of our Gods were the Greeks. We have extensive information on them as well as a civilization we called the Soviesia. We don't know the real name for the Soviesia, but they were a northern country with a great deal of weapons. I'll tell you more about them in a minute. Now before the war, there was a population boom and it was looking like the planet couldn't handle any more people. Many scientists were worried about our atmosphere and the… levels of… pollution."

We all knew Uncle Seth dumbed down his explanations for us. The man is a genius, but he knows how to dumb things down for us without making us feel dumb.

"Like Carbon?" Ardon asks.

Uncle Seth looks down at him quickly. "Precisely! How did you know that?"

"I learned it in school a long time ago," Ardon smiles. "I kept some of my textbooks and read them sometimes."

"I'm surprised," Uncle Seth smiles and nods again. "The education in the Western and Southern Kingdoms has never been known to be the best, but I guess those new laws are finally working, eh?

"Anyway," Uncle Seth smiles at Ardon again before continuing. "Scientists were worried about the air. The sky was beginning to become less blue. One of the last things to happen when an atmosphere is terribly unbalanced is that the sky will turn green."

"*Green*? From what? How does the sky turn green?" Mason asks in disbelief. Penny is still scratching his back but listening attentively.

"Green," Uncle Seth nods, pointing a finger at Mason. "There are all sorts of repercussions from mistreating the planet. The Old World had a lot of machinery and factories that put off toxic gases which affected the planet. After a while, when the emissions from those factories did not let up and the people stop caring, the damage done to the planet will be irreversible. The overall temperature will rise and this global warming will cause the seas to rise. You understand what I'm saying. Anyway, at the same time this was happening, many countries were suffering from hunger and famine. There were three diseases called AIDS, Cancer, and Paraber. AIDS was devastating. People were dying by the millions, but even that many people dying couldn't stop the population boom. Luckily, today we don't have AIDS, but back in the Old World it was a very real thing."

"It's called AIDS?" I ask. That seems like such an odd name. Aids?

"AIDS stands for Acquired Immune Deficiency Syndrome," Uncle Seth says quickly. "It's the final stage of human immunodeficiency virus infection, otherwise known as HIV. It attacks your immune system."

"Oh," Ardon says rather gleefully. "That's what keeps you from getting sick, right?"

"Exactly," Uncle Seth looks at Ardon again. "You really paid attention in school, didn't you? Very good. Yes, your immune system protects your body from diseases and germs."

I grin down at Ardon, who is glowing with pride. I never realized how smart he is.

"Cancer," Uncle Seth says, suddenly grave, "is still among us today. Many people don't know what it is. It doesn't happen very much anymore, but it's still here. It's unavoidable. Cancer happens inside the body. I'm sure you all know what cells are?"

We all nod. We learned about it in school so long ago. Schooling stops when you turn twelve. I don't remember cells in detail, but I remember learning about it.

"Well," he puts his fingers together in a steeple again. "Cancer is when the cells just get out of control. Normally, if you remember, the cells divide and repair themselves. You know, the usual. But, sometimes, the cells sort of mess up. The bad cells don't die like they're supposed to do. Instead, the bad cells keep replicating. Then they can get into your blood, for example, and the cancer spreads."

"It kills you from within," I say quietly. "There was a man in Mika Papa tried to heal, but he never healed."

"He probably had cancer," Uncle Seth nods, looking at me. "Paraber is the final disease. Paraber is a man-made disease. It was made in World War Two. It was discovered just before World War Three. Paraber is the result of a biological weapon that was used on millions of people as experiments. Many people survived and carried it on to their offspring through their DNA. Many are immune to it, but many are not. Somehow it remained dormant until its discovery just before that third world war. It is still among us today – carried through DNA – and, like cancer, there is no cure. Paraber, granted, is rare today because it has slowly been purged from family lines thanks to the stronger DNA of immune people. But it ran rampant around World War Three until the Ravage. It attacks the skin system, producing terrible lesions, welts, pus-filled blisters, and sometimes can make your appendages fall right off."

Penny grimaces, looking ill. Uncle Seth continues without notice. I lean forward. This is all too fascinating.

"Then it attacks the lungs and digestive system," he frowns. "All in all, it is one hundred percent effective in killing its victims. No one, once infected, survives Paraber."

Uncle Seth shifts in his chair. "So when it was discovered, everyone panicked. This was a disease that came quickly and without warning and was highly contagious because it is passed through bodily fluids and is airborne. For example, we know that the disease took out several entire cities in powerful countries, so imagine what it did in poorer countries. In one major city, alone, for example, we know that more than two million victims died in a matter of months.

"All the major countries (they were kind of like Kingdoms) were working on containing the disease. And, as with all major catastrophes, there was a need to assign blame. People began blaming the country that first used Paraber on civilians and, long story short, some allied nations dropped nuclear bombs on the country being blamed."

"I remember learning about those," Penny nods, looking somber. "Terrible. I remember the pictures they would show us in class."

"Terrible, indeed," Uncle Seth says gruffly. "After that first bomb, it was World War Three. We aren't sure who, but one of the countries opposite of our ancestors, Mary and Mason, started using even more advanced biological weapons. We understand that they were banned by the UN. UN stands for the United Nations. It was sort of a government of all nations to keep everyone in check and from endangering others.

"Anyway-"

"Wait," I interrupt suddenly. "Did the UN work?"

"What do you mean?"

"Did the countries listen to the UN?"

"We're not sure of everything because of the Ravage, but I'm inclined to say no."

"Okay." I fold my knees under me on the chair. "Go on!"

"Okay." He crosses a leg over the other. "The biological weapons were very efficient and the infected countries were wiped off the map. But our ancestors won and that country that used the biological weapon was completely destroyed."

"What about the citizens who were innocent?" Ardon asks, looking deeply concerned.

I understand him. How can they bomb a whole country? I'm willing to bet not all of the citizens were happy with the weapons!

Uncle Seth jabs a finger at Ardon, "That's the thing! Some citizens were removed from the country before the bombing. That'll be important later. So World War Three was over and the guilty country was punished. All their weapons were taken away and they were left poorer than even the poorest country.

"After World War Three, many people forgot about that country. At the same time, the atmosphere and the state of the planet was growing worse and worse. Billions were still dying from AIDS, Cancer, and Paraber. Starvation was at its absolute height.

"Then the most powerful country in the world fell. It seems as though there was a collapse in its government. We actually have the president's body during that collapse, for your information. Very interesting. His body was preserved by that great government and they included all the books with the information I am telling you now. That's the only reason why we know what we know. As I was saying, that country fell and it seems like the rest of the world fell, too. World War Four came on suddenly with the rise of a new country in place of the old powerful country. There was warfare all over the world, as well as the return of biological weapons – newer, more deadly biological weapons.

"There was a small group of 'citizens' who had been taken from that one country I told you about before it was bombed. Remember? The one that was destroyed? Well, there was a group that were actually scientists who had been working on the weapons. They perfected their biological weapon and let it loose during World War Four. Keep in mind that those two wars were fairly close together. They were both within forty to fifty years of each other. Like I've said, dates and information are minuscule.

"But the biological weapons were far deadlier than the creators realized. The creators lost control of them and they… mutated. Many countries had biological defenses, but that seemed instead to have made the weapons mutate into far more terrible things. Unspeakables, as we call them, started to form. It was terrifying."

"They're still terrifying," Ardon muttered.

"Indeed," he agreed. "Okay, so picture this: The world is losing control. Everyone is terrified. No one knows what is happening. Unspeakables are multiplying alarmingly fast and nothing the humans do can seem to stop them. Scientists cannot seem to find an antidote and, as a result of being in close contact with captured Unspeakables, are turning themselves!"

"Oh, I'll bet that had to be scary." Mason murmurs into his hands.

Uncle Seth nods slowly. "It was. Then, imagine seeing the heavens open up and beings come down. Many humans tried to shoot the Gods and didn't understand when the bullets had no effect. If you had only believed in one God for centuries and centuries and then suddenly multiple Gods and Goddesses come down from the heavens to help you that would really make you lose your mind. The humans set fire to the earth in an attempt to burn all the Unspeakables. The Grimsah Forest appeared out of nowhere. We believe it was an existing forest that Leibus corrupted. Then the Gods started to separate the lands and part the seas. They were separating the corrupted beings from the humans.

"Angels, Lightnings, Thunders, dragons, werewolves, vampires… you name it. All of them came down to help the humans. The humans were reeling from all these species.

They had thought they were all myths. They couldn't help themselves because they were simply dumbstruck. It was overwhelming for most of the population. But many humans adapted well and fought alongside their new allies. Countries joined sides to defeat the Unspeakables and the Grimsah Forest that was spreading.

"The Gods were able to banish the Unspeakables to their Forest after the Ravage. The Gods disappeared again, but all the other beings stayed on earth. Many humans today have forgotten why or where those beings came from. Many don't accept them as their allies and their equals. It's a pity, really. Because, as a result, there has been an increase in Darke beings and it seems Leibus is beginning to stir.

"Don't forget now," Uncle Seth wags a finger at us all. "Leibus, too, was banished by the Gods to his Forest. But now he's coming back. I'm telling you, kids. There is another war coming. It's not going to be an earthly war. It's going to be a cosmic battle. It'll be between Light and Darke, good and evil, Angels and demons. I'm telling you."

"Like how Leibus is gathering up Darke Angels?" Ardon asks him, elbows on his knees and leaning forward.

Uncle Seth stares at Ardon for a moment. "I suppose Hope told you about that, didn't she? Yes, he is gathering up Darke Angels. Not much is known about his Darke Angels. They're pretty rare nowadays. We all know that Eve and Adam are his most powerful Angels. Beneath them are thirteen Angels who will assist Eve. They have specific names drawn from Old World Christian literature. If I remember correctly, their names are Peter, Mary, James, Andrew, John, Phillip, Bartholomew, Thomas, Matthew, Simon, Thaddeus, and another one named James. There are some who are strong. Joseph is a strong Angel, as well as Luke and Mark. These important Angels are more powerful than other Angels but far less so than Eve and Adam.

Eve is the only thing I personally fear. She will destroy the world, and she will take everything she can down with her. Adam is a force to be feared, yes, but Eve is the force whose powers match some of our Gods."

"She is as strong as a God?" I ask skeptically. "How can that be? She's just a Darke Angel."

"Leibus is fairly powerful for a God." Uncle Seth's fingers lace together again. "But he used to be a good God. He fell from grace, but he used to be good. Eve has no soul and was destined from her birth to be Eve, to be pure evil. There is no good in her. She is the very embodiment of evil and, when that takes form, there is nothing that can stop it."

"Nothing? Nothing can stop Eve?" Mason is alarmed now.

"Well," Uncle Seth shrugs his shoulders, "that is the ideal Eve. No beings are perfect and it's the same with Darke beings. When the first Adam (that we know of) came into being, he was destroyed by Leibus, probably because he was not even remotely close to Leibus' ideal Adam. The possibility of finding a perfect Eve is even slimmer for Leibus. He has to pick and choose which Eves he destroys and which he keeps and grooms."

"Can you elaborate on that?" Ardon scratches his head.

"Yes, I can. Let's say Leibus finds a being and knows she is to be Eve. He'll corrupt her and wait for her soul to disappear. Then he'll take her and groom her. She won't automatically come into her full power. She will develop her skills the longer she is alive. The Gods will try to destroy her as soon as she comes into being. The longer she is alive, the more deadly she becomes."

No one says anything for a moment. The silence is deafening. The rain pounds on the window. It's comforting in the loud silence.

"Why did Leibus fall from grace?" Ardon asks.

"Only the Gods know the full answer to that," Uncle Seth presses his lips together but continues. "But from what I've read it has to do with power distribution. He wants more power and more people to know his name. He thinks power is being feared. He's your typical power-hungry God."

There is another lasting silence. I focus on the rain, listening to the steady pour.

"Well," Uncle Seth stands up. "I'm afraid to say I don't have much in the food department, but I'll bet I can whip something up. I'll go to the store tomorrow."

"I can go right now!" I stand up too quickly. My head spins.

"It's pouring outside, Mary," Mason says before Uncle Seth can.

"Good thing we have things called umbrellas!" I say brightly. "Do you have one, Uncle Seth?"

He nods. "Funny thing, those were invented in the Old World! And I sure do have one. Do you want someone to go with you?"

"Mm," I pretend to think about it. No, I don't want anyone going with me. "I'll be okay. You know me, Uncle Seth. I like being alone."

"I think a walk in the rain might actually be good for you," he smiles. "When you go outside the door, just turn left and keep walking straight. It'll take you straight into the main part of town with shops."

"What?" Mason turns to look at him in disbelief.

"She'll catch pneumonia!" Penny looks at Uncle Seth like he's lost his mind.

"She's part wolf," Uncle Seth laughs. "She'll be okay. Why don't you two lovebirds help me make dinner? Mary, the umbrella is by the closet by the door! There's a little jar of money on the top shelf in the closet. Grab a little bit and tell the grocer you're my niece."

I say thank you with a giggle.

"Grab my raincoat!" he calls from the kitchen.

I grab the strange plastic coat hanging by the umbrella. It's dark green with a zipper and a hood. I shrug it on. It's a little big but it'll do.

"Thank you!"

"I can't believe you're letting her g-" Mason is saying as I shut the door.

I open the umbrella and it explodes open, making me give a little yelp. No one is around to notice. The sidewalks are deserted.

I inhale deeply, taking in the thick rain scent and step off the little welcome mat.

Uncle Seth is right. Rain is good for me.

CHAPTER TEN

Mary

I step into the first shop I see. The shop is dark on the inside with dark purple laces and scarves hanging everywhere. There are crystalline figurines, balls, and birds hanging from the ceiling and covering all the tables. A large bookshelf stands on the farthest wall from the door. Large books both worn and new are in complete disorder on the shelf.

"Hello!" An elderly man pops up suddenly from behind a counter I hadn't noticed, startling me.

"Ah!" I stumble backwards.

"My, my," he says, coming around the counter. "You look soaked, my dear!"

He wears a strange dark green tunic with a purple sash tied around his waist. He has enormous glasses on that make Uncle Seth's huge monocles look small. He wears white pants tucked into worn boots. One of the boots has a small bird figure tied onto the shoe.

He has many bracelets on each wrist and several necklaces on. He has a large watch around his neck, too.

"Some tea to warm you, my dear?" he asks pleasantly, gesturing to a large golden teapot.

"S-sure," I shift uncomfortably, looking around the shop.

There are several candles placed strategically throughout the shop, but it is still dark inside. I watch the man carefully as he prepares the tea. He is surprisingly spry for his age. He has to be at least one hundred. He has a long white beard that is tied in the middle with a thin silver rope. The rope has two round crystals on the ends.

Is he some kind of fortune teller or something? He definitely gives off the vibe.

"What are you doing out in this weather, Mary?" he looks up at me pleasantly and hands me a small white teacup.

I feel my eyes widen. "How do you know my name?"

He smiles. "Is the tea to your liking?"

My hands are trembling as I lift the cup to my lips. I take a sip and discover he has fixed my tea just the way I like it – with honey, milk, and cinnamon. No one else does that accept Connor and me.

"Yes," I resist the temptation to step backwards. "Yes, it is. Thank you."

"Have a seat," he says, gesturing to a chair I had not seen behind me. I sit down rather mechanically.

"Tell me," he leans forward, much too close to me. "Why have you come into my shop today?"

"I just wanted to get out of the rain," I say quietly, looking down into my tea.

"I'm sure you did," the man says. I look up into his eyes. They're silver. I have never seen silver eyes before.

"How is your faith?" he asks.

"My faith?"

"Do you pray and worship our Gods often?"

I think about the Gods, but I don't really pray to them. I just never think to do it. "Yes, my faith is fine."

"You needn't lie to me, dear." The man sits back in his chair.

"Okay." I close my eyes for a moment. This is not happening. I open my eyes to find his face a little closer. "Who are you? How do you know my name?"

The man smiles. "My name isn't necessary. My title is Father Trusie Sulibe. Father Sulibe will suffice. That's the name I go by in this business. Some call me fortune teller and others call me psychic."

"Aren't they the same thing?" I am confused. I thought they were advertised as the same thing.

"No, no," Father Sulibe smiles widely, showing all his teeth – or lack thereof. "A psychic isn't real. Psychics do not exist. There are Seers; however, but I am not one of those either. I am a fortune teller. I can tell you your destiny if you want to hear it."

"What if I don't want to hear it?" I put my tea down on the table I have not noticed before either. Are things just appearing? Surely, I am not that unobservant!

Papa always said never trust a man who can tell you your destiny. Your destiny is something you build, something you make yourself. A man who says he can tell you your destiny is a man who lies.

"That's fine." The man closes his eyes and leans back, linking his fingers together around his tea cup. He opens his eyes and locks mine. "There are some questions I would like to ask you. Would you mind that? I know your secret but, before we address that, I want to know a few things."

"Certainly," I say, not wanting to be rude. My secret? How can he possibly know anything about me? "However," I add, "I will be choosey about the questions I answer. I hope you understand?"

"Of course, my dear." He unlinks one hand to wave it about in a partial circle. He rests it against his cheek, propping his elbow on the arm of the chair. "So have you come to Gedan with family?"

"Yes," I answer, thinking it to be harmless. Did I mention family earlier? I suppose so. How else would he know? "I've come with my brother Mason."

"Is that all?" Father Sulibe wants to know.

"No." I take a sip of the tea. "I came with Mason's girlfriend, two friends from home, my best friend, and Hope. Err… she's another friend from home."

"Lovely name, Hope is." Father Sulibe turns his head sideways, leaning heavily on his hand. "Tell me about her."

I realize I shouldn't have said her name. I should have thought of something. I need to start thinking like a liar. Connor told me that once. I don't remember what incited him to say that. I distinctly remember he was very irritated with me. I feel as though it had something to do with the baker. I just can't remember.

"Oh," I say, trying to find a lie about Hope. "I don't really know her well. She's very pretty. She has blonde hair and blue eyes. She looks like an angel! She's very kind an-"

"She's an Angel?" he suddenly says, leaning forward.

"Did I say that?" I skirt around a direct answer. *Jeck*! I *need* to learn to lie!

"Mary," Father Sulibe raises an eyebrow. "Please do not lie to me or attempt to. Tell me about this Angel. They are quite fascinating. Does she have wings?"

"I apologize," I mumble, "N-no, she doesn't have wings. Someone shot her down and they're not there. I don't know why. I didn't ask her about it. She didn't really want to talk about it. She's so kind, you know. I didn't want to make her uncomfortable."

"She's here on a mission, I see. Do you know who she's protecting? Ah, I see that you do."

"She's protecting Kaleb," I say, starting to feel uncomfortable. Why is he so concerned about Hope? And why do I keep answering his questions?

"I can see something else, Mary." He sets his tea down looking grave.

Instinctively, I sit back. I don't like this. I need to leave now.

"I can see your soul." He leans toward me.

I need to leave right now.

"Take this." He reaches out and gives me a small marble.

"A marble?" In spite of myself, I take the marble and stare at it.

"It's a pearl." He watches me carefully. "And it's not just any pearl either. It will heal what has happened to your soul. Washing off Darkeness doesn't work, Mary."

My head snaps up.

"Am I…?" I cannot bear to finish it. There is no way I could be! Kaleb is the one who's corrupted. He's the reason Hope is here.

"I apologize if I startled you, Miss Stoneburner. There was something sinister about you when you walked in. I had to be sure you weren't some sort of Darke being."

"I'm sinister?" My voice breaks. This cannot be happening. The burn from the Unspeakable was so long ago! Wouldn't Hope be able to tell if I was corrupted? "What about Hope, Father Sulibe? Can she tell I'm corrupted?"

Father Sulibe furrows his brow in thought. "I think not. Losing her wings and surviving such a traumatic injury probably somehow took away from her power. I don't know how to explain it, but she probably is only aware of Kaleb as being corrupted."

I suddenly remember right before the Unspeakables attacked Kaleb, Hope and me on the cliff edge. I distinctly remember her looking at me after saying something like "impossible" or "this can't be."

"There it is," Father Sulibe extends his index finger as though that was the key to everything. "That memory. Yes, I saw it, too. Don't act so shocked, child. But that moment shows that she was very confused. She didn't understand how she didn't sense them coming. Angels, with their wings, can see those Darke beings coming for miles. Extraordinary, really."

"So I'm . . . evil?" I look at my forearm where the Unspeakable scratched me.

"No," Father Sulibe smiles. "That is why I was confused when you walked in. You have a sinister air about you, yet you are so opposite of evil. I do admit you had me confused, my dear. I think that Angel's presence has prevented your soul from being completely turned. There is also the matter of the Unspeakable. Unspeakables really do not corrupt beings well. They usually eat them, to begin with, or they merely scratch their victim. That kind of contact would take years to corrupt a soul."

"So this pearl will keep me safe?" I stare at the marble in my hand. The marble is brilliantly blue with swirls of purple throughout. It seems to sparkle.

"As long as it is with you." Father Sulibe smiles widely again.

A shiver shoots up my spine. As kind as this man is, he still is slightly frightening. Perhaps he is a vampire. Vampires are known to have extraordinary powers for earth bound beings.

"May I have your hand?" He extends a long-fingered hand. I hesitate. "These eyes aren't what they used to be. I just want to be sure of the state of your soul. I wouldn't want to give you a pearl if you were too advanced for it. Pearls can only cover the early corruption stages."

I give him my hand reluctantly. He pushes my sleeve up and grabs my forearm with one hand. His other hand wraps around my wrist. He digs a dirty fingernail into my skin.

"Ouch!" I cry, trying to jerk my hand back. He holds on tightly.

"I am terribly sorry. Just a moment, child."

Blackness swirls under my skin under his nail.

"What is that? What are you doing to me?" I cry, jerking harder.

He finally lets go of me. "That was all of the corruption within. Not much, is it? Yes, I think that pearl will do just fine. I apologize for startling you."

I rub my wrist. There is a small black swirl on it now, like a tattoo. It fades around the edges into my skin. It looks unnatural. I rub it, but it doesn't go away.

"That was bound to happen anyway," he says sadly. He takes my hand again and rubs the swirl gently. "Most corrupted beings develop some sort of mark. Let me advise you to do two things, my dear. Please do not tell anyone of our meeting. It is better for both of us that no one knows what has transgressed here. Secondly, you would do best to cover that up. Perhaps a bracelet or gloves? Actually, here, take this."

He hands me a wide leather band with a button on the end.

"It's just a little cover-up bracelet," he says as I take it in my hands. The band has a black X marked on it. I put it on quickly.

"Right," I say nervously. I adjust the bracelet and look at it. It looks normal. "Cover it up. I won't tell anyone. I don't think I want anyone to know anyway."

"I'll be frank with you," Father Sulibe murmurs, leaning forward. I lean toward him. "They will kill you if they ever see that mark and know you are corrupted. They will kill you if they know about the pearl, too. Those pearls are very valuable and can be sold at a high price. Everything that has happened must be kept a secret at all costs. People will kill you and then they will kill me. This business is terribly dangerous. Most of us are nomads and keep the business under wraps. I hope one day you will find me and return the pearl but, until that day, please keep it. I hope to the Gods that you stay safe. I won't lie to you, my dear, many die… many. Please keep everything a secret. No one can know, not your brother, uncle, friends, or lovers. No one can ever know."

Kill me? People would kill me for this little pearl? I put the pearl in my pocket. I stand up, nearly teetering over with fear. Fear for my death… It's almost too much to think about.

Father Sulibe steadies me. His kind wrinkled face looks concerned. I smile at him.

"How can I ever repay you?" I take both of his hands into my own.

"I work for one of the greatest Gods of all," Father Sulibe smiles widely again, making the hairs on the back of my neck stand. "That is the greatest reward of all! I hope to see you again one day! Good luck, my dear!"

I step toward the door, releasing his hands. I glance at him as I open my umbrella.

"And," Father Sulibe takes my hand again and squeezes it, "I wish you the best of luck. Look for signs. They'll always be there."

"Thank you," I say, a little wary of his strange demeanor. "Thank you again."

I leave the shop holding my umbrella with one hand, the other hand in my pocket holding the pearl. I have a lot to process here. A lot. I've been corrupted this entire time, but Hope's presence has kept me from turning! Oh Gods, I could have been a Darke being by now! Thank the Gods I stumbled onto Father Sulibe's shop.

What did he say about why I came into his shop? He seemed to disbelieve I had just stepped in to get out of the rain. Perhaps it was destiny? Maybe the Gods led me there so that I might be saved. Did he say he was a destiny-reader? I ought to ask him about that.

I turn back, but the shop is empty. I grab the door. It's locked. What? No, this is definitely the shop I just walked out of! I peer into the windows. The inside is dark, empty, and clearly has been for a while. No. No, no, no, no. I was just in that shop.

I turn back to the street again. No one is out on the streets. No one can vouch for me that I did indeed walk in and out of that shop. What just happened? No, no, no, no.

I turn back to the shop and stare at its emptiness. I suppose he is magical. That would certainly explain the appearing furniture. I know I'm not that unobservant. He was making things appear as he needed them. He probably needed everything to appear that way to keep me there long enough.Unconsciously, I pull the sleeve of Uncle Seth's raincoat further down. My mark feels as though it is burning from his touch still. How does this all make sense? I look at my reflection in the grey window.

I'm just going to trust that the Gods arranged that all. Papa used to tell us three never to overthink anything the Gods do. Sometimes they do things that make little or no sense, but we need to just trust in them. Our Gods love us and will always do the best thing for us.

I silently thank the Gods for saving me.

Squinting in the rain, I spy a grocery shop. I hustle across the street to the grocery shop. I step under the awning and close my umbrella. I shake the umbrella, trying to get as much water off of it. I pull the door but smack into it. It's locked. How peculiar! I know it isn't late. Perhaps the rain prevented the grocer from opening today or caused him to close early.

Uncle Seth said he could shop tomorrow. I'll go with him and ask him about the fortune teller's shop. Maybe he just closed up and left for the day as soon as I left? I couldn't have just imagined all of this, could I?

No, I mustn't think of that. It's all in the Gods' hands.

"Mary," a familiar voice says from behind me.

I turn slowly.

Connor stands in the rain behind me. I turn to face him fully.

"C-Connor?" I step backwards into the door. My umbrella hits the cobblestones.

"Why did you leave?" he asks. He doesn't move toward me.

His clothing is soaked and sticks to him. I can see through his shirt. There's a terrible wound on his chest. I swallow hard. Fear roots me to the spot.

"Why did you leave me?" he asks again, his voice breaking on the last part.

A voice in the back of my head warns me this isn't right. Connor would have been hugging me by now. If this was real, how could he have found me? In the middle of downtown Gedan in the pouring rain?

I dare a glance down the street. No one is out. It's all too eerie. In a city large like Gedan, why wouldn't anyone be out?

"Y-you're dead!" I flatten myself against the window.

He takes a step toward me. "How could you know? You didn't see. You left me without even checking. You didn't even give me a proper burial. You did to me what you did to Mother. You let me die! Now I know how it must have felt for her. How could you? How could you do that, Mary?"

I step out from beneath the awning. The rain hits me immediately, pounding hard on my shoulders. No, this isn't happening. The pain in my chest flares suddenly. The pain has always been there, always an aching for Mother and now for Connor and Papa. The pain shoots up exponentially. I clutch my chest.

"You're not real!" I point at him. "You're not real! Go away! This isn't happening!"

"No," Connor steps toward me again. His eyes aren't right. They look darker. "I'm not really here. Because you left me in Mika, choking on my own blood and alone."

"N-no!" I back away from him down the street a bit more.

"You're a coward, Mary," he spits, coming toward me more quickly. "You always have been. Even if you had seen me shot, you would have run away. Coward!"

"No!" I cry. I don't know what I would have done had I seen him shot. "That's not true!"

"Isn't it?" He's malicious now. He cocks his head. "You know it's true. You've always been a weak coward! You think of no one but yourself! Coward! You know it's true. It's your flaw, Mary. Your tragic flaw."

"No!" I point at him again, jabbing a finger at him. "You are not real! This is not happening! Go away! You're not Connor! You are not my brother!"

"You left me," he says weakly. His voice isn't so strong anymore.

He staggers toward me, suddenly not so stable on his feet. Blood dribbles out of his mouth and he falls to his knees in front of me. Blood bubbles at his mouth as he breathes raggedly. The wound in his chest bleeds openly. Blood swirls with the rain at his feet.

"Rot in hell, Mary," he reaches toward me. "Join me."

He falls to my feet in a pool of his own blood. I blink and he's gone. Connor's body has been replaced with Kaleb's. I scream in horror.

CHAPTER ELEVEN

Kaleb

I sit outside the small thatch building. The building looks big enough to only fit two people. I cross my arms, trying to keep warm in the rain. The rain has suddenly turned colder, or perhaps it's my imagination.

Goosebumps rise on my arms. I clench my jaw and squint out into the rain. The rain is so heavy and thick I can't see very far. Large figures pass here and there. Cars? Hope told me not to worry before she went into the little thatch building. She said it is the safest place in all of Gedan.

Anything Hope says I'll believe wholeheartedly, but it is still a little unnerving to see the shapes and figures moving past me. When I gave up on Mary, when I discovered what had become of my soul, when Hope stepped into my life, everything changed. Now I am in love with an Angel. Mary still pains me, but Hope has completely won me over. Gods, I love her!

I close my eyes remembering what happened just ten minutes prior to us finally finding the building.

Hope had stopped walking. It was pouring down by then. Her tunic was soaked and hugging every curve on her. Her face seemed more beautiful in the rain. I thanked her for everything. She has been with me ever since she told everyone what happened to me.

She has slept next to me, kept watch with me, talked with me. She is always by my side.

I suppose it finally dawned on me how much she meant to me then. I grabbed her face and kissed her. Desire drove me. I know it was lust and love that drove me to grab her like that. She kissed me back.

My eyes open and I smile. I blink rapidly as the rain pours on my face. Gods, she kissed me back! She wrapped her arms around my neck as I pulled her against me. Gods, I want her. I bite my lip, reliving the memory.

I always heard my parents talking about how they fell in love at first sight.

I think it's the same with Hope and me. Is it too early to tell her I love her? When can I tell her? I've never kissed a woman like that before. My skin felt on fire. I felt as though we were on fire.

Gods, I'm in love with a woman I've known for less than a couple months. I can't wait to kiss her again. I just can't wait to be with her. I picture her smile, her fair skin, her golden hair, and her beautiful eyes.

"Kaleb?" Her voice wakes me from my reverie.

I turn and look at her. She smiles at me. Her smile is like Mary's, warm and kind. I press my lips together. I can't be in love with two women at the same time. Can I?

"Are you ready?"

The giddiness is suddenly chased away by cold anxiety. My stomach feels strange again. I swallow and nod.

"Good." She comes over and intertwines her fingers with mine. "They're here."

Before I can ask who, three large dragons land in front of me. A silver dragon lands much too closely to me. I jump backwards, dragging Hope behind me.

"Kaleb," she laughs, leading me forcefully toward the dragons. "They're here to take you to the Gods."

"They can do that?" I eye the dragons suspiciously.

"Here." She leads me toward the dark green dragon, which is smaller than the other two. "We're riding this one."

The Riders look amused as I inch nervously away from the dragon. This is the first time I've ever seen a dragon in person, so to speak. I've read about them, but I've never seen them!

The green dragon lies down, as we get closer, making me jump a little.

"Kaleb," she laughs, turning around to face me. "Do you trust me?"

I nod, unable to speak. My nerves are starting to get the best of me. I have to ride a jecking dragon to see the Gods!

"I won't let anything bad happen." She smiles and kisses my cheek.

Then she turns away from me and climbs on top of the green dragon. She settles into the front saddle strapped onto the large lizard. Reptile? I don't know…

I hesitate, then clamber onto the dragon less than gracefully, slipping twice and almost yelling when the dragon's large face turns to see what is taking so long. I swear, the dragon's head is as big as a horse's body!

I scoot onto the saddle behind Hope. She twists in her saddle and begins to strap my legs in. I let her, not bothering to even try to strap myself in. I will never ride a dragon again.

One of the Riders calls to Hope in another language. She answers promptly and takes hold of the horn of the saddle. I wrap my arms around her waist.

"We're taking off as soon as the silver dragon goes first," she says over her shoulder.

The wind is picking up. Rain beats us relentlessly.

Suddenly our dragon jerks upward into the air. I feel my stomach churn dangerously. I cannot vomit on the back of the woman I'm in love with. I cannot! Oh Gods, please protect me until I come to you! Oh Gods, please!

I squeeze my eyes shut, unwilling to look around. I try not to crush Hope despite my desire to hold her tighter. It is an uncomfortable mixture of fear and desire.

The rain lessens as we fly higher and higher toward the heavens.

"Kaleb," Hope says just as I realize the wind isn't blowing anymore. "We're here."

I open my eyes. It's only been about 30 seconds. Did we go anywhere? Are they trying to mess with my head? Is this part of the process? Did we just fly up and land somewhere else?

Hope unstraps me first to let me slide off. I slide off the dragon and nearly fall when I land. I stagger for a moment. The green grass is lush and there are flower gardens everywhere. Lovely trees stand in organized clumps here and there, perfectly placed on the grounds.

The luscious grasses become steep and I glance up the hill to see an acropolis built upon it. I can clearly see a large glittering white temple and smaller white buildings around it. I find myself walking up the hill toward the temple. I am completely drawn to it. I can't help myself. It is so beautiful.

The temple has large white columns supporting the roof, which is richly carved with images of humans and Gods celebrating. I cannot see what they are celebrating. I prop my foot up on the silver flooring of the temple and hoist myself onto it using one of the columns. I walk along the columns. Where is this place? I have never heard of any place like this! Surely, everyone must know about this beautiful place.

"Excuse me," a voice interrupts my admiring. I turn around.

My mouth opens a bit before I catch myself. I close my mouth with an audible pop. A tall, beautiful woman is striding toward me. She wears a white dress, almost like a toga, that seems to flow behind her in slow motion. Or perhaps it's my imagination.

She has dark ebony skin and black hair like the night. She has long and lean limbs. She covers the distance between us quickly. She seems unearthly. I feel the hairs on the back of my neck rise. She has startlingly light eyes. They look like silver.

"Who are you?" she asks me coolly. When she gets to me, I realize how tall she is. She's probably an inch or so taller than I.

She wears no jewelry or any other means of identifying her culture or country. I stare at her in dumb silence. Where is this woman from? Is she from here? Where is here? Where the hell am I?

Oh Gods, where is Hope? I just wandered off without her!

"Who are you?" The woman steps closer to me. "I asked you a question, mortal."

Mortal?

"My name is Kaleb Roth," I manage to say. "I-I don't know where I am."

"You don't know where you are?" That seems to catch her off guard. Should I know where I am? Is it terribly obvious?

"You are above Mt. Irise." The woman shifts her weight onto one hip, displaying a slight curve to her lean body. "In the heavens? With the Gods?"

"Why is there grass?" I ask, looking back where I came from. I can see part of a dragon. If I take off running right now, maybe this mysterious woman won't damn me to hell. I wonder why she's up here.

"Why is there grass on earth?" The woman folds her arms across her chest now.

Oh Gods, she must think I'm an imbecile.

"Excuse me," I say, looking at her closely. "But who are you?"

"My name is Psyche." The woman suddenly seems even more imposing to me. "Are you the man I am supposed to cleanse?"

"I-I think so." I am standing before one of the most powerful Goddesses in the universe. Why can't I think of anything intelligent to say?

I stand before her as dumb as a sheep and as silent as a mouse. She looks me over with an eyebrow raised.

"Come with me, Kaleb," she says, sweeping by me. "I do believe I know you."

"You know me?" I walk quickly beside her. Gods, she's fast.

"I know everyone with a soul, all creatures," Psyche says, turning suddenly into a doorway leading into the temple.

"Your parents were killed," Psyche waves her hand carelessly over her shoulder.

My hands are spread wide in front of me as the ground flies up toward me. Leigh has pushed me. I turn around and see the Unspeakable. The Unspeakable makes eye contact with me. My sister screams at it, trying to draw its attention. She waves her arms and jumps in place.

I shake my head slightly, willing the memory to disappear again. I try to focus on what Psyche is saying.

"You lived in Mika until very recently. You are a werewolf. You have a terrible temper, but you've managed to keep that under wraps. Shall I go on?"

"I understand," I say rather dully.

Psyche suddenly turns, startling me once more with her silver eyes.

"I can see your corruption very clearly now." She walks a quick, tight circle around me. "Yes, I can see it. I apologize, dear Kaleb, but this will be painful."

"Why?" I take a step back from her.

"Kaleb," Psyche steps toward me. "I know you. I know you're brave and strong. You can handle this."

"What are you going to do?" I resist the temptation to step away from her. The Goddess is almost overpowering. I can feel her will becoming my own. I am going to stay here and accept whatever is going to be done to me.

"Unfortunately," she walks a tight circle around me, "the extent of the corruption is irreversible in your current form."

"My current form?" What is she getting at? My current form?

"You are a werewolf," Psyche slows and makes eye contact with me. Her terrifying eyes hold me captive. "But you are also mortal."

"You're going to make me immortal?" I guess.

Psyche nods slowly. "I can't make you a demigod, but I can make you immortal."

Her eyes suddenly fog over, turning into swirling silver clouds. I close my eyes as she lifts an arm.

CHAPTER TWELVE

Mary

"Hey!" Someone's voice suddenly breaks through the fog I have been resting on. The soft fog pops and I'm rushed toward the surface. I can hear myself breathe suddenly. The relief of being off of the fog is greater than the comfort of it.

I blink open my eyes. A well-dressed gentleman is leaning over me. His black umbrella blocks most of the rain from splattering on my face. He looks concerned. His mouth is moving. Is he talking to me?

"Hey, Miss." He cups a hand against my face. "Are you alright?"

"W-what?" is all I can manage to say. I feel the fog pulling on me. I still feel hazy.

I slowly become aware of the pain on the back of my head.

"Do you know where you are?" he asks quietly. My eyes focus on his face. Good gracious, he's gorgeous.

I realize there are a couple other people here, all with umbrellas, hovering around me.

"Um," I blink. Where am I? I don't remember. Wasn't I just in Gedan? "Gedan."

"Yes." The man's kind face gives a smile, but he is still concerned. "Where in Gedan?"

"Um," I close my eyes. I remember the... yes. "Downtown?"

"Yes." The man looks relieved. "Do you know what happened to you?"

"N-no," I say. Why am I lying on the ground?

The last thing I remember is Connor covered in blood and begging me to come rot in hell with him, then turning into Kaleb. I swallow. Did the man see that? Was that a dream?

"Here." The man gently puts a hand under my head. "Let's sit you up and see how you feel."

"Are you a doctor?" I ask suddenly. I don't know why I ask that except that he is gentle and calm like Papa was with his patients.

"Yes, angel," he says, pulling me up gently. "How do you feel?"

"My head hurts," I say quietly. "What happened to me?"

"Do you see that awning?" He points to a collapsed awning. One of the bars that supported it has collapsed and is hanging down in front of the shop I had been standing in front of earlier. The cloth of the awning is hanging down in front of the window.

"Did it fall on me?"

"Yes," he says, examining my eyes as he speaks. "It collapsed from the weight of the rain collecting in the middle. There was a witness who saw it collapse on you. You didn't see it coming."

"What was I doing? I don't remember being in front of that shop. I thought I had moved away." Connor had forced me out from under the awning when he had walked toward me.

Or was that a dream?

"You can ask the woman who saw it if you like." The doctor sits back on his heels. "It looks like a minor concussion. Are you human?"

I blink at him. I have never been asked so directly before. In Mika, it is a don't-ask-don't-tell sort of situation. No one wants to know and no one wants to be ousted. Everything works out better that way. Or, at least, it used to.

"We're in Gedan, angel." The man gives a sympathetic smile. "You're free to express your species. Are you human?"

"N-no," I stammer, still surprised. "I'm a wolf. Half human."

"Alright then," the doctor smiles, unfazed, "You should be fine in less than an hour, I believe. Though I do advise you to stay still for at least a day."

"Okay," I say, unable to think of anything else. Gedan is too strange. I suddenly don't like the city. "Th-thank you, D-Doctor."

He helps me to my feet. "Don't worry, dear. Here, take my umbrella."

"Oh," I say, not accepting it as he reaches out toward me. "No, no, it's yours! I couldn't possibly! I have a rain coat."

"No, no," the doctor smiles and presses the umbrella into my hand. "I insist."

"Thank you," I say. "Thank you very much."

"And I am so sorry to say that I must get going." He gives an embarrassed smile. "I have a funeral to attend. Luckily, a shopkeeper came and found me. You're a lucky lady, Miss!"

"Mary," I smile and extend a hand. "My name is Mary. Thank you very much."

The doctor smiles as someone behind him moves forward to share their umbrella with him. He shakes my hand.

"I hope to see you again but in better health next time," he says with a chuckle.

"Yes," I force the conversation further. "Yes, I hope to see you, too! Thank you again!"

I awkwardly step back and give a little wave. He waves and is rushed on by his older companions. One of them gives me another glance over the shoulder. I wave again.

How bizarre. Do things like this happen in the city often? I hurry back to the house feeling overwhelmed…

Suddenly I bolt up, finding myself nestled into Uncle Seth's couch with a soft blanket thrown over me.

Was that all a dream? A bizarre and vivid dream? I stare wide eyed out the window into the dark rain. No, that was no dream.

I am corrupted but am safe with the pearl in my possession. I can tell no one about Father Sulibe. I can tell no one that Connor came back to tell me I'm going to join him in hell.

But did I really see that or was it really a dream? It had to be a dream. But why would Connor be in hell? And how did I get home and onto the couch? It had to be a dream because I am clearly lying right here on the couch, shoes off, nestled comfortably in the pillows.

What is going on?

My hands shake. I press my shaky cold hands against my face. I'm sweating.

I can hear lively conversation in the kitchen. I pull the blanket off silently, constantly glancing toward the door to be sure no one has heard me. I sit on the edge of the couch, still listening attentively to the voices in the kitchen. Then I dart up the staircase as quickly and as quietly as I can. My socked feet make no noise and I stop when I get to the end of the stairs.

I need a place to think. I need to… to process everything that has happened. Papa used to say that one needs to take time to sort through the day. He used to write in a journal, but he stopped after Mother died.

The upstairs has several bedrooms and a large library. I peek into each doorway, hoping for the library. The first bedroom is a light blue room. It has a large bed with two bags sitting on the edge. The next two rooms are darker with grey and green themes. Aunt Margaret liked to make each room have a theme. I try the very last room. It doesn't have a door, just an open door frame. I should have tried that first.

The library is warm and smells like old books and mothballs. The smell is wonderful. I take in the black cushioned seats and the soft red rug in the center of the room. Tall bookcases cover every wall. Uncle Seth's library is stuffed to the brim. Books are stuffed onto every shelf. Neat piles of books sit on the base of several of the bookcases.

I sit down in one of the black chairs facing the single window. Rain beats against the window creating a soothing sound. I close my eyes and lean back in the chair.

I try to remember how the Unspeakable scratched me. The memory is so hazy, covered up by more terrible and pressing memories. I can't remember how it grabbed me. Just a scratch, just a scratch. Then everything happened so quickly in Mika. Everything fell apart. There was so much shooting and smoke, fire and screaming. It was too much.

I clutch the chair rigidly.

Then Papa and Connor lost their lives somewhere in that smoke and chaos. They died and I didn't even know it until Mason told me in the Forest.

I lean forward and put my head in my hands, slipping my fingers through my hair and clutching it tightly. How has everything come to this?

We fled Mika. I never thought twice about fleeing from Mika. Connor was right. I am a coward. But was that Connor? It could be something out of my subconscious. Connor used to read psychology books from the Old World and tell me the fascinating details. I shake my head, removing his smiling face from my mind for a moment.

Gedan. Coming to Gedan was a mistake.

I'm corrupted but am safe with this pearl in my pocket. Wait, if it was just a dream. . . I jerk my sleeves up to look at my wrists. They are both bare with no signs of any marks. I breathe raggedly and swallow. I slowly slide my hand into my pocket. My fingers close around a perfect sphere. A lump rises in my throat and my stomach seems to contract in on itself. I bring out the pearl to see it, to believe it's really there, to believe that all of this has not been a terrible dream. The pearl is bright blue with beautiful purple swirls.

I can feel my breathing starting to increase. I feel lightheaded. I stare down at the pearl. It'll keep my soul from turning. Did he say if it would heal me? I can't ask anyone. I can't even show it to anyone. Can I show it to Hope? Probably not. She would take me straight to the Gods, and I am not good enough to be in the presence of the Gods.

I rub my face hard. Father Sulibe said it would keep me safe, and I will trust him. But he didn't say anything about Connor. If he knew everything else about me, would he not have predicted or told me of Connor coming? Perhaps he didn't because that wasn't Connor. Yes, that wasn't Connor. It was just a dream. It was a very vivid dream. Gods, it seemed so real, but it wasn't. I know it wasn't. Connor would never talk to me like that. Even if he was right, he would never say it. I am a coward and I know it, but he would never say things like that to me.

I rub my face harder. Why do I have to convince myself of this?

This is all too painful. It's all too real! That actually happened!

Is this what hyperventilating is? My breathing is out of control and I may vomit. I flail my hands for a moment to distract myself. Mary, you're okay. You're okay, I tell myself. You're okay.

The pain in my chest lurches again. What Connor said about Mother was true... I did leave her. We were attacked by Darke beings. She fended them off, but her wounds were too much. It was by the cliff edge. I was so young and so afraid. I should have gotten help, but I didn't. I stayed next to her, so afraid the Darke beings would come back for me. They were clearly after me. Darke beings often go after children.

Mother died next to me. Jon, the blacksmith's son, told me if I had gotten help she would have lived. He was a medical student at the time. The blacksmith scolded him for telling me that. It's haunted me since.

Papa said that wasn't the case, but I know it was. If I had gotten help, she would be alive today. Now Papa and Connor are dead, too!

What if I could have helped them! Riley's comment about the silver bullet echoes in my mind but that doesn't matter. They could have still been helped.

I slowly become aware of a quiet sobbing. My chest heaves and I realize I'm crying. I fold over my knees and bury my face in my hands, sobbing.

Papa and Connor are gone! Just when the pain from Mother's death was starting to heal, they leave for the heavens! They're gone!

I sob. I can picture them in my head and it does nothing for me. I can see Connor's silly smile and Papa laughing. What is happening? Why is this all happening? Why the dream? Do I even deserve to be helped? Look at me! Gods!

A warm hand touches my back and gently rubs it. I look up blurry eyed to see who it is. Uncle Seth pulls the other fluffy chair over and sits next to me.

"Oh," I wipe my eyes. "I didn't mean to... Sorry... I-"

"Why are you apologizing?" Uncle Seth shakes his head. "There is no need to apologize for grief. We are all grieving."

"How did you know I was up here?" My voice is still shaky from crying. I sniffle.

"I didn't." Uncle Seth smiles and hands me a handkerchief from his pocket. "I saw the empty couch and wondered if you were up in your room. I wanted to make sure you were okay."

"I don't really remember what happened. I don't remember falling asleep. When did I do that?"

Uncle Seth actually laughs. "Oh, you fell asleep after Mason got up to get some food. Are you okay, pumpkin?"

His childhood pet name for me nearly drives me over the edge to hysterical crying. I fight back more tears, but my mouth turns into a frown against my will and my eyes let a few tears escape. "N-no!"

He pulls me into a hug and holds me while I cry. He rubs my back and tells me everything will be alright. I can't help but wonder how he could possibly be right.

I cry for a long time until I am simply hiccupping. I can hear the others downstairs talking and laughing. Mason has done his mourning. I have a hard time letting go. I suppose that's why he's the one with a better spiritual relationship with the Gods.

Uncle Seth pulls away and wipes a tear from my cheek. He smiles and stands up. It looks like he's been crying also. I didn't notice when he did, but his eyes are red.

"I promise you, Mary," he takes my hands in his own, "that everything will be okay."

"I hope you're right," I say rather pathetically.

"Now," he clears his throat and smoothens out his tunic "Go get cleaned up and we'll have supper. Kaleb should be home before long."

I had forgotten about Kaleb. He went to see the Thunders with Hope.

Uncle Seth trots down the stairs and I walk into the bathroom. My face is fairly clear. My eyes are a little red. I flush my face with cold water and pat my cheeks. I look into the mirror. I look pretty normal. Maybe no one will even notice my red eyes.

I sigh loudly and start to go down the stairs just as Hope and Kaleb come in through the front door. Kaleb suddenly grabs her and pulls her into a kiss. I clap a hand over my mouth. He slides a hand down the small of her back and pulls her to him. Her arms twist around his head and they are locked in a passionate embrace for a long moment. Both seem to be glowing. It's probably the kissing.

I freeze, unsure what to do. I step backwards, out of sight. Oh my Gods! When did that happen? I should have known Kaleb would never love a girl like me. That was so silly of me to even think that could happen!

"We're home!" Kaleb suddenly cries.

I take a deep breath and come down the stairs, trying to put a little bounce in my step. I will not let anyone see how I feel. Kaleb turns and sees me come down the stairs.

"Mary!" he cries happily. He pulls me into a tight hug. He is definitely glowing. His skin is too hot. He's a little fire!

"Kaleb." I force a smile and a laugh. "Are you glowing? Gods, your skin is so hot!"

Kaleb gives Hope a knowing smile. "I have big news."

"I do, too," Hope gives me a dazzling smile.

Oh Gods! Are they engaged already?

"Kaleb!" Mason yells happily. "Is that you I hear in there?"

Mason appears around the corner followed by Penny, Uncle Seth, and Ardon.

"How did it go?" Uncle Seth asks, walking into the living room and sitting down.

We all follow him into the room. I sit next to him as usual and Ardon takes the floor in front of me.

"Are you ready for this?" Kaleb asks. Good Gods, he is literally glowing like fire. He is giving off his own light.

"Um," Ardon puts a finger up to get his attention, "Kaleb, you are literally glowing. What did they do to you?"

"They made me a Lightning Child," Kaleb says proudly.

"What?" Uncle Seth's voice snaps like a whip. "You're a Lightning?"

Kaleb grins. "I'm immortal." He doesn't sound as sure of himself as he says this.

"And I have my wings back," Hope smiles and turns. "I'll show you."

Everyone claps and smiles as her glittery wings appear. They flutter and reflect spectacular colors. Her wings are beautiful. I glance at Kaleb to see his reaction. He is looking at her like he's in love with her… already. Is it possible to fall in love with someone so quickly?

I can only hope to have someone look at me like that one day. I had hoped it would be him, but I should have known better.

"So tell us everything!" Mason says. "Both of you! How did everything happen?"

Kaleb and Hope exchange a smile and Hope begins first.

She says that when they landed in the heavens, Kaleb disappeared so she went looking for him and ran into Zeus in his temple. Zeus was so proud of her for successfully finding her target and bringing him to the heavens to be purified despite having been shot that he restored her wings right then and there.

Her story is short and simple, but everyone smiles and congratulates her.

Kaleb tells us how he was confused when they landed. He wandered off and accidentally wandered into Psyche's temple. He describes the temple and the temple grounds and how beautiful they are. He tells us Psyche is beautiful and tall, with dark skin and light eyes. She is scary, he says. He doesn't tell us what they talked about, only that she said the only way to heal him was to turn him into an immortal so she turned him into a Lightning Child. They called for Zeus and together they made him into one of the Heaven's elite.

"I have to travel to Mt. Irise," Kaleb ends. "That's the bitter part to all of this wonderful news. I have to go and meet with the Guardians and begin my training as a Lightning Child. I-I'm not a werewolf anymore. I'm a Lightning Child, and I have duties to the heavens now. Everything… Everything is different. I'm so happy to be pure and cured, but I know it has come at a cost."

No one speaks. Hope takes Kaleb's hand. Kaleb looks unhappy for the moment.

"Someone," he says, looking unhappier and unhappier as the silence continues, "please say something."

"What can we say?" Ardon suddenly says. "Listen, I'm happy for you, but at the same time I understand what this all means. I know what immortality means for the rest of your life. You have to go to Mt. Irise, and I might not ever see you again."

"You'll see me ag-" Kaleb begins to say.

"Kaleb," Penny hugs him tightly. "I'm so happy for you, but what if we never see you again?"

Mason crosses his arms and frowns. He is not happy about this. I'm not either. I can't lose someone else. Even though he is alive, he is gone, and we'll never know if anything happens to him.

He may be immortal, but other immortal beings can destroy him. Gods can easily destroy him. Being an immortal being does not automatically mean one can live for forever.

"Now listen here," Uncle Seth suddenly says. Everyone has been talking except me, but we all turn to face him. "Reason is just south of Mt. Irise. My sister and your aunt, Aunt Imry, lives there. I have been promising to visit her for ages. When do you need to go to Mt. Irise, Kaleb?"

"I leave tonight," Kaleb presses his lips together.

I turn and leave the room. No, I cannot cry right here. Something between anger and misery boils up inside me. I storm out.

CHAPTER THIRTEEN

Kaleb

Mary suddenly runs out of the room. I start to run after her but she has reached the front door. She flings the door open. She can't go out in that weather! When Hope and I arrived, the rain had turned to sleet. It will probably be snowing soon. A blizzard, perhaps! Winter is coming fast!

"Mary!" Uncle Seth yells after her. But the front door slams shut.

Mason is right behind her. He flings the front door open and yells into the darkness. Sleet and snow blow into the entrance room. Mason yells for her again. His clothing suddenly bursts, and we see his dark brown tail disappear into the night after her.

"Mason!" Penny yells after him.

Ardon grabs her. "Don't!"

Penny yanks her arm out of his grasp. "What?"

"Don't go after them." Ardon steps in front of her. "Do you know how mad Mason would be if you went out there?"

"I don't really give a jeck!" Penny pushes him aside.

I've never heard her use that kind of language before.

"Penny," Seth says. "Please sit down. Mason will find her. I know my nephew and I know he'll find her." Seth suddenly looks very weary. The lines in his face seem more pronounced now.

"Can't you do something?" Ardon looks at me, stressed. Hope squeezes my hand and releases it. She sits down, looking calm.

"I can't do anything!" I say, feeling utterly helpless. "I have no control over my powers! Psyche told me not to do anything!"

I turn to Seth. "What do we do?"

Seth shakes his head and sits down on his chair. "We wait for them to come back."

I sit down on the edge of the couch and stare at the door.

"Why did she run?" Penny's voice cuts the tense silence.

Seth frowns and crosses his arms. "There are a lot of reasons. Mary is a lot like her father in many ways, but she isn't able to adjust to change like her mother. Mary's life has been turned upside down and inside out within a couple weeks. I think she believes she's at fault for her mother's death and she probably feels some sort of guilt for Connor and James' deaths."

"Why would she feel any blame?" I ask, confused. Mary couldn't do anything. She didn't know they had died until Mason told her in the Forest.

Seth shakes his head. "I don't know. She probably thinks she ought to have done something."

"That doesn't even make sense," I shake my head. "I'm going to strangle her later. How can it be her fault?"

"When you've lost so much," Seth shrugs, "it begins to seem as though it may be your fault."

It seems to me he's speaking more out of experience than speculation. Mason has told me Mary and Seth are very much alike. I wonder if they share similar experiences, too. He seems to understand her more than any of the rest of us.

"Then," Seth continues, "you come and announce that… She's lost so much and now, in her mind, she's losing you too. Just like what Ardon said, we may never see you again. You're her best friend, aren't you?"

"Yes," I say without hesitation. "I always have been and always will be."

Seth raises his eyebrows.

"I'm like her brother," I say slowly. I look at him. Mary has been falling apart since Connor and Mr. Stoneburner died, and I've been too blind and too self-absorbed to see how she was deteriorating. Gods, I'm such a terrible friend. I have been so focused on myself and on Hope, I have been blind to Mary's suffering.

"Mary has always been so quiet and so shy." Seth laces his fingers across his stomach. "Her way to express anything is to be alone."

"I'm so stupid!" I stand up, throwing my hands up. "How did I not notice?"

I'm in love with Mary, so why didn't I notice that? I have always loved Mary. Usually nothing escapes me, but I've become distracted with Hope. Oh Gods. How did I not see?

"Kaleb," Hope touches my arm. "You were occupied with other things."

"I know," I rub my face with a hand. It's because I was occupied with you, I want to say. "But I should have seen her suffering. I should have helped her. I should have-"

"Kaleb." Hope grabs my arm. "You were corrupted! That would weigh on anyone's mind! It's not your responsibility to look after everyone. You had so much on your mind. I'm sure Mary understands that!"

I pace anxiously. Hope has a point, but I still should have kept an eye on Mary. I was corrupted, but I'm still in love with her. I'm in love with both of them. My heart pains me. How can it do this to me? You can't split a heart between two amazing and beautiful women, can you? My thoughts race back and forth between Hope and Mary. Oh, Mary. She must be so fragile at this time. She has lost everything and now she probably thinks she's going to lose me.

The door suddenly bursts open and hits the wall hard. Two large werewolves appear in the doorway. The larger brown one barks at the smaller black one. Mary trots up the stairs, her hackles straight up. Mason trots up after her.

I bounce on my toes for several seconds, waiting for them to find a change of clothing. Will they come downstairs or will they stay upstairs? I can't stand it anymore!

I rush upstairs before anyone can say anything. I hear Seth tell the others to stay.

I get to the top of the stairs as Mason's door opens. He emerges fully dressed and looking furious. He face is angry and he's tense. He gives me a hard glare but looks back at Mary's door, waiting for it to open.

"I know it doesn't take that long!" Mason roars. I jump, not expecting him to yell like that.

Mary wrenches the door open and gives him such a furious look that he actually takes a step back.

"What?" She stands in the doorway positively huffing with anger. "What do you have to say to me?"

Something else happened out there while he was looking for her. I don't understand where all this anger has come from.

"You can't just take off like that!" Mason flings an arm out, getting redder and redder. "You can't just take off running without anything to say or telling us where you're go-"

"I'm not a child, Mason!" Mary yells right back. "I am not a *child*!"

"You're *my* little sister," Mason steps closer to her. "And you cannot *do* that!"

"I can do whatever the hell I want!" Mary screams, her fists clenching. "You can't control me!"

Oh Gods, what have I just gotten myself into. I can't back out now. Mason's blocking the stairway. This argument has been coming for a long time, it seems, and now I'm a part of it.

"I'm not trying to control you!" Mason grabs his hair in frustration. "I just- I just- I just need to know where you are! You can't just take off like that in a strange city!"

"I was in my form!" Mary steps toward him, looking up at him. "I *dare* someone to jeck with me when I'm a jeckin' wolf!"

"Why did you run off?" I say quietly. My voice is barely audible. Both siblings whirl on me. Oh, that was a mistake. I should have stayed silent.

"*Why*?" Mary is shaking. "Why the hell do you care? You're leaving! With Hope!"

I shake my head. "But I have to. I have to do all of this because I was *corrupted*. Psyche told me I was supposed to be a very powerful Darke Angel. Leibus could have come for me any day to take me. I was so far gone and didn't even know it! Why would that make you run off like that?"

Mary splutters. "Yes, but you're leaving! I just… I had to get out of there!"

I feel irritation rise in me. That was so irresponsible of her. I don't know if I'm agreeing with Mason because I love her or if because he really is right. Could it be both?

"Did you not just hear me? I was *corrupted*! There is nothing I can do! I have to go! Running off isn't the answer! You can't just do that!"

Mary gives an angry huff. She glares at me powerfully. I can feel her irritation, her anger boiling up. I can feel my own starting to bubble and boil.

"Are you really going to get angry over this?" I demand. I can feel the irritation turning into hot anger. My temper, so carefully kept quiet, is rising again. So easy to rise and so hard to keep under control. I can feel myself rapidly losing control of my temper.

"I was corrupted! Corrupted, Mary!" I am suddenly shouting.

"Whose fault is that!" Mary yells back at me, pushing Mason out of the way.

Did she really just say that? How could she say that?

"Are you jeckin' kidding me right now, Mary?" I shout. My temper is officially out of control. I can feel something I'm going to regret coming on quickly. "Can you stop thinking about yourself for once and realize what is happening right now! This happened to me and I didn't choose it! The only thing I can do is stop it!"

"Stop thinking about myself?" Mary spits. "Yes, I can see you were really concerned about the state of your soul while you were snogging Hope! I saw you! You were all over her!"

I feel my face grow red hot. "Don't bring her into this! She has nothing to do with this!"

Oh, Gods. She has everything to do with this. It's because of my infatuation with Hope that I didn't see what was happening to Mary. I could have stopped this argument before it had formed had I just watched Mary.

"She has everything to do with this!" Mary screams. Her voice breaks. "You're corrupted and you find time to kiss her? And then you try to tell me how concerned you are about me? Please!"

"That doesn't even make sense, Mary!" I yell back at her. "Leave Hope out of this! I don't know why you're so angry about this, but you need to get over it!"

I instantly regret saying that. I don't mean it. I don't want her to get over it. In a way, I want her to be jealous. I want her to scream at me. I want her to tell me she wants me for herself.

"Get over it! Get over it?" she shoves me suddenly. "Go! Just go! Get out! Leave with your precious Angel and go! Go save your jeckin' soul!"

"Mary," Mason touches her arm. "You're being irrational…"

"*I'm* being irrational?" Mary whirls on him now. "You're the one who won't let me be two feet away from you! To hell with both of you!"

"Mary!" Mason rubs his face. "So help me I will-"

"You're being ridiculous!" I shout, my temper raging out of control. "You're not going to lose me! I'm not going to disappear! Why do you care so much that I'm leaving? You didn't seem to care earlier! Fine! You know what? Just fine! I'll leave and I'll take Hope with me! It's not like you care!"

"That's a bald-faced lie and you know it!" Mary jabs me in the chest. Her green eyes are ablaze with anger and her red hair almost seems like fire. "How dare you say that! You know that I love you more than anything! You're… like a brother!"

"Then why are you so-" I start to say, my voice lowering. *Like a brother*, she said. My heart feels like it could shred itself into pieces. Why can't I choose a woman? I feel myself wanting to go back down to Hope. I want her to comfort me.

"I am not the irrational one here!" Mason bursts out. "You're the one who can't handle people leaving or whatever and disappears! You can't just do that!"

"Why can't I just do that!" Mary screams again, turning on him. He takes a step back. "How dare I have the audacity to do something of my own will!"

"No! You-"

"No!" Mary jabs him in the chest hard. "I can leave whenever the hell I want to leave! That's how I handle things! You throw temper tantrums and I leave for a while! That is how I do things! You want to know why the jeck I left? Huh? Do you? It's because I can't have him leave! What if something happens to him! I left and Papa and Connor were killed! No matter what I do, someone I love is always going to get hurt! There is nothing I can do about it!"

"Mary," my voice softens. "I'm going to Mt. Irise. I'm not going to die. I'm immortal. You will not lose me. I'm always going to be your best friend. Nothing will change that. Not even this stupid argument. I love you."

I try to put as much meaning as I can into those last three words. Mary is so angry right now she probably won't catch it.

"Besides," Mason struggles to keep his voice calm. He takes a breath. "Uncle Seth just said we are going to stay in Reason with Aunt Imry. It's not like you'll never see him again."

Mary looks between us, shaking her head. Tears are welling in her eyes. Her fists are still clenched and she's unable to say anything. She and Mason are both irrational when they're angry, but that's the first rational thing Mason has said.

She looks up at Mason, forcing eye contact with him. "But you don't have to come after me like that. I am not a child."

Mason grabs her by the arms and shakes her. "I know you're not a child! Quit saying that! I know it! I know you are not a child! Okay? I understand that you're not a jeckin' child! I just can't let you run off like that!"

"I can do whatever the hell I want to do!" Mary is shouting again. She jerks herself away from him and bumps into the wall behind her. "You are not my father!"

Mason's mouth clamps shut abruptly. Mary looks away. She shouldn't have said that. I look down. Oh Gods. Oh Gods. This is not going anywhere good fast.

"I," Mason's voice is shaking dangerously. "I know I'm not Papa. I can never be anything like Papa."

"Mason-" She starts to say but he continues.

"I'll never measure up to Papa," Mason's eyes are welling over with tears. "But I can't lose you, Mary. I can't. I just… I don't think I could handle losing you. We've lost so much, Mary, so much."

Tears drip down his face. I feel tears well in my own. This family has been through so much. They've become my family now… I look down. I just can't look at them. I can't.

"Mason-"

"I cannot lose you," Mason grabs her again and pulls her into a hug. "I promised Papa I would never let anything happen to you, Mary. I was there when he died. I was right there, and I promised him."

"Mason!" Mary bursts into tears and cries into his shoulder.

He hugs her tightly and I look around awkwardly for a room to back into. I back into Ardon's room behind me. I'll let them hug and talk together. I can hear muffled voices and sniffles as they talk.

There is a silent moment. I poke my head out of the room. Mary looks up. Her face is a little puffy from crying, but she looks fairly normal. The redness from her anger has disappeared and she opens her arms up, inviting me in for a hug.

I go to her and hug her tightly. "I am so sorry."

"No," Mary pushes her face into my chest. "I'm sorry. I was… I wasn't thinking. I wasn't making sense. I was just mad. I was mad and afraid of what is going to happen to all of us."

"I'm sorry that I," I swallow, struggling for the right words, "didn't keep you in mind when I broke the news. I should have found a better way… I should-"

"Kaleb," she looks up at me with her brilliant green eyes. "You don't have to apologize. I'm the one who was behaving like an imbecile."

I smile down at her and she smiles up at me despite herself. Mason gives a quiet laugh.

"I don't remember the last time I've gotten so mad," Mason laughs. "But I think Papa would have found this whole thing amusing."

Mary smiles at him. "I think so, too."

I laugh. "I have been working on my temper, but it really didn't take much for it to come all out."

"Your temper used to be foul!" Mason laughs.

"Yeah," I scratch the back of my head, feeling sheepish. "I'm sorry for what I said."

"I am, too," Mary looks up at Mason.

"Me, too," he hugs us both.

"Well," I say as we release each other. "Now there's the awkward task of going downstairs."

Mason wrinkles his nose. "Oh Gods, that'll be awkward. I'm sure they could hear us arguing all the way to Chiksaw."

Mary shifts her weight uncomfortably. "What do we do?"

I burst out laughing. "There's nothing to do but to say nothing. I'm sure they heard every bit of it."

"Well," Mason pats his stomach. "How about dinner? That sounds like a good icebreaker, no?"

Mary nods and smiles at me.

"I think that's perfect!" I laugh again.

CHAPTER FOURTEEN

Mary

"Where are we?" Ardon asks as we walk into a large town.

It's been a month since my argument with Mason and Kaleb. Kaleb and Hope left after dinner. The rest of us, except for Uncle Seth, left for Reason the next morning. He will come in the spring. Winter is lasting longer than usual and he can't handle the cold like he used to.

Mason greets the gate guards as we walk in. There should be a hotel somewhere. Uncle Seth gave us money. The guards eye us uneasily.

"I think this is Roarsh." Mason squints at the faded town sign on the bell tower, oblivious to the guards watching us. "The Ciarian Mountain range is just east of us."

Ardon glances toward the guards. "Can I help you?"

The guards have been following us. They stop and exchange a glance. "What species are you?"

"What species are you?" Penny says rather irritably, folding her arms across her chest.

The guards frown. "We've had a lot of trouble lately with the Forest," the older guard says. "What species are you?"

Mason looks between Penny and the guards. "Excuse me, what is going on?"

"They're being unprofessional and violating my right to withhold my species," Penny spits. Good gracious, she's in a mood today.

Mason gives Penny a long hard look.

"We're all werewolves," Mason says, giving Penny another look. "What sort of trouble lately?"

The older guard frowns, but the younger guard pipes up. "It's been active lately!"

"What do you mean?" Ardon asks.

The older guard glares at the younger guard but to no avail. The younger guard continues to talk, unaware of the glares from his older companion.

"Oh, we've seen large packs of Unspeakables moving through. A lot of Darke beings moving in packs; more times than not the packs aren't even all one single species!"

"That's unusual. I wonder why that is." Mason scratches his chin thoughtfully. Papa used to do that.

The older guard finally relents and shakes his head. "We're not sure. Several days ago we had a vampire come into town and kill several people. He was a Darke being. We… we had no idea."

"I'm sorry for your loss," Mason and Ardon say robotically. I remain silent.

The Forest has been more active lately; it seems to have more life in it. I knew that wasn't my imagination. Perhaps the Forest is preparing for something? Like another war? Oh Gods, what if another Ravage is coming?

"I'm surprised we didn't hear news about it." Penny's frown seems permanently glued on her face.

The older guard responds to her, but I barely hear him. He says something about the Gods. My eyes catch a baker throwing a man out of the shop. I find myself walking over to see what the commotion is about. The baker and the man begin screaming at each other. Travelers and villagers begin to gather. I stand behind the first line of observers.

"You have n-" the man shouts.

He has dark skin and is wearing a white tunic. He is dressed nicely but appears to be sweating profusely. The baker is a large man with pale skin tending toward pink. He shakes his fist at the man, interrupting him. His face is either pink from anger or pink from the cold.

"It's my shop! My rules!"

"I have rights!" the other man shouts, balling his fists up.

"Amazing, isn't it?" A cool voice close to my ear makes me jump. "Decades pass, centuries pass, and still some things never change."

I turn to find a man standing very close to me. I step away from him. He is much too close in proximity to me. I decide to humor him and feed my own curiosity.

"What never changes?"

"Racism, my dear." He smiles brilliantly.

"What's that?" I ask, confused by the term. Racism? The term doesn't make sense.

"Way back when," the man begins, watching the two men scream. I watch him. He's too handsome. "Before you or I were born, there were just humans. The Gods had yet to intervene and the Ravage had not begun. It was before even World War Two – way before then, actually. Humans divided themselves based on skin color."

"Skin color?" I'm skeptical. Skin color? Why would that be a dividing point? I look at the man with darker skin bowing up to the large pale baker.

The man nods. "Skin color. The paler skinned humans seemed to think they were better than the darker skinned humans. Side note: the funny thing is that the paler humans later hyper focused on tanning their skin to be darker. Heh, I always thought that was amusing."

"Wait," I blink hard, trying to process this. "So this baker is practicing racism?"

"He's a racist, my dear." The man smiles at me again. He has tan skin and contrasting white teeth. He has dark messy hair and dark, nearly black, eyes. Dimples touch his cheeks when he talks and he has a handful of freckles splashed across his nose. Good Gods, he looks like a God! He also seems very familiar to me.

"I'm sorry," I blink hard again. I know I know him! "Who are you?"

"You don't need to worry about it," he says, smiling brightly again. Good Gods, if he smiles one more time at me…

"Excuse me?" I squint at him, confused. "Wait, who are you?"

"Don't worry about it." He smiles coolly. "I'll see you soon."

He gives an obnoxious smile and slips between two other people. I try to follow him out of the crowd but, by the time I push myself back into the open, he's gone.

I shake my head and start to walk aimlessly toward the other side of the town. I need to think.

CHAPTER FIFTEEN

Kaleb

I stand outside the Great Hall where the Greater Gods meet, waiting for Psyche to show up. She finally appears from around a corner. Perhaps it is her dress, but she seems to actually glide across the marble floors.

"Kaleb." She puts a hand on my shoulder. "When did you arrive?"

"Another Lightning came and got me about five minutes ago. I haven't been here long."

"Do you know where you are?"

"Erm," I glance around. I have no jecking idea where I am.

"You're above Mt. Irise in the heavens," Psyche glances behind me then catches my eyes again. "When in doubt, guess Mt. Irise. Oy. The Greater Gods are about to meet in here. You will walk in with me. Say absolutely nothing unless spoken to… wait, do you know your Greater Gods?"

"Yes," I say, slightly proud of myself, "I know every Greater and Lesser God."

Psyche smiles. "Excellent! Do you know what they look like?"

Before I can answer her no, a man appears around the corner. His skin is bright, nearly glowing, and his tunic is made of fine material. Strange as it is, I want to touch it. It looks so fine. He must be a God!

"Hermes!" Psyche greets him. "How are you? How is Echo?"

"How did you know I was just there?" Hermes laughs. He runs a hand through his red curls. He turns to me. "She always knows everything before I can even deliver the message! I swear, Psyche! You ought to take my job."

Psyche playfully slaps his arm. "No, you do a fine job!"

"Echo is fine," Hermes sighs, smiling. "Today wasn't her best day, but she's still trying to tell us something. Maybe you should stop by and see her later. You know how she adores you."

Psyche nods. "Yes, I haven't seen her in while."

"Have you seen your daughter recently?" Hermes asks.

"No," Psyche shakes her head unhappily. "I haven't been able to check in on her for a while what with Leibus stirring up all this trouble. You'd think he'd pick better timing to try and take over the universe!"

Hermes laughs again then stops. "Oh, I'm sorry, Lightning. I failed to introduce myself. I am Hermes and you are?"

"K-Kaleb," I say nervously, unsure if I should stick out a hand.

"Zeus and I just made him," Psyche smiles.

"Ah," Hermes nods. "And you're already attending a Meeting of the Gods?"

"Well," Psyche answers for me, "we have some important information for the Gods regarding his former being. It looks as though you have important information, too? I gather that you are not just here to report on Echo, are you?"

My former being? Did I die? I'm still the same person. Right?

"No, I'm afraid I bear grave news. The meeting should be starting at any moment." Hermes forces a smile. "Let's take our seats, shall we?"

"I heard about Ares," Psyche nearly giggles to Hermes as they turn to the huge white marble doors behind me. She changes the subject effortlessly. "Is he coming today?"

"I doubt it," Hermes rolls his eyes. He is clearly forcing himself to be light and unstressed. "The dolt got himself injured pretty well. He's in the Infirmary."

"Well," Psyche drops her voice to a whisper. "I'm glad Hephaestus finally got to show Ares who's boss. It's about time someone put that moron in his place."

I follow awkwardly behind. I didn't know Gods could be injured. I look around the Council room. There are fourteen huge throne-seats. There are smaller seats for people my size near the entrance. The ceilings are high sky windows.

Psyche gently moves me to the center of the room. I glance behind me to see that other people, presumably Gods, are filling into the room. They take the smaller seats behind Psyche and me.

"What do I do?" I lean over to ask her as I examine the huge marble thrones. Some of the thrones have silk thrown over them and others have elaborate carvings around the base.

"Just answer honestly if asked a question," Psyche doesn't look at me. "Otherwise, please stay quiet."

"Got it," I say, looking down at my feet. Are the Greater Gods going to fill those huge thrones?

Suddenly Psyche jabs me hard with her elbow. I look up to see spectacularly colored dust and mist spinning down from the sky windows. The Greater Gods materialize in their thrones in front of us. But two thrones remain empty. One of them must be Leibus' seat. I had heard he used to be a Greater God but was disgraced and banished to the Forest. It must be true!

The first God to completely materialize is Chaos. It has to be!

Chaos sits in the center seat, the most elaborately carved throne, and casts an imperious eye upon us. I instantly feel like a grain of sand before an ocean. His huge form makes him seem even more powerful. He wears a white tunic with breeches and he's barefoot. If he were smaller, no one would ever guess he is the greatest God in the universe. He has dark skin, like ebony, that contrasts with the white marble. Otherwise, he's very unassuming.

Gaia appears beside him and then the rest of the Gods appear. Chaos and Gaia are the only two I can guess. Gaia has silver hair with green vines woven into her hair like a small crown. She has on a light green dress and sandals. Gaia seems so calm and so unthreatening.

"Let the Council come to order," Chaos' voice booms, making me jump. I turn my attention back to Chaos.

Hermes stands up and walks to the center of the room to stand with Psyche and me. "We are discussing the grave matter of the War between the Angels and Demons. We have new information for you. Before we address the new Lightning in the room, I have two pieces of bad news. First, Echo is not making any progress and we are not any closer than we were a decade ago. The second piece of news is concerning Hades' disappearance, and it is terrible. It seems as though Leibus has taken him hostage. Due to the large concentration of bodies and souls gathering near the Grimsah, we have surmised that Leibus has Hades."

Chaos rubs his temples with his fingers. "I want you to consult with Nyx, Erebus, and Lesypyx after the meeting. We will speak on this matter privately. Lightning, step forward. Psyche, what do you have to say?"

"This is Kaleb," Psyche begins as Hermes retreats back to his seat. "Zeus and I made him a Lightning Child without permission, Chaos."

"Excuse me?" Chaos sits up and glares at me. Do I make eye contact? I look down out of reflex.

"A particularly phenomenal Angel, despite having her wings injured, brought this being to me." Psyche begins to pace in front of me. She stops in front of Chaos. "He was to become Adam."

Several of the Gods gasp.

"I have reason to believe Eve has been found and will soon become Darke," Psyche's voice drops. The atmosphere in the room suddenly becomes stiff and tense.

"What evidence have you?" Gaia asks, leaning forward. Her silver curls swing forward.

"Leibus has a tendency," Psyche gestures to me, "to create Adam after Eve. He always forms Eve first because her corruption is much deeper and takes longer. Adam is… far more simple than Eve. His corruption is simply based on power or something material. Eve's corruption is deeper, and I have yet to find the root of it."

"So Eve is out there right now?" another Goddess asks. She seems like she should be Nyx, the Goddess of the night. She has dark hair, black eyes, and dark clothing. Her eyes flicker toward me and I swallow.

Psyche turns. "Yes, I believe so."

"Why have we not detected her? Have you detected her?" Chaos asks, leaning back in his throne. He strokes his chin.

"Leibus knows who she is, Chaos," Psyche looks down. The other Gods in the room shift in their seats. Obviously, that isn't good. "He's shielding her from me. I have no idea who she is or where she is. I have to wait for him to slip up. She has no idea she will be Eve, but Eve will rise before the Winter Solstice."

"Oh heavens," Gaia puts a hand to her forehead. Psyche takes my wrist and we back up to the seats behind us. She and I sit down in the front row. The Gods watch us, but their thoughts are elsewhere.

"The winds tell me," a God suddenly says, breaking the small momentary silence, "that Leibus is beginning to collect his forces. It is coming, Father." This must be Zephyrus, God of the wind.

Chaos turns to him. "So the Darke Angel was telling the truth. This war is coming and it is coming fast."

"Father," Zephyrus says, almost hesitatingly, "the war will be here in less than a week. The winds do not lie."

"It has finally come to this!" Chaos sighs. "Leibus has gone too far. The long dormant war between the heavens and his hell has risen again, my children! This war will be the final war. Gather the forces; rally the mortals! Bring the Thunder, the Lightning Children, the Elite! Bring every being we have! This war will not end without Leibus' defeat and ultimate death."

"Death," Gaia repeats quietly to herself.

"Yes," Chaos beats his fist on his throne, making the Council Hall shake. "I will kill my own son or one of you will kill your brother. It is a command. Do you understand?"

"You're willing to kill your own son?" Psyche pipes up. The other Gods stiffen.

"She's the only one, the only being other than Gaia, who can talk back to him," Hermes leans forward and whispers to me.

"Why?" I whisper back as Chaos says, "Excuse me?"

"She just can," Hermes says. "I suspect it is because she is the most powerful God aside from him."

I look up at Psyche with a whole new respect.

"I thought she was a Lesser God?"

"She is because she was created by another God," Hermes whispers. "Eros created her."

"All souls can be turned," Psyche stands up and walks to the center of the room. One of the Gods rubs his head in exasperation.

"Only beings with souls can be turned," Chaos retorted.

"She is extremely powerful and," Hermes glances up to make sure we aren't being disruptive, "no one knows how she is so powerful. We don't even know the full extent of her power."

"Surely there is another way?" Psyche folds her arms and shifts weight to one hip.

Chaos presses his lips together, making them disappear in his dark beard. "We have given Leibus chance after chance as well as ample time to come back to us. He has chosen the Darkeness over Light."

"He believes that the Darkeness will overcome," a Goddess pipes up. She must be Lesypyx, Leibus' twin sister. "He thinks that the universe is a set balance between good and evil. Good, he thinks, has reigned far too long and he fears evil will take over. So rather than be destroyed, Leibus chose the Darkeness and gave up his soul to evil for more power and for guaranteed life after evil takes over. He thinks you've been disrupting the balance. You intervene in every evil in the universe instead of letting some play out. The Ravage of this planet was the moment he turned. He had long been telling me to open my eyes. He begged me to go with him. That is, as you all know, the moment he tried to destroy me. Psyche, he must die."

None of the Gods speak, but it is understood. Leibus will die.

Outside the temple, Psyche moves quickly toward her temple. I follow behind her, practically jogging to keep up with her.

"So the war is on?" I ask, panting with effort.

"Yes," Psyche says. "The war has begun."

"Psyche!" Two Gods appears beside us. I jump. Good heavens! How do they keep appearing? One of them, the older one, asks her attention. "You called for me?"

"Yes," she stops and I nearly walk into her. She glares at me. "Yes, this is Kaleb. He's the new Lightning Child you saw in the meeting."

"Ah yes." The God's eyes fall on me. "I'll take care of him."

"Goo-" Psyche starts to say but she suddenly stiffens. Her eyes swirl over in silvery clouds, her mouth parts slightly, and she looks as though she's about to fall.

"Psyche," the other God steadies her. "I'm here."

She struggles to breath for a moment. "I can see her. I can see Eve!"

The God holding her whirls on the other God and me. "Go get Chaos! Now!"

The God beside me disappears. I look around, unsure of what to do.

The God holding her lays her down carefully. "Just stay here! Pay attention to what she says."

"I can't see her face." Psyche grips the grass forcefully. She spits each word out. "I can see her corruption, but I can't see who she is. The corruption… it's faster than it's supposed to be. No, no. Wait… Now… Now I'm in Sesaru. Why am I…? Oh, there's a Darke army forming here. They're going to attack Halley. Oh, oh, there are Darke disciples there. Leibus already has his twelve Darke Angels for Adam and Eve. Eros! Eros, where are you?"

She reaches up blindly, feeling for him. The God with her, Eros, reaches for her.

"I'm here, darling," he says, taking her hand. Oh, they're together. I should have remembered that story. But I don't remember if they ever had a daughter together. Who is the daughter Hermes asked about?

Psyche grabs Eros' forehead with both hands and he gasps. His eyes fog over.

"I see now," he says.

"Step aside, Lightning," Chaos' voice says. I feel his hand move me sideways. I stare, gaping. He's my size now!

Chaos leans over them. Psyche suddenly recovers herself and releases Eros. She blinks several times. The fog retreats under her eyelids. Her silver irises dull in intensity. She finds Chaos and reaches up for him.

"There is an army forming in Sesaru," she breathes. "It's a distraction. They're going to attack Reason in less than a week. I almost caught sight of the new Eve. He is somehow advancing her corruption rate. I saw an Angel beside the prospective Eve. I don't know who, but Leibus has seen her, too. This Angel will be dead by tomorrow."

"Aigaion." Chaos doesn't take his eyes off of Psyche as he speaks. "Take this Lightning and begin training. Rally up as many new Lightnings as you can. Send Zeus down to gather the weak and crippled. Do what you can with them. But forming Lightnings should be your last option. Psyche, I want you to find that Angel. We cannot lose her. Use any means possible to find this Angel. She is our key to finding the prospective Eve. Eros, I want you to find Nyx and Erebus and have them collaborate with Ares. Our forces need to be built up before the full moon."

"Yes, Father!" Aigaion grabs me. "We're going to transport. Don't panic."

Suddenly I feel as though my skin is going to be sucked off of my very body and then, all at once, it stops. I stagger sideways. Aigaion grabs my upper arm and steadies me.

"That's what it'll feel like when you learn to transport," Aigaion says rather gruffly. "I am the God of storms and, although the Lightning are under Chaos, they report directly to me, and beneath me is Zeus. Excuse me a moment. Grace! Grace!"

My hands are spread wide in front of me as the ground flies up toward me. Leigh has pushed me. I turn around and see the Unspeakable.

A bolt of lightning strikes the ground in front of us and pulls me out of the sudden memory. A woman gives a slight bow to Aigaion. She looks a little irritated. She has the nerve to be irritated by a God?

"Yes?" She puts a hip out and shifts her weight to one leg. She has long platinum blonde hair. It's straight and goes down to her waist. She has dark eyes and a sharp nose. She has a very intimidating beauty. I swallow.

"He's yours to train," Aigaion says and promptly disappears.

"Hello." Grace extends a hand. "My name is Grace. I am an Elite Lightning Leader. You are a new Lightning Child?"

"Kaleb Roth." I shake her hand. "Nice to meet you."

CHAPTER SIXTEEN

Fritz

Athena points to the map. Her finger presses hard against a point on the map labeled Vidian. The tip of her fingertip is white from the pressure of her force. The point is in the green blob known as the Grimsah Forest.

Gwendolyn elbows me sharply. Athena is speaking to me. Oh dear. She's speaking to me. I glance around. Did she address me? Holy fire, I'm going to be destroyed by her. I'm an idiot.

"Lightning," she looks angry. "Are you having a problem?"

"N-no!" I stammer, startled by her sudden attention directed on me.

"What's your name?" she looks me over, raising her chin.

"I'm new," I say.

She stares at me. "Your name is New?"

"It's Fritz," I say suddenly, shutting my eyes briefly. Good gracious. I'm going to burst into flames right now. Right this very moment.

"Well," Athena crosses her arms over her armored chest. She purses her lips. "Fritz, you have been moved to the third wave. As I was saying, the first wave will come in quickly. Anything that moves that isn't a Lightning will be struck dead. Do you understand? Leave no survivors other than the hostages.

"This is a rescue mission. There are many captives there being tortured and being experimented on. We know of several demigods and Angels that have been taken. They are all being held here in Vidian. Vidian is a known capital of a group of people known as the Atys. For you new Lightnings," she glances at me and I feel my face grow hot. I feel like I'm on fire. Shouldn't I be on fire? "The Atys people are mortal beings who worship Leibus. There is an underground prison here. The second wave is in charge of finding the prison while the first wave is in action. The third wave will come in directly after the second wave has located the prison and remove the prisoners. You are to take at least two at a time and no more. They will be weak.

"It will be very chaotic." Athena looks around at all of us. "Many of you will switch waves quickly and that is fine. We have a light organization, but I want you all to do what you need to do. Are there any questions?"

I dare not raise a hand despite the questions flooding through my brain. Why are the captives there? Why does Leibus want these captives? What does this have to do with the war?

Athena clears her throat. "The war is upon us and it will be the fight of our lives. This is truly the battle we have been talking about for centuries. This is the battle between the Gods, between the angels and demons, between good and evil, Light and Darkeness! Leibus knows the war is about to erupt. We have been looking the other way for too long! But now Leibus will be punished for his crimes!

"Don't you see? He's frightened! Why wouldn't he be? The power of the Gods alone is enough to defeat him. He has created new Gods, new beings, and new forms of evil to defend himself. These captives are his newest experiments. He is splicing souls. From conversations with Psyche, I understand that the splicing means taking a part of the soul and trapping it in the Forest. Leibus owns them and can control them. He is making an army of half-dead slaves.

"This mission is important for many reasons." Athena grips the table in front of her. "We need to weaken him as much as we can. We need to stop this growth of Darkeness. You will go and you will bring our people back! For the Gods! For goodness! For Light! For all of time!"

Athena raises her sword in the air. Cheering erupts around us. I look up at Athena in her glittering armor. She looks terrifying.

"Go!" She screams and points her sword forward. The first wave of Lightnings disappears.

"You are the Lightning children for a reason!" Athena yells. Her voice rises over the cheers. "You are the future and you will keep the future! For the Gods! For goodness! For Light! For all of time!"

People are screaming wildly. We are doing a good thing. My fear is replaced with a strong sense of responsibility. I can do this. We can do this!

"Second wave! Go!" Athena points her sword again. The Lightnings disappear with a clap of thunder.

"Fritz," Athena is looking down at me again. I stare at her wide eyed. What did I do now? I've been paying attention and listening! I'm ready to go! I have no fear now. "I know you will make a difference.

"For the Gods! For goodness! For Light! For all of time! Third wave!" She screams. "Go!"

I launch myself up and over the edge of the heavens. We race through the clouds toward the Atys people's Vidian. We light up the stormy skies. They know the war has begun and they will know the pain they have inflicted.

Anger rises in me. How dare they take innocents and submit them to this kind of torture. How dare Leibus. I hope he dies painfully. I hope he feels the pain of the world. I hope he feels the pain he has inflicted on every being indirectly and directly.

We curve down and jet toward the small city buried in the Forest. My feet slam into the ground. A Darke arrow lands at my feet. I look up to see a Darke Angel hovering in the sky. I grit my teeth and blast him backwards with lightning. I zip over to where the prison entrance is. Two Lightnings are guarding the entrance, screaming at the third wave to get in and out quickly.

I strike another Darke being with a flick of my hand. Athena is with us. I can feel her power. She's with us.

I sense another Darke Angel descending on me. I twist in the air, my feet leave the ground, and I throw a bolt of lightning toward the Darke Angel. She evades my blast easily and has the audacity to smile at me. I throw another bolt at her, but she deflects it with her hand.

"Fool," she says coolly. Her crystalline voice sends shivers up my spine. "Do you know who I am? The greatest there is. I am the end of everything you know."

Eve. The thought slams into my mind. Fear starts to leak out, affecting me but something stronger pushes it back.

You can do it.

I throw a particularly powerful bolt at her. Other Lightnings rush in.

"It's Eve!" someone screams.

"Oh Gods!" a Lightning beside me screams.

Eve lunges forward suddenly and grabs the Lightning by the neck. She digs her fingernails into his neck. Dark liquid seeps out from under her nails and the Lightning goes limp. I back away in horror.

Suddenly there is howl from behind us. The werewolves are here. The huge wolves launch themselves against the Atys archers, taking them by surprise. The wolves tear their heads off viciously. Serves them right.

I flash over to a wolf who has fallen victim to several vampires. I blast the vampires off of the wolf. The wolf gives me an appreciative nod and tears after another. I turn to find another Darke Angel behind me. I react quickly and send a bolt through the Darke Angel's stomach. The Darke Angel doubles over but manages to dish out a dusty Darke wave of energy. The wave knocks me off of my feet. I scramble to my feet and flash behind him. I stab him in the back, in the heart, with a bolt. The Angel deteriorates into dust.

I flash as quickly as I can into the prison. I land in the prison and stumble sideways into bars. The prison is pitch black. Another Lightning lights up the prison temporarily.

"Find someone now!"

I look to my right to see a man lying on the floor. There are two men in the cell. One is chained up and the other just lies on his stomach on the floor. I flash inside, startling the two men.

"Who are you? What's happening?" the chained man asks me.

I blast his chains off of him. The man pulls his feet close and rubs his ankles.

"I am a Lightning Child of the Gods," I say, my voice sounding strong. "They never forgot about you. I'm here to bring you home."

I take his forearm and pull him to his feet. The other man rolls over and looks at me. Both men have been beaten severely.

"What are your names?" I ask them, still looking down at the man on the floor. Why has he not stood up?

"Manuel Stout," the previously chained man says, taking one of my hands in both of his. "Bless my soul. The Gods are saving us!"

"And you?" I look down at the man on the floor. I extend a hand toward him.

"Connor Stoneburner," he says weakly. "I can't get up."

I need to get him back quickly. I grab the man on the floor by his arm. I pull him up into a sitting position.

"Brace yourselves," I pull them close to myself and shoot through the ceiling to the heavens.

Stoneburner lets a moan escape. He must be in a lot of pain. Those evil, evil sons of swine. They will pay. They will pay.

I land in the Infirmary, startling several nurses.

"Are these the last?" one of the nurses asks as another Lightning appears.

"No," the Lightning says, breathing hard. He has two captives hanging on him. "These are the last."

Three nurses take Stoneburner and two more take Stout from me. I watch them carry the two men down the hall to intensive care. I swallow.

I flash back to the clouds, travelling back to Vidian. There are Darke Angels to be killed. Eve needs to be destroyed.

CHAPTER SEVENTEEN

Mary

When darkness sets in, I head back to the only hotel in town. Mason is probably there and waiting for me. I can picture him standing there, feet apart, arms folded, with a hard glare molded on his face.

"Well," a familiar voice suddenly sounds beside me, "hey there, angel!"

"Um," I turn to see the man from the bakery walking beside me.

"How's it going?" he asks brightly. He looks me up and down. I feel goose bumps race down my back.

"Good," I say uneasily but I can't help but feel trusting toward this perfect stranger. "How are you?"

"Oh," the man smiles again at me. "I'm well."

"So," I pat my legs as we walk, "are you going to tell me your name? Don't you want to know mine?"

"Oh, angel," he laughs. "I already know yours but you are answering to Mary presently, aren't you?"

"Um," I furrow my brow, "sure. My name is Mary. How did you know that?"

"I heard your brother call you that," the man says simply.

"So I can't know your name?"

The man taps his chin. "I suppose you can, but you and I won't be friends until later."

I stop walking. "What are you talking about? You sound insane right now. Are you insane?"

"No, I'm Còiseam." The man's mouth twitches, a ghost of a smile playing on his lips.

"Ugh!" I groan and take two steps away from him. I turn around again. "What are you jeckin' laughing at, huh?"

"My, my," Còiseam laughs. I want to strangle him. "You're a little tense today. Relax, I didn't want to spoil the fun so quickly, but it appears I have to appease you."

"What?"

"Remember Father Sulibe?" Còiseam says, watching me carefully. "He sent me."

I am careful to not let any emotion show. I stare at him blankly.

"I don't know what you're talking about." I shake my head. Father Sulibe told me to tell no one about him. Didn't he? Was any of that real? I pull my coat around myself tighter. The cold wind seems to have revved up.

"I know," Còiseam steps toward me. "This is all very confusing. After you passed out, I took you back to your house and put you on the couch. Everyone's minds were touched just a bit so it seemed as if you never left."

I don't say anything. How can I? Can I believe this?

"I'm sorry, angel," he says, using the annoying pet name again, "but it had to be done. You were not yet psychologically ready to handle the reality, so we made it seem like a dream for you. This happens to all corrupted souls like your own." Còiseam looks so sincere. I can't help but feel slightly relieved to have him with me. He kicks snow off his boots. "This is the system used. I am your Guardian and will keep you from corruption if you let me."

"If I let you?"

"Father Sulibe created my species," Còiseam says. "I'm not really a species. There are too few of us to be recognized by the Gods. It doesn't help that the Gods cannot see us. Only two Gods can see us… You are the only person on the earth that can see me. No one else can see me because I am your Guardian. When I appear to you, no one else can see or hear me. In fact, you can talk to me without anyone noticing because I touch their minds to mask my presence. But you don't have to accept me. It's a choice to accept me."

"This is a lot to take in," I say slowly.

"I know," he says. "I'm going to leave you to think and mull over that. I'll see you again soon. If you need me, I'll find you. I'll be searching for more pearls. The more the merrier!"

"Wait!" I call into the darkness, but he's disappeared. Why do I need more pearls? Why would I need more pearls? Father Sulibe said that the one pearl should suffice. Didn't he? Oh Gods, I can feel myself doubting the entire thing again.

I stand there a moment. Father Sulibe has sent me a sign, a Guardian! Còiseam does look familiar. He is the doctor who gave me the umbrella. I recognize him now.

I turn and find myself in front of the hotel. I sigh heavily and walk in to find Mason in the lobby with his arms folded, feet apart, and a glare on his face.

"Sorry," I say, "I was walking with Còiseam."

"Who is Còiseam?"

"Oh, he's just someone I met," I say, rubbing my chin. How would Còiseam find me if I needed him?

"You were walking at night with a perfect stranger?"

"Mason," I sigh again. "I'm not in the mood, ok? I have a lot on my mind."

Mason says nothing.

Then he turns and starts to walk away. "What are you waiting for? I got a room for all of us."

The room has two beds, a couch, and way too many pictures on the walls. Penny and Ardon are each laid out on a separate bed. Penny is turned on her side, fast asleep, and Ardon is reading a book. He doesn't glance up when the door clicks behind me.

"You're sleeping with Penny," Mason says. "As soon as we're up tomorrow, we are moving out."

I walk around to the other side of the bed closest to the window.

"Okay," I yawn suddenly in the middle of the word but Mason understands me. He smiles and blows out the candlelight.

"Hey!" Ardon says.

"We have to get some sleep, ya jeck," Mason laughs at him. "Apparently the war between the Angels and Demons has started up again. We have work to do."

I hear the book plop on the bedside table and Ardon groan. "Fine. You wouldn't have turned the light off if you were reading this!"

"Sleep is more important," Mason says, sounding considerably sleepier.

Penny turns over in her sleep.

Mason says it so casually it takes me a minute to process what he has said. There's a cosmic war that has just begun again?

CHAPTER EIGHTEEN

Hope

I carefully uncover the pearl, pushing snow away from it. I'm careful not to let my flesh touch it. Oh stars, I need to get to Psyche. The pearls are in action! I stare at the perfect pearl. What do I do? How can I pick this up? How do I get to Psyche? Oh stars, what am I going to do? I look up, hoping somehow she'll see me. I look back down and uncover the pearl more.

As I look back down at the pearl, I hear the snow crackle as if someone is walking toward me. But I see nothing but vast whiteness. The wind is picking up and I need to go before it'll be too hard to fly in.

"Excellent," a voice suddenly says. "You've found it for me."

I swing my arm up and over, casting glittering light between the Darke being and myself. The being laughs but still burns himself on the shield. The being throws a handful of Darke dust at my shield. The dust and the glitter begin to eat at each other. My shield falls and I look up at the being. The being smiles at me. He looks like some mortal Darke being. Human? Vampire? His species is unclear.

I throw a handful of light at him as I draw up another shield. The light glitters gold and explodes on him. The being gives a yelp and angrily throws his robes down. He begins attacking. I step backwards, holding my shield against him.

The being throws a massive Darke shield over both of us.

"Psyche!" I cry out in desperation. "If you can hear me, my name is Hope. I'm the Angel who delivered Kaleb to you!"

"Your Gods can't hear you now. Your pearls are going to a good cause, to a good creation, but I need to know if Psyche knows about the creation."

I draw my shield tighter around myself. The shield glitters brilliantly and appears to be strong, but I know I won't last much longer. This being is much stronger than I am.

"Do you know if she knows, Angel?" The being swipes my shield away easily. I gasp as my shield disintegrates. "You know a lot, Angel. You took my Adam from me. Now I'm going to take you."

He smiles suddenly. "Yes, you can't hide from me. You do know. But I need the specifics on Psyche's range of power. You have the answers, and I will get them out of you. Khermes!"

A large black dusty cloud appears. Good stars! It's Leibus' assistant! Khermes engulfs me. I scream, trying desperately to do some damage to Khermes.

The being sends a shockwave of Darke energy. My sight is fading. I look back as Khermes begins to lift me. The being bends down and picks up a pearl.

"No!" I say, but my voice is too faint to be heard.

Khermes carries me high over the Forest. I'm going straight to hell, straight to Leibus.

CHAPTER NINETEEN

Mary

Kaleb knows we were expected at Aunt Imry's house by now. Uncle Seth told him where it was and he should be arriving at any moment. Should I wait here for him? Should I leave and come back to find him?

Mason says Aunt Imry apparently left several months ago but left the house to us. She left a note saying she'd be back soon.

Mason doesn't seem bothered. I'm not really surprised. I didn't really expect to find her here, although it would have been nice to see someone familiar. She is Mother's sister after all, but we never knew her well. Papa said Aunt Imry was always a flighty one. Honestly, it doesn't really bother me if she never comes back. I'm numb to everything anyway. Besides, Aunt Imry is always gone. I'm just numb.

I wander through Aunt Imry's house. I sigh and sit down in an overstuffed chair in the sitting room.

Reason is surprisingly big. It's much bigger than Gedan. It has huge temples with spiraling towers and beautiful sculptures dedicated to the Gods. There have to be millions of people living here, and I haven't seen any of it. I need to go outside!

I stare out the window, watching people busily hustling down the street back and forth. Carts, people, wolves, and all kinds of beings moving. I watch a small pack of five wolves slink down the street.

"Hey," I yell to Mason from the front of the house. "I'm going to go explore!"

"Okay," Mason says, sounding strange. His voice sounded muffled. I hear Penny mumble something. He is probably kissing Penny. "Be back in an hour or so. Kaleb should be here by now!"

I leave the house and bounce down the front steps. Aunt Imry lived only a couple minutes' walk from the heart of the city.

I round a corner and collide with a girl running around the corner. She and I stare at each other for a moment. She has white-blonde hair, fair skin, and silver eyes. Is she blind?

"Excuse me!" She scrambles to her feet, suddenly remembering she was running, and disappears.

"Hey!" Two men run up to me. "Did you see a blind woman come through here?"

"Who?" I say without thinking. "I apologize. Yes, she ran off. I think she went that way."

"Gah!" the two men turn the same way the woman went and sprint after her.

I've been in Reason for less than a day and I've literally run into a blind woman! Why was she running? I pause on the sidewalk, thinking about the excitement that had been on the woman's face. Was she really blind? Why was a blind woman running? And why were those men chasing her? I pick myself up and look over my shoulder. The men and the woman were gone.

My excitement for Kaleb suddenly smacks into me. I hesitate to explore any longer. Kaleb could be here any moment! I would rather wait at the house and be an unwanted presence by Mason and Penny than wander out here. I turn and run back to the house.

I run past another pack of wolves. This one is larger, about ten of them. I nod to them and one of them barks a hello to me. As I near the house, I can see Mason standing on the front porch, undoubtedly looking for me.

"Mary!" Mason yells from the front porch "Kaleb is here! Come quickly!"

I run up the steps as Kaleb comes through the front door. "Kaleb!"

He opens his arms and pulls me in for a tight hug. A woman is standing behind him smiling pleasantly. Còiseam suddenly appears behind them. He gives me a little wave and leans against the doorframe. He eats a bagel and watches me. I swallow and try to focus on what's happening. He said no one would see or hear him but me. It's weird, but I find his presence comforting somehow.

"No time for questions," Kaleb looks frantic with happiness. He has a silly grin on his face. "You are not going to believe what I have to show you. We're going to transport you. Oh, and this is Grace. Grace, this is Mary, Mason, Penny, and Ardon. Mason, is Hope still gone?"

"Yeah," Mason says. "We haven't heard anything from her."

"Okay," Kaleb nods. Còiseam eats the bagel slowly, watching all of us. It's hard for me to focus when he's lounging over there. I open my mouth to talk to him, but he shakes his head.

"You'll feel force pulling on you as we transport." Grace tosses her platinum hair over her shoulder. "It is a normal feeling. Do not panic."

"Mary," Kaleb reaches for me. "I can only transport one person so you're coming with me.

"The rest of you are with me," Grace reaches for the other three. In that moment, I recognize her self-confidence as the source of her power and poise. Gods, she is strong. It seems like she would be brave, strong, and smart.

Kaleb wraps an arm around my waist, pulling me from my admiration of Grace. Còiseam frowns and I give him a smile. He finishes the bagel with several angry bites and intense chewing. I snort. He folds his arms across his chest.

"Ready?" Kaleb looks at us all eagerly. "Let's go!"

I feel my body jerked in all directions. I hold onto Kaleb harder. My limbs are being pulled on and my skin feels like it's stretching to the limit. Then Kaleb releases me and it stops. I make a strange gurgling noise and fall over sideways onto a hard marble floor.

Ardon falls down on top of me. "Oh!"

"I never want to do that again!" I shout through the nausea rolling my stomach over.

"That was horrible!" Ardon makes a dramatic puking noise.

"Would you two shut up!" an all too familiar voice says quietly. "Bunch of babies."

Ardon and I look up as Mason and Penny turn around. Ardon is already on his feet.

Behind us is a small cot with a very weak looking man on it. His face has dozens of cuts and bruises and his arms have wraps on them, too. His legs are completely wrapped up in casts. The man gives us a weak smile, but it reaches his mossy green eyes. The man is almost unrecognizable. Almost.

"Connor!" Mason screams and nearly tackles him.

Connor cries out in pain but laughs through it. Before I realize it, I'm beside the bed and kissing his face. Connor swats at me weakly. He laughs which instantly fills the room with a happiness that I thought I lost forever.

"You're alive!" I exclaim right as we hear a solid thud from behind us.

Penny passes out. She's so sweet, but she's such a flake.

Mason turns around. "Penny!"

"I'm alive," Connor says as though he's shocked, too. His face seems almost foreign. I had long erased it from my mind. It had been too painful. Connor smiles up at us.

"You passed out?" Mason laughs at Penny.

"I didn't expect to see Connor!" She says, slightly irritated.

"I thought you were shot?" Ardon says, mussing Connor's hair.

"I'm alive," Connor says as though he's shocked, too. His face seems almost foreign. I had erased it from my mind. It had been too painful. Connor smiles up at us.

"Hey, I thought you were shot," Ardon looks down at Connor adoringly but his expression immediately changes to concern as he adds, "but if you don't want to talk about it…"

"I was," Connor says, his voice very quiet and very weak. "He shot me in the thigh, so I fell down and pretended to be dead until it was all over."

"No one checked?" Ardon asks in disbelief.

Connor shrugs. "There was a lot happening."

"How did you get here?" Mason asks, supporting Penny. Penny manages to get to the bed. She smiles lovingly at Connor, squeezing his hand.

I take in his face, every cut and every bruise. He's alive!

"Well," Connor's jaw clenched. "I haven't told anyone yet."

A nurse comes into the room. She has blue skin and is about seven feet tall. She's a Faerie. She looks at all of us in the room and the dark look on Connor's face. The nurse gives us a sheepish grin and leaves the room.

"I'll be back later for your medicine, Mr. Stoneburner," she says, poking her head back into the room.

"Thanks," Connor says in a forced pleasant tone.

"I-I was taken from Mika by some Darke beings." Connor looks away from us. He stares at his feet. "They tortured me… for a long time. They paralyzed my legs. I c-can't move them. They did it with Darkeness, so no one here can fix me. Then the Lightnings came and rescued me and everyone else they had captive. They brought us here to the Infirmary and I've been healing since."

"What about the Gods? Can they fix you?" I ask. How can they not fix him? They can't leave him paralyzed!

"There's a war going on," Connor sighs. He gives me a brave smile. "They don't have time for every single person, and they can't always fix Darke magic. I'll be okay. I'm getting used to it."

"How long have you been here?" Mason asks.

"Little less than a week." He smiles at all of us. "I promise that I am much, much better than I was before! In fact, let's go for a walk! Mason, will you bring my chair to the side of the bed?"

"Of course," Mason pushes over a red wheelchair. "Do you need help into it? It's only been a week since you started recuperating."

"Uh," Connor stares at his chair for a moment.

You'd better say yes!" The nurse pops her head in. "I know you're strong, Mr. Stoneburner, but you are still healing!"

"Yes," Connor groans. "Help me in."

We walk around the Infirmary grounds. Connor isn't allowed to get too far from the Infirmary. Although he is part werewolf and heals quickly, the nurses are still trying to see if anything can be done for his legs.

"So where have you guys been?" Connor asks eagerly, looking at all of us with a love like Papa's.

Mason smiles at him. "We ran into the Forest after everything…you know."

"I know a way to save him." Còiseam suddenly appears beside me.

I jump a little. No one notices. They are listening to Mason tell our story. Còiseam gives me an obnoxious smile.

"You seem a little jumpy, angel," he smiles.

"Well, I didn't expect you to show up! You startled me is all," I growl at him. I look at the others.

"Oh, we're cloaked," Còiseam says as if I should have known. "They can't see you or me. Our conversation is private. When you return to their vision, their minds will be touched and they'll think you were there the whole time."

"You can do that?"

Còiseam nods smugly. "Of course! It's quite easy."

I roll my eyes. "Now you say you know a way to save someone?"

Còiseam's expression changes rapidly from smugness to sincerity. "Those pearls that protect your soul also have profound healing powers. You could heal Connor's legs. I actually found a pearl for you."

"Oh!" I smile and look at his hands. "Did you?"

Còiseam nods. "I looked into Connor's injury, however; and we're going to need ten more pearls."

"Ten?" I'm skeptical. Why do I need that many? It only takes one to keep corruption at bay within me. It shouldn't take ten to heal Connor! How would he know anyway? "That seems excessive."

"Well," Còiseam folds his arms, stopping. The others continue to walk without a glance behind them. "This new one I found is for you. Two is always better than one when it comes to protecting your soul. Two pearls will halt the corruption until the Gods can heal you."

"So then why ten for Connor?" I say, looking at the back of his wheelchair. Connor already seems to be adapting to his new condition.

"Four or five is the number for injuries inflicted by Darkeness," Còiseam explains. "I had a conversation with Father Sulibe about this very thing. Connor's injury, however, is spinal and very much a traumatic injury to his body and general well-being. Father Sulibe thought it would be wise to double the amount of pearls to insure his perfect healing."

I think in silence for a moment. How would we even find these pearls? Còiseam looks at me earnestly. He has a slight smile on his face. He's clearly pleased and proud of himself.

"You're a good guardian," I smile up at him suddenly.

Còiseam smiles sweetly. "Thank you. I try to be the very best I can be."

"So how do we find these pearls?" I clap my hands together.

"Leave that to me." Còiseam points at me and winks. "I can handle that. Every once in a while I can tell you where to find one. Do you have your pearl on you now?"

"Yes," I say, reaching into my pocket. I extend my hand toward him.

Còiseam jumps backwards. "You can touch that?"

I pull my hand back and stare down at the pearl. The beautiful little thing sits harmlessly in my palm. "Should I not be able to?"

"Those things have too much power for most mortals! I can't even hold them. It would destroy me," Còiseam stares at the pearl. His dark eyes flicker to my face. "Did Father Sulibe give that to you?"

I nod.

"He must have blessed it or something." Còiseam touches my fingers but doesn't touch the pearl.

The pearl gives a little twinkle of light, and Còiseam pulls his hand back. "That's the only one you should touch. Don't touch the rest of the pearls, okay? In fact, I'll hold onto the other pearls for you until I have all of them."

"Will I still be protected?" I swallow hard. If he leaves with the others, then what? Will I still be safe?

"Of course," Còiseam smiles and starts to move toward me but holds himself back. "As long as you have me, you will always be protected and under my cloak."

"Thank you."

"Well," Còiseam flushes slightly and looks toward the others. They've walked farther than I realized. "We better get you back over there. Their minds are touched and ready to go. I'll see you soon."

"Wait," I say to him. "Why do you always have to leave so suddenly?"

"Well," Còiseam shifts his feet. "I guess I don't have to go. I just don't want to bother you."

"Bother me?" I laugh out loud. "How could you bother me? You're saving my soul! I like having you around. I-I want you around."

"You do?" Còiseam smiles and my stomach flips suddenly. I take in Còiseam's face. His dark eyes and long dark eyelashes seem so perfect. With his tan skin and dark thick hair, he looks like a God. He's so attractive... and kind. His eyes make me feel as though I could melt right through the clouds.

"Yeah," I say for lack of better words.

"Well," Còiseam touches my chin and angles my face toward his. "I like being around you more than I should. I need to go. I'll see you soon, angel."

Còiseam disappears suddenly and I'm standing next to Kaleb. Kaleb seems to be standing closely to me. I can feel his warm skin.

"Whoa," I mumble to myself.

"Did you say something?" Kaleb looks down at me.

"Nope." I grin at him. "Not a word!"

CHAPTER TWENTY

Mary

We leave Connor at the Infirmary to get something to eat. Happiness seems to make us all glow. I feel so lightweight. He's alive. My Gods, he is alive! Although I cannot say anything to the others, I know I can save his legs! Còiseam and I can give him his legs back.

I find myself smiling the entire walk back.

"What the-?" Someone suddenly says as we top a small hill.

There are tents of all sizes and colors, beings are everywhere, and there are blacksmiths working overtime. The war has officially come.

"The war is here," I say quietly but everyone hears me.

"Yes," Grace suddenly says. Her bright eyes fall on each of us. "I knew of this. I didn't realize it was happening today, though. I must have missed something."

Grace turns and faces the camp. From the hill we have a good vantage of the entire camp. There have to be at least a million people. The camp extends back further than we can see.

A God suddenly appears beside her making us all jump. His skin glows slightly, giving away his God status.

"There you are!" Grace turns to him. "Would you make that announcement now? Chaos said everyone is gathered here in the camp. We need to organize immediately."

Another God suddenly appears. "Aether, Grace, so good to see you two. I have a report for you straight from Zephyrus."

"Nice to see you, too, Hermes." Grace smiles politely. "What is the report?"

"The Darke forces are up in arms and moving through the Forest toward Witchen in the Eastern Kingdom. We are to take up arms in Persephone's Forest and attack from there. Athena, Ares, and Erebus are coordinating below, but we have to get all beings to their correct areas."

"That announcement would be good right about now, Aether." Grace raises an eyebrow smirking. How can they be so lighthearted about everything when there is a war about to begin? I look up at Kaleb. He doesn't look down at me. He's focused on the conversation.

Còiseam suddenly appears beside me again. He puts a finger to his lips and watches Aether work. My skin prickles with excitement. I want him around me way too much. Còiseam glances at me sideways without turning his head. He smiles smugly.

Aether raises his arms and begins working them, twisting the air. He twists the air and seems to ball up wind before him. I can hear the air thrashing wildly in his hands and I can feel the force of it. His arms are flexed as he holds the air close to himself.

"Lightnings, Angels, and immortal beings are on the north and west sides," Aether says to the thrashing air. "Humans and mortal beings are on the south side. Dragons and their riders are on the east side. Everyone report to their designated areas accordingly and wait for further instructions there."

Aether releases the air over the large camp. Suddenly, his voice booms over the huge camp as the air moves through and over the tents and beings. Aether turns and gives Grace a self-satisfied smile.

"Ahem," he says with a slight smile. "I have things to tend to now."

"I'm sure you do," Grace retorts, folding her arms and smiling. Còiseam makes a loud gagging noise. Of course, I'm the only who can hear him. I stifle a laugh.

Aether disappears with a chuckle and Hermes takes off.

Grace turns to us, and her smile has disappeared. "You heard the God! Go report to your spots. Kaleb, you're with me. Let's go."

Grace leaves in a flash of lightning that seems to come from nowhere but herself. Kaleb disappears in the same manner. I look over at Mason. Còiseam looks over at him, too.

"Let's go," Penny laughs. "Looks like we've just been recruited."

"Whoa," I stop as they all take a step forward. "Wait, what? No! What if we don't want to be killed?"

"I've always wanted to be a part of the Gods' army," Ardon says quietly. "It is an honor to die for the Gods. I have always known I would die fighting for goodness to finally win this world."

We are all silent for a moment. Mason turns to Ardon and claps a hand on his shoulder. "You are probably one of the smartest and bravest men I have ever had the privilege of knowing. You have always been one to defend the innocent and to take on Darkeness."

Ardon smiles. "Thank you. That's one of the greatest compliments I have ever received. Especially because it has come from you."

I'm starting to feel like that coward again. I am a coward. I need to...not. I need to stop being a coward. Cowardice and apathy will never change anything for the better in this world. Gods, I need to think more like Ardon. At the same time, I don't want to die. I don't want to leave this world. My soul may be on the rocks, but I still have a chance. I can still live.

"I don't blame you," Còiseam nudges me with an elbow.

"I'll fight, too," Penny nods to herself, drawing my attention back into the conversation. The two men turn to look at her. I shake my head. Why would she fight?

"Mason," she takes his hand. "We've always talked about what we would do if this war ever came. I mean, your Uncle Seth even said himself that the war was coming. Your Papa always knew it was coming. I think we did, too. Why else would we talk about it?"

"We knew," Mason nods.

"So I want to fight." Penny makes eye contact with me and then with Mason. "If anything, I will fight in Mr. Stoneburner's name. We have this gift. We're werewolves. We need to use our gift. Our species wasn't spontaneously made. Our species was made to fight evil and Darkeness. I'm going to fight."

"I will, too," I sigh. She's right. They're all right.

"You don't have to," Mason says, looking down at me. "I don't want you getting hurt. No one ever wants their loved ones in war. I don't want Penny going to war either, but I know her and I know I won't change her mind. I love you both too much to want you to go to war. Yet, I know I can't change either of your minds"

"It'd be nice if you tried," Penny snorts, folding her arms. Mason laughs and gives her a little push. Then he pulls her in for a kiss.

Còiseam makes a loud gagging noise complete with expressions. I glare at him. Mason sighs heavily, making me look at him.

"Mary," he turns back to me, his brown eyes are very serious. "You could stay here and help nurse Connor."

I frown. "Mason, you saw Connor. He'll be fine in another week. He's recovering quickly, and he doesn't need me babying him. I want to fight. I've never fought for anything in my life. I've always been a coward-"

"Mary," Mason starts to say.

"No!" I shake my head. "You all know me. I know me. I've always been too afraid of everything. Papa used to say that apathy and cowardice never helped anyone. I want to be the person Papa would be proud to have as his daughter. I'm going to fight and I'm going to kick some demon-ass!"

"Mary!" Penny bursts out laughing. "I've never heard you say anything like that!"

I laugh in spite of my dignity. "I wanted my point to be clear."

"Crystal clear!" Ardon laughs.

Còiseam winks at me. "Very nice, angel."

We all start down the hill with a clear understanding of what our fates could be. Our hearts are set, and we each have a will to fight the Darkeness that destroyed Mika and almost killed our family. I can feel Mason's will mixed with anger and righteousness radiating off of him.

A wolf howls below, calling to all other wolves to come toward him. Còiseam salutes me and disappears. We break into a jog and run down the hill toward the camp.

CHAPTER TWENTY-ONE

Connor

I push myself down the hallway, turning down several offers from nurses to help me. I need to build my strength. I need to develop my muscles and not let them atrophy. I need to be able to push myself around. This is what the rest of my life is going to look like, and I must be fully adapted to it.

At first I was devastated when my nurse, Natalya, told me the condition of my legs. It ate me up for several days. It still bothers me, but I hold it at bay. There is no use being mad and frustrated with something that has already been done and cannot be undone. This is my life now and I have to deal with it.

It seems a little melodramatic to say it that way to anyone. I don't think I could ever bring myself to say anything like that to Mary or Mason. Gods, it was fantastic seeing them. I thought they were dead. My arms still ache from being attacked by them with love and affection.

I round the corner to see Natalya waiting outside my room.

"There you are, Mr. Stoneburner," she says happily. "You look much better. All it took was a visit from the family, huh?"

I can tell Natalya would be a very large being even if I were standing. I mean, she's a Faerie, but it seems like she's a giant from my vantage point in my chair.

"I feel much better," I smile up at her. "And, please, call me Connor."

Natalya sighs as she follows me into the room. "If you insist. Now, here's your medicine. This is the last of it. But we plan on keeping you here for a couple more days for observation and so you can rest."

I frown. "But I feel fine!"

"Better to be safe than sorry," Natalya smiles and lifts me onto my bed without asking. I feel like a child. This is an indignity I need to keep to myself. I need to accept that I'll be needing this kind of help.

"Excuse me," a woman sticks his head in the doorway. "Nurse, I'm sorry to interrupt. Could you help me after you assist him?"

"Certainly," Natalya smiles. "I'll be right with you."

She turns back to me and hands me a large cup full of the bitter orange medicine.

"Drink this up and I'll be back," she says and leaves the room.

I sigh and gulp down the medicine as quickly as I can. I shudder and lick my lips. Revolting, absolutely revolting!

"How can I help you?" I hear Natalya's quiet voice outside the room.

"Yes," the woman says. "I need some patch powder for my dragon."

I sit straight up. She's a Rider! She has a dragon!

"Oh," Natalya's voice is suddenly louder. "You're a Rider? How interesting. How did your dragon get hurt?"

"Oh," the woman's voice is lighter now. "She clipped another dragon during a practice."

"So," Natalya is rummaging through something. "Are there a lot of new dragons? I heard there was a hatching a couple months ago. How do you find Riders for the new ones?"

"Yeah," the woman sighs. "We still haven't found Riders for about five of them. Not just anyone can be a Rider. We have to match the perfect Rider with the perfect dragon. Sometimes dragons will die never finding their match. Sometimes dragons will settle on someone less perfect. It's been really difficult because one of the dragons is pretty rare, and it's a shame he hasn't been matched yet."

"Maybe I should go try to imprint!" Natalya laughs.

"You should! I wish more beings would try to imprint," the woman laughs. "What with this war and everything, everyone has seemed to forgotten we have dragons to be matched."

I look down at my chair. It seems to me that Natalya is hinting. Why else would she be talking so loudly? She wants me to go and try! I suppose from our many conversations this past week, she knows I'm serious when I say I want to help in the war. I want revenge from the sons of swine who stole my legs from me.

I lean out of my bed and reach for my chair. I push off the bed and land rather ungracefully in my chair. I shift myself and lift the brakes. I push myself out of the room.

"Natalya," I say as I wheel into the hallway. She and the Rider look down at me. "I'll be back in a bit. I'm going to go outside."

Natalya smiles a knowing smile and waves me on. "Be back before dinner or the others will worry. Be safe."

"Will do!" I say, pushing myself toward the nearest exit.

"Wait!" the Rider is running to catch up with me. She meets me as I get to the door. She holds it open for me. "The nurse told me to escort you while she's getting the powder."

"Did she?" I ask, holding back a snort. She is too much!

Natalya suddenly appears behind us. "Here you are, Rider. Oh, and if it's not too much to ask, would you escort him to the Dragon cages? He wants to imprint. Thank you!"

She disappears behind the doors before the Rider can say anything.

"You want to imprint?" the Rider looks down at me. She purses her lips thoughtfully. She has olive skin, tanned from the sun, and her black hair is in a tight bun on top of her head. Her large dark eyes stare at me skeptically.

"I do," I say. "I know I don't look like much, but I'm part werewolf and I heal quickly. You don't know what I've been through, but I know I have to try to imprint. I have to fight in this war."

"I believe you, I do," the Rider sighs. "But I'm going to speak to you rather bluntly. Your legs are useless, right? It's going to be harder for you to do certain things as a Rider. Your dragon will have to compensate a lot for your legs, which will put both you and your dragon in danger."

"You speak as if I've already been matched to a dragon." I furrow my eyebrows together. "Who knows! I may not be matched at all. I wouldn't blame the dragons if they didn't want me as a Rider, but I have to find something for myself. I am not the man I used to be so I need to find a new man to be. A life doing nothing is not a life worth living. I want to do something with my life and I will not let this injury hold me back. You don't have to escort me there, but I will go and I will try."

The Rider is silent for a moment. She regards me calmly with a kind eye. She finally nods.

"Let's go. It's not too far off," she says softly. "I will, however, insist on pushing you there because you need all your strength to imprint."

"If you insist," I say, as she gets behind me.

"Will you hold this?" she hands me the small white container of patch powder and begins pushing me quickly through the grass.

The Dragon arena is large. The walls extend about twenty feet up but there is no ceiling. There are dragons and Riders everywhere. Only a few give me a passing glance as most are occupied with their dragons. Riders are preparing their armor for both them and their dragons. A large silver dragon spreads her wings, making me jump. Her armor gleams malevolently and she eyes me. The silver dragon seems unkind. We pass and I avoid her gaze.

We exit through the back of the arena to a large open dirt plot. There are three rows of six cages. The first row has five dragons; the other cages are empty. Several Riders are facing a sleek black dragon. All of them turn to glance at me and the Rider pushing me.

"Soleil," one of the Riders turns and walks toward us. "Did you get the powder?"

"Yeah," she points to the container in my lap.

"Who is this?" the Rider asks Soleil.

"Connor Stoneburner," I extend a hand and shake his.

"Keith Amor," the Rider gives a brief smile that doesn't reach his eyes. He has red hair and blue eyes. He seems young to have this amount of authority. "I'm the Dragonmaster. What brings you here? Did you just get out of the Infirmary?"

"I'm here to try and imprint," I say with as much confidence as I can muster.

The red dragon furthest from us looks up and gives a snort.

"I don't mean to offend you," Keith gives me a skeptical look. He scratches the red scruff on his jaw and chin. "It looks like you've got broken legs or something, am I right?"

"They're paralyzed."

"Oh," Keith seems a little startled. "So why are you here? How do you think you're going to be able to ride? Let's say you imprint successfully, how are you going to fight?"

"I think that would be between him and his dragon," another Rider suddenly says.

I do a double glance at the Rider. He looks just like Keith. Are they twins?

Keith's jaw clenches and he nods. "Let's give him a try."

Soleil pushes me toward the dragon cages.

"Keith," Keith's twin steps closer to him. "If he imprints and the match is successful, this could open up a whole new world to us. If he's a successful rider, this could open up so much."

Keith crosses his arms. "I just don't see how this is going to work."

"Have a little faith," the twin says.

Soleil pushes me in front of the first cage. A huge green dragon is lying inside. She gives me a lazy look and puts her head down.

"This is one of our largest females we've ever had," Keith says. "She's a Levisalean Ridgeback. She's a real beauty."

"Huck!" Soleil suddenly yells, making me jump. "Bring some meat over here!"

A Rider named Huck throws a hunk of meat into the cage. The dragon seems unimpressed.

"I think she's sick," Soleil says to Keith.

"Take him to the next one," Keith says. "Huck and Rogan, go see what's wrong with her!"

Soleil wheels me over to another large green dragon. The dragon snarls at me and I grip the chair nervously. Out of the corner of my eye, I see Huck and Keith's twin go toward the sick dragon.

"Okay," Soleil says quietly in my ear, bringing my attention back to the dragon in front of me. "We're going to try her out. This is also a Levisalean Ridgeback and they can be pretty nasty. One of two things could happen: She could accept you and mark you as her own…"

"Or?" I eye the large green snarling dragon in front of me. She snarls again and gives me a look meaner than Leibus.

"Or she could kill you," Soleil says flatly.

"What?" My voice cracks.

Soleil laughs. "Don't worry. See those two men on either side of the cage? They'll stun her before she can do anything to you. Just try and relax. I know this can be… a bit unsettling, but try and trust me."

"Why are you doing this?" I twist in my chair and look up at her. Soleil looks down at me. "Why are you helping me? You don't even know me. I'm in a wheelchair, for God's sake!"

"You seemed so eager a minute ago. Are you having second thoughts?"

"No," I hold her gaze despite my back aching and my rib hurting. "I just want to know why you're helping me. You heard Keith. I could end up killing myself and a dragon that could have been for someone else."

"There are very few men and women in this world who would dare to try and imprint on a dragon," Soleil says as she looks up at the dragon. I turn and watch the dragon pacing in her cage, watching me. "Many people fantasize and dream of being a Rider but, when they're placed before a dragon, all but a few lose their nerve. The idea of putting your life at risk before a huge animal such as this," she motions to the dragon, "is downright terrifying. Couple that with the fact that you may never imprint on a dragon. You're putting your life at risk for no reason. Being a Rider is a privilege, an honor that most will never accomplish. The Dragonmaster is very choosey. I am to become the next

Dragonmaster, and I feel that your heart is pure and brave and your intentions noble."

Before I can say anything, Soleil pushes me forward as the cage is opened. The black dragon two cages down begins thrashing wildly in its cage. For a moment, the two men at the entrance of the green dragon's cage are distracted. The green dragon leaps forward and I gasp out of reflex. Her eyes tell me all I need to know. She is going to kill me.

There is a loud crash and several screams. A green tail slams into my chair, sending me flailing into the air. The ground rushes up to meet me, but something yanks me away from it inches before I make contact.

Zenyo.

Zenyo?

Zenyo.

The unfamiliar thought seems to echo inside my head.

I open my eyes, realizing I had shut them, to see that I am hundreds of feet above the ground. I scream and then realize that the green dragon is below me, still on the ground. If she's down there, then who has me?

My eyes scan the cages. The black dragon is gone and the cage has been demolished. It looks as though the dragon burned it down. Now I'm in its clutches! I squirm in vain, struggling against the dragon's talons wrapped around my torso. But the black dragon seems to be lowering me back to the ground. I can hear its wings beat the air and I can feel the force in its powerful wings. But it isn't hurting me. Is this imprinting? Am I a Rider?

It seems too good to be true.

The dragon lowers me down gently and sets me on the ground as though I were made of glass. He curls around me protectively and I can't move. The dragon arches his head and looks me in the eye, bringing his face close to mine.

Zenyo. That's the dragon's name! He's my dragon. He has to be!

His face is close enough to touch. I swallow hard and reach out. Either he really is my dragon or he's about to devour me. The dragon suddenly makes a horrid choking noise. I jump and pull my hand back.

"He's laughing," a voice yells from the cages. "Touch his face!"

The dragon stops laughing and watches me calmly. He has large green eyes the color of moss. I close my eyes and touch his nose. A powerful force blasts out from under my hand, but it seems to pull Zenyo and me closer together and pushes the others back. The force blasts out in a purplish ring. I see dragons and their Riders coming out from the arena. Did the force have a noise? How do they know what is happening?

They can feel it. The thought isn't my own. Other Riders and dragons can feel the bond that has been made. They can feel the power of a perfect match. I open my eyes and stare at the dragon, at Zenyo. I feel a sting on my hand. I stare at my hand but there's nothing there. I look back up at Zenyo, at my dragon.

I am a Rider.

CHAPTER TWENTY-TWO

Mary

I bare my teeth and circle the other wolf. Yet another one of these training sessions. I want to go see Connor. I haven't heard from him or seen him for two weeks. I know there's a war going on and everything, but Connor matters a little more to me. Call me selfish but it's true.

The other wolf lunges at me and I evade the attack easily. I am getting quite good at attacking in my wolf form. I have neglected to go to any of the training sessions for the humans. We're supposed to go so we can learn how to fight outside of our wolf forms.

I snarl and swipe at the other wolf with a fast paw. I leap just as he does. We collide in the air and hit the ground rolling. I manage to get myself on top of him. I put my teeth against his throat. Someone blows a whistle and I jump off of the wolf.

Mason and Penny are next to fight. They were paired randomly and neither of them are happy about it. They've never fought physically or verbally. The whistle is blown again and they begin circling. Penny growls and Mason snarls back.

Penny is clearly worried about the size differential. Mason is huge compared to her. She pins her ears back and licks between her teeth. She growls deeply.

Suddenly Mason lunges at her and she ducks out from under him. He turns quickly but she has jumped on top of him. He throws her off and she hits the dirt with a cry. Mason stops immediately. His head jerks up, ears pricked forward, and his eyes are worried. He walks over to her and nudges her.

The whistle blows.

"Get these two out of here!" Ares folds his arms and jerks his thumb over his shoulder. Penny and Mason leave the little practice corral with their heads down. "And give them new partners!"

Còiseam suddenly appears beside me. I look up at him. His unexpected appearances are having less of an effect on me. I always expect him now.

"I know where a couple pearls are. We need to get to them eventually," he says.

I nod.

"I can understand your thoughts." Còiseam smiles. "I'm your guardian, aren't I?"

That's true. How many pearls do we have?

"We have one," Còiseam counts on his fingertips. "Two, three! We have three! But we need to hurry and collect as many as we can. It appears others have discovered the power of the pearls. Others are collecting them."

Are they really? I look up at him. Why would other people want them?

"People," Còiseam sits down beside me and gives me a solemn look. "People will always take something good and turn it evil. The enemy is taking the pearls for their own gain. We have to collect as quickly as we can. The problem is that you can't get the pearls because you're up here and I can't get the pearls by myself because of my being. There are some things I simply cannot do."

Còiseam is so good to me. I'm so undeserving. He is getting himself all worked up because he cannot collect all the pearls for my brother. Why do I get a guardian? Why do others not have guardians?

Còiseam smiles. "Shall we go on a walk? You do deserve me."

I get up and walk toward the tent Mason pitched for us. Còiseam suddenly reaches out and pets me.

"Is it weird to say your fur is really soft?" Còiseam almost laughs as he asks me.

I laugh, making a horrid choking noise.

"Are you laughing at me?" Còiseam asks me, appalled. He grunts and bends down and to look me in the eye.

It's never wise to look a wolf in the eye. Còiseam stands up suddenly and raises an eyebrow. He bends down again to crawl into the tent. I walk in and sit down.

Would you mind putting that blanket in the corner over me and hand me the pile of clothes you're sitting on?

Còiseam stares at me a moment. He puts the clothes in front of me and puts the blanket on top of me. I close my eyes and send out my senses. My skin retracts back into me and I can feel the coldness of the air again. I fumble beneath the blanket, trying to put on my clothing without flashing Còiseam. I manage to get my shirt on so I stand up and jump into my pants. I tie them tightly and throw the blanket off.

Còiseam looks me over. He swallows hard.

"Are you okay?" I ask, sitting down in front of him.

"Would you pardon me for a moment?" Còiseam asks, blinking rapidly.

"Certainly," I say, worrying. Is he going to be okay?

He suddenly grabs my face and brings me forward. My stomach seems to do several backflips in a row, my heart beats wildly, and my skin doesn't feel like my own. I close my eyes and follow his lead. It's like I'm not in my own body.

I can feel his soft lips on mine. His fingers venture into my hair, pulling it tight against my scalp. I sigh between kisses and he lets out a soft sigh between his lips. I reach out to feel his body. My hands find his chest and my fingers crawl their way up and around his shoulders. They grab his hair and he makes another sound, more like a groan, and pulls me closer to him.

He suddenly stops kissing me and pulls away from me.

"Oh dear," he suddenly says, swallowing audibly. "I shouldn't have done that."

"Wh-why not?" I feel as though I should be hurt, but I can still feel his lips on mine. I can barely focus on what he's saying.

"A guardian shouldn't have relations with his-"

"What?" I close my eyes and put a hand to my head. I open my eyes and look at him. "Why not?"

"Because it complicates things," Còiseam stammers, running a hand through his hair nervously.

"It probably makes you a better guardian if you have personal… interest," I say slyly. The words come out of my mouth before I have time to stop them. This is completely unlike me to say something like this, to be so forward.

These… Those… Those words aren't mine.

"I suppose you're right," Còiseam says and pulls me onto my cot and begins to kiss me again. My thoughts are foggy and disappear.

We roll over, me on top of him, and we just kiss.

"Why do you think you don't deserve me?" Còiseam says, lying beside me. I play with the tassels on his tunic. The black tassels are frayed at the end.

I shrug. "Why me? Why did I get you?"

Còiseam smiles. "You were corrupted and needed a guardian to watch over you. People all over the world who are destined to become something great and terrible are given guardians."

"What?" I smile, looking into his eyes. "Am I going to be Eve or something?"

Còiseam's mouth twitches. "Didn't you hear Eve has already come into being? The Lightnings that went to Vidian think they saw her."

"I think I did hear something about that," I say, trying to remember who said it. It was another werewolf, I know.

"You could be the Darke Angel named Mary or Esther for all I know," Còiseam leans in for another kiss. "All I know is that you were a high priority for Father Sulibe and I'm grateful I have been assigned to you."

I kiss him back. "Me, too."

CHAPTER TWENTY-THREE

Psyche

I brace myself against the window. Breathing out slowly, I close my eyes waiting for the vision to take me. As always, my breath is taken from me and I collapse to the floor. I'm swept out of my temple and taken down to the snow-covered lands between Reason and the Atys lands, to the past.

I see an Angel with golden hair bent over something. I move around her, craning my neck to see. She looks up as though she knows I am there. She brushes snow carefully off of the object in front of her. This is the Angel from my other vision!

"A pearl!" I gasp out loud, hoping Eros is listening. The Angel brushes the pearl off but suddenly looks up again. "The Angel has a pearl."

Suddenly Leibus appears in front of her. He is well disguised but not well enough for me. I knew exactly who he is. "Excellent. You've found it for me."

"Chaos!" I cry out. "Chaos! Chaos!"

The Angel jerks an arm up, putting a glittering shield between them. She backs up and stumbles to her feet. He flicks some Darke dust at her effortlessly and it eats away at her glitter. Her shield collapses and falls to her feet. The Angel looks up at Leibus, terrified.

"No!" I cry, gripping something cool and hard. "No! She can't fight Leibus!"

She throws up another shield, more powerful than the last. It is unstable though and explodes. The glitter is thrown onto Leibus and he yelps as the light eats into him. Leibus jerks off his robes and throws a handful of Darke dust at her. This time he isn't playing. Suddenly he throws a shield over both of them. I push myself inside before it closes me off.

"Psyche!" the Angel cries out pitifully. She looks for me in desperation. How did I miss this? How did I miss this Angel calling for me? What was I doing that I didn't hear her? "If you can hear me, my name is Hope. I'm the Angel who delivered Kaleb to you!"

"No!" I scream loudly. "No! No! No, you can't say that in front of him! Hope!"

"Your Gods can't hear you now. Your pearls are going to a good cause, to a good creation, but I need to know if Psyche knows about the creation," Leibus smiles at her. He then mumbles to himself. "I'm sure she does, but I need to know what she knows."

The Angel doesn't appear to hear. She pulls her glittering shield tighter around herself, looking more and more terrified. She knows she won't last. It's written all over her face.

Leibus glances at her and, with a swish of his hand, destroys her shield. The Angel, defeated, looks up at him.

"Do you know if she knows, Angel?" He smiles again. Goosebumps shoot up my arms. "You know a lot, Angel. You took my Adam from me. Now I'm going to take you. Yes, you can't hide from me. You do know. But I need the specifics on Psyche's range of power. You have the answers and I will get them out of you. Khermes!"

Leibus' assistant appears. The large Darke dust cloud appears at his side and suddenly snatches the Angel. She screams and struggles against Khermes. Leibus throws

Darke energy at her, stunning her for a moment. She whimpers as Leibus bends down and picks up the pearl.

"No!" the Angel cries in vain.

Leibus looks at the pearl as Khermes lifts the Angel and carries her away. "For every great power, there is the equal potential for good and evil. It just so happens this good side has taken control."

I pull out of the vision to find Eros above me. His beautiful face is twisted into anguish. He holds me closely.

"What did you see?"

"The Angel that is connected to the prospective Eve is with Leibus now." I look up at him sadly. "She's going to be dead soon if not already.

He strokes my face gently. There is something else bothering him. I can see it.

"What is it?"

Eros frowns and the muscles in his jaw flex. "The Darke forces have taken Sesaru. We're about to engage them in Naem. I fear they know we are coming. We don't have the element of surprise anymore. I think Aigaion is sending down the Lesser Gods to assist."

He helps me to my feet. I sigh heavily. "Why we haven't been preparing for this war is unknown to me. I have been telling Chaos for centuries now…"

"This is no time to say 'I told you so', dear." Eros cocks his head sideways. His hazel eyes penetrate me as they always do. "What are you going to do now?"

"I have to find every person that Angel has been with recently." I put a hand to my head, trying to calm the rush inside. "The Angel I saw is the same one from my other vision. She was in the presence of Eve and didn't know it. There is another layer to this. I just know it."

"How do you mean?" Eros pulls me toward our bed and sits on it.

I sit down next to him. "That Angel should have known Eve was beside her but she didn't. She sensed Adam but not Eve. That Angel was right next to Eve in my other vision. She should have sensed the corruption within her."

"Perhaps she wasn't corrupted at that time?" Eros sticks out his lower lip slightly in thought.

"No," I shake my head. My eyes are fixed on an imperfection in the marble on the wall across from us. "No, I saw her corruption quite clearly. She was most definitely corrupted at that time. She's nearly gone. That Angel should have sensed her, but she didn't. The Angel was completely and utterly unaware of the state of the soul beside her."

"That's not right," he blinks slowly. "No, she should have sensed her. The prospect must be cloaked or something. Leibus has more than just a hand in this."

"This prospect is different," I say quietly. "I couldn't sense her identity. Leibus is doing something else."

Eros is quiet for a moment. "This is not just another Eve. This is *the* Eve. This is the true Eve."

I nod slowly. "This is the most perfect Eve Leibus will ever hope to create."

"So he's taking precautions," Eros looks at me intensely.

"He's cloaking her."

"Or something," Eros finishes my thought for me. "Leibus has been planning this all along. He has his twelve disciples for her lined up. He has the armies organized. He has Hades, and he distracted us with Adam. He has been planning this for centuries."

I shake my head in awe. "We never knew."

"But now we do." Chaos' voice makes us jump. We both turn to find him standing in the doorway. "I heard you call out for me. You had a vision."

"Father," Eros stands. "How long have you been there?"

"I heard the whole thing," Chaos comes into the center of the room and folds his arms. "I have something to tell you now."

Eros steals a glance toward me. Chaos' tone is different.

"You are my oldest son," Chaos says, moving closer to him. He claps a hand on Eros' shoulder. "Leibus is far more powerful than I could have ever imagined. I am taking your mother to the high cosmos to protect her. I will remain there with her. The last thing we need is for her to be destroyed."

He says it so matter-of-factly. I blink.

"You and Psyche are the most powerful Gods on high now," Chaos says. His voice breaks slightly. He breathes deeply. "You are in charge now."

Eros says nothing.

"What?" My voice snaps out, breaking the momentary silence.

"I cannot risk Gaia being destroyed," Chaos presses his lips together. Dimples dent his cheeks briefly. "She is still so weak from the Old World pollutions and destruction and then the Ravage nearly killed her. She is not strong enough to fight off Eve or Leibus. Leibus knows this, and she will be the target. He will kill his own mother."

"You're right," Eros looks up at Chaos. "I accept the responsibility."

"I never thought I would have had to ask this of you." Chaos sticks his hand out. "I am relinquishing to you the power and responsibility of all the cosmos and all the worlds until you see fit to return it to me. You are now the God of Gods, the God of worlds, and the God of everything and nothing. Do you understand and accept this power?"

"I understand and accept." Eros grips Chaos' hand and light explodes across the room.

I fall off of the bed, sliding ungracefully to the floor. Chaos and Eros separate and the light fades. Eros is shining brightly, brighter than Chaos.

"I will be watching from above," Chaos says. He grabs Eros suddenly and hugs him. "I am so sorry."

"Protect Mother." Eros hugs him tightly.

"Always." Chaos smiles but it doesn't reach his eyes. He disappears.

"You are my wife," Eros looks at me and reaches out a hand. "Which means you have the same power as I do now."

"Oh stars," I take his hand as he helps me up. "We're in charge of this war now?"

Eros stares at me blankly.

"Can it be this easy? Did he just give it to you like that?" I start pacing. "We're not ready for this kind of responsibility! How can he just leave us like this? Oh stars, we're in charge now!"

Eros grabs my arms above my elbows and jerks me. "Stop it! Now you're just rambling! You know we can handle it. You have never listened to him before and now you don't have to. You have always acted above the rest of us and you have always talked back to him. This is no different. He is gone and you are in control as usual! I will handle everything, and you keep doing what you always do!"

"I'm sorry." I hug him. "I lost my mind for a moment there. I was acting like a mortal and I apologize."

"Of course, dear," Eros chuckles and hugs me again. "Now you follow the Angel-Eve connection and I will go handle everything else. You are in charge of everything related to Eve."

He kisses me and disappears with a small pop.

Now I need to find Kaleb and break the news to him. I close my eyes and search for his soul through the layers of the world. I find him fighting near Sesaru. Eros must have just sent them.

I push myself out toward him. Kaleb strikes down a Darke Angel right as I appear before him. Kaleb jumps backwards.

"Psyche!" He wipes Darke dust off of his hands. "What are you doing here?"

I send out a shockwave of energy, pushing back all the Darke beings momentarily.

"I need you to report to my temple immediately," I say, right before I pull my projection back. I don't even hear his response but I can feel his soul rushing toward me.

CHAPTER TWENTY-FOUR

Mary

The Gods delivered us to Naem, just south of Varlet but just north of Persephone's Forest. The Lesser Gods seem to be in charge now and have divided us all into groups. Artemis was put in charge of the wolves.

She divided us into small armies, but now we all sit here awaiting further orders. Naem has been evacuated and the wolf armies of the Gods are the only inhabitants. Artemis doesn't wait with us but appears to us when she has orders.

Penny sighs heavily. "So have you heard anything from Connor lately?"

I shake my head. "I went up to the Infirmary about a week ago, but Natalya told me he didn't want to be seen."

"He's probably having a hard time with…" Penny trails off. "I don't really blame him, but it's been nearly two months since we've even heard from him."

"Give him some space," Ardon says from under the pile of blankets in the corner. "Imagine if you lost your legs and recently learned your family is alive. He thought you guys were dead."

"Yeah, but two months is a long time for space," Penny breaths and we're silent. "Well, Mason has been writing him letters. So I guess it's not a complete-"

"Mason has been writing him?"

Penny opens her mouth to say something just as Mason steps in to our tent.

"So what exactly is going to happen?" I ask Mason. He brushes snow off of himself.

"Yeah," Penny furrows her eyebrows and looks up at him. "You're one of the leaders, aren't you? Did Artemis tell you anything?"

Mason rubs his hands together. The bitter cold has turned his cheeks and nose a bright red. The cold sleet outside patters lightly on our tent and there is an unsettling chill that seems to muffle everything.

"Well," Mason says, as he pulls off a pair of gloves. "She just told us that the wolves would be the first to attack. We are to run through Persephone's Forest and to take the Darke forces by surprise in Naem. They're heading there now but they haven't arrived yet. We believe there is an injured Angel there vital to the discovery of the identity of prospective Eve."

"We're the first?" Ardon pokes his head from out of the covers.

"The thunders will come after us, then Ares' forces, followed by the Lightnings." Mason takes his boots off and rubs his feet.

"Ugh," I say before I can help myself.

Mason rolls his eyes. "They're just feet."

I make a face at him as Penny asks another question. "How big do they expect the Darke forces to be?"

Mason shrugs. "I haven't the faintest idea."

We're quiet for a moment.

Mason clears his throat and turns to face Penny. "Penny, well... err... everyone, this war is just beginning. I have been listening to the discussions with the Gods and the Lightnings and, frankly, I'm scared. I am scared because I don't know what is going to happen. I am really worried… and… I… uh…"

Penny and I exchange a glance. What is he doing?

"Penny," Mason's face pales. "I want you to know how much I care for you. I have never met anyone who is quite like you. I love you with all my heart and soul."

Penny claps her hands to her mouth.

"You complete me," his voice croaks on the second word. "I would like to know if you would marry me? I know this is not the time nor pl-"

"Yes!" Penny tackles him before he can even get the ring out. He fumbles it. "Yes! Oh Gods, yes! I love you!"

"Oh my Gods!" I exclaim, looking at Ardon and Kaleb. "Did you know?"

They both shake their heads.

Penny slips the ring on her finger. It is beautiful.

"I had it specially made," Mason says softly. "When you change into your wolf form, it will stay on your finger when you turn back into a human."

"Gods," she breathes and kisses him again. "I love you so much!"

A horn sounds suddenly and brings us all back to reality. We're in a war. The air in the tent is ice cold once more. It is silent. Penny and Mason are hugging each other.

Ardon buries himself back under the blankets and he's nothing but a small heap in the corner. The wind seems to go right through the tent. Penny pulls a blanket around herself and Mason. I pull a blanket around my own shoulders. We pull the blanket tight around ourselves.

"So now we just wait?" Ardon's muffled voice comes from behind us. Apparently the blanket heap had moved behind us for shelter from the wind.

"I'll change so I can hear. The others are in their forms," Mason stands up. "Avert your eyes, people."

"Done," Ardon's voice rises up again.

I look down and can't help but notice Penny doesn't look down. I can hear Mason taking his clothes off.

"Ugh," I say again.

Mason snorts and there is a slight shift in the air in the tent. I look up to see Mason's clothing piled neatly in front of a large dark brown wolf. The wolf lies down with a groan and crosses his paws in front of him. Penny sticks her feet out and puts them against his fur.

"So warm," Penny nearly giggles.

"This is stupid," Ardon says from under the blanket. "There's no point in sitting here freezing in my jeckin' skin."

There is a large amount of rustling and tossing beneath the blanket. Finally the blanket is blown off of him and a large grey wolf appears from beneath the blanket. Somehow he manages to have a satisfied, almost smug, expression on his wolfy face. His blue eyes radiate contentedness and he settles down behind us.

"He's right," I say to Penny. "Why are we sitting here shivering when we could be warm and fluffy like these two jecks?"

"Here." Penny picks up Mason's pile of clothing and stuffs it into his hip bag. She ties the small cloth bag around his ankle. Mason watches her carefully.

She turns, swinging her blonde braid as she goes, and ties Ardon's clothes up in the same manner. "Go on and change, Mary."

She hands me the blanket and I get underneath it. I struggle to take my clothing off while keeping out of sight. I take the pearl out of my pocket and put it into the sack I hang on my belt. I wonder what is happening with the other pearls.

"I'm here," Còiseam's voice suddenly sounds. I jump. "Don't worry. I heard you were wondering about the pearls. I'm keeping them safe for you."

The blanket I'm holding against me drops a little, revealing my pale skin. Còiseam winks at me.

"Nice, angel," he smiles crookedly with the smallest of blushes and disappears.

I feel my face grow hot. I feel my senses burst outward and I feel warmer and safer. The blanket drops off and I shake out my fur. I stretch, flexing each toe in turn, before lying down.

"Hey," Penny pokes me. "Gimme a foot here."

I extend a foot and watch her as she ties my clothing onto me. I shake my foot, testing it. What is she going to do? I whine at her to get her attention. She doesn't pay attention to me and undresses beneath the blanket. I see her hands appear from under the blanket and tie a wide loop around her ankle. She ties the loop off and disappears beneath the blanket. The air in the tent shifts again as she changes.

Penny shrugs the blanket off and lies down beside me. I nose her foot and she gives me a wolfy smile as another wolf howls loudly not too far from our tent.

Mason stands up quickly and leaves the tent without a look to any of us. Ardon rushes after him, knocking Penny into me. She huffs and follows him.

Còiseam suddenly appears again. "Follow them and do what you need. There are pearls nearby and I'll get you when we can get them."

I nod and he slides a hand down my back as I leave the tent. He pats my rear as I leave. I leap out and look back at him. He winks and disappears.

We are organized into packs of thirty with three alphas heading each pack. My pack will take the left flank. Penny is in the right flank pack. Ardon and Mason are heading the center pack. Twelve more packs will be behind us in different waves in the same pattern. Lucky me gets the first wave.

My heart is thumping too loudly and too quickly. My pack slinks through the tall grasses approaching Persephone's forest. I can feel their fear, their bravery, and their righteousness. My fear is probably the loudest among us, but I force my feet forward. I don't even really want to be here! Why bother fight? The Gods will win anyway! They always do.

The tall and massive flowers loom over us. We have entered Persephone's forest. The pack moves silently other than the quiet rustling of our bodies against the grasses and stems of the flowers.

On my signal, charge forward and engage the enemy. Protect any Angels you see at all costs.

The thought echoes through the pack's mind. We have just cut through a small portion of Persephone's forest. I can see the light parting through the flower petals and grasses. Despite the bitter cold and snow, Persephone's forest stays alive and vibrantly colored but it provides no shelter. Snow sneaks through the petals and soaks into our fur. I shiver slightly. The flower forest may be able to stay alive, but I may not if I have to stay out in this cold any longer.

A wolf howls and we charge forward. My heart leaps and my body suddenly feels lightweight. I burst out of the grasses and we race down a slope toward the charred city of Naem. The city has been burned by the Darke forces.

My paws barely touch the ground as we charge down the hill. We yip, bark, snarl, and howl in panicky excitement. Suddenly, Darke wolves appear. They were ready for us. We were deceived.

They charge toward us and I feel a moment of panic right as the first lines of wolves slam into each other. There is a loud clap of thunder and I feel my body shake. I look up and realize the Riders and the Thunders have arrived. Lightning strikes are suddenly everywhere as the Lightning Children come down.

Enemy dragons and Riders appear from the Forest. This battle is much larger than we were told. Suddenly the dark clouds part and several Gods on fiery chariots descend. I recognize Artemis immediately with her famous bow and arrows. She begins rapidly firing arrows, felling Darke wolves and other Darke beings.

I leap over a dead wolf, enemy by the looks of it, and continue after my pack. We are clearly looking for the Angel. Suddenly, something tackles me hard, knocking me to the ground. I struggle for air for a moment. Another wolf circles me, snarling and licking his teeth.

I jump to my feet immediately. I press my ears against my head unconsciously. Maybe he won't kill me. I'm clearly being submissive. I lick my lips nervously. He takes a step forward. He is going to kill me.

I bark at him, challenging him. Gods, I hope I'm not making a mistake. He lunges at me and I avoid him easily. I turn quickly and leap on top of him. I get a hold on his neck and sink my fangs into it. I hear him squeal in pain and anger. He tries to rub me off. I scratch and claw, fighting to stay on his back. He turns, trying to bite me. I scramble off of him, still growling.

A lightning bolt is thrown at him, nailing him right on his spine. I see life leave the wolf's eyes immediately as he slumps and rolls over. I look up right as the Lightning Child who rescued me runs to engage another enemy.

I look back to see Athena destroy a Darke Angel. The Darke Angel explodes in a burst of Darke matter and dust. Athena yanks her sword back and screams a battle cry. She rushes forward, pushing Darke beings out of her path effortlessly. Ares knocks a Darke low-flying dragon out of the air and cuts the head off. I almost scream. Ares, covered in blood, looks up and smiles. His bloodlust has taken control of him now. He charges forward beside Athena and both attack several Darke Angels who have been terrorizing a small group of trapped humans.

The humans scatter as another Goddess appears. She scoops them up in her power and disappears with them. I look back to see wolves attacking each other, dragons mingling in the air, ripping at each other's throats. The Darke Angels are falling left and right to the might of the Gods. All of this is for one Angel?

There is an explosion to my right much too close to me. I yelp and tuck my tail in and run. I run toward the center of the city, away from the main fighting. I hear another battle cry from Athena.

The rain is pouring now and so hard to see clearly through. I turn a corner blindly and smack into another being. I get to my feet quickly, squinting to see who or what it is. It's a Blood elf. I snarl and circle him. The elf crouches, ready to pounce on me.

"What are you doing so far from the fight, wolf?" he spits at me. "Are you looking for something? Someone?"

I bark at him. He jumps slightly, not expecting a noise from me.

"Are you looking for an Angel?" His lips curl into an unflattering smile. His mouth is stained red. Oh Gods, it's stained with blood.

I growl and snarl at him, baring my teeth at him. He whips out a long and crooked dagger. My ears flatten against my head. I'm terrified out of my wits. The dagger doesn't help! It is crude but clearly sharp. The elf is balding with a few stringy black hairs. He has a bony body with long gangly limbs. His sharp teeth bare themselves to me and I swallow. I take in his weaponry: long nails, more like claws, and a knife. He also has sharp teeth and a longer reach.

He suddenly swipes at me, barely missing me with his knife. I jump backwards but force myself back forward. I duck below another swing and manage a solid bite on his shin. He howls and brings his knife down between my shoulder blades. I let go in pain. The elf suddenly drops to his knees and onto his face. Còiseam stands behind him looking horrified. His hands are glowing a light blue.

Did he just kill the elf? Còiseam nods in response to my question.

"Are you okay?" he asks me, coming toward me.

I shake my head right as he discovers the answer for himself. He gasps loudly.

"Oh God," he touches the fur surrounding the fresh wound. "Don't change into a human. Whatever you do, do not change. I can heal this. I can heal this. I can. I can do it. Oh God."

I lie down as the pain is finally sinking in at its full power. I whimper as he presses a palm against the wound. Something more painful than the wound surges through me, and I cry out again. Then, all at once, it stops.

I look up at him. He smiles down at me, relieved and tired.

"Let's get in here." He points to a partially charred building. "You need to change because I've located two pearls."

I follow him into the building.

"I won't look," he says, turning around.

I collapse my senses in to myself. This is getting smoother and smoother. I quickly unfold the makeshift pack Penny had made for me. My clothes are all wet with little patches of mud on them, but I pull on my clothing quickly. The cold wet clothing clings to me, and I shiver.

"Ready," I say with a little shudder.

He turns and frowns. "Your clothes are wet."

I say nothing.

"Here," he pulls a coat out from nowhere. "Put this on."

"Where did you-?" I start to say, but he puts a hand up.

"Don't question." He smiles his old obnoxious smile. "Just accept."

I glare at him and shrug the coat on. I can accept things as they are. I'm good at that.

"Where did you find two pearls together?"

"Someone else was collecting pearls and had two of them," Còiseam looks out the broken window. "They were either killed or forced to leave. Their loss is our gain, Mary. I can sense they are near. I think he hid them in a couple buildings over."

"How many do we have so far counting those two additional ones?" I ask as he takes my hand.

"We will have six." Còiseam takes my other hand. "Okay, we're going to transport. You may feel a little dizzy."

I groan right as we transport. We suddenly appear in a new building and I start to lean one way. He steadies me until the dizziness passes.

"Let's see here." Còiseam lets go of me and walks around the room. "They're in here. I can feel it."

I look across the room. Chairs are overturned, papers and books are scattered all over the room. It looks as though the book shelf is smashed entirely. The table is split into several pieces on the ground. Glass covers the ground.

"What happened here?" I look around the room. Is that blood on the wall? There is a large dark stain on the wall beside me with clear drippings onto the red carpet that has been wrinkled against the wall. It looks as though someone slid into the wall on the small carpet.

The pale yellow wallpaper is peeling with the blood. I wrinkle my nose. Còiseam comes to stand beside me. He looks at the wallpaper and then down at me.

"This is called war," he says sadly. "Someone died here and the body was removed. We need to get out of here quickly."

Còiseam walks back to the center of the room. I watch him carefully. What is he doing? His eyes are closed and his hands are raised. He must be feeling, sensing, for the pearls in the room. He suddenly opens his eyes and walks toward the split table. He moves some large pieces, tossing them aside.

"Did you find them?" I ask but I remain where I am.

"Yep," Còiseam pulls a white cloth from his tunic and picks up one pearl. He drops the pearl into his sack. He picks the second one up and looks at it with a smile. "Here's number six."

"Six," I breathe to myself. "That's a lot. We could heal Connor now if we wanted!"Còiseam drops the pearl in the sack and ties it to his belt again. He walks over to me and puts both hands on my shoulders. "Mary, I know you want to save him as soon as possible, but now is not the time we stop looking because we're impatient. We have to heal him right. We're halfway. We have to find six more. I know where five are, but I'm not sure that you're ready to get them."

"Wait," I close my eyes and step back from him. "We're only halfway? I thought we had six."

"Yes," Còiseam lowers his chin, looking at me imploringly. "But we have two for you, remember? So technically we only have four for Connor right now. Mary, we have to stay on track and find the rest of them. It's the only way to get his legs back. We can do it."

I step forward and hug him. "You're right. We have to keep going. Where are the others?"

He separates from me. "There are five in the Faerie District. I have yet to locate the last pearl."

"Where is the Faerie District?" I have never even heard of it.

"It's in the Northern Kingdom in the Grimsah," Còiseam says the last part quickly and waits for me to respond.

"Will you be with me?"

"Of course," Còiseam laughs. "I'll even be visible to others."

"Then let's go," I say and before I can stop myself I manage to plan the rest. "No one will miss me in the heat of all this fighting. They'll just think I went and hid or something. Let's go quickly. It shouldn't take too long. Right?"

"Right," Còiseam kisses me. "You just planned it all out, didn't you?"

I smile as he kisses me again. "Ready?"

"Ready," I say as he kisses me again. He wraps his arms around me and transports us.

CHAPTER TWENTY-FIVE

Hope

"Your Gods are coming for you," the being says, walking circles around me. "How does that make you feel?"

I say nothing, staring at the ground. My arms shake even with the small effort of holding myself up. My legs are folded awkwardly beneath me. I look up at him with, I hope, a murderous look.

He gives me a glance and laughs. "Are you mad at me?"

I still say nothing.

He suddenly flips a switch and kicks me in the chest, knocking me over. My head bounces against the cold ground with an audible crack.

"You would do well to answer me when I speak to you." His face is very close to mine. My eyes aren't focusing. I've lost too much blood.

He stands back up and smoothens his white tunic out, looking down at me with a pleasant smile.

"It's all too perfect really," the being smiles and sighs. He examines his nails. "After I kill you, the message will be very clear to my brothers and sisters on high. Hope is dead."

He laughs with delight at his own created irony. As he smiles at me, I suddenly realize who he is. As it dawns on me, it must show on my face for Leibus laughs loudly.

"I wondered when you would see through my disguise," he laughs. He waves a hand in front of his face, removing his disguise. The dark hair becomes blonde and wavy. The dark eyes lighten into an icy shade of green. His pale skin tans and his body lengthens and muscles up.

"Hope," he smiles. "Do you know why you're still alive?"

"Because you're out of your mind," I say between gritted teeth.

He gives me a smile and slaps me suddenly. "No, not that reason. You're alive because we need a witness to your death. You have given me all the information I need. I really have no more use for you. You're not responding to pain anymore and you're not responding to me anymore. You're no longer pleasurable for me. It's no fun to torture someone who won't play along."

"You are insane," I spit at him. I feel something warm runs down my chin. Blood, probably.

"I have one final question for you," Leibus smiles. "Well, actually I have several. I can sense someone coming to try to rescue you. I have time."

I wait.

"How does it feel knowing you have destroyed everything you hold dear?" Leibus squats in front of me. If I could, I would hit him, but I am far too weak to even move. "No one came looking for you until recently. How does it feel knowing that?"

I say nothing, but he raises a hand and I flinch.

"I don't know," I manage to say.

Leibus smiles amusingly at me. "Surely you have to feel something? You told me all about Psyche. You told me all about this Kaleb fellow. You told me all about prospective Eve. You almost told me everything."

"I told you nothing!" I raise my voice.

He slaps me harder this time. "Don't raise your voice to a superior. It's rude."

I cough and blink hard. Stars dance in front of my eyes. I cough again, bringing up blood.

"You're not superior to me," I say in a low and shaky voice. "You are the lowest of scum. You are the worst thing ever to have come into existence. You are a coward and a bully. You are nothing."

Leibus' mouth twitches. He slaps me again. "I do believe you're the one being tortured here. I have more power."

I felt myself snort. "That may be but I will always be more than you."

"Well," Leibus stands up and walks around me again. "Ms. High and Mighty, you have just told a scum like me everything you know."

"I told you nothing," I spit. My voice echoes in the room. I receive a swift kick to the stomach again. I curl over, coughing.

"Mm," Leibus muses above me. "That is true, I suppose. I extracted the information while you were unconscious. You tried so hard to stay conscious. You knew what would happen. But I knew that you could take only so much pain. It's elementary knowledge, Angel."

"Leibus," I say, struggling to push myself back up. "You will never know everything I know."

Leibus throws me across the room with a wave of Darke energy. I hit the back wall and crumple into a pile at his feet. He bends over and forces himself to speak in a normal tone. He voice shakes. "My name is Lucifer."

Suddenly a light appears in the cell, blinding both of us. Leibus stands up and faces the light.

"Just in time," he says.

"No!" I scream.

In a swift motion, he twists around and stabs me in the stomach with an iron rod. He sends Darke energy and dust down the rod, conducting it into my body. I remember this iron rod. I had held onto it early on when my legs were failing me. He twists the rod inside me. I can't stop myself from screaming. I can feel my soul losing its grip on my body. A light brightens as the original light dims. A Goddess screams and rushes toward me as Leibus disappears.

Her hands find my face. I'm fading. Her hands are so warm and kind. She's helping me leave my body. I can't resist. My body is too weak to return to and I let her lift me to the light. She is comforting.

I give a final sigh and loosen my grip. Sobbing, she lifts me to the light.

"Thank you, Psyche," I say to her as I pass from her hands to the light.

CHAPTER TWENTY-SIX

Mary

We land in the thickness of the Grimsah. The trees seem Darke and leaning over of us. Pale green vines run all over the trees and ground. It's like a temperate jungle. The darkness from the trees makes the Forest seem all the more wicked.

Còiseam looks down at me. He suddenly smiles. It isn't a pleasant smile. It's almost wicked. I instinctively take a step backwards.

"No," he grabs me. "This is good. The Faeries have five pearls. I can sense it."

"Why do they have five?" I'm instantly engaged again.

Còiseam shakes his head. "Some sort of ritual, I imagine. Mary, the Faeries are very strange creatures. Don't let them manipulate you."

"Manipulate me?" I ask him, but he seems distracted.

Còiseam is leading me down a path clear of vines. He's holding me tightly, almost too tightly. I look up at him and notice the muscles in his jaw working.

"Còiseam," I stop him, taking his wrist. "What's wrong with you?"

Còiseam looks down at me. "Something is about to happen and we cannot intervene. The Forest works in its own way and if we intervene it will turn on us. Do not react. Do you understand?"

"I-" I shake my head unconsciously.

"Do. Not. React." Còiseam's face is close to mine. The intensity scares me.

Suddenly, a being stumbles onto the path in front of us. The being looks to be a human man. His forearm has a large gash in it and blood drips down his fingertips.

"Help me!" he cries, running toward us. Còiseam steps in front of me. "Please help me! For the love of God, help me!"

God? Singular? I look around Còiseam at the man. Còiseam and I are silent. I'm too terrified to move or say something. I feel like I should help him, but Còiseam told me not to react. I also don't want to anger whatever is chasing after him and become its next victim.

He starts to come forward but is shoved sideways by a blast of Darke energy. I dig my nails into Còiseam's arm and bite my tongue. Do not react, he said.

My skin crawls as a Darke Angel descends from the trees. The Angel looks at us and I feel my stomach turn. The Darke Angel has long black hair that seems to dust off into nothing. Her wings flutter lightly, scattering Darkeness around her. The plants wilt and blacken around her. She has white skin, pure as snow, with black eyes as soulless as Leibus himself. The Darke Angel's eyes flit to Còiseam and then to me. She smiles briefly before turning on her prey.

The human scoots backwards, trying to find footing to get up. He screams wordlessly. His face, white with terror, turns to us.

"Please help me!" he screams. His voice breaks. "God, save me!"

The Darke Angel suddenly appears on top of him and drives a shaft made of Darke dust into his heart. He screams again and the hairs on the back of my neck stand. The human dies after a few minutes. The Darke Angel stands back up and looks at us. The silence in the Forest is horribly loud. I dare not move. She looks back down at the human, sending dust everywhere in just that simple movement. She raises the human up, his body limp in the air. She lifts her arms up and Darkeness pours out of her and into him. The Darkeness swirls out of her hands and wrists gracefully.

Suddenly, his body begins to thrash and he begins screaming again. Oh Gods, I thought he was dead! I grip Còiseam's arm harder and I bite down on my tongue. Blood fills my mouth as I watch the body twitch and thrash in the air.

The human's back arches and he emits an ear-splitting scream. His skin seems to pale and his hair darkens. It's no longer the honey-blonde color; it is black as coal. The human's feet touch the ground and he curls in on himself. Darke wings burst from his back and dust flies everywhere. It stops just short of Còiseam and me.

The human rises up and screams again. The muscles in his arms are flexed and the veins in his neck are prominent. Some of his skin darkens, forming some sort of tattoo. Tendrils and swirls race up his bare back, disappearing into his hair. The tattoo spreads to the side of his face and down his chest. I knew Darke Angels have markings and tattoos such as this, but I have never ever seen a marking as extensive as this. Most Darke Angels have these dark markings to identify who they are. I knew from impromptu history lessons with Kaleb that the markings are an identification system. Leibus likes to name his Angels after an Old World religious book. I can't quite remember the name of the Old World book, but I know it was the book of the Christians. The mark on the human is still swirling into intricate patterns, some sinking into his skin and some remain on top of his skin, staining it permanently.

I have never seen a Darke Angel being formed.

The human stops screaming abruptly and turns to look at us.

"In due time," the Darke Angel says. She takes his hand and they disappear in a shimmer of Darke dust.

For several long minutes, Còiseam and I do not speak. I clutch his arm as tightly as before, staring at the Darke dust on the ground where they just stood.

"C-Còiseam," I say, my voice hoarse.

"Mary," Còiseam says without looking at me. "Let's keep going."

"Aren't we going to talk about what we just witnessed?" I take several big steps to be at his side rather than behind him.

"No," Còiseam says stiffly. "This is the way of the Forest."

"That doesn't mean it's right," I say quietly to myself.

Còiseam whirls on me. "No, here it is right. This is the Grimsah Forest, Mary. Here, things happen the way they are supposed to happen! The only thing we can do… well, we practice self-preservation!"

"That sounds like cowardice to me," I say, looking away from him.

Còiseam's jaw twitches. "It's not cowardice. It is self-preservation. This is the Grimsah Forest, Mary. If we had intervened, we would have met the same fate. Not reacting was our best option."

I am silent. I suppose he is right. I didn't really want to intervene, but I just have the feeling that I should have. I know I wouldn't have, but I'm surprised Còiseam didn't intervene. He seems so honorable and brave. He just seems to have so much wisdom and courage. I don't know if I'm surprised or disappointed. Or both.

I look up and realize we are closer to the Faerie District than I thought. Tall thatch houses nearly blend in with the forest. I see pathways and bridges between the tall, thick trees. Houses are built on the ground and in the trees.

"This Faerie District used to be the greatest in all the world," Còiseam says grimly. "But the Forest has been eating it."

"Eating it?"

"Sometimes," Còiseam looks down at me. His face is a mask. I can't read it. "Sometimes, a house will disappear overnight because the Forest took it over as its own."

"It can do that?"

"Mary," Còiseam stops for a moment. "I don't ever want you to forget this. The Grimsah Forest is not just a forest. It is a being. Everything about the Forest is alive and connected to one soul, or rather, lack thereof. The Forest is a single being and it knows every being's movement within it. It takes anything that isn't like itself and it perverts it. The Forest eats Light or neutral beings and spits out Darke beings."

"Like that human?" I ask. My voice is almost inaudible. I feel sick.

"Like that human," Còiseam looks up at the Faerie District. "But that human was different. He was a Christian."

"What's a Christian?" I ask and we slow down to a stop.

"A Christian is a human, usually," he looks anxiously toward the houses again, "who believes in only one supreme God. Christianity ruled the Old World."

We start walking again. Còiseam really wants to get out of the Forest. I don't blame him.

"Christianity was almost lost during the Ravage." Còiseam's eyes are scanning the Forest. The Forest knows we're here. I wonder if it'll try to attack us. "Despite seeing the Gods, many humans still believe that their Messiah will come rescue them."

I don't say anything.

"Faith," Còiseam looks down at me suddenly, "is a powerful thing once established soundly. It blinds the mind and makes hope seem bigger than it actually is. Faith and hope are two things people must cling to."

I look down at my feet as we walk. I almost can't believe some people don't believe in all the Gods. We've seen them. We've all seen them many times. How can someone be so blinded that they stop using their reason?

"How do the Christians explain the Gods?"

Còiseam smiles down at me. "I knew you'd have a question. You're so curious, Mary. You always have to find closure, always have to know the answer, always have to complete something," he chuckles. "The Christians believe that their God created these other, and in their belief, 'lesser' Gods to rescue them. They believe their God made and sent all these beings that weren't present in the Old World down to protect them. They believe the new beings are here to serve and protect them."

I snort. "How presumptious!"

"It's the only way to explain something they don't want to accept," Còiseam shrugs. "Most believe Chaos is the true God. The original God."

I nod. "Why do you know everything?"

Còiseam gives me my favorite smile. "I just do."

I plant a peck on his cheek as we step into the Faerie District.

"Okay," Còiseam says in a low voice. "The Faeries know why we're here and they won't give the pearls up easily. They are probably using the pearls for Darke magic. That has to be the only way they have survived; otherwise, the Forest would have eaten them by now."

"Oh," I look around, suddenly uneasy. "I didn't think of that!"

Còiseam nods. Fear seems to fill his eyes. I watch him carefully. He looks down, but his mask has been drawn up. No fear. No emotions. Nothing.

"The Faeries will try to manipulate us," Còiseam is still speaking in a low voice. He looks around constantly. "If we need to, we will have to kill them."

"What about the Forest?" I ask fearfully. "Won't it be angry with us killing part of its creatures?"

Còiseam shakes his head. "If anything, it'll help us. These Faeries aren't native to the Forest. The Forest wants them gone and it also enjoys kills. If anything, it'll assist us. Do not attack the Forest or any of its creatures if they assist us. Do you understand?"

I nod slowly. "Còiseam, I'm scared."

Còiseam hugs me tightly. "I know, angel. I know. But we have to do this. For Connor, right?"

"For Connor," I swallow, feeling brave for the first time in a long time.

"Step away from the girl, evil spirit!" a voice suddenly sounds from behind us.

We turn around quickly. Còiseam still has me in his arms. Several Faeries holding staffs are watching us warily. Their blue skin and light hair stands out in contrast with the dark forest. They move forward slightly. An older female with white hair beckons to me.

"Come," she says, motioning me over. "Please! Come here, child! That man isn't who you think he is! He is an evil spirit and he will destroy you. He's only after your soul!"

Còiseam hugs me tighter. "Don't listen to them. You know how I feel about you."

"He will destroy you!" the Faeries beseech me. "Please, child, come! We can heal your soul!"

"Lies," Còiseam hisses under his breath.

"How can they see you?" I ask, looking around at the approaching Faeries.

"The Forest reveals all things," Còiseam says. He starts to continue but stops when a Faerie takes a bigger step toward us.

I grip Còiseam tighter. The Faeries even seem threatening now. What would they do to me if they got me away from Còiseam? They seem so evil with their long gangly limbs, wicked green eyes, and horrid voices. Their voices sound like they belong to the dead.

The Faeries start to inch closer to us.

"Mary," Còiseam says. He sounds fearful.

Faeries are circling us, moving in closer.

"Mary," Còiseam swallows. "We're going to have to attack and hope the Forest helps us."

"Do you really think it'll help us?" I eye the Faeries moving in on us. Còiseam hugs me tighter. Fear pumps my blood faster.

"The Forest doesn't know our intent," Còiseam says. "It just knows that we wandered in here willingly. If we attack non-native beings, maybe it'll think we are on its side."

"I'm not hearing anything definite," I say. "I kinda need something definite."

"I can always transport us ou-" he cuts off and suddenly looks directly at a Faerie in front of us. "You. I can sense the pearls on you! For what wicked purpose do you have five pearls?"

"Silence, evil spirit!" the Faerie snaps back. "These pearls are protected. They shall not fall into Darke hands!"

"They will be used for a good purpose!" Còiseam yells back. His arms are still tight around me. "Hand them over or prepare to have them taken from you!"

"Over my dead body," the Faerie hisses, stepping dangerously close.

"Mary," Còiseam whispers to me. "Change into your wolf form. You're strongest then. We have to attack them and hope for the best."

"I trust you," I say, looking up at him.

"And," Còiseam hesitates, "I love you."

Before I can say anything, a Faerie grabs my arm and yanks me out of Còiseam's arms. Còiseam falls onto his hands and knees and looks up at me. The Faerie is dragging me backwards. I collapse my knees and send my senses outward. I breathe out and land on four paws.

I turn on the Faerie with a snarl. Courage, I think to myself. Courage is what it will take now. I lunge forward and sink my teeth into a Faerie. I taste the salty-tasting blood in my mouth. The other Faeries react violently. Two jump on top of me, forcing me onto my stomach. I thrash, trying to bump them off of me.

"She's too far gone!" one Faerie shouts, approaching me slowly with a long dagger in hand.

"She has spilled innocent blood," another says from above me.

I thrash back, trying to get a look at Còiseam. Several Faeries are on top of him and kicking him. I howl and bark, thrashing harder.

Suddenly the Faerie with the dagger is thrown backward into a tree. A Darke Angel appears behind him and snaps his neck. There is a shattering scream and the Faeries around me are lifted off of me. The Darke Angels rip into them, tearing them apart and blasting them with Darke energy.

I turn and run toward the group of Faeries on top of Còiseam. I jump on the back of one of them and sink my nails into the skin. I close my eyes and clamp my teeth down on the Faerie's neck. With a single jerk, I pull the head off and jump from the Faerie's back.

I snarl and leap at another Faerie. A house collapses nearby and several screams follow. The Darke Angels are killing each and every Faerie. The Faeries surrounding Còiseam and me are blasted off their feet by two Darke

Angels. The Darke Angels don't even give me a passing glance but instead converge on their prey.

Còiseam grabs my fur and helps himself up. He has a cut lip and a bloody nose. He wipes the blood from his face with his wrist. He points to a Faerie lying on the ground dying. The Faerie's abdomen is being eaten out by Darke dust. I grimace.

Còiseam stands over the Faerie.

"Over your dead body," he says with venom.

Còiseam stretches his hand out over the Faerie and clenches his fist suddenly. The Faerie's neck is wrenched sideways with an audible crack. It is a sickly crack, one that goes straight through me to my core. The sound is eerily beautiful. It is an ugly beauty. The sound almost resonates within me. I'm frozen for a moment. My eyes feel stuck on the Faerie's body. I take in the broken form and then my eyes move up to Còiseam. I catch a strange look on his face, a crooked smile creeping across his face.

Còiseam spreads his hand again and a pouch from the Faerie's belt unties itself and lifts into Còiseam's hand.

"Let's get out of here before the Forest decides to turn on us," Còiseam leans over me and hugs.

I feel myself fading out from the Forest. The familiar sucking sensation of the transport grips me and I squeeze my eyes shut. It'll be over in a second.

CHAPTER TWENTY-SEVEN

Mary

Còiseam transports us back to our tent in Naem. Còiseam collapses onto the blankets. He gives me a smile which splits his lip again. Blood dribbles out.

I take hold of my senses and collapse them into myself. I fall forward in front of Còiseam. I don't even care that I'm naked. I grab one of my shirts and shrug it on quickly. I jerk pants on and sit down in front of him. Còiseam smiles again and more blood dribbles down his chin.

"You have a cut on your forehead," he says, reaching up. "It's bleeding pretty badly."

I grab one of Mason's shirts and hold it up to Còiseam's lip.

"You were so brave," I smile at him. "I can't believe we did it."

Còiseam gives me a smile, but it doesn't reach his eyes. "I killed someone."

I finally recognize the look. Pain. He's in pain and not just from the brutal kicking. Còiseam drops his gaze and won't make eye contact with me. He holds the wadded up shirt to his mouth and stares at the corner of the tent.

"Còiseam," I say, taking his face in my hands. "We did what we had to do."

Còiseam looks up at me. His eyes are watery. "I make beings. I protect beings. I guide beings. I don't destroy them."

"Còiseam," I say gently and stroke his face with my fingertips. "I killed someone, too. We did what we had to do."

I can't believe what I'm saying. Am I so callous now to war that taking my first life means nothing to me? I feel indifferent. Those Faeries were evil and I vanquished them. If anything, I have done a great deed.

The pale yellow tent makes Còiseam's face seem worse and paler than it should be. Còiseam holds my gaze.

"I'm sorry." He looks away again. "You must think I am unreasonable."

"No, no!" I say, catching his eyes again. "It's perfectly reasonable! It is very traumatic taking a life. Còiseam, it is normal for you to feel this way!"

Còiseam smiles again. "You are the perfect being."

"That's you," I say, leaning in and moving the shirt out of the way. I kiss him softly on the lips.

Còiseam smiles at me again. "Listen, I have to go soon. Father Sulibe can heal me. I'll keep the pearls together and try sensing out the last one."

I nod slowly. "That's right. We only have one left."

"The others will be here in about an hour," Còiseam says. "Just tell them after they found the Angel, you came back here with another pack. You've been waiting for them to return since."

"Got it," I say. "May I have one more kiss?"

Còiseam leans in, takes the shirt away from his mouth, and kisses me. I sigh and his kisses immediately become more urgent. I feel something within me stir and I grab him. He moans in pain and in pleasure. I have grabbed his sore side.

Còiseam rolls on top of me and kisses me hard. We're breathing harder and his hands are all over me. I kiss his mouth, his jaw, his temples, and his neck. He almost frantically kisses me as if he's trying to fit all his love in at this moment. I can feel his lips on my ear, my jaw, then my mouth, my cheekbones, and then my mouth again.

He jerks my shirt up and I fumble with the tassels on his tunic. He smiles, unties them, and then helps me out of the rest of my clothing. I swallow and look up at him. He smiles reassuringly.

"Just keep the shirt." I push the shirt back to his mouth which has started to bleed again. "It's stained anyway."

"So is this," he says, holding up my own shirt. I didn't realize it had been under us. It has some blood on it. "But it's probably blood from your cut." He winks.

I put my clothes on gingerly, putting on a new shirt from out of my pack. I move carefully, newly sore in a very new place. I smile up at Còiseam. He gives me a happy smile back. His smile begins to fade and his eyes focus on some unknown point behind me.

"Oh no," Còiseam frowns. "Father Sulibe knows what we just did."

"What?" I frown. I look around the tent. "How?"

"He sensed it," Còiseam frowns.

"How?"

Còiseam shakes his head. "He just did. I'll go see what he thinks. Recently, he told me you and I could... have relations."

"He won't change his mind, will he?" I ask, scooting closer to him.

"Unless something changed that is better for you," Còiseam tucks a strand of hair behind my ear, "then no."

"Okay," I wring my hands.

"I'll be back."

"Okay." I smile mischievously. "See that you are."

He vanishes.

I stare at my hands in my lap. Is something wrong with me? I kill someone and then make love to Còiseam? What's wrong with me? I stare hard at my hands, almost believing there will be some sign of my killing on them. These hands have killed. I bit someone's head off. I swallow. Now alone, I am the victim of my thoughts and conscious. Guilt begins to fill me and, to my surprise, tears land on my hands.

Suddenly, a blinding light appears in the tent. I scream and fall backwards, kicking up blankets accidentally. Kaleb stretches his hands out. I stare blankly at him.

Why is he here?

"It's just me!" He spreads his hands out. "I'm sorry I scared you! Man, this transporting thing has some getting use- What's wrong? Are you okay?"

He leans forward and looks sincerely concerned. A few more tears roll down my cheeks. He takes my hands into his. "What's wrong, Mary?"

Oh Gods. No. This is not happening! He cannot do this to me now!

Unless something changed that is better for you...

"I," I look down, avoiding his eyes. This is just too much. I need to focus on one crisis at a time. I killed someone. Can I tell him? He is so noble, so honorable. How can I tell him that I have killed someone?

"I killed someone."

Kaleb's fingers lift my chin up. My eyes reluctantly find his.

"Mary." His face is so kind and understanding. "War is death. It is alright. You have helped the cause."

I sniffle. "I've never killed someone before."

"Neither have I," Kaleb pulls me toward him. "But these things must be done. We're fighting the good fight for our Gods."

I nod. I let him pull me close to him. I lean against his chest. My skin feels like it is on fire now. Good Gods, can I make up my mind? Here I was just kissing Còiseam and now I'm with Kaleb! Sure, I'm not supposed to be kissing Còiseam now… maybe… but I feel loyal to him now.

Còiseam suddenly appears. I jump visibly and Kaleb holds me tighter.

"It's alright," he says soothingly. He rubs my shoulders. "You liberated that soul you killed. That soul is now released and can be good."

I sniffle and watch Còiseam. Còiseam looks hurt, but his stony mask takes over. He gives Kaleb a long, hard look. He looks at me and my heart feels weak.

"Father Sulibe," Còiseam sounds as though he could cry, too. "He sent me here to tell you that we can no longer have a relationship. It is the best for you. The best that is for you has already arrived." He stares again hard at Kaleb. I try to detach myself from Kaleb but he holds on tighter to me, thinking I'm still upset about murdering someone.

I give him a pleading look.

"I will be your best friend," Còiseam says with a small smile. "Don't worry about me. Father Sulibe has healed my heart, too. Let Kaleb heal yours. He has come to form a relationship with you. Tomorrow you will wake up with no feelings for me other than our friendship. You'll forget. Don't worry, angel, it will be the same for me."

I shake my head slightly. I don't want to forget his love. I don't want to forget! How can this happen? How can we make love like that and the next day forget? How can Father Sulibe do this to me? To us?

"Mary," he says. I close my eyes. "Mary, it has to be this way. Kaleb loves you. He can heal you, and he is the man you need. He is a part of your destiny, of your future. I am just your guide to your destiny. Don't worry. All will be well and all will be as it should."

But how can this be so sudden? How? Why?

He gives me a sad look. "We will have forgotten about our relationship tomorrow when we wake up. Don't worry. Be happy. Kaleb loves you and you know you love him back. Mary, I know we had something, but you've always loved him. Now the tides have shifted and it's Kaleb's time now."

Còiseam suddenly disappears without another word. I cry a little more. I have killed someone and lost a love all in one day. Somehow, losing a love seems to hurt more. Kaleb rubs my shoulders.

"Mary," Kaleb says, rubbing my shoulder. "Do you want me to stay?"

"Yes," I say between little sobs. "I want you to stay. Um, but what about Hope?"

"She's still out on her mission," Kaleb says. "We're not together anymore."

I sit back and look at him. "I'm sorry. What happened?"

"Don't be," Kaleb smiles and a dimple appears on his right cheek. I restrain myself from touching it. "Hope and I agreed to be friends. I realized that I didn't really love her. She and I realized that we weren't meant for each other. Then she left on her mission and I think she's doing well. I'm doing well. I think the separation has given us time to breathe and think."

"Oh," is all I say. Kaleb is worse than me! He can't make up his mind either.

A hand suddenly pulls the flaps of the tent back and Mason appears.

"Oh Gods!" He cries happily and looks behind him to a pair of legs. "She's in here! Mary, how did you get here? Kaleb… what are you doing here?"

I feel Kaleb shrug. "I felt like I should be here. It turns out I was kind of needed. Mary's a little upset…She killed someone today."

Mason's face softens. "Oh, Mary. Don't be upset. You killed a bad guy!"

I look down. Bad guy or no, I didn't want to kill anyone.

"You did kill a bad guy, right?" Ardon says jokingly as he comes in behind Mason. He folds his legs and sits down. He instantly pulls the blankets around himself. Mason snorts.

I nod my head. "Yes, I killed a bad guy."

"Then did you run back here? How did you get here?" Mason asks, sitting down across me.

Penny comes in and sits down next to Ardon. She steals a blanket from him and focuses her attention on me.

"I came back here," I force the lie out. "I was scared."

"It's alright." Penny smoothens my hair against my head. "I'm fairly certain we won the battle."

"With a great cost," Mason murmurs.

I don't say anything. Honestly, it doesn't matter to me. There is too much going on in my own little life for me to worry about the war. Of course the Gods will win. I don't see why everyone is adamant about fighting for the Gods, fighting the good fight! The Gods will win. They always do.

CHAPTER TWENTY-EIGHT

Psyche

"Goddess! Psyche!" Someone suddenly calls out from behind me.

I turn and look down the long marble hallway. I have just come out of a meeting with the Greater Gods. A lanky Faerie is running after me. I recognize her from the Infirmary.

"Goddess," she calls, putting a hand up as if it could stop me from moving. "Goddess, please!"

"I hear you," I say, turning toward her.

The Faerie is breathing heavily. She's still in her uniform and has her black hair tied neatly back.

"My name is Natalya," she says between quick breaths, "I work in the Infirmary. I recently took leave to go visit my family in the Faerie District in the Grimsah and it's gone!"

I frown. "Gone? What do you mean by that?"

Natalya's face suddenly floods with despair. She puts a hand against her face.

"It's gone, Goddess!" Natalya looks as though she may burst into tears.

I can feel her soul. It's suddenly quite vulnerable. Something terrible has happened. I try to sense around her, trying to find a feel for the tragedy she is trying to relay to me. I haven't felt any disturbances lately. Have I missed something?

"Let us walk somewhere and speak in private," I say, guiding her with a hand on her back.

"Yes, Goddess," Natalya's voice is significantly quieter.

We walk out of the temple and toward my temple, which is close by. We walk through the small garden area dedicated to Gaia. Natalya looks at everything we pass carefully, taking in everything. I watch her just as carefully. Something has definitely happened.

We enter into my temple and I lead her past the statue of Eros and me and into my rooms. Natalya takes in everything. She looks at each painting carefully and seems very attentive to details.

I gesture toward the pale purple couch in my consultation room. Natalya sits down, looking slightly uncomfortable. She looks at me pathetically.

"If I may," I begin, clasping my hands together. "I think it would be easier for you if I go directly to your memory. If I'm correct, you probably have an excellent memory?"

Natalya nods. "How will you do that, Goddess?"

"All you have to do," I say, smiling encouragingly, "is trust me. When I put my hands on your head, think of what you are trying to tell me and I will do the rest."

Eros suddenly walks into the room from the hallway leading to our bedroom.

"Oh," he takes a half step back, "I didn't realize you were with someone, my dear."

"No," I beckon him to come toward us with my hand. "You actually are needed here. Would you please put her at ease while I go through her memory?"

"My God," Natalya says, bowing slightly.

"No need, child," Eros smiles and sits down beside her. He takes her large hand into his and Natalya visibly relaxes.

I put my hands on her head, sinking my fingers beneath her hair and onto her scalp. I'm pulled into her memory and find myself walking on the path that leads to the Faerie District. I recognize everything I pass and so does Natalya.

Natalya begins to feel confused as she draws nearer to the village. She doesn't see anything, no houses, no buildings, and none of her people. The Forest is too quiet. Natalya steps into what would be the entrance to the large village.

Bodies. Bodies are everywhere. Natalya grabs her face and nearly screams. She looks left and right and sees only bodies. Her people are lying in disarray everywhere. Darke dust and blood cover the bodies and the buildings. Natalya feels panic shooting up her throat. Her hands begin to shake.

However, the bodies have already started to decompose. This happened a while ago. I can feel Natalya's sadness and panic mixing into anger. Natalya looks around the bloody scene. She sees her family, her friends, and her leaders. Everyone is dead. Children are dead. The elders are dead. Everyone she knows and loves is dead.

Natalya drops to her knees and looks up at the wicked trees. How could this have happened? she thinks. Then Natalya knows who is responsible.

Father Sulibe. She knows he is responsible for this.

Then Natalya sees it. I can feel her anger come to a peak when she spies the wolf print. She squats down and puts her hand against the print. Werewolf print to be sure. Natalya stands up suddenly.

I sense no more in the memory and I pull my hands from her head.

"Did you see it?" Natalya says suddenly.

"I saw it," I say with terrible sorrow. I pause for a moment to recount the recent souls I have ministered to in the heavens. Their souls are not here. "I saw it."

"How could this have happened?" Natalya leans forward. Her anger is still alive and well within her.

"When did you go and discover this?" I ask her.

Eros sits quietly. He knows I will tell him later what I saw.

"Three days ago."

I nod and pace about the room. Both Eros and Natalya watch me in silence. I ignore them and think. Something Darke must have attacked those beings.

"Who is Father Sulibe?" I turn and ask Natalya. That thought from her memory did not escape me. It captured me.

Natalya's face darkens and her accent is thickened when she responds. "He is a demon."

"Tell me about him," I push her a little.

She looks away from me and fixes her eyes on the corner of a table holding eternal flowers.

"When I was just a girl," Natalya begins, "my mother told me stories before bed. Most of them were made up or silly, fanciful, and wild tales of princesses and princes, but this story was real. This story was one all the mothers told their children. Father Trusie Sulibe was a mortal human until he made a deal with Leibus. Sulibe, you see, was cursed by a demigod when he tried to steal the demigod's wife from him. My mother never went into detail over that, but Sulibe was cursed. His appearance changed every day and no one ever knew him. He had no family, no friends, and no woman would ever take him. Sulibe gave up the Gods, convinced they would never forgive him for his lust. After many years, he realized he could use his curse to his advantage. He could make his curse a blessing in disguise. He knew the only way to get what he wanted was to make a deal with a God. Leibus was the only God who would hear him. Sulibe wanted immortality. In exchange for immortality, Sulibe gave up his soul and his life to Leibus. Sulibe's name was also changed. Trusie Sulibe was not his first and original name, but my mother never knew his first name. We only know his new name. Trusie Sulibe is an anagram for Leibus is True. Leibus made Sulibe his direct slave, almost. This, of course, was back when Leibus was struggling to be his own God, his own ruler. No one knew Leibus was truly dark and evil. Sulibe made a deal with him and then Leibus changed."

Natalya looks up at me. "Sulibe was stuck. He was soulless and forced to do Leibus' commands. Leibus put him on standby, told him to wait for a prospective Darke Angel to come along. Then Sulibe was given the thirteen pearls to set up the legacy of Eve."

I sit silently, stunned by this story of a being I never knew existed. Natalya is staring at the floor as though she is frightened. I watch Natalya for a moment. Eros moves slightly, drawing my attention. I make eye contact with him and he nods. I need to ask her more questions.

"You mean to say," I begin, "that this Father Sulibe is a direct line to Leibus and to Eve?"

Natalya nods. "Yes."

"Why would Sulibe attack your village?" I frown and cross my arms. Eros, in the corner of my eye, seems to finally be making the connections.

"Sulibe," Natalya says slowly. She looks up at me. The pause between the words is killing me. It's too much.

"Yes?" I push her.

"Sulibe is after the pearls. He's collecting the pearls for Eve. Our village had many pearls, but he has killed everyone and the pearls are gone."

"Eve is here?" Eros asks, his voice steady and controlled.

"Eve is coming," Natalya looks at both of us separately. "Eve is coming and unless we find the prospective or Sulibe, she will be here before the solstice."

"Why the solstice?" Eros asks and then looks at me as though I may know. "Why the solstice?"

"The solstice," Natalya folds her hands in her lap, trying to control the shaking that had taken over moments ago, "is when Sulibe became immortal. The winter solstice is when he is his most powerful."

"How do you know all of this?" I ask her. "Did it come from your mother?"

"Yes," she says simply. "The legend of Eve itself comes from my people. Because we live in the Forest, we are privy to all its secrets. The legend of Eve is true, but it's not really a legend. It is a prophecy, and it will come true."

I close my eyes. This all makes sense. I know Eve is out there right now and I perceived she would rise before the solstice. Perhaps she will rise on the solstice by Sulibe's hand. This all fits together.

"Sulibe will raise her?" I ask Natalya. "According to the lege- err, prophesy, Eve will rise from a betrayal in her mortal form. The betrayal will be parallel to a wonderful event. Eh, Eve will rise in the hands of a being who is not a being."

I put my hand against my forehead. That seems to be all of the prophecy I can remember.

A being who is not a being...

"A being who is not a being?" I ask Natalya before she can answer my previous question.

"Sulibe will not raise her," she says abruptly as if she is trying to spit the words out as quickly as she can. "Sulibe will not raise her directly. Alongside his immortality, Sulibe was given power over his own creation."

"What does that mean?" Eros asks, slightly irritated. "Only Gods can create."

"Sulibe can create his own beings." Natalya squints her eyes, searching for the right words. She presses her lips together. "He can create beings out of dust, but they aren't full beings. They only exist when he calls them. They are only solid when he wants them to be seen by those he wants to see, and known by those he wants to know."

"So these beings cannot be detected by me?" I start pacing the room, deep in thought.

"Yes," Natalya sighs. "They can be detected by you, but it'll be by chance. You can't search for them."

"Basically," I say, stopping in my pacing, "I won't find them unless they want to be found."

"Correct," Natalya says, watching me continue in my pacing.

"We need to call another meeting," Eros stands up, turns, and looks down at Natalya. He looks between us. "Natalya, you need to tell all of this to Chaos."

CHAPTER TWENTY-NINE

Mary

"Mary!" Mason comes into the tent. Kaleb, Penny, Ardon and I look up. Mason seems even more pleased to see everyone in the tent. "I got a letter from Connor! He wants us to meet him in the Infirmary!"

"He can see us?" Ardon seems extremely excited to see his best friend.

"Oh my Gods!" Penny exclaims, jumping to her feet.

I get to my feet and push past Mason. "What are you waiting for? Let's go!"

The five of us rush out of the wolf campsite and up the grassy hill toward the entrance of the Infirmary. We step off of the grass and onto the white marble sidewalk. We follow the sidewalk around the temple and toward the infirmary. Mason and Ardon are talking excitedly, Penny is quiet, and Kaleb and I walk beside each other.

Our hands brush against each other every couple steps. Each time it gives me a small shock of pleasure. I don't know if he's doing it on purpose or if it's just chance. I would like to think he's doing it on purpose. Ever since he told me in the tent that he and Hope weren't together anymore, he's been closer to me. Ever since he comforted me after killing someone, it's been different. Perhaps he has realized that he actually may love me.

His hand touches mine again and I dismiss the thought. The sidewalk is small. He's not doing it on purpose. How could he love me? No, Kaleb doesn't love me.

Kaleb takes a couple larger steps suddenly, putting himself in front of me, and opens the door for us. We all enter and he follows behind. I stop short when I see the nurses, the Faerie nurses. Will they know I have killed one of their own? Sure, it was an evil Faerie, but it was still their species. I eye the nurses nervously.

"Mary?" Mason turns and looks back at me. I didn't realize I had stopped walking. The others turn and look back at me. "Are you ok?"

I nod stiffly. "Just nervous to finally see Connor! I wonder how much he's changed!"

Mason speaks to one of the nurses at the front desk.

Ardon grabs me and jiggles my arms. "I'm *so* excited! It's been *months* since we've seen him!"

"I know!" I say, bringing out my enthusiasm. I am practically bouncing in my boots. "I can't wait to see him."

"Right this way," the nurse's voice carries over ours, grabbing our attentions. We look to her eagerly, waiting to see him. "He's outside with Zenyo."

"Who is Zenyo?" Ardon suddenly asks.

The nurse turns and looks back at us. "Did he tell you to meet him here?"

Mason frowns, but Penny answers. "Yes, we haven't seen him in months. He told us to come here. Is he alright?"

The nurse smiles a knowing smile as though she is privy to something we don't know. She continues walking and leads us down the hall and toward the door to the outside. She doesn't say anything but briskly walks ahead of us. Kaleb holds the door open for me again and follows me as we step outside.

"Hey," Kaleb suddenly says, brushing closely against me again. "I think that's Connor's chair!"

We look sideways to see his empty chair sitting in the grass pressed against a bench. The nurse smiles and begins to walk back into the Infirmary.

"He'll be down shortly," she smiles.

"Down?" Mason turns to face us. "What does she mean by down?"

I suddenly become aware of a dark shadow growing larger and larger over us. Ardon looks around in alarm and looks up. Penny looks up and screams. I shield the sun with my hand and look up. A large, black dragon is descending nearly on top of us. I yelp but am pushed backward by Kaleb. He shields me with his body. Ardon stands beside me, holding onto my sleeve. Penny is behind Mason and beside me.

The dragon's wings beat the air more powerfully, slowly lowering itself down to land. Two enormous legs touch down delicately. The beast flaps its wings one last time before tucking them against its sides. The dragon regards us with one large green eye, turning its head from side to side, examining and analyzing us.

Kaleb's body is tense. I can feel the muscles in his back through his skin. I tighten my hold on his shirt, peering over his shoulder. My eyes catch something silver glinting off of the black dragon's back. A Rider in full leather and metal armor sits regally atop his dragon. He has a quiver of arrows tied to his back and a bow slung over his shoulders. The Rider suddenly laughs at us.

"You people look terrified!"

"Connor!" Penny suddenly squeals.

The Rider laughs. I blink, trying to really believe this is my brother.

"Connor?" Mason steps forward but is still holding onto Penny, unwilling to let her go.

"Hello!" Connor laughs again. "Would you mind pushing my chair closer to me?"

I look at the chair beside me. I push it through the grass and between Mason and Kaleb toward the dragon. Kaleb touches my shoulder.

"Relax," Connor flicks his wrist and begins to unstrap his legs from the saddle. "Zenyo won't harm you guys."

I push the chair until Connor tells me to stop. He smiles and tells us to step back. I stare, open mouthed, as the dragon's tail sweeps over our heads toward Connor. Connor grabs onto the dragon's tail and pulls himself up.

"Oh," Penny says involuntarily.

The dragon's tail carries him directly over his chair and lowers him gently into it. We all watch with our mouths agape. Connor settles himself. He is not the same broken person he was when we last saw him. His skin is healthy and tan, his hair is shiny, and his face is happy. He looks strong and confident again. He looks like Connor.

"Thanks, Zen," Connor says to the dragon. He turns in his chair to face us and lifts an arm, gesturing to the dragon. "Guys, this is Zenyo. Zenyo, this is Mary and Mason, my siblings, and my friends Ardon, Kaleb, and Penny."

Zenyo lowers his head to our level. He suddenly lies down and the ground trembles. Mason steadies Penny who had lost her balance. She runs over and hugs Connor suddenly. Zenyo doesn't move or seem the least bit perturbed by his master being attacked with kisses. Mason grabs Connor's head and musses his hair. I kiss him solidly on his cheek and hug him around his neck. He laughs and hugs us all.

"This is why I have been unavailable the past couple months," he laughs and looks up at Zenyo. Zenyo doesn't move his head but his eyes roll over to see his master. "I've been learning and training. Zenyo and I have had to take longer in our training because he has to compensate for me."

Ardon suddenly walks over to Zenyo's face.

"You can pet him," Connor says, watching calmly. "He doesn't mind. I'm sure he'd like a new friend to know."

Ardon reaches out hesitatingly while Zenyo watches him lazily. Ardon finally touches Zenyo's face and suddenly is blown off of his feet. Connor sits up suddenly. Ardon is sprawled out in the grass. Zenyo lifts his head and looks at Ardon.

"Wow!" Connor says, pushing himself over to Ardon. Kaleb and I exchange a glance. "He must really like you!"

"What?" Mason bursts out. "What?"

Connor looks back at Mason. "Zenyo likes him."

Ardon lifts his head and looks at Zenyo. "I like him, too."

Mason starts to laugh. "You people have lost your minds!"

"So," Penny sits down on the ground and crosses her legs. "So what now? What does this mean for you?"

I sit down beside her and Kaleb sits beside me. Mason sits, but Ardon is still sprawled out in the grass. Zenyo lays his head back down and watches his Rider.

"I am to fight in the next battle," Connor says. "Zenyo and I have passed everything and we are going to fight."

Mason shakes his head. "I really don't like that."

Connor presses his lips together. "You don't have to like it."

"But it'll be dangerous," I say.

"It's just as dangerous for every other Rider as it is for me."

"B-but-"

Connor smiles grimly. "I know what you're going to say. You're going to say that it's different for me because I'm paralyzed. It may be different in the sense that I can't do any ground fighting or any sort of ambush attacks. Yes, you'd be right if you said that. But when I'm in the air with Zenyo, we're better than all of the others. We are the best Rider and

Dragon in the heavens. We have proved it over these past several months. Zenyo and I are the best."

Connor smiles. He is so proud and happy. I glance at Zenyo who appears to be sleeping now. I look back at Connor.

"Well," Mason gives him a meaningful look. "I can't control you or keep an eye on you constantly. I guess I'll just have to trust you."

Connor raises an eyebrow. "You wouldn't have been able to stop me even if you hadn't come to that brilliant conclusion."

Mason rolls his eyes. "Alright, then. But if you get killed or hurt, I will kill you!"

"Again?" Ardon laughs from his spot in the grass. He's still lying on the ground.

"Again," Mason says in a mock threatening voice.

"Ardon?" Penny walks over quietly and stands over him. "Are you okay there?"

Ardon laughs. "Oh, I'm alright. I'm actually a bit sore from the battle, so I'm content to not move for a while."

"Battle?" Connor pipes up and Mason sighs exasperatingly.

"Yeah," Mason shrugs. He starts to say something else but shuts his mouth.

"You were worried about me?" Connor folds his arms. "Yet, all of you were in that battle? I heard about it. The Battle of Persephone's Forest? We all heard about it."

"What do you mean? What's with the tone?" I ask. I thought we had won.

"The Faerie District in the Grimsah Forest was completely destroyed and all the villagers were killed at the same time." Connor turns his head slightly, confused by our expressions. We don't know what he's talking about. "Did you not hear about it? The Gods think the battle was a distraction from the Faerie killings."

Faeries?

"I thought those Faeries were Darke?" I say slowly.

Mason and Kaleb turn to look at me. "Where did you hear that?" Kaleb asks.

"Oh," I stammer, searching for a lie. "I just heard they were Darke. Are they not?"

"No," Mason shakes his head slowly. "Who told you that?"

I shrug. "I don't know. I just heard it around the camp."

Mason and Kaleb exchange a glance. "We need to find who is murmuring these things. You probably should let your head Lightning lady know."

"Grace?" Kaleb nods. "Yeah, I should let her know. She'll take care of it."

I look between the two of them. The Faeries were good? I need to ask Còiseam about this later.

"I'll be back later, Mary," Kaleb says and starts to move forward as if to hug me but thinks better of it. His body thins into a bright light and he explodes from the ground, disappearing into the sky.

Penny gives me a look, raising her eyebrow and smiling knowingly. I smile back, slightly uncomfortable. Is she smiling at me because of Kaleb? She finally looks away and down at Connor who is talking with Mason about the saddle on Zenyo.

Còiseam suddenly appears. He looks worn, sorrowful. He has circles under his eyes and he seems paler than his usual glowing tan.

I frown.

"You can talk," Còiseam gives an effort to smile but it doesn't reach his eyes. "The others won't hear you."

"What's wrong with you?" I ask. I try to give an effort to be playful like he does to me when I'm flustered or something. "You look awful. You really look as though some Unspeakables were playing Grinma with you!"

Còiseam gives half a smile. "Nah, it's just been a long night. I've had lots to do."

"Oh," I say. He seems to indicate that he would rather not talk about it. "Alright."

"I overheard what Connor told you all," Còiseam folds his arms and looks over at Connor. His eyes roll toward me again. "He's mistaken. The Gods are scrambling right now because they aren't sure who killed those Faeries."

"But," I frown, "I thought Faeries were good? There were some working in the Infirmary."

Còiseam nods. "It's the same case as with all species. Some are good and some are not. We killed the ones who weren't worshipping the Gods, the ones who were wrongly residing in the Forest. It seems to me that anyone who lives in the Forest is questionable."

"I suppose that makes sense." I fold my arms and shift my feet. I don't like thinking that either Connor or Còiseam is wrong. I've known Connor much longer, but I feel an unspoken loyalty to Còiseam now. "I guess it's just hard to accept that."

"It's alright," Còiseam cocks his head, trying make eye contact with me again. I look up at him and he smiles. "I know why you're asking. We were justified in killing them. For one thing, we only have one more pearl to acquire for Connor."

Mason and Connor are laughing about something. Penny is standing over Ardon, talking to him in a high voice, and laughing. Ardon is still lying on the ground.

I close my eyes trying to focus. "So we did kill the right people? Err, the wrong people?"

Còiseam nods. "Yes, we killed beings who shouldn't be living and now they aren't. I can tell you're still upset about that. Do you remember anything else from that day?"

"No," I look down, rubbing my arm. "All I can focus on is those Faeries..."

"That's okay," Còiseam reaches out and touches my shoulder. I look up at him and he drops his arm. Why is he acting so strangely? "I'm glad that's all you can focus on. It shows that you have morals and a soul. But you shouldn't worry about killing creatures like that. You've made this a better place for us all."

"Thanks Còiseam," I smile at him.

"I'm always here for you," he takes a step back. "Just call me when you need me. I'm going to go scout around for that last pearl."

"Okay," I give an awkward wave as he shimmers out of sight and disappears.

"Mary?" Connor suddenly asks me, his eyebrows arched. "Did you hear me?"

"Uh," I shake my head. "No, sorry. I was thinking."

"I asked if you were okay." Connor gives a partial smile. "You seem quiet."

I put my hands on my hips. "I'm always quiet, Connor."

"Ma-" Connor starts to say but is interrupted with a loud crash. I jump. Mason grabs me reflexively.

Zenyo is awake and has his tail over Connor. Connor reaches up and grabs onto the tail. Zenyo lifts Connor onto his back. Connor lands in the saddle softly and immediately begins to strap himself in. He tightens the thick leather bands around his legs.

"Where are you going?" Mason yells to him. "You're not going toward that sound?"

There is another crashing sound. Smoke rises above the white temples of the Lesser Gods. Smoke is rising from Aphrodite's temple. I can hear distant screams. The clouds suddenly darken and the grass seems to recede away, revealing the greying clouds beneath us.

Lightnings are streaming across the dark skies toward the source of commotion. Kaleb might be one of those streaks of light. Then the dragons fly over us. It occurs to me suddenly that Zenyo is rather small compared to the other dragons.

"Connor!" I look back down toward him. He's putting his helmet on. "Don't go!"

"Guys," Connor pats Zenyo's neck. Zenyo spreads his massive wings. "I have to go. This is my job now."

Ardon stands up. "I'm going to run beneath you. I'm going with you."

"Ardon!" Penny claps her hands to her head. "No, why are we all splitting up!"

He laughs. "Penny, I'll be fine. I'm sure Connor will watch over me."

"That doesn't make me feel better," Penny mumbles.

"Gods," Mason mutters then yells, "Gods, what can I say? You better remember what I said! If you get hurt or something…"

"Always! We'll be fine!" Connor smiles and Zenyo gives several mighty pushes and they're in the air. Zenyo snaps his wings and they take off quickly toward the smoking temples. The gust of wind produced by his wings nearly knocks us over. Ardon scrambles to his feet and takes off running after Connor. He bursts into his wolf form. One of his boots, now destroyed, explodes off of him and nearly hits Penny. Penny ducks and glares after him.

She looks at Mason. "We have to go, too."

Mason shakes his head. "I don't like that idea. I really don't want either of you in any more battles or action."

Penny shakes her head. "Quit being a sexist. We have to go help. What if one of our Gods is in trouble? They have given us grace, and they deserve all of us."

I had not realized how devout and religious Penny is. I personally don't invest a lot in my Gods. It seems to me our supposed 'grace' is deserved on our part. We deserve their saving.

Mason sighs heavily, interrupting my thoughts. "I'm not being a sexist and you know it, Penny."

"I know," Penny laughs but the laugh isn't genuine. "We still have to go, though. You know we do."

"Let's go," Mason turns and starts to run. "Stick close together."

He shifts and lands on all fours. His clothing is shredded. Penny shifts after him and I transform on the spot and run after them.

We run around the Infirmary toward the temples of the Lesser Gods. There is another loud explosion. A blue wave or energy pushes upwards into the sky. A Lightning is struck by the energy and fades out. I see the small body falling from the sky. Another Lightning intercepts the body and disappears into the dark clouds.

Mason reminds us again to stay together. His large body is ahead of me with Penny flanking him. I'm behind both of them. Mason, with his dark coat, will be easy to keep an eye on next to the white temples. Penny, however, will be more challenging to keep an eye on. Her silver fur will be harder to see.

We run straight into an oncoming cloud of dust and smoke. The screaming is getting louder. I can hear conflict, clashing metals, and bodies. I can feel Penny's uncertainty now. Mason is strong, brave. I'm sure though that his fear is there. There can't be bravery without fear. I just wish I could mask my fear like he does.

He masks it with his love and concern for others, Penny thinks. She has been listening to me. Penny is an exceptional communicator in this form. She always knows what everyone is thinking. Penny seems to think I can do the same. She retreats from me then and I don't feel her being next to mine anymore. I glance at her, running just ahead of me.

I block off my thoughts from her. I can't mask my fear like that. I only have a concern for myself. What if I get hurt? I can't get hurt. I have so much to do in this life. Of course, I'm concerned for those important to me, but I just don't see why we had to come out here. The Gods don't even know my name, and here I am risking my life for them.

A small pack of wolves comes up from behind us and joins our group. I can feel their beings being added to our pack. I can sense Penny searching through the pack and telling them what we know, which is little.

Suddenly, the dust cloud we have been running through clears up. Mason stops abruptly and I run into him.

Darke beings are everywhere. Darke Angels are in the air fighting with Angels. Dragons are everywhere and I can't tell which dragons are ours. I recognize Zenyo immediately. He is the only black dragon in the air. Zenyo twists in the air, avoiding the liquid fire from another dragon. The fighters below yell out and run out from under the falling fire. The fire falls and catches the grass. The fire is extinguished by a Lightning who flashes over it immediately.

Another Lightning lands in front of us, struggling with a Darke Angel. The Lightning narrowly avoids a ball of Darke dust. The Lightning turns and viciously stabs the Darke Angel with a bolt through the stomach. The Darke Angel's knees give out and he falls before the Lightning. The Lightning kicks it over and turns.

Kaleb!

Something is wrong with him. He appears angrier than he should be and his body is completely tensed. His face is pink and I can see his eyes are tearing up. He gives a fleeting glance toward us before disappearing again.

Mason runs forward and weaves suddenly, avoiding tangled Angels fighting each other. Penny and I follow. The rest of the pack follows behind us. One of the wolves behind us yelps. I turn to discover the Darke Angels are attacking us now. I suppose the cloud had hidden us for a while.

I bolt forward and past Mason but am tackled by a Darke being. I hear Mason's barking immediately. We roll sideways and down the hill toward the camp. I know vaguely where we are judging from the quick moments I see a building. Grass, tents, sky, temple, grass, tents, sky temple, grass, and then tents are what I see. We roll all the way down the hill and crash into a tent.

I struggle to turn over, but the creature is on top of my chest. I squirm and fight against the creature. I feel a cold hand press against my throat, forcing my head backward. I can see Mason running toward me. The sky has become the ground. Mason's feet run toward me on the upturned ground. Suddenly Còiseam appears, at least his legs do, and I feel the creature lifted off of me.

Còiseam disappears again and Mason's body sails over me. I flip over and watch Mason rip into the being's throat. It appears to be a human or a vampire. It is some two-legged being.

How can the Darkeness attack the heavens? This is a sacred and holy place! I thought only goodness could stand here in the presence of the great Gods!

I look around, panicked. It is pandemonium everywhere.

The Great Temple where the Gods have meetings has been partially destroyed. A large Darke dragon and its Rider sit atop of it, occasionally torching passersby with fire.

Connor! Penny's thoughts interrupt mine loud and clear. I look up at the skies, looking for Zenyo's black body. I see the dragon then. Zenyo is racing toward the Darke dragon on top of the Great Temple. The Darke dragon turns and sees Zenyo racing toward him.

The Darke dragon, a blood red color, spews out hot fire right at the last moment. Zenyo cuts sideways around the fire, making a sharp turn around the dragon. I can see

Connor, poised and arrow loaded. The arrow shoots out from his bow and finds its sure way into the side of the dragon. The dragon roars loudly, drawing attention from across the fields.

Zenyo doubles around and back again toward the dragon. The dragon spits out fire again. Zenyo shoots out his own fire, a light green color, and counters the blood-red dragon's orange fire. Connor shoots an arrow into the flames, into the mouth of the other dragon. Zenyo turns again, revealing a belly with several arrows stuck in it. I gasp. Does Connor know Zenyo is injured?

Several more arrows arch over Zenyo and Connor, barely missing him. The Rider of the other dragon is shooting rapidly. Then, in the instant of a second, a Lightning sweeps the Rider off the dragon. The Rider bounces down and rolls off the roof. The dragon dives after its Rider but Zenyo collides with it, allowing Connor to take his sword and stab the dragon in the neck. I gasp again, horrified by Connor's brutality. I did not realize he had that within him!

The dragon makes a horrendous sound and slides off of the roof. It lands with a heavy sigh and breathes its last. The Rider has not moved. Zenyo and Connor take off and disappear into the low-lying dark clouds now. They appear to be pursuing another dragon and Rider.

The Lighting doubles back and I recognize the Lightning to be Grace. Grace finishes off the dragon and the Rider each with a bright flash of lightning to their hearts.

Grace disappears just as quickly as she appeared, jetting upwards into the dark clouds again. I can see flashes of lightning and light as the unseen battle ensues. A body flies out of the dark clouds toward us.

The body of a Darke Angel plummets into the ground, hitting several tents and lying limply there. I exchange a glance with Mason.

Another loud crash reverberates through the ground. Everything trembles. Rubble from the Great Temple falls off the building and bounces down the hill.

There is an explosion to the right of the Great Temple, near the Lesser Gods' temples. Aphrodite's temple has been destroyed. We watch it crumble and collapse. I squint my eyes. A Goddess is standing on top of the newly destroyed temple.

Mason starts to run toward her but stops when she is struck down by a powerful being. It isn't a Darke Angel. I can't tell what or who it is. The Goddess collapses spread eagle on the rubble. The Darke being converges on her and takes her, easily picking her up.

Another Goddess appears from behind the Darke being and sends a powerful wave of energy his way. The being drops the unconscious Goddess and turns to face the other.

"Psyche!" someone cries from behind us. "We have to help her!"

"I don't think that's Psyche!" someone else says. I turn to see who is speaking but someone else suddenly yells out who the being is.

"That's Artemis!"

CHAPTER THIRTY

Psyche

I follow the unknown being as it moves around the heavens. This must be the nonbeing Natalya spoke of. I watch it as it suddenly picks up speed. I follow the being as it rushes toward the Werewolf campsite on the north end of Irise. The being moves and suddenly makes itself visible to a Darke being on top of a Light being. The nonbeing pushes the Darke vampire off the werewolf. It seems to have used a Darke-based force. Why would it use it against its own brother?

The vampire falls off of the werewolf and is killed by another wolf. The black wolf stands up and looks around. Much to my confusion, the black wolf doesn't seem the least bit perturbed by what just happened. Can the wolf see the nonbeing?

The others don't seem to see it. The nonbeing must be cloaked somehow to remain unseen by the wolves. The nonbeing lingers for a moment longer, watching the wolves. The nonbeing suddenly looks up and straight at me.

It pushes me back into my own mind, into my own perception. I fall backwards physically and into the arms of someone. I open my eyes. The silvery clouds ebb away from my vision.

I blink rapidly, focusing my eyes. Eros looks down at me. I jerk up and away from him, getting to my own solid feet. He is in his war gear. Silver robes and dark britches. He has his scepter tied to his belt. He looks grave and in no mood to be trifled with. I can see the burden of taking Chaos' place is starting to take its toll.

"What are you doing?" Eros snaps at me. "Are you aware we are under attack right now?"

"Are you?" I fold my arms. Why am I being scolded in here already? He should be out there. "You're the Supreme God now! Aren't you supposed to be saving this place? I was in a vision!"

Eros folds his arms in turn. "We don't have time to be fighting right now. What did you see?"

"I was following that nonbeing Natalya was talking about," I say. "The nonbeing pushed me out of my vision."

"What?" Eros' head jerks involuntarily. He steps closer to me. "It *pushed* you? *It pushed you out of your vision?*"

I nod slowly. "This is very, very bad."

"This nonbeing is powerful," Eros murmurs to himself. There is another explosion and we both jump.

Suddenly Hermes bursts into the room. His robes are torn and the sandals on his feet, usually pristine and clean, are covered in mud, dirt, and something that looks like blood. I swallow. "Chiemon and Theros have been taken!"

"What?" Eros whirls on him. "By Leibus?"

"Leibus!" Hermes looks over his shoulder as if fearful he would be heard, "Leibus is here! He is here on Mt. Irise! Lesypyx has gone to confront him! You have to stop her! He is far too powerful!"

"Powerful?" Eros repeats rather dully.

"This is the most powerful I have ever seen him!"

Eros turns to me. "Where is he getting this power source from? I thought he fell from grace in a weak state?"

"Eros," I shake my head. "That was centuries, eons, ago! He has probably been biding his time and building up his strength!"

Hermes waits, anxiously dancing from foot to foot, for instructions from us. I scratch my head in anxious thought and stare at our feet. The only question is the basis of his power. Leibus has to have a power source. Being banned from the heavens comes with a price. His power source used to be inherent. As a fallen God, he now has to create energy from Darkeness and worship from mortals. Where is he getting this significant power source? Last I checked, the majority of mortals worship the Greater and Lesser Gods on high.

Eros makes a noise and I look up at him.

"Is Aigaion still working?" Eros asks, scratching his chin in thought.

"Yes," Hermes wrings his hands. "He has worked up a fine storm. The Light beings are using it to their advantage. The Lesser Gods are protecting him from the Darke beings."

Eros nods slowly.

"Where are our ground forces?" I ask.

"On the ground," Hermes affirms. "Ares and Athena are on Earth waiting for orders."

"We want them to stay down there," I say. Eros looks at me. "Give them command over the ground forces. Leibus may try something. Hermes, I need you to find me Connor Stoneburner."

"Right now?"

"Right now," I say. "I don't care if he's fighting. I need him now."

"I'll be back," Hermes says. He flies at the wall and goes through it.

I stare around my bedroom, looking for some sort of inspiration. The cool marble walls stare back at me indifferently. The grand bed, draped in silken green curtains and sheets, is just as uninspiring as the walls.

"Stars," I throw my hands back in frustration. "Where are the muses when you need them!"

"Who is Connor Stoneburner to you?" Eros asks me. "I recognize the name, but I do not know him."

"He is a Rider," I rub my temples. "His legs are useless but he imprinted on the Black Lunar. I have foreseen that they will be the greatest dragon and Rider we have ever seen, but they are not ready right now. I want them out of harm's way. Connor and his dragon have much ahead of them. They are perfect for this job. Stars! Where are the muses?"

"I told them to hide," Eros says. "The muses are not strong."

Ever since the death of creativity in the late Old World, the muses have been weak. They nearly died during the Old World era. Luckily, there has been a revival in creativity and inspiration due to the Ravage and the destruction of Old World technology.

I shake my head. "It's a damn miracle the Old World didn't destroy all of us."

"Will you see what is happening now?" Eros asks me. His blue eyes are anxious and I can see the stress of being the Supreme God now in his face. I oblige.

"Let me put my hand on your head but keep an ear out for Hermes," I say just before I slip into the silver mists.

I find myself by the werewolf camp where I left. The wolves are long gone and so is the nonbeing. I hear explosions and screaming very clearly now. I turn and find the Great Temple has been damaged. A large and very dead dragon and its Rider lie near it. I move above the rubble and the dead bodies toward the Lesser Gods' temples. Aphrodite's temple has been destroyed completely.

I gasp. Artemis stands on top of the rubble, on top of another Goddess who appears to be unconscious and lying on top of the fallen marble and wreckage. She is furiously shooting. Several Darke Angels have surrounded her. I can't see who the fallen Goddess is.

Artemis twists sideways sharply. She lands an arrow in the heart of a Darke Angel. I push myself into the reality and sweep away the Darke Angels with a blast of energy. The red waves shoot out of my hand and slice into them. They fall before Artemis. She pauses and looks up at me.

"Thank you," she says. "Leibus has taken the other temples. I think he's going after Echo."

"Echo?" I say, my voice barely audible above the roar of the battle. "Why Echo?"

Artemis shakes her head. "I'm not sure. The only person who knows why is right here."

She steps sideways and I recognize the Goddess as Lesypyx.

"What happened?" I ask, alarmed. I can feel Eros pushing me. He wants to see more.

"Leibus did something to her," Artemis frowns. "She won't wake up. He was trying to take her away, but I distracted him and he dropped her. Then he just disappeared! He is so powerful now, Psyche!"

"Thank you," I say. "I want you to go guard the Valley of Ashes. Leibus may have a side plan for the souls there, too. I'll send another Lesser God over there with you."

"Of course," Artemis gives a slight bow and dashes away. I watch her go for a moment as she picks her way through the debris.

I sweep over Lesypyx and gather her into my arms. I retreat back into my reality with her in my arms. We collapse to the floor as her weight becomes real in my arms and as the silver mists leave my eyes. Eros lurches forward and catches us.

"Put her on my bed," I say. "My temple is protected from Darkness. No one will get her in here."

Suddenly, Hermes bursts into the room. "I have him and his… assistant."

"Assistant?" Eros asks, but Hermes is distracted by Lesypyx's unmoving body.

A young man with dark hair rolls into the room in a wheel chair. I take in his appearance. Here is the man I have seen in my visions. I have heard rumors too of his growing power. I have also heard of his accident. I can see immediately that he is still self-conscious about his new weakness. Connor stares up at us, jerking his chin up. His expression is almost defiant in its effort to prove something to us, to prove his worthiness.

"Connor Stoneburner," Eros says. I look at him quickly. Eros does recognize him! Eros gives me a slight smile. "I wondered if I would be seeing you."

"My gracious Gods," he bows in his chair as another young man walks in. The other young man bows as well.

"Ardon Darmer," Eros smiles and Ardon looks up. I look at Eros. He is a fine God, indeed!

Hermes is slowly walking over toward Lesypyx. He touches her hand and looks intently into her face. The expression on his face… I recognize that affection. Oh, Hermes.

I turn back to look at Connor and his assistant in front of me.

"My Gods," he bows again.

"You two are to travel to Keishahn," I say and both men snap their heads up. "It has come to my attention that the only kingdoms on the earth invested in this war are those that share land with the Grimsah Forest."

"I mean no offense," Ardon begins to say.

I interrupt him. "Then do not interrupt me. Hear me."

Ardon bites his lip and looks visibly upset with himself.

"Keishahn is the wealthiest nation on Earth," I say. Eros is watching me closely. "With wealth, comes great influence. You need to convince the Keishahn king to send aid to the Eastern and Northern Kingdoms.

"Leibus' forces are becoming greater and greater, and we need more mortals in the field. This is now a world and cosmic war. We need everyone. Do you understand?"

"Highness," Connor rolls forward in his chair tentatively. "Gracious Goddess, I accept. But may I ask why now? Why during this attack?"

"At this moment," I look over at Hermes again, "Leibus will not expect us to be planning ahead. He will expect us to react to his attack and recover. He may even expect us to retaliate. But he will not expect us to start recruiting.

"We know he has been recruiting mortals, promising them power, immortality, and wealth. Then he splits their souls and forces them into war. But he cannot recruit a soul who has no interest in his offers or a soul promised to the Light. Are you understanding what I am trying to say?"

"Why have you kept this information from me?" Eros asks slowly. Hermes turns to look at the two of us.

"It was not intentional, love," I say, touching his arm. "I only recently figured this out. The Battle at Sesaru was my indication to start looking, but then the Battle at Persephone's Forest and then one in Mika told me that he was recruiting this way."

Connor suddenly stiffens in his chair. I ignore him for the moment. Ardon appears even more distressed. I ignore both of them.

"There was a battle in Mika?" Ardon asks, still looking flustered.

"Yes," I nod. "I would like for you both to leave immediately."

"At once?" Connor asks, interrupting Ardon who had begun to ask another question.

"At once," I say.

Connor turns in his chair and begins to roll out. Ardon follows him closely.

"We won't fail you, Highnesses," one of them says.

"We know," Eros says.

The rolling of the chair fades and I look into Eros' face. Still looking at him, I command Hermes to find a nurse for Lesypyx, preferably Natalya and he leaves quickly.

"Now we need to find Chiemon and Theros immediately," Eros says. "You stay here and find them. I'm going to get Echo before Leibus does."

"Please be careful," I say and the moment is suddenly intimate.

Eros comes closer to me. He kisses me on the forehead. "I always am. You be careful, as well."

He disappears, shimmering into nothingness. I close my eyes and let the silver clouds roll in from behind.

CHAPTER THIRTY-ONE

Grace

"Kaleb!" I roar at him. He comes closer to me and I yell in his face. I push him and grab his arms and shake him. "Get it together! This is war now! There is no time for grief! None! Get it together now! Channel your grief into anger! It is these beings who killed her! These beings did it!"

Kaleb blinks slowly and looks at me. I can see the pain in every line on his face. His blonde hair seems to glow in comparison to his dirty face. I can see tear tracks down his cheeks through the dirt, blood, and Darke dust.

Another explosion sounds above us in the clouds. I exhale heavily.

"I know you loved her," I say, but he interrupts me.

"I didn't love her," he says almost aggressively back. "But I still care for her. I-I should have known… I should have felt something!"

Another explosion sounds and lasts longer. I can feel waves of energy pass through my body. I yell over the loud crashes. "Kaleb, how could you have felt her death? Do not take this as anything except a tragedy! A tragedy that could not have been stopped by you! She died for this cause! She died for the very cause you're fighting for."

Kaleb shakes his head. "I'm sorry, but I just can't let this go. She saved me! She saved my life!"

"Then avenge her death!" I scream at him. "I know who you are, Kaleb Roth. The Gods know who you are! Don't you understand all of this? Any of this? Don't you recognize that soon you will be beside me in leadership? Why do you think you're the only Lightning Child that has been with me?"

Kaleb looks up. His blue eyes are electric and piercing. "What?"

"You will soon be one of the Elite Lightnings and one of their leaders!" I shake him again. "Get it together! The only way you're going to feel better is if you accept her death and then avenge it!"

He looks away from me, looking off the edge of the heavens and toward the earth. His eyes flicker to different points and then back to mine. I can see wetness trapped between his eyelashes. I think about the Angel who saved me. I was to become a Darke Angel named Ruth. A very powerful and frightening Darke Angel. She saved my life.

The only difference between Kaleb and me is that my Angel is still in the heavens. I see her often…

I focus on Kaleb again. "Can you do that? Can you channel your emotions? This is part of being an Elite Lightning Child."

Kaleb hesitates but nods slowly. "I can do it. You're right. Hope chose me for a reason, and I won't have her die in vain."

I am unsure what to do. I know I need to show him some sort of affection. I jerk him into a hard hug. In this moment, I am so proud to be his mentor. I can feel Kaleb relax slightly in my arms. I suppose he needed the affection.

"Stay with me," I tell him. "We're a team. I'll stay with you, too."

I burst from the ground and into the dark skies. A vicious wind is cycling within the cloud, capturing Darke beings and throwing them off their courses. A Lightning suddenly tackles a Darke Angel from below us and pushes her into the center of the winds. The winds violently tear at the Darke Angel, but she appears unfazed. The Lightning attacks again. Kaleb and I converge onto the Darke Angel with the other Lightning.

I recognize the Lightning to be Fritz, an up and coming Lightning like Kaleb. Fritz snaps the neck and pulls a bolt, hot and white, across the Darke Angel's neck. I catch the Darke Angel in my arms before she falls. I quickly analyze her tattoo which identifies her as Rebekah. I sigh and let her fall away, disintegrating into Darke dust. She'll reincarnate eventually as a new being unless Psyche finds her.

At least she isn't a terribly dangerous being.

Kaleb suddenly races across the clouds, a bolt of lightning. I follow him immediately. He plummets into the belly of an enemy dragon and out the other side. The dragon falls lifelessly from the sky, with its Rider holding onto the saddle screaming helplessly. I dash across the sky and intercept the Rider. I kill her quickly.

Kaleb and I work together, knocking Riders off their dragons and killing the dragons. Other Lightnings catch on and we take the storm. I can feel Aigaion struggling to maintain control over the wild storm. The Lightnings form a V-formation behind Kaleb and me. Fritz is on my right, lightning bolt in hand. He slices the neck of a Rider as we pass, killing the Rider and her dragon.

The storm pushes us apart slightly with its warring winds. The V formation comes apart and the Lightnings separate when a large body of Darke Angels appears before us. We scatter into the dark clouds, almost hiding from the Darke Angels. The Darke Angels, suddenly larger in number than before, swell and scatter like a swarm of bees into the dark clouds. The clouds have formed a sort of clearing between the darkest of clouds. The battlefield is endless.

Then I hear the screams of Lightnings, Angels, Furies, and Darke Angels. Beings begin to fall from the sky, either dead or dying. Suddenly, a Darke Angel appears before me. I instantly recognize him as Joseph. I give a malicious and forced laugh.

"I wondered when I would see you again!"

I killed Joseph right after the Ravage when Darke Angels were trying to form and take over the new planet. I knew he would come for me again after his reincarnation and I know he has come with vengeance in mind.

Joseph lunges forward, pushing Darke dust toward me. I avoid the Darkeness, twisting down and out the bottom of the storm clouds. Joseph follows me. Joseph has become stronger since I killed him. I lead him away from the clouds, away from where Kaleb is. I know if Joseph figures out Kaleb is my mentee, he will kill him.

Another Lightning soars out of the clouds with a thick black line trailing him. He appears to have met a Darke Angel, too. We part from each other, not wanting to complicate the individual fights.

Joseph suddenly tackles me and scratches Darke dust into me with his gnarled nails. I scream, pushing him away from me. I veer sideways at the last minute, avoiding the Great Temple, which appears to be in shambles now.

Joseph narrowly avoids the ruins and tears after me. I twist in the air for a moment and send a bolt of lightning at him. Immediately after, I switch directions. He avoids the bolt and looks into my eyes as I slam into him. There is an audible sound of our bodies slamming into one another.

We tumble in the air and crash into the ruins of the Great Temple. Joseph rolls on top of me and wraps his fingers around my neck. My lightning speed builds up within me and I let it loose, hoping to peel him off of me in the speed.

He holds on tighter. My back is scratched from the rubble and the speed. Joseph struggles to get his arms around my neck. He wants to break it. I struggle against him in a slow moving but deadly embrace. I can feel him growing stronger or I'm losing energy and strength. He slips an arm around my neck, putting the crook of elbow near my nose. His hand sinks into my hair, pulling hard. I slip a hand between my neck and his hand. I knee up, trying to push him off of me, but he holds on and yanks down on my hair. I hear the strands being pulled out of my scalp.

He suddenly croaks, making a terrible gasping sound. Hot black liquid seeps out of his stomach and onto mine. He looks me in the eyes and I watch as he struggles to keep a hold on the captive soul and body. The eyes are fading from black to their former color of green. I watch as Joseph leaves the body and the soul assumes its place and then dies.

I push the body off of me. Never look into the eyes of a dying Darke Angel. I never want to see the eyes of a dying soul again. I have seen it too many times.

Kaleb is standing over me, lightning bolt in hand. The bolt disappears and melts into his flesh. He extends the same hand to me and helps me to my feet. He looks me over.

"Are you okay?" He is frowning. Any answer I give him will not suffice.

"I'm fine," I say and he frowns deeply. "Kaleb, thank you."

He looks up toward the clouds again. The angry, swirling clouds are raining bodies. Goose bumps rise on my arms as I watch dead Angels, Furies, and Lightnings falling from the clouds. I can see Darke Angels' bodies falling, although some disintegrate into Darke dust. It's usually the weaker Darke Angels that disintegrate.

"That is so…" Kaleb trails off as we watch the bodies fall.

There is a loud screeching sound unexpectedly. Kaleb and I cover our ears. We both look around for the source of the terrible noise. The screeching is loud and terrifying. Darke beings pour out of the clouds and over the edge of the heavens. The Dragons and furies pick up non-flying beings on their way out.

The clouds immediately whiten and dissolve into rain. The rain pours down, cleaning the heavens of the blood, Darkeness, and death. The blood around us is seeping into the ground and disappearing. Bodies are disappearing into the ground, swallowed by the clouds. The bodies will be taken to the Valley of Ashes.

Kaleb and I look at each other.

"They came for a reason," he says, squinting in the rain.

I nod slowly. "They must have achieved whatever their goal was. They retreated too quickly for it to be anything else."

Kaleb looks out over the battlefield. "Now what?"

I look away from him and over the destroyed heavens. Temples lay in ruins. Smoke rises from the rubble. The rain is putting out a fire that had been started in Athena's Temple.

"We need to get to the Great Temple and see what will happen next."

CHAPTER THIRTY-TWO

Mary

The screeching has stopped. I uncover my ears and look around and begin to crawl out of my hiding spot within the ruins of the Great Temple. The Great Temple is mostly intact but the main Stial, the meeting room, is in ruins from the roof falling in. I push a ring from a column off of myself. I had used it to hide myself.

Còiseam told me to hide and I did. I hid there for hours. Is the battle over already? I expected to hide there for more than just a couple hours. Còiseam even said he would bring me food while I hid.

My hands are cut with shallow scrapes and nicks and they're stained with my blood. I suppose the ruins were sharp. I'm too numb to really feel anything. Còiseam told me he would watch over my family, but I am still worrying. Where is he?

Còiseam shimmers into view in front of me. He smiles and helps me up to my feet.

"Thank you for listening to me," he says. His body twitches, as if he wants to hug me. One of my arms is crossed in front of me, holding onto the other arm.

"Of course," I say. "You are my guardian, after all. Are the others okay?"

Còiseam nods and turns to walk beside me as we make our way through the rubble. "Connor and Ardon are on their way to Keishahn. I don't know why. I think a God gave them orders or something. It's not clear to me.

"Mason and Penny are alright. They were fighting by Aphrodite's temple, but they're both okay. I think they managed to kill a vampire together. Kaleb is okay but he's upset," Còiseam looks at me sideways without turning his head. "Hope is dead."

I stop in my tracks and look at him. He turns right as I ask what he just said.

"Hope is dead." Còiseam's expression is a mixture between sorrow and disappointment. "Something Darke killed her a couple weeks ago."

I cover my mouth in shock, unable to speak. "Is Kaleb okay? How is he dealing with this?"

"Better than you would think," Còiseam shrugs. "The only reason he's okay is because he… loves you."

"Còiseam," I step past him and walk out of the Great Temple. "That's ridiculous."

He doesn't say anything but walks quietly beside me. I look around the battlefield. The werewolf encampment which had been at the base of the hill leading up to the Great Temple and Infirmary is completely destroyed. The tents are destroyed and torn, the armories are scattered, and the weapons are all broken.

I look sideways toward the Lesser Gods' temples. Some of the temples are still standing while others are completely decimated and smoking with small fires scattered throughout. The clouds are white now and it appears that it has rained.

A large group of Angels and Lightnings are approaching the Great Temple from the other side. Kaleb may be among them! I can see other beings coming in behind them.

"Mary!" someone calls and comes running toward me.

"Mason!" I yell and run toward him. We embrace and he kisses my forehead.

"Where did you go?" Mason holds my head his hands. "I was so worried! We couldn't find you!"

"Lie," Còiseam suddenly says. "You don't want him to think that you were just hiding and being useless."

I give him a look.

"You weren't doing that!" Còiseam spreads his arms emphatically. "You were hiding to keep from being corrupted. Remember what I told you? I told you that if a Darke being were to detect your corruption, they would have turned you immediately. Just tell him you were on the west side of the Temple."

"Oh," I say, giving an apologetic smile, "I was on the western side of the Great Temple fighting. There wasn't as much action over there though as there was on the eastern side."

"That's fine with me," Mason hugs me again. "I'm glad you were over there."

"Where's Penny?" I ask, looking over his shoulder.

"She's with Kaleb right now," he says, turning to scan the crowd of beings. "We're all going to the Great Temple to see what Eros will say."

"Eros?"

"Yeah," Mason raises an eyebrow. "He's the new Supreme God. He replaced Chaos. Chaos is protecting Gaia in the upper cosmos."

"Oh," is all I say. Còiseam cocks his head.

"Chaos isn't in charge?" he asks me.

I shrug and he scratches his chin. He points a finger at me.

"Don't get into any trouble," he laughs mirthlessly. "I'll be right back!"

He disappears as Mason tugs me along back to the crowd. We weave through the crowd until I recognize the back of

Kaleb's golden head. I call out his name and he turns and sees me. He hugs me immediately, but I instantly detect his sadness. Còiseam must be right. Hope *is* dead.

"Are you okay?" I ask him quietly.

He frowns down at me but says nothing. His blue eyes are the only thing in his stony face that give away his pain and sadness.

"I know what has happened," I say lowly, still holding his arms in mine.

Kaleb looks away from me. "I'm fine now."

I don't say anything and look away. Several Lesser and Greater Gods have appeared in front of us. They face us but say nothing. I recognize Hephaestus, Erebus, Aether, Chronos, Ouranos, Eirine, and Hestia among them. The other Gods are covered in ashes and soot making them unrecognizable to me.

Eros suddenly appears and the crowd grows quiet. Psyche appears from behind him. Her silver eyes make me shiver as she scans the crowd. Eros clears his throat and takes a small step forward.

"I am sure you all have realized the Darke forces came here with a goal in mind," Eros pauses and takes a couple steps sideways, looking down at his feet. "They have kidnapped several Lesser Gods. They have kidnapped Chiemon and Echo.

"We understand they have kidnapped Chiemon to make winter last longer. Echo's kidnapping, however, is still a mystery to us. If anyone has any information concerning Echo and her relationship to Leibus, please see me."

He starts to turn but is stopped by a voice.

"What do we do now?" Someone calls from behind us.

Eros turns again. "Right now we are repairing and mending the heavens. We will be sending down several forces to try and retrieve Chiemon and Echo. Our main concern is Echo. You will be updated accordingly."

Eros disappears without anything further. Psyche stares out at all of us. There is a moment of silence, but then she opens her mouth to say something.

"Lightnings will report to Athena and Ares now. Each Lightning will take at least two non-flight beings with them. The following beings will be reporting to Athena and Ares: Riders and their dragons, Lightning Children, werewolves, and mortal beings."

She disappears without a final word or a signal for us to begin. Beings start to murmur among themselves. Do we start now? What are we supposed to do?

Erebus suddenly begins to speak. His voice is loud and it silences the crowd. We had begun talking and organizing, but we have fallen silent now.

"If you are injured in any way," he says, "report to the Infirmary. If you have knowledge of any being that has been corrupted, report to Hermes. Hermes is in Aphrodite's temple at the moment. If you are unable or unwilling to fight, please speak to me. These are your orders. Obey these orders until you have been given further instruction."

He disappears and the rest of the Gods fade into nothingness behind him. Lightnings begin gathering up the non-flying beings for transport. I had forgotten I was standing next to Kaleb. He looks down at me suddenly and I look up.

"I'll transport you and-" Kaleb looks around suddenly. "Where's Ardon?"

"He and Connor were sent to Keishahn on a mission," I blurt out without thinking. I instantly regret saying that. Mason, Penny, and Kaleb are all staring at me now. I only know that because Còiseam told me. Would I know that otherwise?

"How do you know that?" Kaleb asks me. "When did they leave?"

"I was eavesdropping on some beings talking outside the Great Temple," I shrug. "I knew they were talking about Connor and Ardon. A God sent them for some reason."

Kaleb starts to ask me another question but is interrupted by another Lightning. I recognize her as Grace, Kaleb's mentor.

"I'll take Mary," she says, "if you'll take Mason and... Penny, is it?"

Penny nods.

"Right," Grace nods and pulls me closer to her side. "This is an excellent time for you to practice carrying two people. I'll be right beside you."

"Where are we going?" Kaleb blinks hard as though he is still trying to think about what she said.

"We're going to Roarsh," Grace puts an arm over my shoulder. "It's at the base of the Ciarian Mountains and a little north of the Forest. Just follow me, ok?"

Kaleb nods and puts both arms around Mason and Penny who have moved closer to him. Grace turns into me and wraps her other arm around me. I bury my face in her hair and close my eyes.

I feel the familiar tugging on my body, the familiar need for release and for air. Then, all at once, it stops and Grace lets go of me. I stumble sideways and pitch over. I remain on the ground, trying to get my bearings.

"You alright?" she asks me, smiling kindly. She extends a hand toward me.

I focus on her face. "Um, I'm okay down here for a little bit. Unless you're doing some strange dance right now, I think I'm going to sit here for a moment."

"Dizzy?" she laughs.

I nod, closing one eye to look at her. "Yup."

"That's pretty common," she smiles as another Lightning lands beside us. I jump.

Mason and Penny immediately stumble away from Kaleb. Penny nearly falls over but Mason catches her. He seems to have his balance alright.

"You okay, Mary?" Mason stands over me. He chuckles softly. "You've never been one for moving quickly."

"What do you mean?" I raise my eyes slowly.

"Remember when we were kids and Mother took us to ride horses?"

"No," I shake my head. Oh, I regret that immediately. I'm not going to move my head for a bit. I keep one eye open and fixed on him.

"Well," he laughs again, "we all got on the horses and your horse started to walk fast. You started to cry and then fell off your horse. You sat there for forever because you didn't want to get up."

"I have no memory of this," I open the other eye, feeling brave.

"Connor will back me up later on this," Mason says.

"Where are the Gods?" Penny asks Grace.

"They should be-" Grace turns to point toward a small army campsite.

"What are you doing?" Còiseam asks, interrupting Grace. No one notices him, of course.

Còiseam is standing in front of me with his arms folded. He's wearing a dark tunic and trousers. He has an apple in his hand and is casually eating it while watching me.

"I'm dizzy from the Lightning transport," I scowl at him. "Help me up."

He extends a hand, slightly sticky, and helps me to my feet. He eyes me for a minute, casting a gaze up and down my body. I fold my arms across my chest.

"Can I help you?"

Còiseam laughs at me. "You are edgy today. What happened? I was only gone for a little bit."

"Meh," I say, not giving him a straight answer.

I look past him across the snow-covered land. In the distance, the dark Forest looms. I turn and look toward the Ciarian Mountains. Their sharp and rough peaks reach into the sky, peaking through clouds. I turn back to Còiseam.

"Why are we here?"

"The Gods want everyone here." Còiseam raises an eyebrow as though it were a stupid question.

"No," I shake my head. "What I meant is why do they want people here? What is so special about Roarsh?"

Còiseam glances around the depressing landscape, lips pursed. He walks away from me, still looking around. He looks up at the grey skies and then down at his own feet. He stares at the Forest for a moment before turning back to look at me.

"Maybe it's just a good location for military tactics?" he shrugs and crosses his arms. "Oh, I think the Gods are here. Looks like they want to start organizing. They probably want to get Chiemon and Echo and stuff."

I turn to look at him. "Why do you say it like that?"

"Lucifer kidnapping Echo and Chiemon is so random," he says.

"So?"

"Don't you think it's just a distraction?" Còiseam gives me a knowing look. "Knowing Lucifer, this is probably just a distraction from his real intent, his real plan."

"Do you think the Gods know?" I look back at the crowd forming around Athena and Ares.

Còiseam pauses before answering. He glances at the Gods. "They probably don't know... They're so occupied with getting Chiemon and Echo back, they're failing to see the big picture."

I frown. "Well, we should tell them! What if we're walking into a trap now?"

Còiseam nods. "Oh, they are walking into a trap. I can almost guarantee it. Why would he take Echo anyway?

She's pretty much useless what with her curse to repeat anything you say… And Chiemon? Well, I guess I can see why he chose her."

"Why?"

"She's the winter Goddess. She's one of the more powerful seasonal Goddesses. She and the summer Goddess are pretty powerful. Lucifer probably wants to make the winter solstice last," Còiseam glances at me.

"We need to tell the Gods," I say, starting to walk toward them.

Còiseam grabs me, "Why? Don't do that!"

"I think it'd be the right thing to do," I say quietly, a little less sure of myself.

He shakes his head. "No, that would draw attention to you! Then they'd wonder where you got that idea. Eventually, they would see the state of your soul."

I shake my head slowly. "You're right. I can't tell them. I just have to watch this happen."

CHAPTER THIRTY-THREE

Kaleb

"As the elite leaders in this operation," Grace tells me as we walk away from the larger group, "you and I are to break into the prison where Echo and Chiemon are being kept and transport them out of there." Grace turns and faces me. "Athena has informed me that we are to get Echo first. She is a higher priority because of the information she holds."

"Echo has information?" I ask. I thought Echo was a joke among the Gods for being useless.

Grace nods, her eyes cutting toward the group behind me momentarily. "We don't know what yet, but Psyche and Lesypyx have been working with her to extract the information."

"I had no idea," I say quietly, mostly to myself.

"Go get some sleep," Grace touches my arm before turning. "We are striking tonight."

"You, too!"

I turn and walk toward the camp which had been raised before we arrived. Do I just pick a tent and go in? I have long last track of my personal possessions. They were probably destroyed anyway in the Irise battle in the heavens.

I see the Unspeakable through the crack of my door. It walks through the living room silently. I catch my breath and its head turns sharply at the noise.

I pause outside of the tents and turn around to face the Forest.

My hands are spread wide in front of me as the ground flies up toward me. Leigh has pushed me. I turn around and see the Unspeakable. The Unspeakable makes eye contact with me. My sister screams at it, trying to draw its attention. She waves her arms and jumps in place.

I blink.

The Unspeakable rushes toward me and I can hear my own scream rip up my throat. It was white eyes, almost silver, fixed on me. It has slimy black hair that hangs in thin strands from the top of its head. It reaches for me.

I shake my head. The Forest stares back at me. It offers me nothing, no compassion, no hatred… nothing. I turn away from it and walk through the tents. I call out quietly for Mason or Mary. By now they would have chosen a tent. Darkness has fallen and everyone is getting rest.

"Hey," a voice comes from behind me. I turn to find Mason's head sticking out of the flaps of a tent. "We're in here."

I turn around and walk over to him. He holds the tent open and I crawl inside. Penny is already asleep, as is Mary. Mason lies down between Mary and Penny. He turns toward Penny and puts an arm over her.

"Don't forget to pray," Mason whispers just before slipping into sleep. His breathing becomes slow and even.

I lie down on the other side of Mary. I find myself turned toward her. My arm lays awkwardly on my side. I peek over her sleeping face at Mason then put my arm over her. She sighs in her sleep automatically, making me jump a little. She nestles closer to me and sighs again.

I close my eyes and will sleep to come for me.

I wake up suddenly. I heard something in the house. I stand up slowly, straining to listen. There is a quiet groan of the wooden floors as someone moves across it. I swallow and move silently toward my door, avoiding all the spots in the floor that usually creak.

I peek through the crack in the door. I cover my mouth to keep from screaming. An Unspeakable is in the house! It walks through the living room silently. I catch my breath and its head turns sharply at the noise.

It moves quickly toward my door. It has sensed me now. I was too loud! I scream wordlessly as it crashes into my bedroom. I scramble under the bed, pushing myself into the small space. I feel pain suddenly invade my senses. It has scratched my leg. I scream again.

"Kaleb!" Someone screams.

I look up to see Mother. She is standing in the doorway. The Unspeakable is tearing at my bed, trying to get it off to kill me. She rips her shoe off and hurls it at the creature. The Unspeakable turns around to find a full-grown werewolf in the doorway. The Unspeakable snarls and Mother disappears from the doorway. The Unspeakable, easily distracted, tears after her.

I hear another scream and realize there is more than one Unspeakable in the house. I see Leigh run by my doorway.

"Kaleb, stay there!" she yells.

There is a crash in the living room and I pull myself out from under the bed. I get to my feet and run toward the doorway. I come out of the room just as an Unspeakable swings at the wolf. The wolf dodges the swipe and growls menacingly. Mother looks injured. The other Unspeakable is watching me. It knows it can't get past Mother. This one seems to be smarter than the other one.

I don't realize the scream is my own until Leigh turns to look at me. She has a spear in her hands. She is standing over a body. Oh Gods, it's Dad. Dad is lying on the floor dying.

"No!" I scream, dropping to my knees. I crawl toward him without thinking. "Dad? Daddy? Please don't go!"

His eyes find mine and he smiles at me. "You're a brave boy, Kay. You will grow up and do many great things."

"No," my voice breaks and I hover over him. "You'll be okay, right? Right? No, you can't go! You... You'll be okay! Right? Right, Dad?"

Dad reaches up and touches my face. "Don't ever forget who you are or where you come from. You're a Roth, Kaleb. I love you so much. You were born for greatness. Do you understand that?"

The Unspeakable snarls. I look up for a moment. Its eyes are fixed on me.

"Dad?" I look down, but he has already passed. "Dad! Daddy? No!"

Leigh looks down at me. The wolf suddenly cries out and collapses. The Unspeakable jumps on top of it. I scramble to my feet. It's going to hurt Mother!

My hands are spread wide in front of me as the ground flies up toward me. Leigh has pushed me. I turn around and see the Unspeakable. The Unspeakable makes eye contact with me. My sister screams at it, trying to draw its attention. She waves her arms and jumps in place. Then I notice the spear laying in front of me. Leigh has dropped it to push me out of the way.

I look sideways. The other Unspeakable has started to come after me. I grab the spear and leap to my feet. I stab the Unspeakable on top of mother in the head. Black blood pours out of the wound instantaneously. It collapses and rolls beside Mother's body. I can't tell if she's alive or not.

"Mommy?" Leigh asks. She is distracted for a moment.

The Unspeakable rushes toward me and I can hear my own scream rip up my throat. It has white eyes, almost silver, fixed on me. It has slimy black hair that hangs in thin strands from the top of its head. It reaches for me. Leigh stabs its arm with her pocket knife. The hideous thing screeches and knocks Leigh sideways into the wall and leaps on top of her.

I scream and charge it with the spear. The spear sinks into its side. It staggers sideways and turns around to face me. It charges me but falls two steps in. The Unspeakable dies without another sound.

"Leigh?" I look at her. I can't tell what is her blood and what is Unspeakable blood.

She's covered in dark liquid. Her breathing is shallow. Her eyes slide toward me but she makes no sound. I can see fear in her eyes. She's terrified. I crouch in front of her.

"Leigh?" I feel a tear roll down my cheek as I stare at my older sister.

"It's okay," she manages to say. The edges of her mouth are a strange color. "You'll be okay."

I shake my head. "Please."

Leigh suddenly gives up her bravery then. "I'm scared, Kay."

"Me, too," I say. I touch her face, wiping the blood from around her eyes. "Please don't leave me."

"I don't want to leave," she says, beginning to cry tearlessly. "I'm scared."

"No, you'll be okay! You will!"

Her breathing is getting shallower and shallower. Her words are becoming more of an effort for her. Her eyes don't leave mine. I take her hand and squeeze. If I can hold onto her, she won't leave me. She won't die if I hold onto her.

"I," she breathes raggedly, "I don't want to... want to... die... S-stay..."

Leigh doesn't say anything else. Her eyes seem to be looking somewhere I can never look. I wave my hand in front of her face. I look down at my hand holding hers. She can't leave! I was holding her hand! I was holding her here!

"Leigh?" I shake her suddenly. "No!"

I turn, wildly and desperately. "Mother! Mommy!"

I crawl toward her, sliding in the blood on the floor. "Mommy!"

"I'm here, baby," she says.

She has changed into her human form. I take a throw blanket from the chair behind her and lay it over her body. She smiles at me and reaches up to touch my face.

"Mommy," I say, tears streaming down my cheeks. "Will you be okay?"

She blinks rapidly, fighting tears.

"I don't think I will, baby," she strokes my face gently. "I think you will have to be strong for me now. Can you do that?"

"No," I bite my lip. "No, Mommy. P-please... please stay?"

"I'll stay as long as I can, honey." Her eyes are welling up with tears. A tear escapes and leaves a clean track down her face.

I lie down beside her. "Can Mr. Stoneburner help you? Should I go get him?"

She shakes her head. "No, baby. He can't help me."

"Can I stay with you?"

"Of course." She smiles at me. "I'll never leave you either."

"What's going to happen now?" I ask her, terrified of the unknown now. I had known what my life would be like. I had known. Now I don't know. I don't know anything. "What if I'm not... enough? What if I can't be strong?"

"You will be," her eyes flicker all over my face. "You have always been so brave and strong. You always will be, too. You are my son and you always will be. I love you so much, Kay."

"I love you, Mommy." I touch her face one last time.

Her eyes glaze over then.

"Mom? Mommy?" I sit up and look at her closely. "Mommy! You said you'd stay! No! Please come back! Mommy!"

I shake her body, trying to bring her back. I scream for her. I hold myself, rocking in place and crying. I look over at Father lying on the floor and Leigh slumped against the wall Her eyes are blankly fixed in my direction.

Suddenly the door bursts open. Mr. Stoneburner stands there for a minute. His eyes take in everything in the room and then they fall on me. He drops to his knees and opens his arms.

"Kaleb," he says urgently.

"Kaleb," someone says urgently. "Kaleb!"

I jerk awake and jump again. Mary is leaned over me. Her hair tickles my face. I blink several times. Her face is concerned and she doesn't lean away from me. I become aware of my senses. I'm soaked with sweat and my hands are shaking.

"Kaleb?" Mary touches my forehead gently. "Are you okay?"

"I need some air," I grunt and start to sit up. She moves away from me and watches me, looking concerned. I don't look at her and crawl out of the tent. I didn't notice if Mason or Penny are awake or not.

The winter air is cold and biting. It wakes me up fully and I blink. I fold my arms tightly and look up at the stars. Someone comes out of the tent and stands silently beside me. I look down to see Mary. She's already looking up at me.

"It was a nightmare," she says simply. It isn't a question. She looks up at the stars.

I nod and look up, too. "It was a nightmare."

"What was it about?" she asks me. "If you don't mind talking to me about it…"

I sigh heavily. "It was the one when my parents die."

Mary doesn't say anything for a long time. "Sometimes I have nightmares about my mother's death. I understand if you don't want to talk about it."

"I don't."

"Neither do I."

This moment lasts for a long time. We both stare up at the sky in miserable silence. Mary suddenly hugs me. She presses her head against my chest. I hug her back.

"I'm sorry," she whispers.

"Me, too," I whisper back.

She looks up at me and I lean in and kiss her suddenly. I don't know what takes control of me, but the urge to kiss her comes on strongly and suddenly. I hold her face gently and tenderly.

"Mary," I say, moving her lips, too. "I think… I think I love you."

"What?" Mary moves her head to look at me.

"I, uh," I say uncertainly, "I think I'm in love with you. I always have… been. I love you."

"I love you, too," she says and my heart flips in my chest. My stomach twists and I swallow. "Why do you love me?" she asks.

I touch her face gently. "I don't know. I always have, though."

"Me, too," she says and I smile.

I kiss her again. I feel a familiar feeling creeping upon me: happiness.

CHAPTER THIRTY-FOUR

Mary

The next morning, we all ate quickly and prepared for the attack. All the wolves changed and were ready for transport. The plan is that a new wave of Lightnings will come in and transport us out when we have Echo.

One werewolf is assigned to one Lightning. Due to the massive size of the wolves, only one can be transported by a single Lightning at a time.

Kaleb leans over me and wraps his arms around me. My stomach flips again with the thought of what happened last night. He loves me! When I had told Còiseam this morning, he seemed irritated. I told him he was jealous and he just disappeared. I'll have to make sure he's okay later.

Suddenly my body is jerked and we're transporting. The giddiness from Kaleb's kiss is quickly replaced by ice cold fear for my life. Why am I here? Why am I fighting for Gods I don't even like? I feel a sense of resentment toward these Gods. Why am I fighting their battle? Surely they are strong enough, all together, to defeat one rogue God? Lucifer, Leibus, whatever his name is, surely isn't that strong!

We land and immediately my mind is filled with orders from the alpha of our pack force. Do not attack unless given orders to attack. I look around. Where are we? The Forest is its absolute darkest, but I can still see. Sunlight is streaming in random spots through the canopy.

Dark buildings are scattered around a clearing. We're standing in the clearing. Perhaps it's a plaza? We look around. There are no Darke beings in sight.

Lightnings strike the ground and are instantly on alert. Grace walks past me. I watch her as she goes. She walks like a cat, confident and cool. Her long blonde hair is pulled back into a ponytail. Somehow having her hair pulled back makes her look even more severe.

Kaleb moves over to her, stepping sideways and squeezing past large wolves. He nearly stumbles, trying to move past them. Grace turns toward him. They begin talking in low voices and pointing to various buildings.

Suddenly, I hear a crack. It sounds like a stick being snapped beneath a foot. All the wolves turn their heads. The Lightnings look at us and then look where we are looking. The Forest is too dark to see into.

They're attacking! Assume the defensive position! The thought almost screams through my head. I run toward Kaleb and Grace. I do not want to be on the outside and vulnerable.

The Lightnings react, forming an oblong wall around us, facing the dark Forest. Then, as predicted, Darke beings begin appearing out of the darkness. Their bodies are painted black and they are screaming as they charge us. Lightnings immediately engage the first enemies to appear. Kaleb snatches up a Darke being and disappears into the sky. He'll probably drop him from the sky and let him die. Kaleb strikes the ground again, knocking several Blood elves over, and attacks another Darke being. Grace's ponytail grabs my attention. She has a bolt in hand and stabs the stomach of a Blood elf. The elf doubles over and falls to the ground. She ducks a blow from another elf and twists around, her ponytail flying, and stabs that elf, too.

An arrow whizzes past me and strikes the wolf behind me. I hear a sharp cry but I don't turn around. The wolf is as good as dead now that he's injured. Although war is fought between groups of beings, each being is for him or herself. It is a group of individuals fighting each other. It is a sad reality, I think. I watch another wolf in front of me fall. No one gives her a second glance.

A vampire suddenly attacks the wolf beside me. The wolf fights with him, leaving me exposed. Oh Gods! I look frantically around me. Wolves are engaging in small fights all over the clearing. I am one of the few who isn't fighting. Suddenly someone screams and I look up. Fallen and Darke Angels are descending from the sky, sprinkling Darke dust all over everything. I panic. If the dust touches me, will it affect my soul? I have to find a way out of this. Gods! Where is Còiseam when I need him?

Còiseam suddenly appears. He looks around us and glares down at me.

"What are you doing?" he is shouting over the roar of conflict. "Go hide!"

Where am I supposed to hide?

Còiseam grabs the fur behind my neck and pulls me toward the darkness of the Forest. He points to a gnarly looking bush. The bush is planted just outside the clearing and just inside the darkness.

"Hide here," Còiseam pushes me into the bush. A twig jabs my eye. "I'll stand here and protect you. If anything Darke touches you, it may overthrow that precarious balance within your soul. That could be the final straw for your soul. We have to be careful. Why do you keep putting yourself in these positions?"

How am I supposed to say no to Kaleb or Mason when they declare they have to go fight again? They really love the Gods, and I don't.

"Then why fight for them?"

I don't know. I sigh heavily but flinch suddenly when another coven of vampires runs past us. They didn't even look at us.

Suddenly an army of Lightnings smash into the ground. A blast of energy ripples through the ground out from them. Beings, both Light and Darke, fall down. Several Lesser Gods appear, too. A majority of the army and the Gods attack the furthest building from us. They overtake the security forces outside the building and swarm the building. Two Lightnings stand outside the building with a bow and bolts. The Lightnings are superb archers, taking out enemy archers and fighters while still guarding the building.

What is in that building that is so important?

Còiseam opens his mouth to answer but the roof of the building explodes open. Bricks begin falling at random, hitting anyone in the wrong place.

"I don't know what is in that building," Còiseam yells over the screams and fighting of the other beings, "but it must be important!"

CHAPTER THIRTY-FIVE

Psyche

Erebus slams a Vidian aside. The Vidian crumples and doesn't move. Nyx blasts through an iron bar cell, releasing several Faeries. The Faeries don't say anything to us and run. Nyx sends out another blue-purple shock wave. Vidian soldiers fall at our feet. Nyx grabs one that isn't fully unconscious.

"Where are Hades and Echo?" She shouts in the Vidian's face. "Where is Chiemon?"

"I-," the Vidian struggles. Nyx shakes her hard. "They are downstairs being guarded!"

Nyx throws the Vidian aside and she hits the bars to another cell. Nyx and Erebus move ahead of me. The Lightnings behind us are silent, listening for sounds of attack. I am, too.

We descend down a dark spiral staircase. Nyx sends out another shockwave. We hear several bodies groan and hit the floor. We come out of the stairwell and into the main cells, dimly lit by a torch on the wall. The light flickers in the darkness, but it flickers just enough to reveal several Darke Angels waiting for us.

"My Gods," one of them says. Her voice is high and melodic, like bells. It sends shivers down my spine.

"Angels," I say, acknowledging them. "Step aside, please."

One of them snorts and folds his arms. Darke dust sprinkles across the floor in that simple movement.

"So be it," Nyx says and acts immediately. She throws a ball of energy at one. The Darke Angel struggles to get it off himself but the ball explodes, throwing Darke dust and matter all over the cells. I feel the dust land on me but I wipe it off.

"That appeared to be Adah," Nyx says. "She was weak."

Erebus engages one and I send a couple Lightnings in. I still have several behind me, protecting our back. The Lightnings quickly kill one Angel and move to the next. Erebus decapitates the Darke Angel before him.

"That was Jonah," he murmurs to me. I nod.

"Help!" someone cries from a nearby cell. I can't see who is in it.

"Shut up!" The Darke Angel closest to the cell whips the victim with Darke energy. The being cries out.

I push out with my sense and strangle the Darke Angel from within. I crush the evil inside and release the soul. The Angel disintegrates into a little pile of Darke dust.

"Please help!" the voice cries as the Lightnings kill the last Darke Angel.

Nyx wrenches open the cell and moves inside. Her dark tunic and pants almost disappear into the darkness of the cell wall. I brush past the solid cell wall. It wasn't made of iron bars but rather a protected solid wall. The wall seems to have a stunting effect. I can sense it.

"Hades!" I push into the cell just as Nyx hugs Hades.

He is chained to the back wall. His back, bare and scarred, is toward us. I can see scars and fresh wounds on his back. He has been beaten many times.

"I can take him," I say. "Find Echo and Chiemon!" But I can sense that they are not here.

I wrap my arms around Hades and feel myself fading from the room. Hades' hands are freed from the wall and we suddenly collapse in the Infirmary.

Nurses jump backwards from us.

"Psyche?" One of them says and then looks down at who I have brought. "Oh my heavens! It's Hades!"

Natalya suddenly appears. She looks at me first and then at Hades.

"I need eight nurses here now! Bring the Gods' kit and a syntyn!"

I look down at Hades. He blinks at me slowly without saying anything. His skin is pale and his hair is greasy. There are deep circles beneath his eyes and the skin around his mouth seems strained and sallow.

I touch his face gently. "What have they done to you?"

He moans slightly and looks at me sadly. "I couldn't-"

I shake my head. "Don't worry about anything. Don't tell me anything until you are feeling a little better."

The nurses gently push a mat beneath him. They raise him up and transport him to another, more comfortable bed.

"I will come see you tomorrow," I say, squeezing his hand.

He nods slowly and relaxes visibly. As I watch him disappear around a corner, I feel the fog coming. I hold a hand to my head. Not now!

"Eros!" I cry out. "Eros!"

Two nurses turn and look at me. They move toward me, concerned. I put a hand up.

"If Eros isn't here before I start talking, remember everything I say," I tell them. "Write it down if you have to! Do you understand?"

The nurses nod. One of them gets out a notebook as I sit on the ground, waiting for the fog to take me. Eros appears just before the fog covers my vision. My hand slips into his and I fall into the fog.

I find myself over the battle in the Grimsah. I can see the Lightnings are overwhelming the Darke force for now. They need to leave soon. Hopefully, Erebus and Nyx have found Echo and Chiemon.

I'm suddenly jerked to Sesaru. The Darke Angel disciples are moving. The realization suddenly slams into me. They're preparing to recover Eve! I struggle with the vision. I need to get out of it to tell Eros!

I'm jerked back to the Grimsah battle. I rush forward and find a lone werewolf hiding behind a tree just outside the battle clearing. I watch her for a moment. She's alone and none of the Darke beings appear to pay her any attention. Oh stars! This is Eve! If she stays in her wolf form, I can find her! Suddenly that being that seems to hover around her is there. It pushes me violently out of my vision. I struggle and fight with its strength. It's power is too much.

I pull out of my vision. My face is hot and I'm sweating profusely.

"I know where Eve is!" I shout. The Infirmary grows quiet and cold. The nurses pause to stare at me. Eros looks panicked. He grabs my other hand and transports us out of there.

We land in our bed in our bedroom. Eros rolls off of me. I sit up.

"She's a werewolf and she's in the Grimsah battle right now!" I cry. "We have to get to her now! I don't know her human form! If she changes, I will have no idea who she is!"

"I'll gather the Gods," Eros reaches across the bed and squeezes my hand. "You get down there now and be safe!"

He disappears and I push myself down to the battle again. The kidnapping was all a distraction! Leibus wanted to distract us while he tries to make Eve! I picture the black wolf in my head. I picture her eyes. I won't forget her!

CHAPTER THIRTY-SIX

Mary

Còiseam suddenly panics and grabs me by the fur on my neck again. "We're transporting now!"

I can't protest because we are suddenly transporting. The familiar feeling of suction and coldness makes me feel nauseous again. We land and I stumble sideways into a bookcase. Books rain down on me, bouncing off of my head and back. I blink rapidly until the books are done falling.

The bookcase is one of many in a grand library. Great Gods! Are we in a castle or something? A palace?

"Change! Change into your human form now!" Còiseam says urgently. "I'll go get you some clothing!"

He disappears, leaving me standing in the library. He suddenly appears again with a blanket. He glares at me.

"Change!"

I don't want to change with him right here!

"Mary!" he holds the blanket up. "Dammit, it's not like I haven't seen you naked before!"

He has? I look up at him, horrified!

"Change right now!" Còiseam shouts. His voice echoes in the large library. "This is a matter of life or death for your soul right now! Do you understand?"

I nod my head and change. My senses compress and I stand unsteadily on two legs. Còiseam wraps the blanket around me without looking.

"Now we have to get you sent to the Infirmary."

"What do you mean?" I say, trying not to be distracted by all the books.

"I'm going to give you an injury so you can be transported up to the Infirmary," Còiseam says. "Psyche suspects you are corrupted which means she'll expose you! She only knows your wolf form. We have to injure you so there will be a reason for you to not be on that battlefield. It wouldn't surprise me if Psyche came down to analyze everyone. So I'm going to have to injure you, ok?"

"Okay," I nod slowly. "Then leave me out on the battlefield for a Lightning to transport me up?"

"Yes," Còiseam nods and takes my hand. He pulls me close to himself. "I'll make sure that it's Kaleb that takes you."

"Thank you," I say to him. He smiles down at me right before we transport.

We land back in the same place outside the trees. He frowns, hesitating.

"I'm so sorry for what I'm about to do to you," he says. "Forgive me?"

I kiss his cheek. "I know you're looking out for me."

"Turn around and close your eyes," he says.

I take a deep breath. I've always had a fear of pain, but the fear of being exposed is greater. I close my eyes and wait for the pain.

I feel the blanket ripped away and then something hard hits the back of my head. I cry out and fall to the ground. My fingers sink into the snow and I try to hide in the bush again. Còiseam pushes me over onto my back. He holds down my arms. Something slices across my left arm and I instantly feel warmth spread out over my arm. I cry out in pain. He smears my own blood over me. He cuts my cheek and then my stomach. I try to crawl away from him. He gives me another cut on my hand before letting me go. No more! I don't want any more injuries!

I crawl out toward the field where the fighters were still engaged. I see Còiseam appear beside Kaleb and say something in his ear. Còiseam appears to be dancing or wiggling? The trees dance and waver. My vision is blurry. I can't see anything. I roll over onto my back, still looking at Còiseam and Kaleb. The world is upside down and wiggling. I blink hard, trying to focus.

Kaleb's arms are suddenly beneath me. We transport without a word. Luckily, I'm in his arms. I don't have to worry about falling sideways.

His arms… warm. My eyes can't see. I don't understand. The light is really bright. I blink up at him. He's saying something to me. No, he's yelling. He's yelling? What is he yelling?

I close my eyes just as I'm laid out on a bed by gentle hands.

CHAPTER THIRTY-SEVEN

Psyche

"She's gone!"

My anger flashes white-hot. I knock a bust of my own head with the back of my hand off of a plinth. It shatters upon impact and the pieces scatter across the floor. Eros looks up at me, barely moving his head.

Eros steps forward and tries to touch me. I slap his hand away and whirl on him. I am not angry with him or at him. He watches me calmly, waiting for me to calm myself down. I'm not really angry at anyone, not even myself. I am mad at the situation. Nevertheless, I yell at him.

"I knew where she was!" I yell. I backhand a vase off of a table. "I knew where she was! She's gone now! Leibus may have gotten to her! Hell, I don't know! I got there in the middle of the battle and she was gone! I looked all over for her but she had disappeared! Agh! That was our only chance!"

"I can think of something that is more important right now," Eros says. I turn on him. Now I am mad at him. What could be more important than the end of the world?

His expression stops me short. I turn my head. His expression is grave, a mixture between fear and resentment. He takes my hands.

"Leibus knows about Kahtya," he says quietly.

"Where is she?" I try to take my hands from his.

"She's still in Leis," Eros hugs me suddenly. "I've already told Kaisa. Connor Stoneburner is down there. I've already sent him to get her and bring her here.

I stare at the shattered bust pieces laying at my feet. The pieces sparkle and glitter. I shake my head. This is more important than the end of the world!

Eros touches me hesitantly on the shoulder, turning me toward him. I tear my eyes from the glittering marble pieces and look up at him.

"At least she'll be okay," I murmur quietly, hopefully, momentarily paralyzed by fear.

Eros hugs me and we stand quietly like that.

"We ought to go check on Hades," Eros says into my hair. He runs his fingers through my hair, making my scalp tingle pleasantly. "He ought to be stabilized by now."

"Right," I nod. "I want to see if Echo or Chiemon made it to the Infirmary."

Eros holds me tightly and we shimmer from the room to the Infirmary.

Several nurses jump when we shimmer into view. I roll my eyes. Eventually, they have to get used to people shimmering in!

"Did Echo or Chiemon arrive yet?" I ask the nearest nurse. She stares at me with huge eyes. Obviously, she must be new.

Another nurse spares her and answers, "No. They have not arrived."

I frown and look up at Eros. He nods. "I'll go find out where they are."

He shimmers out, leaving the two nurses and me in the hallway. The new nurse looks completely terrified of me. Just because I judge souls does not make me someone to fear!

I smile at her but that doesn't seem to help.

"Nala," the other nurse pushes the new one down the hall. "Why don't you go check on Mr. Patters?"

The new nurse scurries away.

"She's new," the nurse says, giving me a sympathetic look.

I nod. "I could tell. So how is Hades doing? Do you know?"

The nurse sticks her hand out, switching her notebook to her other hand. "I'm the nurse in charge of him actually. My name is Sai. Yes, he has stabilized, but he will be very weak for a while. He's definitely vulnerable. There is also a chance he could be injured permanently."

"Injured permanently? In what way?"

Sai presses her lips together. "His power to guide and watch over souls has been damaged. He was tortured with Darkeness directly from Leibus. The Darkeness, although not permanent, has damaged his soul. As you know, it's the basis for his power. Some of that damage may be irreversible."

"May I speak to him?"

Sai nods and walks past me. I turn and follow her down a narrow hallway. The hallway is short and has only one door at the end. Paintings of various Gods line the hallway toward the door. I recognize the Gods and Goddesses as those who had died during the Ravage. I swallow. Hades, hopefully, will not earn himself a painting here.

Sai opens the door and lets me in. She shuts the door behind me and leaves me alone with Hades. Hades turns his head toward me and gives me a weak smile.

"Psyche," he says. "I have some information for you, if you already don't know it."

I sit down in a chair beside the bed. His skin is pale and covered with bruises. There are deep circles under his eyes and his parched mouth is covered with slits of dried blood.

"Only if you're ready," I say gently, touching his arm. "If you need to rest, please do. I can wait on information. We're at a standstill anyway until I can locate Eve."

"It's about Echo," he says quietly. His voice is a little higher than usual as if he's trying to speak louder.

"Are you sick as well?"

He nods. "Yes, but I know why Leibus has taken Echo."

"What are you sick with? Are you well?" I ask him. I'm not focused on Echo so much. She isn't an essential Goddess.

"Psyche!" Hades closes his eyes. "Please do not waste my energy. Leibus has taken Echo because she knows where to find Eve. Echo knows how to create and destroy Eve."

"H-how is that possible?"

Hades opens his mouth to respond just as Sai comes in through the door. Another nurse pushing a cart full of medicines follows her in.

"I am terribly sorry, Goddess," Sai bows slightly. "Our dear Hades needs some rest as well as another round of medicines. You can come back to see him tomorrow."

Hades smiles at me. "Eros knows a bit more information about Echo than you do."

"I'll go talk to him, then," I say. I squeeze his hand and stand up to leave.

"Just focus on a speedy recovery," I say as I shut the door.

I arrive at the Stial of the Great Temple just as Hermes is leaving. He seems stressed and in a hurry. He only gives me a wave before disappearing in a blur of speed toward the Greater Gods' temples.

"Eros!" I call out. He has to hear me!

Eros shimmers before me and grabs me before he has completely solidifies. "Psyche!"

"Did you visit Hades earlier?"

He nods quickly. "Yes. Did you?"

"I did," I can feel the intensity between the two of us building. I can use this energy to my advantage and look for Eve again. "He didn't get to tell me much before the nurse came in. He told me that Echo knows the secret of Eve?"

Eros nods and releases me. He throws his arms up. "She's known all this time! She's been right under our noses! Somehow we missed it!"

"Now Leibus has her!" I shake my head. "He would have only kidnapped her if he knew she knew."

"Of course!" Eros turns toward me. "He would have only taken her if he feared her somehow telling us! We didn't even know until he took her. Hell, we don't even know how Hades found out!"

I breathe in slowly. "There is something else at play here. There is something we're missing. It's something we're missing that Leibus thinks we're not... does that make sense?"

Eros nods. "It does. So far everything that Leibus has done is calculated and for a reason. I understand why he took Echo but why would he take her now? Why didn't he take her long ago when he began creating Eve and Adam?"

"Why didn't he take Echo when the very first Eve made a deal with him?" I close my eyes and rub my temples. "Something is missing."

Eros doesn't answer me. We both stand there in silence, our thoughts racing. I can almost hear his brain turning over rocks and thinking. Where did we go amiss? When? I shake my head. When did Echo come into contact with that information? She must have gotten the information after the first Eve. If Leibus knew she had the information, he would have taken her sooner. She must have figured it out right before he kidnapped her. That has to be the only reason why he kidnapped her. It has to be!

"Have you visited Theros lately?" he suddenly asks. I hadn't realized we were both standing in silence.

I shake my head. "No, I haven't talked to her since the attempted kidnapping. I don't think Leibus was going after her. I think he was just trying to get to Chiemon. Oh, do you know where Chiemon is?"

Eros nods. "She's somewhere beneath the Grimsah."

"Beneath?" I have never detected anything beneath the Grimsah. Never, not once!

"That's what Hades said," Eros sighs. "Hades doesn't know for sure where Echo is, but he suspects she is with Chiemon."

"Why does Leibus want Chiemon?" I do not like not understanding my enemy's movements. What is Leibus planning? He has to have a side plan alongside his master plan concerning Eve! He always has a counterplan or something going on.

Eros spreads his hands out wide. "Don't you see? It's all coming together! Chiemon is the Goddess of winter, yes?"

"Yes, but doesn't Demeter have control over that?"

"No," Eros points a finger at me. "That's what I thought! I went to talk to Demeter and she apparently gave full control of winter to Chiemon after the whole Persephone-Hades drama."

I shake my head. "So he wants control over winter?"

"Eve will rise on the winter solstice," Eros says. "He wants to prolong winter!"

"Why? How does that benefit Eve?" I rub the side of my face hard with a palm. "Stars! Why does he have to be so difficult! I don't understand his movements!"

"I think he gives away more than we realize," Eros says quietly as I stomp off to the window to look over the knoll.

The knoll, once covered in tents and war camps, is clear and green. It disappears into wispy white clouds at the base – the edge of the heavens.

"That doesn't help us," I mutter. He hears me.

"I think he is prolonging winter because his forces will fight better than our mortal ones," Eros says softly. His voice gets louder as he works out Leibus' plan out loud. "Yes, he is prolonging winter for his own benefit because he knows we have the advantage. We have more Gods, more power, and more allies!

"He is going to find leverage wherever he can. So far he has found Echo, Chiemon, Hades, and his strange cloaking ability over Eve." Eros nods and grabs me again excitedly. "This is it! Leibus has a weakness! There is a hole somewhere in his plot that he fears we will find!"

"It has to be Eve!" I exclaim, grabbing him in return. We hold each other's upper arms and stare at each other intensely.

"It is Eve!" Eros is nearly shouting now. "Leibus took Echo from us because he thought there was a chance we would find out. Echo was right under us! The prospective Eve has to be right under our noses!"

"Oh my dear stars!" I push away from him. "It can't be this easy! It just can't! If this is true then she must be within our reach!"

We both pause, staring at each other.

The thought hits me and I burst into excited half-yelling. "She's in the forces! That would explain why I caught a glimpse of her at the battlefields!"

"We have to get every single wolf that was in that battle here above Mt. Irise!"

"I'll get Hermes!"

"We will find her!"

CHAPTER THIRTY-EIGHT

Kaleb

Ares comes into the room from his kitchen. We are in the most intimate part in his temple, the rooms no one is ever allowed in uninvited. Ares offers us all a hot cup of faix, but none of us want any.

Grace is called out of the room and we all wait for her return. Eros himself has called her away from the strategy table. We had been discussing the losses and winnings of the last battle.

I stare at the little pawns and pieces sitting on top of the three maps on the table. One of the maps is crinkled and worn with four heavy paperweights weighing down the edges to them keep from curling in. The map is an old but accurate rendering of the underworld, of Hades' realm. The second and largest map is that of the world. I stare at the red pawn in the middle of the Grimsah Forest. That is our most recent battle. We achieved our goal but suffered many losses. The last map is the smallest and a pristine white. It is a map of the heavens in limited detail.

I stare at the little block labeled "Infirmary." I long to check on Mary. I haven't seen her since I dropped her off. She looked like she had been maimed by a vampire or something. When I returned to the battle, Psyche had been blasting the enemy to pieces. She was absolutely terrifying to watch.

Suddenly, we hear a Lightning strike the ground. One of the other Lightnings is staring through the doorway.

"The Greater Gods want us to round every wolf up," Grace says as she comes back into the strategy room.

The other Lightnings and I look up. Ares folds his arms. We exchange glances.

"From which battle?"

"What?" another Lightning says, frowning. His name is Fritz. He is one of Athena's favorite Lightnings. He folds his arms across his chest.

"The most recent one," Grace says. "She says the prospective Eve is among them. We have to locate every single wolf so Psyche can single her out and destroy her."

"Prospective Eve?" I gasp. "I thought she- What? How can she be here?"

Grace shakes her head. "Leibus has been working behind the scenes it seems."

"Of course he has!" Ares sets his steaming mug of faix down rather roughly. The brown liquid spills over and stains part of the map.

Fritz moves the map away from the stain.

"When has Leibus ever been straightforward with any of us, Grace?" Ares seems to be angry. He turns and faces us. "You all don't know because you're young. Leibus always has a trick up his sleeve. He always has a second show in mind. Always. This should surprise none of you that Eve is rising.

"Kaleb, it should surprise you the least since you were to become Adam! Eve always comes after Adam unless Adam's rising is stopped!"

I shake my head. "I'm confused because only the wolves and the Lightnings were in on this fight. I know nearly all of the wolves and all of the Lightnings. It can't be anyone I know!"

"Don't be ignorant," Ares snaps. "It could be anyone. It could be one of the wolves you don't know or one of the wolves you do know."

"It cannot be a Lightning, correct?" Fritz looks worried.

"Correct," Grace nods and Fritz relaxes. Grace continues talking. "The prospective Eve has been with us this entire time. Psyche is unsure of how long she has been corrupted, but she does know that the prospect is being shielded from her."

"Wait, what?" Fritz closes his eyes for a moment as though he were trying to process what she had said. "What do you mean?"

Grace's nostrils flare slightly as she breathes out through her nose. Her patience is wearing thin.

"The prospect is being covered, shielded, from Psyche. Psyche is usually able to detect corruption like that. I mean, even angels can detect corruption like that. Kaleb, your angel was able to detect your corruption. My angel detected my corruption. As a result, Psyche purified us by making us into L-"

Psyche suddenly appears in the room. There are other Gods behind her. She looks furious. I swallow. I understand why Grace just stopped talking. Psyche's fury is written all over her face and seems to take over the room.

"If you are not a God or a leader, please exit the room," she says. All kindness within her seems to have exited the room as well.

I stand up but Grace lays a hand on my arm. "You are with me."

The other Lightnings, including Fritz, leave quietly without a second glance. Ares, for once, is completely silent. Gods file into the room. Athena, Artemis, Hermes, Apollo, Poseidon, Zeus, Morpheus, and Hera come into the room.

Then Nyx steps into the room. I hold my breath. Are the Greater Gods here, too?

Erebus is followed by Aigaion, Aether, Ouranos, Zephyrus, Chronos and Hemera. Finally, Lesypyx steps through the door. Her usual disposition is light, warm, and kind, but her expression today is completely opposite. The air in the room suddenly becomes air tight. The tension becomes so thick I wonder if it could be punctured.

Some of the Gods are sitting and some are standing. Grace keeps a hand on my arm, keeping me in place. I would have offered a seat to someone but Grace remains seated and still. Everyone is looking at Psyche.

Eros suddenly appears in the room, shimmering into view. I glance over at Grace. She shakes her head slightly.

Suddenly a single Thunder walks into the room in her human form. A vampire walks in after. Then an Elite, an Angel, a human, another human, a Rider, and a Star come in. Then Mason walks in. I open my mouth but Grace digs her nails into my skin. I stay quiet. Lastly, a spirit comes in.

Mason must be the leader or representative of the werewolves.

"Are we all here now?" Psyche looks around the room coolly. My thoughts scatter and focus on what she has to say. Whatever she has to say, it will be important. I have never seen all the beings and Gods gather in one spot like this.

Has something happened with the war? Did they find Eve? Or did Eve take over the prospect's body already?

"I thought that we should all get on the same page information-wise," Psyche says as she looks around the room. "Before we begin, where is the human?"

One of the humans raises his hand. The other human must be a demigod. Psyche's face softens slightly.

"We will not be needing you, my dear man," Psyche clasps her hands together. "I do not want any humans to engage in this war until I need them. The information you will hear in this meeting will not reach the human population. Do you understand?"

The man nods. "I understand."

"The humans will only be casualties in this war," Psyche says. "This war has reached cosmic proportions. After the meeting, I will tell you what to tell the rest of the population."

He nods again. "Yes, Goddess."

"Now we will begin," Eros steps forward. "Psyche and I are going to relay to you what we know currently. I know some of you have bits and pieces of information but now you will have the whole picture. It is a dire one.

"Psyche recently caught wind of the prospective Eve. I'm sure you are all aware of the consequences if the prospect is taken over. Leibus has already created an assembly of the disciples of Eve. There are twelve of them. Psyche has foreseen their rendezvous. We know it will happen on the winter solstice. Unfortunately, Leibus has found a way to block Psyche's visions partially. She does not know the location.

"The winter solstice is approaching rapidly. It is in less than a week and we still have yet to find the prospect. However, Psyche has located the prospect in her form. We know she is a werewolf and that she was in the battle against the Vida in the Grimsah. If she enters her form again, Psyche will know immediately.

"To our Lightnings in the room, we are a step ahead of you. We have other Lightnings and spirits out gathering the werewolves who engaged in that battle together. Psyche will analyze each of them," Eros pauses. He steals a glance at Psyche before continuing.

"Unfortunately," he presses his lips together momentarily, "we know that the prospect is being shielded from us. The shield is apparently a being. It thinks and moves of its own accord. We do not know the origin or the name of this species. We have never seen a being like this one. It is quite powerful. It 'pushed' Psyche out of her own vision."

Several of the Gods gasp. The Elite in the room begins to shake her head.

"I know," Eros puts his hands out as if he were quieting us. "Echo and Chiemon have been kidnapped. Lesypyx was injured in their kidnapping as she was trying to defend them. I see, though, that she has recovered."

I look back at Lesypyx. She looks worn but angry. She doesn't look at me but I can sense she knows she is being stared at. I turn around and face Eros again.

"We have met with Hephaestus and together discovered, with the help of spirits, that all thirteen of the Pearls of Life have gone missing. We can only surmise that Leibus has taken them to aid Eve in taking over the prospect.

"Psyche, through her brief examination of the prospect, has determined that the use of these pearls is unnecessary for the corruption. In fact, the prospect is unaware of her corruption and seems to be welcoming it. We are not sure that she is aware of this. Psyche and I suspect that the shield is also her guardian. The guardian may be deceiving her and leading her to her corruption. The use of the pearls, we can only guess, are being used as some sort of safeguard for Eve's take over. Or perhaps the pearls are for after the corruption. Perhaps they will somehow make Eve more powerful."

"I don't understand," Athena suddenly speaks. Her voice is loud and sure. "How did all thirteen Pearls of Life disappear without any of us detecting it?"

Psyche shakes her head. "It is the shield. This being clouds my vision and clouds all of our senses regarding Eve and the pearls. The shield is a one of a kind. I haven't had an opportunity to view it, but it seems to be visible only to the prospect. It has been in the heavens and none of us detected its Darkness. It looks like a male human but moves like a spirit. It has great power, too. I am still tracing its roots. It leaves little marks where it goes. I'm not sure if the shield is aware of its traces that it leaves behind. The shield has also left a trace upon the prospect. I see within the prospect that the shield has consummated Darkness… meaning it has lain with her."

Psyche opens her mouth to continue but instead looks to Eros. She inclines her head, urging him to continue.

"The prospect is in her final stages of corruption," Eros looks away from Psyche and again around the room. "The guardian may or may not have influenced her to do so, but she has taken innocent blood as well. We have traced her to the massacre of the Faeries in the northern Grimsah region. That is apparently when the pearls guarded by the Faeries were taken."

"Why have none of us heard of this information?" Artemis crosses her arms. Her brother Apollo crosses his arms, unconsciously mirroring his sister.

"This information is only hours old," Eros says. "Everything has just begun coming together. We are still figuring out new information."

"What about Echo and Chiemon?" Hera asks.

"I'm getting to that," Eros spreads his hands. He seems flustered. "As I was saying, the prospect is in her final stage. Unless we can find her before the winter solstice, which is any day now, Eve will rise."

"Any day now?" the Rider shakes his head. "How do we not know the day of the winter solstice?"

"Chiemon usually informs us when the day is," Psyche shakes her head.

"I thought it was a set day," the Rider frowns. "From what I understand, the winter solstice has to do with the rotation and positioning of the earth relative to the sun."

"You are correct, Rider," Eros nods. "But Chiemon has a pull, an influence, on the earth. She does have the ability to change it. She set it long ago, but Leibus can force her to change it."

"Essentially," Psyche's voice is soft, "we have no idea when Eve will rise."

"This information is not new to us," Eros continues. "We have all known that if Eve were to rise, she would rise on the solstice. Leibus also knows this. It should not surprise anyone that he would take away a possible source of information.

"Yes, under our noses this entire time has been someone who knows the story of creation of Eve. Echo knows how to create and destroy Eve. We didn't realize this, but Hades was still captive when Echo and Chiemon were taken. He was privy to information that was not meant to reach the heavens. Leibus has handicapped us through Chiemon, Echo, and Hades. Unfortunately, Leibus has injured Hades in such a way that the pathways to heaven and hell are not being guarded. Hades has his spirits guarding the pathways, but they will be no match for Leibus if he attacks. We're not sure yet, but we fear that Leibus has done this so that he may reuse his soldiers. Basically, by injuring Hades, he has ensured that his mortal army can become immortal. There are too few Gods to kill every single mortal in his army."

Psyche squeezes Eros' arm.

"Back to Echo," Eros looks around the room. "Echo knows everything but because of a curse someone put on her," Eros glares at Zeus. Zeus says nothing but looks away. "Because of the curse, we never knew what she knows.

"Chiemon was taken to keep winter going. Not only Darkeness is more powerful and potent in the cold, but Leibus can extend the winter solstice to allow Eve to rise. Leibus knows he is outnumbered so he has resorted to these kinds of tricks.

"Because Chiemon is so much stronger than her sister seasons individually, her sisters cannot stop winter; they cannot overpower her together for fear that they will kill her. We have to rescue Chiemon physically-"

"And what of this prospect?" the Thunder asks. "Will you change her if you find her?"

Psyche nods. "If I can purify the corruption, she will be made into a Lightning. If I cannot bind the corruption, I will destroy her."

"Where are the werewolves being gathered?" I ask suddenly. All eyes are on me for a moment. I swallow and look at Mason. Mason gives me an encouraging nod. My eyes find Psyche again.

"They will be gathered together on earth," Psyche answers me. "I will not risk having such corruption here in the heavens anymore."

"Are you sure she is one of the werewolves that was supposed to be in the battle?" Lesypyx asks. "Are you sure this isn't a trick of Leibus' to throw you off the trail?"

Psyche nods slowly. "I thought of that but the shield seemed to be surprised I was there and pushed me out of the vision. When I returned, she was gone. I'm thinking there was a mistake and I just happened to know where to go. There are other factors here that Eros and I have yet to piece together. The shield is obviously a part of something bigger that we have yet to expose. The other factors now... well, they are definitely a part of this but we aren't sure how they apply.

"For example, we all know of the death of the Angel named Hope. Leibus has always had a need for symbolism. He has named all his Darke Angels after characters in the Old World Christian Bible. We could dismiss the Angel's death as being a symbolic killing, that Leibus has killed Hope.

Psyche glances at me. "However, this same Angel was the Angel that brought the prospective Adam to me. At first I suspected that this was a revenge killing, but I couldn't imagine why. Other Adams and Eves have been destroyed but those Angels that brought the prospects to me are still alive today."

She nods to the Angel in the room.

"This Angel, Hope, knew something regarding either the pearls or the prospect. Leibus kidnapped her when she was handling a pearl. Hope was kept alive much longer than I would have expected. Leibus is cruel, yes, but keeping her alive that long doesn't make sense. He kept her alive to question her. I doubt he was questioning her about the pearl. If anything, the pearl had been planted to snag her attention. I am almost positive that the Angel knew something about the prospect. There is the slim chance that she knew the prospect herself. I-"

Psyche's eyes suddenly fog over and the room grows quiet. She's having another vision.

The fog disappears and her silver eyes look over us all.

"They have been gathered. Hermes, Mason, and Grace," she is speaking and walking out the door, "you are coming with me. Everyone else stay in the heavens. This meeting is over."

Psyche disappears through the doorway. Grace, Mason, and Hermes run after her.

CHAPTER THIRTY-NINE

Mary

Còiseam sits across the room from me. He watches me with a sad expression on his face. He has apologized so many times for injuring me. I have assured him just as many times that the injuries were necessary. I have to avoid Psyche or she'll see my corruption. If she sees my corruption, she may make me into a Lightning or she'll destroy me.

The thought of either is terrifying. Besides, as long as I have a single pearl, I can keep the corruption at bay. I have twelve pearls extra now! When Connor returns from his mission, Còiseam and I can cure him!

"What are you thinking about?" Còiseam asks. I realize that we had been staring at each other in silence.

I open my mouth to tell him but there is an abrupt knock at the door. Còiseam and I look up to see Kaleb coming in. Kaleb smiles at me and comes forward quickly.

My stomach flurries suddenly as if butterflies had been captive within. "Kaleb!"

He takes my hand in his. "Why aren't you down on earth?"

"What do you mean?"

"They're rounding up all the werewolves who were-"

Còiseam interrupts and talks over him. "Tell him that Psyche has already been by to see you."

I look at him. Kaleb is still talking, but I cannot focus on the words coming from his mouth. Còiseam looks distressed.

"I know," he frowns. "You have to lie to him though. If you don't, he will get Psyche up here and undo everything we have done!"

"What?" I say out loud.

Còiseam stands up and leans over the bed. "Lie! You have to lie!"

"What?" Kaleb frowns. "Mary, are you okay?"

I blink rapidly at him. "Y-yes, I'm fine. Psyche came by to see me earlier."

"And you're pure?" Kaleb asks me. He is looking at me strangely.

My eyes flicker to Còiseam. Kaleb looks to where Còiseam is. It looks as though Kaleb is staring straight at him.

"As snow," I say. The lie is easy. It comes easily out of my mouth. I used to be a terrible liar. I have become a good liar now.

Is this a good or a bad thing?

Kaleb hugs me gently. "I'm so grateful that you are okay, Mary."

"Me, too," I say and he laughs.

"Gods," he caresses my cheek, his fingers moving down my cheek bone to my jaw. "I love you."

I smile at him. "I love you."

He looks me over. I can see the love in his face, in his eyes. I watch his eyelashes move as his eyes search all over my face. They are so long.

"Most of your wounds have healed," he touches my forehead gently. "The perks of being a wolf!"

I smile. "I should be fine by tomorrow. That's what my nurse said."

"Kaleb," a Lightning hovers in the doorway. "You're needed."

Kaleb sighs heavily. He leans over me and kisses me softly on the lips. Lying to him makes me feel guilty and the guilt burns on my lips. He is so kind and so trusting. He believes me without batting an eye.

"I'll be back."

"I hope so," I smile up at him.

He leaves the room with one last glance and smile at me. I look over and catch Còiseam's expression an instant before he erases it. His expression is miserable. Sadness lines his face. Misery, pure misery, is in his eyes before he masks it.

Now he looks at me with his usual expression: knowing and arrogant, with the ghost of a smile on his lips.

"Còiseam," I say, sitting up with a wince. He raises a hand.

"Don't sit up," his voice is gentle, gentler than I ever remember it being.

"Còiseam?" I lean back in the pillows. "Are you alright?"

Còiseam sighs. "No, I'm not okay."

I don't know what to say. I stare at him.

"May I be selfish for a moment?"

His words touch me. "Còiseam, you have been nothing but selfless to me. You are... you are my best friend. You're like my brother. You can be selfish any time you want."

"I'll be right back," he stands up. "I have to speak to Father Sulibe. I just can't stand this anymore."

"What do you mean?"

"I'll be back," he says.

He comes over to the bed uncertainly. He presses his lips together. I furrow my eyebrows together, confused by his actions. Còiseam leans over me and gently kisses my mouth.

I do not react. I watch him as his disappears. I gingerly touch my lips with my fingertips. Why did he kiss me?

I stare at my hands lying in my lap.

Kaleb suddenly comes in again.

"Hi," I say, smiling.

But my thoughts are elsewhere. My thoughts linger on Còiseam's sadness.

"I can't stay long," he says. "As soon as you are ready and healed, you need to get down to earth. Psyche analyzed the rest of the troops and prospective Eve wasn't there! Psyche thinks she is loose in the heavens. We think Leibus is going to try to raise her up here. So get down to earth as soon as you can!"

"Wait, wha-" I start to say but Kaleb interrupts me with a kiss.

"I love you," he says before disappearing a bright light.

Prospective Eve? Eve is here? She is in the heavens?

Còiseam suddenly appears right next to my bedside. I look up at him, still shocked by the news Kaleb has told me, and he leans over me. He grabs my face and kisses me passionately.

I am instantly hit with memories. I gasp between his kisses.

I remember everything. I remember him saying he loved me. I remember saying it back. I remember our kisses. I remember that night. I remember what Father Sulibe made me forget.

Còiseam releases me and stares at me.

"I have loved you all along," he breathes, looking unkempt and wild. His hair is messed up and his cheeks are flushed with color.

"I-I don't know what to say," I whisper.

"I know it's a lot to take in," Còiseam says, looking down. "This is my incredibly selfish moment. I don't expect you to choose me over Kaleb, but I wanted you to remember. I just wanted you to remember. What are you thinking right now?"

"I-" I close my eyes, "I'm on overload. Kaleb kisses me. You leave. Kaleb comes back and tells me Eve is here and in the heavens. You come back and kiss me. Now I remember all these things, and I don't even know if it's real."

Còiseam kisses me again. "It was real and it is real."

I close my eyes again. "I know."

"Wait," Còiseam frowns. "Did you say Eve is here?"

Did he just hear what I said?

"Yes," I say. "Kaleb came and told me that Psyche thinks Eve is in the heavens since she wasn't down on earth with the other troops. I- Còiseam, what is he talking about?"

"We need to get to earth now," he grabs my arm which is still wounded.

I cry out but the pain ebbs away. I whimper, staring at my arm. He removes his hand and I see that my wound has healed.

"What?" Confused, I looked up. "Why haven't you done that before?"

"It's better for your body to heal itself naturally," Còiseam says, but he's distracted. "We need to get out of the heavens."

"Will Eve come to the Infirmary?" I ask him, panicked.

"Yes," Còiseam is helping me out of the bed. "So we have to get out of the heavens because Psyche will be up here looking for any form of corruption."

"She doesn't give up, does she?"

Còiseam shakes his head. "No, she doesn't."

He wraps his arms around me and I feel the familiar transporting suction.

We appear in a large tent. We look around the tent. There are several cots neatly lined in two rows. There are tables near the entrance with medical supplies covering the surface.

Còiseam helps me into a bed.

"You were transported here earlier by a Lightning because you were strong enough to be moved. Eve is in the heavens."

"That's my story?" I ask him.

He nods. I stare at him for a moment. I analyze his handsome face carefully. I take in his dark eyes and his dark hair. I look at his mouth, the mouth that has kissed me so many times.

He leans over the bed, bracing himself on the frames.

"I know it's a lot to take in," he presses his lips together, creating dimples in his cheeks. "I'll let you think about it. I'll be near if you need me. I'll influence Kaleb to come check out the medical tent."

He kisses my forehead and disappears before I can say or do anything. Why would he have Kaleb come see me? Is it because I love him? Why would Còiseam do that? Còiseam loves me, but lets me see Kaleb?

Còiseam must really love me.

Would Kaleb do that?

Kaleb suddenly peaks into the tent. He pulls his head out of my view and then suddenly looks back in again.

"Mary!"

"Hi," I smile weakly. How much more lying can I do?

"What are you doing here?" He comes in and looks around. We are alone in the tent.

"I was transported here because I was strong enough," I shrug. "Eve is in the heavens."

"You know that for a fact?"

"I don't know," I shrug again. "I overheard some nurses speaking."

"Oh," Kaleb hesitates. He kisses me on the forehead. "I need to go speak with Psyche. I'll send Mason and Penny your way. They'll love to see you!"

"Oh," I say quietly, "okay. Yeah, I'd love to see them, too."

"What's wrong?" Kaleb instantly detects the tone in my voice.

"There's just a lot going on," I say. "Please be careful."

He kisses my mouth. "I will. I'm sorry I can't stay. I'm second in command over the Lightnings."

"Because you are brilliant," I say just before he disappears through the tent flaps. I hear him transport.

I stare at the tent flaps. I swing my legs off of the cot and stand up. I move toward the flaps.

"Um," a voice behind me makes me jump. "Are you aware that you're only wearing an Infirmary gown?"

I turn around to see Còiseam. Còiseam is calmly nibbling on a buttered roll.

"Why are you always eating?"

Còiseam looks at the roll in his hand. "Because I need to eat food?"

"Ugh!" I roll my eyes. "Okay, what am I supposed to wear?"

Còiseam points to a pile of clothing on the table. "I brought you your clothes."

"Well," I say, picking up the clothes, "turn around!"

Còiseam sighs and turns around, facing the tent flaps, and licks his fingers.

"Where do you think you're going to go?"

"I feel fine and I want to see where we are," I say, yanking on my pants.

"We're stationed in Roarsh right now," Còiseam leans over and scratches something off of the bottom of his trousers.

"Stationed?"

"Yes," he sighs, almost exasperated, "This is where Athena's troops are stationed."

"My leader is Athena?"

Còiseam turns around just as I'm fixing my tunic. "Còiseam! What if I wasn't dressed!"

"It's not like I haven't seen you before," Còiseam says affectionately. "Yes, the God overlooking the troops you are a part of is Athena."

I glare at him and fold my arms across my chest. The knowledge that he has seen me naked is still bothering me. The knowledge that he… and I… That bothers me even more. I can't even think about it.

Yet, I do.

I look at his handsome face and I think about the sacrifice he tried to make for me. Why would he change his mind? Is something coming?

"Còiseam," I begin softly, "Why did you tell me?"

Còiseam's eyes dart away from me, staring just past me. His dark eyes find me again and bore holes into me. His face is like stone; it reveals nothing.

"Is something going to happen soon?"

Còiseam turns his head this time, looking away from me.

"Còiseam," I take a step toward him.

He takes a step backward.

"Còiseam, please tell me. I don't understand."

I close the gap between us in six strides. I stand directly in front of him, looking up at his face. He reluctantly matches my eyes.

"Things are happening," he says simply. His voice is strained, though. "This war is just beginning. I fear that things are about to get really, really complicated. This war is going to bring out the worst in people. I can see… I can see that millions will die."

"M-millions?" I look toward the tent flaps. My mind leaps to images of fire, destruction, screaming, and blood.

Còiseam nods. "I love you."

I look back up at him.

Còiseam takes my face in his hands. His hands are warm and I can feel his pulse in his palm on my cheek. "I love you. I'm afraid of what is going to happen to you. You're going to change. War always changes people, but I'm afraid… I'm afraid that you will become great. You will become great."

"What are you talking about?" I slide my hands over his wrists. "I'm no one special."

"Yes, you are. And you will be even more so!" Còiseam's eyes dart back and forth between mine as if he is trying to catch one moving. "There is something in you, Mary! There is something in you that makes you special! Why would Father Sulibe choose you to protect?"

"He doesn't save everyone?" I pull slightly away from him but he steps forward.

Our bodies are close together. I can feel an energy between us. It is electrifying.

Còiseam shakes his head. "No, he doesn't choose just anyone."

"Why would I become great?" I hold onto his wrists. "Why are you afraid of that?"

"Everything great has an end to it," he says rather darkly. "Both Lucifer and the Gods are great in their own ways. One of them will be ended with this war. Something great will end. Everything great is broken down after a while."

I shake my head. "What if I never become great?"

"You will," Còiseam says and kisses me hard on the mouth.

His kiss makes the back of my knees feel like rubber. Memories of our intimate time together rush to the surface and play before my eyes.

He releases me and steps back.

"I'll be back later," he says. "Do not change into your wolf form. You're not ready for that yet."

He disappears with a kind smile.

I touch my lips again.

Is it even possible to love two people? Can I be in love with two people? Who was I in love with first? Kaleb? Did I love Kaleb or did I just like him? When did I start loving him?

A feeling deep within me tells me it was Kaleb who I loved first. I loved Kaleb first. I gave up on him when he became corrupted and developed feelings for Hope, I think. Did I really give up on him? If I did, then why would I take him back so quickly?

Then there is Còiseam. He is my best friend, like Kaleb. He and I have… done more than Kaleb and I. Còiseam is more passionate. He shows me how much he loves me.

If I fell in love with Còiseam after Kaleb, did I ever really love Kaleb?

CHAPTER FORTY

Kaleb

I land on the grassy knoll where the Lightning told me to be. I look around. No one is here. I frown. Did I hear the Lightning correctly? Just before I went into the medical tent where Mary was, a Lightning approached me and told me there was a meeting on the knoll in front of the Great Temple.

I picture the Lightning in my head. He had dark hair, dark eyes, and tan skin. He was wearing dark clothing but addressed me as another Lightning would. He knew I was a leader. He seemed honest. Why would a Lightning lie? Perhaps he was mistaken. Who gave him orders to tell me where to go?

I transport immediately down to Roarsh again just outside the medical tent. I step inside but find Mary is gone. Where could she have gone? I notice her Infirmary gown lying on the table beside the door.

Where did she find clothes?

No, I don't want her to meet up with Mason just yet! I have to find Mason first! I clear my mind as Grace tells me to do. Trust the Lightning in you, she says, the Lightning will find the person you seek.

I transport and land beside Mason. Mason jumps back with an unflattering squeal. He recovers himself and clears his throat, but the damage has been done. Penny roars with laughter beside him. He glares at her.

"Nice of you to pop in," Mason says flatly.

"I wanted to ask you something before Mary finds you," I swallow. My hands are already shaking and sweating. Mason is my friend. So why am I terrified?

"Mary is here?" Mason sits up a little straighter. Penny stops laughing.

"She's here," I nod. "She's well and looking for you."

"Why don't we go find her?" Mason looks at me sideways. He hasn't figured out my intentions yet.

I swallow again and nervously sit down in front of him. I had not realized I was hunched over until the wind blows the tent and hits me.

"You are Mary's older brother," I say and Penny suddenly squeaks.

Mason looks at her. He still doesn't know.

"I wanted to ask for your permission and blessing," I continue. "I want to ask for Mary's hand in marriage."

Mason doesn't say anything. He stares at me blankly.

I continue babbling. "I know people say not to do anything drastic before a war like get married and stuff like that, but-"

"Of course," Mason finally smiles and something unclenches my stomach. I can breathe.

Penny grabs Mason in pure delight. She hugs him tightly. Then she grabs me.

"When are you going to ask her? Do you have a ring?"

I pull the ring from my pocket and shake it from the little velvet pouch I have been keeping it in.

Penny takes it from me and looks at it with careful hands. "Kaleb, this is absolutely beautiful. Where did you get it?"

"Hephaestus owed Grace a favor and she cashed it in for me," I smile. "It's perfect for her."

"It's simple and so elegant. It's perfect." Penny hands it back to me. I slip it in its pouch again and smile. She clasps her hands in front of her face in complete glee. I notice her own ring shining on her finger.

"Let's go find Mary," Mason stands up. "How about you ask her later tonight?"

I nod, feeling sick to my stomach again.

We leave the tent and walk through the maze of tents. There is no rhyme or reason, no organization to the tents. We step through them, looking over them for Mary's red hair.

"Mary!" Penny yells.

We turn to see Mary just a few yards away. She is facing the other way and nods. I don't see anyone else in front of her. She nods again and then turns to see us. She smiles immediately and runs toward us. I don't recognize the coat she is wearing.

Mason reaches her first and hugs her tightly. Penny hugs her next. Mary turns and looks at me. Her expression is unfathomable and she seems less warm to me. I hug her anyway and look at her. She smells differently. What is that smell? It isn't unpleasant, but it isn't pleasant.

"Are you alright?" I hold her at arm's length. "Do you feel okay?"

She nods. "I feel strange but otherwise okay."

I frown. "Are you sure?"

She forces a smile. "My thoughts are everywhere, but I am alright. I just feel… different today."

"You probably just feel healthy!" Penny hugs her again in pure delight. She makes eye contact. "Maybe today is just a great day!"

I roll my eyes.

"Oh wow," Mason suddenly says. "I didn't realize it was getting so late."

We all look up at the skies which have become dark and heavy. Light snow is falling all around us. I frown.

"It isn't that late," I look toward Athena's large tent in the center of the camp. "I wonder if a storm is coming in."

We all stand there for a moment, staring at Athena's tent. People are out and looking up at the skies. Many are staring at Athena's tent. Surely, she will come out and tell us Aether or Aigaion is brewing up a storm. Is Leibus on the move?

"Should we go and find out?" Mason asks me. "We are commanders."

I nod. "Let's go now."

Penny kisses Mason. I lean over and kiss Mary's cheek.

"We'll be back," Mason says and we turn to walk toward Athena's tent.

Suddenly, the skies burst open and several Gods descend in flaming balls of light. I recognize Psyche immediately. They plummet to the earth and land, sending a circle of energy out and through the camp.

They enter the tent and Mason and I begin to run toward the tent.

CHAPTER FORTY-ONE

Mary

Còiseam suddenly appears behind Penny. He stabs her in the back and she gasps. Her hands touch her stomach. Her eyes find me and her lips form a perfect 'o' shape. She reaches out for me, but I don't take her hand. I'm too afraid to move. Her hand falls as she collapses onto her knees. Her hand sinks into the snow and she drops onto her stomach and lies in the snow without a sound.

I open my mouth to scream, but he clamps his hand down on my mouth. I look at him. He just stabbed her! He just stabbed Penny!

"Trust me!" he yells at me. "Don't scream! Just trust me!"

I stare at him in terror. Why did he just stab her? He takes my hand and tugs me through the tents. I look back at Penny and her blood staining the snow.

"She is a danger to you," Còiseam tugs me through the tents.

I stumble over a tent rope. My eyes have filled with tears and I cannot see. In the darkness, this does not help my vision. The sun has disappeared and the moon is rising. Còiseam tugs me harder, almost in a panic.

"What's going on?" I stop, wrenching my hand away from his.

He turns around and stares at me. This is the first time I have ever defied him or raised my voice. I swallow. He looks angry.

"We have to keep moving! Mary, they are coming for you!"

Còiseam grabs my hand again and pulls me along. I run blindly behind him, still trying to look back. Tents block my view. I can't see her body. Suddenly a tree passes me. I look forward to where he is dragging me.

"Why are we in the Grimsah?" I ask as he lets go of my hand.

I look around us. We appear to be on a pathway. The trail leads deeper into the forest.

"This is the only place they won't think to look," Còiseam breathes. "Don't worry. The Forest will not harm us. We have not come here with evil intent."

I swallow. "Who is after me? Who is *they*? Còiseam, I'm very scared!"

He takes me in his hands. "I know. I know you're scared."

He hugs me and for a moment I feel safe. He releases me and looks over my head toward the camp.

"The Gods have figured you out, Mary. They're coming for you now," he says. His expression has changed. I take a step away from him. "Do you have your pearl?"

I nod as he takes out the pouch with the rest of them. He throws the pouch at my feet. The pearls spill out in front of me and roll around me, forming a circle around me.

"Drop your pearl," he says.

"Why?" I drop the pearl anyway as I ask him. "Còiseam, what is going on?"

Còiseam pulls out a black bladed knife from his pocket. The blade is curved with curls. He takes a step toward me.

I take a step away. "Còiseam, you are scaring me! What is going on? What are you doing?"

"Mary," he closes the gap between us. "Just shut up and listen to me."

"No," I step away from him but he grabs my wrist. I start to raise my voice. "No! Còiseam! Let go of me n-"

Còiseam jerks me close to him and sinks the knife in my chest. I gasp.

"Why scream now? You've never had a voice," he says and twists the blade.

Ah, there is the pain I didn't feel at first. A small croak escapes me and I fall backwards. I land hard in the snow. White snow dust powders upwards.

"Welcome to the Forest, Mary," Còiseam leans over me.

His lips touch mine and immediately burn. My eyes are wide open. The white snow that had blown upwards with my fall turns black, turns Darke. The snow converges on me and, now Darke, crawls up my arms and sinks into my skin.

Darke energy from the pearls spirals upwards and forms a force field around me. Còiseam smiles down at me. His once handsome face is suddenly terrifying and evil.

I scream as loud as I can, but the Darke snow pushes itself down my throat and silences me. Pain rips through my veins and then an intense pain slices twice down my back.

Còiseam is suddenly gone.

I claw at my face. I can feel it. I know what I'm becoming. All this time. All this time he was with me. I realize then who Father Sulibe is. Trusie Sulibe. Oh Gods, it is in his name!

I arch my back and scream. The snow pushes me to my feet, and I feel myself collapsing in. I see her rising. She's coming through.

If I let her through, the pain will stop. The pain will stop for me.

I let her through and everything changes.